In Justice Found

In Justice Found

by

K. Scot Macdonald

Kerrera House Press

K. Scot Macdonald is the author of:

Novels

The Shakespeare Drug

Non-Fiction

Rolling the Iron Dice

Propaganda and Information Warfare in the 21st Century

Cover image by Ian Britton.

Macdonald, K. Scot.
In Justice Found/K. Scot Macdonald—1st Edition
p.   cm.
ISBN 978-0-9859650-3-7

Kerrera House Press
Culver City, CA
www.KerreraHousePress.com

First Printing: 2013
Printed in the United States of America

10 9 8 7 6 5 4 3 2 1

For Kira,
for all the times you say,
"It isn't fair."

"…when we cease to consider what the criminal deserves
and consider only what will cure him or deter others,
we have tacitly removed him from the sphere of
justice altogether."

C.S. Lewis

Chapter 1

Monday, August 4, 2008

"Hurry up," Arden Jeffries urged the red traffic light as he finished the *Los Angeles Times* crossword in his head and drummed a rapid tattoo on the worn steering wheel, even as he savored the thought that he had just 361 days to work before he could retire.

"On reports of an SEC investigation and several clinical trial deaths, Antioch Pharmaceuticals plummeted 35 percent today."

For once, Arden's attention telescoped down to a single point: his orange 1974 Kharmann Ghia's push-button radio.

"Antioch CEO Richard Sloane said his Boston-based firm is cooperating fully with the SEC. Sloane said adverse outcomes are not unexpected given the clinical trial's subject population. In a conference call with media earlier this afternoon, Sloane said, 'My team has every confidence our new lab-grown heart valve will prove revolutionary and a boon to the 45,000 Americans every year who face the terrifying prospect of major surgery to repair or replace a defective heart valve.'"

Arden gasped. He dropped the blank crossword. His heart thumped as if it would erupt from his chest. His ears buzzed. His senses fell away, as if the world was fading into oblivion.

How many Antioch shares did he own? About 4,000. A 35 percent drop meant....one hundred and twenty-six thousand dollars.

"As recently as last week," the radio announcer said, "according to the CEO, Sloane, the project's principal investigator reported the trial was on schedule and under budget."

The car behind Arden honked. The light had changed. Arden slammed his car into gear. Letting out the clutch, the engine stuttered, coughed and hesitated before catching again. As he accelerated across the intersection, Arden waited for his coupe to return to a more normal grumble before jabbing black buttons on his radio in rapid succession. The fifth station confirmed the devastating news: Antioch was down 35 percent.

As Arden drove in a trance toward his Santa Maria home in West Los Angeles the figure rampaged through his mind: one hundred and twenty-six thousand dollars, one hundred and twenty-six thousand dollars., one hundred and twenty-six thousand dollars.

Closing his eyes, Arden shook his head to clear it of the devastating figure. When he opened his eyes, he was parked in his driveway. He stared out at his house. Was he home already?

One hundred and twenty-six thousand dollars. One hundred and twenty-six thousand dollars. One hundred and twenty-six thousand dollars.

Years of savings, of not replacing his 34-year-old car, visiting relatives for vacations, rarely eating out, and bringing lunch every single day to work, all gone in a day. Holding his right index and third fingers against his carotid artery, Arden stared at his watch with the nicked face. After a long minute, he was relieved to find that his heart beat was steady and regular. At least he would live to tell Marisela the bad news.

One hundred and twenty-six thousand dollars. One hundred and twenty-six thousand dollars. One hundred and twenty-six thousand dollars.

His fury rising, Arden slammed his palms against the steering wheel and let out an anguished scream. He only succeeded in causing a stabbing pain in his throat and a numb, prickly sensation in his palms.

Arden dragged himself out of the car. Under a brilliant sun, he trudged up the walk to the front porch, from habit a wad of blank newspaper crosswords wedged under his left arm. As his neighbor Harry's ancient coon dog, Rusty, wheezed and woofed at him from one side of his lot, Arden's unfocused gaze fell on the redwood fence on the other side of his property. In the shade of a magnificent American ficus, the wood fence leaned over like the side of an ancient Egyptian pyramid. He would have to arrange with the neighbor—what was his name? Duel? No. Sowell? No. Buell, that was it—to repair the fence before it toppled over.

Turning back to his house as Rusty fell silent, Arden noticed that the front blinds were drawn: odd. Marisela usually left the blinds open so her plants would have sunlight. Arden closed his eyes and leaned his head back to bathe in the sunlight that cascaded down onto his face. How could anything bad have happened on such a glorious day?

Forcing himself not to think about the $126,000, he stepped to the door, slid his key into the lock, turned the deadbolt and opened the front door. He set the newspaper crosswords on the hall table and hung his keys on one of the hooks near the door, hooks he'd installed so Marisela wouldn't lose her keys so often. Unfortunately, stocks didn't have hooks from which to hang them.

Arden heard a thunk. He froze. Straining, he heard first one and then another whispering voice from the rear of the house.

"Hello?!" Arden yelled. "Marisela? Sam?"

Silence.

Who could be in the house? Sam should be at swimming and Marisela at work.

Whispers.

Burglars. He shouldn't have called out. Now they knew he was alone. But was Marisela still at work? Was Sam still at her swim-team workout? Had either of them been home when the burglars broke in? Were they hurt? Were they safe?

With all thought of financial loss driven from his mind, fear flooded his body, glazing it with sweat and drying his mouth. Arden felt the suddenly dry, hard ridges on the top of his mouth with his tongue. Marisela and Sam could not be home. Please, God, no, not yet, no.

Call 9-1-1? He reached for his cell; missing. In his daze he had left his cell, laptop and bag in the car. He had remembered the newspaper crossword puzzles; what a sense of priorities.

Arden's gaze flitted across the darkened living room to the phone. He baulked. If thieves were in the house, he didn't want to be there making a phone call. Losing $126,000 was bad; getting shot by a burglar was exponentially worse.

His heart thumped. It had to be beating irregularly now. His hands quivered. A bird outside sounded obscenely loud as Arden swallowed hard. His gaze darted around to inspect as much of the ground floor as he could see from just inside the front door. His ears strained to listen and analyze every sound. If Marisela or Sam were home, they weren't making a sound. They must be somewhere else—safe.

Even so, Arden felt cold, his body still. His senses were acutely tuned to every stimuli. What to do? Get his cell from the car, or had he left it at work? Run next door and use the phone? Would anyone be home this early? Harry should be. He was retired. That was the best plan; let the police handle it.

Whispers from the back of the house.

Maybe having heard him, the burglars would slip out the back door and leave him be.

It was a negotiation. Even as he realized it, Arden smiled. He could handle this type of situation. The parties: he and two or more burglars. Goals: Arden wanted them out of his house; the burglars wanted his belongings. Reservation values: the burglars, now detected, would be happy to escape; Arden would be happy to evict them with no injuries to anyone, even if they took a few things. The reservation values suggested that a mutually beneficial outcome could be negotiated. His evaluation eased Arden's fear and calmed his body.

The key to negotiation was communication; time to establish an opening position. As he opened his mouth to yell an offer, a male voice with a Hispanic accent pre-empted him.

"*Vamos juntos.*"

More whispering.

"We go, mister. We no take your stuff."

Arden agreed with that plan wholeheartedly—for about a second. His professional view of the situation as a negotiation vanished, replaced by a rage that fired every nerve in his body. How dare someone break into his house and rob him? Son-of-a-bitch bastards. And now they just expected to slip away scot-free after having scared him enough to throw his heart beat off. No way was that going to happen. Not a chance. Not today. His reservation value had just changed.

Time to alter the party's relative bargaining positions. With the utmost care and gentleness Arden slid open the front hall closet door. He felt it jiggle as it slid along its aged track, his ears keen for any noise. They should have replaced the rollers, but why spend the money when they still worked, even if they were as noisy as a vengeful ghost rattling its chains? Watching the hall leading to the back of the house, Arden felt for his golf bag. The 9-iron had the greatest heft, but it gave up a great deal in reach to the driver. The bubble-headed driver, however, felt like an oversized Popsicle; not the most reassuring weapon to carry into battle. Compromising between heft and length, Arden selected his 5 iron. He always hit it well.

He swallowed, set his lips in a determined line and advanced down the ochre tiled hall toward the back of the house, the 5 iron clenched in his right hand, held high, ready to strike.

Arden started as he heard the fridge compressor start; at least they hadn't stolen the fridge.

"Okay," Arden called, his anger still winning the war within him against his terror. "You go ahead and leave. I won't stop you."

Arden stalked down the hall lifting and setting each foot down with great care and deliberation. His eyes never blinked as he scanned the darkened kitchen—the microwave, coffeemaker and toaster were gone—and the part of the den he could see: no one in sight. He smelt dust in the air, as if someone had been moving things long sedentary. With the blinds closed, he could just see the photos of the turreted, white adobe house in Las Cruces Marisela had put up with New Mexico souvenir magnets of roadrunners and a Zia on the fridge—their long-dreamed-of retirement home.

A car door slammed. They were in the garage. Now Arden knew the site of the negotiations. Every piece of information helped in a bargaining situation; you just had to know how to use each piece to your greatest advantage.

The garage door's ½ horsepower motor rattled and hummed. Arden heard the door groan and clatter, like the rickety drawbridge of an ancient castle as it opened. He stepped from the hall into the den. The television was gone, leaving only dust-coated white cables behind. Arden looked through the open doorway to the garage.

His rage was ebbing, beginning to lose the battle against the fear that was rising from his stomach to engulf his brain, threatening to seize control of his body.

The door from the garage into the house hung askew on its hinges, shattered. The molding on the inside of the doorframe was hanging off, splintered into two long, jagged pieces and a multitude of shards. The door hung open, splinters sticking out on the inside as if a bomb had blown it open. Someone had kicked it in. Arden eyed the lock, copper-colored and gleaming, hanging from the doorframe attached by a single screw, which had been partially ripped out of the frame. If Sam or Marisela had been home, they would have heard the noise and run, hid or at least called the police. They must be somewhere else, safe.

Arden saw two men in jeans in the garage loading his 30-inch flat-screen television into a white moving van. Both men wore work gloves and baseball caps. The bills curled down on both sides, casting the tops of their faces into shadow even as sunlight flooded through the now open garage door. Clustered around their feet were Arden's possessions: two old cathode-ray-tube televisions, a laptop, computer, printer, DVR, and a pillowcase bulging with what Arden could only guess. He discerned the outlines of the microwave, coffeemaker, Sam's skis, stereo, and lamps stacked in the cave-like darkness of the truck's interior. At the sight of his stolen possessions, his anger flared, banishing his fear to the farthest reaches of his mind.

"Hold it right there," Arden barked, brandishing his 5 iron with both hands. It was only then that it crossed his rage-filled mind that the burglars might be armed with something far more lethal than a 5 iron. The second it occurred to him, his anger shoved the worrisome thought from his mind. Justice must win out.

Still holding the television between them, the pair turned their heads toward Arden.

"*Vete al diablo*," one of the thieves, his arms shaking, blurted out. In his twenties, he sported a smudged Virgin Mary tattoo on his forearm that bulged from lifting the television. The veins, arteries, muscle, and bone in his sinewy arms stood out in stark relief. His glittering silver necklace jangled as his head jinked back and forth like the head of a threatened cobra. His white sneakers shuffled this way and that, kicking dust up into the sunlight behind him, as if he planned to flee as soon as he could let go of the television, but for some reason his fingers remained fused to the set. "No harm, no foul, *comprende?* Let us go, *sî?*"

The other burglar appeared younger, but whereas his partner's end of the television waggled and shook, his end, held by arms the width of Arden's thighs, didn't move so much as a hair's width.

Even as Arden opened his mouth to order them to stay where they were, he smelt chocolate. Puzzled, Arden heard a muffled crack as someone stepped on one of the door shards in the carpet behind him. As he spun around to strike whoever was behind him with his club, something heavy and hard slammed down into the back of his head.

Chapter 2

"Six people died," Chen Yu, MD, PhD said. His high forehead wrinkled with anxiety, concern and, Antioch Pharmaceuticals CEO Richard B. Sloane hoped, fear.

"How many would have died without the new valve?" Sloane demanded as he spun around from the view of Lake Geneva and the Swiss Alps that the 5-star Beau Rivage Palace Lausanne had offered discriminating guests since 1861. "Six out of how many already seriously ill patients? Sixty?"

"Fifty-eight." The Asian-American researcher sat at an antique butterfly table. Sloane owned two just like it at his Newport home on Rhode Island. A laptop and a pair of black binders bulging with protocol data sat incongruously on the 250-year-old circular table, which formed a delicate buttress between Yu and Sloane. "Six out of 58 patients who were indicated for mitral valve replacement surgery within six months."

"So we hit a patch of bad luck," Sloane said, dismissing the setback with a wave of his tanned hand. He noticed that he needed a manicure when he returned home to Boston; only Roxanna did his discriminating nails. "Find out what screwed up the works and fix it."

"It's not that easy. We experienced some morbidity with the animal trials during the phase I trial," Yu began to explain.

"Then you've had plenty of time to figure out what the fuck is screwing this up," Sloane interrupted. Sloane knew the history of the trial as well as anyone. He had gone back to school to earn a master's degree in biochemistry from Boston University as soon as he had realized the top position at Antioch was within his grasp, but only if he patched a couple of holes in his resume.

"Maybe," Yu said, as a sour expression marred his youthful-looking face.

"Maybe?" Sloane loathed how this meeting was progressing. With the stock plummeting like a brick down a well, his job as Antioch CEO was more precarious than an ugly whore's at a brothel. There was no way on God's green earth some researcher was going to cost him his position. He only had a short time to put things right, a very short time, if he had any time at all.

When news of the trial and the SEC investigation reached Sloane, he had been at Cowes Week on the Isle of Wight. He had missed racing his new 40-foot Saber racing yacht, *Midas*, in the challenging waters off the Solent against some of the finest yachtsmen in the world, not to mention missing his first holiday longer than four days in three years.

When Sloane told his wife, Maddy, he had to leave Cowes, she'd been furious. In a snit, she stayed behind to go with that born-to-wealth snob Edgar St. Pierre to the formal dinner at Osborne House, the summer retreat of the late Queen Victoria. Prince Charles and Camilla were scheduled to attend. When Sloane asked Maddy to accompany him to Switzerland, she replied with her surgeon-sculpted nose held high, "Your next job might be managing a start-up in Bombay, so I better partake of the chance to associate with royalty when I am presented the opportunity." His reply that they had plenty of royalty in India from maharajahs on down had just stoked her anger to a glowing intensity. Her sole interest had been whether "we" were in trouble. Sloane had ignored the suggestion that his success was shared even one iota by her, and responded that in one bloody week in 1993 the CEOs of IBM, Westinghouse and American Express had all been axed because of poor financial results, largely related to tumbling stock prices, and none of them had suffered anything near a 35 percent drop in their stock price.

Leaving his angry wife behind to St. Pierre and the Royals, Sloane jumped on Antioch's Dassault Falcon 7X to catch the clinical trial's PI in Lausanne. The PI and his team were in the Swiss city for a previously scheduled meeting with an expert panel to review their preliminary findings. Maddy could find her own way home to Boston.

Sloane didn't wait until Lausanne to start the task of salvaging his job. As he waited for a car to the private airport near Cowes where the Falcon was going through pre-flight, he called Dan Laycock, Antioch VP for Research and Development.

"The trial just had a hiccup," Laycock said from Chapel Hill, where he was investigating a new biotech start-up Antioch was considering purchasing. "The stock fell because of the SEC investigation, not the clinical trial."

"Six dead is a hiccup?" Sloane asked, sounding astounded, even though he agreed with Laycock.

"They were heart-valve patients. Heart-valve patients die. It wasn't my fault. It wasn't anyone's fault."

"I disagree, as does the board." The board would agree with Sloane, he knew, as soon as he spoke with them. "I want your resignation on my desk in Boston by 8 am tomorrow."

"Richard, I don't—"

"First thing tomorrow, Dan." Whatever the letter said, Sloane would ensure everyone knew that Laycock had taken complete responsibility for the trial's 'hiccup.'

Through a series of phone calls from Cowes and then from the Falcon, Sloane convinced a bare majority of the board that ditching the CEO right after news of the SEC investigation broke and a major clinical trial went south would confirm that the company was guilty of misdoing and that the trial was dead, the last things any board member desired. Sloane argued that sacking the VP for R&D would show Wall Street that there had been a failure of a single member of the executive team, not the entire executive team, let alone the board.

Even though he had bought time, Sloane knew he had to fix things fast. If the stock hadn't rebounded and reached new highs in a couple of months, the board would announce that Sloane was retiring to spend more time with his family and pursue other interests. No one quit being a CEO to spend more time doing anything, except maybe to die of a terminal disease, but it was what was always said. Sloane never wanted to "spend more time with his family and pursue other interests."

"We developed hypotheses about why the rats died, but we lacked sufficient time to test them with any degree of rigor," Yu explained in the Lausanne hotel suite, sweat beading on his broad forehead.

"Why the hell not?"

"Only seven rats died, which, with more than 100 rats in the study, was well within the statistically expected morbidity range, although we did suspect there might be a common cause."

"Fantastic." Sloane pursed his lips, turned and looked out at the vista across Lake Geneva. He was furious. He had a researcher who couldn't be bothered to figure out why rats were dying, even if it was just seven of the vermin. Worse, it seemed far from certain Yu could ever figure out what had crippled the human trial.

"It's funny," Yu said.

"What's funny?" Sloane spun on his heel to glare over at the pudgy researcher, who was wiping his brow with a blue, linen handkerchief.

Yu swallowed and said, "I sometimes wonder if we're wasting our time with rats."

"Every lab in the world uses rats for animal modeling."

"Yes, and doing so has great advantages. The Wistar rat is small enough to be housed in large numbers in relatively small spaces. Since they're mammals, they share many characteristics with humans. They can be outbred so they don't share identical genotypes for random-population studies or inbred so each rat has an identical genotype."

Sloane loathed being lectured to like one of Yu's students at Boston University, where Yu was an adjunct. The academic position looked good on his resume for soliciting funding from investors.

"But if a cure for atherosclerosis, for example," Yu said, warming to his argument, "is to be found in something unique to humans or, at a minimum, not found in rats, then we'll never find that cure."

The thought of starting a research lab using animals other than the standard Wistar rats or rhesus monkeys flashed across Sloane's mind, but he couldn't see the profit in it. It would be impossible to get government funding to test drug treatments on anything other than the standard lab animals, given that 'government creativity' was an oxymoron.

Sloane glanced at his Patek Philippe watch, which he had seen in Zurich last winter and just had to have. He liked it, even if it was last year's style and it was time to replace it.

Walling off his anger at Yu's digression in the back of his mind, Sloane refocused on the devastating issue at hand. "You know as well as I do how important this trial is, Yu," Sloane said, stalking across the suite's deep-pile carpet to loom over the stocky principal investigator. "Our stock went into the crapper when news leaked about the patients."

"I don't know where the leak came from."

"I don't give a damn where it came from. Companies leak more than a drunk after an all-night boozer. That's why we have a PR department." Not that they did shit with this one, Sloane thought. "Regardless of who spoke out of school, I want the trial fixed soon; now, today, yesterday."

"My team and I are working on a number of possible causes of the fatalities."

"Good," Sloane said, gripping the back of a Chippendales chair. "How long?"

Yu frowned.

"How long?" Was the man dense? Did they hand out PhDs like after-dinner mints at Stanford?

"It isn't like…It isn't predictable."

"You're a smart man, some have even whispered in my ear you're brilliant. You must have a guess based on your vast experience." From long practice, Sloane made the compliment sound sincere.

Yu swallowed, tapped his stubby fingers on the top of one of the bulging black binders. "A month to analyze what happened and determine the cause, if it is a single cause. Another month at least to figure out how to remedy the problem, if it can be fixed, and then time to test the solution on animal and then human subjects."

"It bloody well better be fixable." It was too long, far too long. Sloane needed the problem solved now, within a month at the most—or he needed more time. "This report of yours," he said, picking up a slim, bound volume off a cherry side bureau as if it stank. "Very thorough and extremely well written." Yu nodded, but there was wariness behind the carefully modulated movement. "But not exactly the soul of optimism."

"No, sir. The problems inherent in growing a heart valve are far greater than those found in, say, growing a kidney from stem cells."

"I'm fully aware of that, but can't we be just a tad more optimistic about our prospects?" Sloane sat across from Yu and offered his most encouraging smile as he crossed his legs to appear relaxed; just two friends discussing a minor, solvable problem.

Yu considered and after a moment said, "Maybe."

"You sound like day-old dishwater: lukewarm, but at least you're heading in the right direction." Uncrossing his legs and leaning forward, Sloane rested his elbows on the delicate butterfly table. His white shirt displayed his monogram on either cuff beside gold cufflinks with ruby inlays—a gift from his wife, Maddy, which she'd picked up on Santorini last summer. He adjusted one so it showed the ruby inlay more prominently. "Sanjeev is leaving Antioch," Sloane said, his voice lowered to sound friendly and reassuring, yet confidential. "That leaves the liver and kidney projects without a PI. Not many men can lead those projects. I need someone with stem-cell and solid-organ donor experience, and someone who lives and breaths optimism."

Sloane waited. He let the implications sink in. He could have gone the threatening route, telling Yu his job was on the line, not to mention his reputation, but Yu was already scared. The bastard was sweating like a fully clad Eskimo in a sauna. Heaping on more fear would accomplish nothing. Yu needed some positive motivation.

"You lead three projects, you'll notice a nice bump in compensation," Sloane promised with an enticing grin.

Yu nodded, but his uncertainty was clear.

"You'll publish more papers." The PI got his name on every paper published by every researcher in his research groups. "More papers, more research grants, which leads to even more papers and more grants, which all lead to more prestige and a bigger name. In a few years, you'll be able to write your own ticket, anywhere you want to go: Harvard, Princeton, back to Stanford as a full professor or to the Scripps Institute for the sun and a beach house in La Jolla. Antioch can arrange an endowed chair wherever you want."

Yu nodded, running the tip of his tongue over his dry lips.

"You think you can rework this report, just a little?" Sloane held out the slim volume. "A touch less pessimistic? Acknowledge the problem, identify some possible causes and—the key—some possible solutions? Show your brilliance to the board."

Yu looked down at the report, but his pudgy hands did not move.

"Maybe say what you just told me: a month to analyze the problem, a month to come up with some solutions—just the truth. No need to mention how long to test the solution. Everyone's aware of the timeline for a clinical trial."

"Could be longer," Yu said, meek as the smallest mouse in the litter.

"Could be shorter. You're smart and your team is chock full of brilliant researchers, I'm told. Maybe phrase it as four weeks instead of a month; sounds better."

Yu still hesitated, but at least he nodded.

"Antioch Pharmaceuticals was founded on succeeding where others have failed," Sloane said, still holding out the report. "Our mission statement is to push the boundaries of medical science for the common good. I don't have to tell you, Yu, if this heart valve works, thousands, no tens of thousands of people every year are going to be healthier and happier, not facing the terrifying prospect of having their sternum cut open, their ribs spread apart like Texas BBQ, and their hearts stopped to replace a failing heart valve."

Yu kept nodding.

"Not to mention helping our shareholders," Sloane said, "including you, me and every single one of our colleagues."

Yu still didn't reach for the report, but he kept nodding like a bobblehead Buddha. Some of the researchers certainly had autistic tendencies.

"The board just wants something to give them hope. I know you have a tremendous amount to contribute to medicine. Fix this and you're still a PI, soon with two more research projects to shepherd along. If you don't...." Sloane's gaze met Yu's dark eyes as he let the dire implications sink in. "Just a little optimism, just a little, that's all we need; all both of us need."

Sloane held the report out closer to Yu.

"Just a little," Sloane prompted.

Yu took the report from Sloane's outstretched hand.

Chapter 3

"I tole you, that's the split," Angel Morales proclaimed in the alley behind *El Tigre*'s shop. No way was he going to give up even a penny he wasn't forced to give up.

"It was no routine lick," Diego Lopez insisted. From inches away, Angel could smell the chocolate bars, which Diego inhaled like air, on his homeboy's breath.

"Right," Angel agreed, "you fucked up."

"*Mierda*, without me, that dude had you iced."

"Chester have me out already."

"With shit to show for it, 'cept for a court date."

"And a free city lunch," Cesar chipped in, then added, "Diego did save our asses."

Angel glared at Cesar, who pursed his lips and looked down, although he kept shuffling his feet and tapping his fingers on his blue jean-clad thighs. Cesar was always in motion.

The homeless couple who watched the shop for *El Tigre* at night sat on two plastic Pepsi shipping cartons watching the show, sharing swigs from a jug of cooking brandy. With no apparent regard for Diego, Angel made an act of looking through the shop's open back door, taking in a room whose walls were plastered with posters of Jesus, Mexican boxer Julio Cesar Chavez, and bare-chested women with breasts the size of speed bags. A circular table held remnants of the poker game from the night before: cigarette butts heaped in thin, bent metal ashtrays; empty, crushed beer cans; cards and chips; and an open spiral notebook for tallying debts. Angel could smell the odor of flat beer, acrid cigarettes and deep-fried pig's ears. Stereos, TVs, computers, laptops and DVDs teetered in stacks everywhere—none in boxes. A nice lick, Angel thought, if he could unload it all without *El Tigre* knowing; something to keep in mind for the future. Not that he feared *El Tigre*. The tailor had earned his nickname not because of any inborn ferocity but because his clothes were so poorly made, his customers might as well shred them.

Angel turned back to Diego as a car backfired next door at the muffler shop: *El Pedorrero*, the farter. Angel said, his voice flat, cold and final, "Same split."

"No."

Angel's right fist slammed into Diego's gut, just above the gold belt buckle he'd taken from a house in Southgate they'd hit. One of the buttons on the tartan wool shirt Diego wore over a white T-shirt gouged into Angel's knuckles. It stung, but didn't slow his attack. Angel shoved Diego against the wall of the loading bay that was covered with Evergreen gang graffiti. Angel delivered three quick punches to Diego's head.

"Same split?" Angel demanded as Diego collapsed. "Same split? *Justo?*"

"*Sí, sí,*" Diego wailed from a fetal position on the chipped, dirty and soda-stained concrete. He cradled his head in his hands to protect himself from Angel who kicked him in the back, legs and head. "*No mas. No mas.*"

"Next time, take the dude's car." Angel kicked Diego again. "Next time, don't hit the dude's shit-box car with the van." Another kick. "Next time, don't question me." A final vicious kick.

Gasping, Angel sat on a plastic Coke shipping case and shook a Marlboro Red out of a cigarette pack from his front shirt pocket. Hard to breathe with the smog today.

The unlit cigarette in his mouth, Angel counted out 25 twenties from the lick's $2,200 take and tossed them with disdain onto the prone Diego.

"Got enough for trade school?" Cesar asked Angel.

"Soon." In Phoenix, electrician school beckoned. Then a real job, real money and no more hanging with these *pendejos*.

"Bad luck that dude coming home." Cesar lit Angel's cigarette with a silver lighter, which shook as Cesar held it out. Did Cesar shake even when he banged a girl?

Cesar said, "Knocking on the front door always worked before."

Angel took a satisfying drag from the Marlboro. He glanced at Diego as the fallen homeboy scrambled to his feet and collected his cash off the filthy ground. He shot Angel an angry look, just short of being a challenge, and brushed off his black jeans.

"At least all he had was a golf club." Cesar giggled at the memory. "He'd had a gun, we'd all be in the dirt."

Angel asked, "What's on tonight?"

"Party at Felicity's. Kickin' it," Cesar said as he staged an enthusiastic little dance of glee.

Angel nodded; it might be fun, but he doubted it.

"Nothing like today though." Cesar stopped his dance when he saw Angel's lack of enthusiasm. "That garage door opened easier than a can of refried beans. You looked like the Blue Demon kicking in the door. One kick and we're in, like a free-for-all at WalMart."

Angel nodded. It had been great.

"Nothing like it, but sex," Cesar said, relishing the memory with a broad smile.

"Only if it's done right," Diego said as he leaned against the chipped cinder-block wall of the shop, shifting his back to get comfortable after his beating. "Me and Ms. Rollinson could really do it right."

Cesar giggled at the mention of an English teacher at their school.

"Only you'd do it wrong," Angel said and glared at Diego. Their eyes met. After a moment Diego lowered his gaze to the loading bay floor. Angel tossed a wad of cash at Diego and barked, "Get Modelo's for tonight."

Chapter 4

"If you want to go get something to eat, go." It was the voice of Arden's mother.

"I don't want to leave Arden," his stepfather said. His voice dropping, he added, "And I don't want to go alone."

"For Heaven's sake, why not?"

"Please keep it down," Marisela said.

Arden could tell his parents had been arguing for some time. Creeping farther out of the dark pool in which he had been immersed, he forced his eyes open the narrowest possible slit. He saw his parents' tense faces glaring at each other across the bed on which he lay. His head, right arm and shoulder ached. It rushed back to him: the stock loss, the burglary, the blow to his head. His gaze flicked around. He must be in an ER. Marisela stood at the end of the gurney, her face marred by a concerned, worried frown.

Even with slit eyes, the fluorescent light above him burned into Arden's retinas. Closing his eyes tight, he tried to rid his head of the throbbing behind his eyes, which shot miniature lightning bolts of pain throughout his head as if every neuron was screaming.

"I'm starting to get a headache," his stepfather said. "I need something to eat. You know I'm pre-diabetic and pre-diabetics have to eat regularly."

"Then go," his mother said, exasperated.

"Where? I'll get lost. This place is a maze. Every hall looks the same. You'd think they'd paint each hall a different color. That would make it easier, unless you're colorblind. They'd have to use primary colors."

Arden wished he was up to talking. He could have resolved the budding argument. He always had. As the youngest child, he'd been the one left home alone with his mother and stepfather when his older siblings escaped to college. He had been the one left to weather the arguments when his parents, no longer with young, impressionable children, slid into open warfare. Without him, they would never still be married. Arden "Never-Fail" Jeffries, the finest negotiator in the country. Why couldn't he summon the energy to say something?

"I'll go with you," Marisela said.

"No, no, no," Arden's mother cut in. "You stay with Arden. I'll go with him."

"I can stay with Dad, if you want," Arden's daughter, Sam, offered. Arden heard a page turn. He wanted to open his eyes to see Sam, but he couldn't. The pain was already too much even with his eyes closed. He felt nauseous.

"How can you do homework at a time like this, Samantha?" Arden's mom asked.

"It's not homework."

"What is it?"

"A scholarship application for Georgia Tech; due Friday."

"Isn't Georgia Tech in Atlanta?" Arden's stepfather asked. "I'd detest going there; horrendous muggy summers and bugs everywhere."

"Thirty percent of their engineering students are women," Sam said, her voice as confident as ever. "They graduate more female engineers than anywhere else in the country."

"I'm hungry," Arden's stepfather said. "Feeling a little faint."

"Let's go then," his mom said, anger rising through her self-imposed role as martyr.

"No, you don't want to leave Arden," his stepfather said.

"If you won't go alone, I'm not going to ask Marisela or Samantha to leave Arden," his mother said. "Let's go."

"I can wait."

"Let's go."

If only he was up to talking, Arden thought. If only.

Chapter 5

"Arden," Marisela's strained, yet urgent voice intruded upon Arden's sleep. "Arden." Sharper this time.

"Yeah," Arden said, forcing his mind to surface from its slumber, even as he kept his eyes closed. "What?"

"What's your name?"

"Arden." She'd just said it; how bad could his memory be?

"Your *full* name."

When Arden remained silent, Marisela gave his shoulder a shove that rocked him as they lay in bed.

He squinted as he took in the darkness in the bedroom and the absence of light coming through the blinds. Under the covers it was wonderfully warm and he could smell Marisela's shampoo; sweet, clean and fresh. "What time is it?"

"An hour since I last asked you your name—your full name."

"I'm fine." He rolled back toward his edge of the Queen-sized bed and feigned sleep. His head throbbed. His shoulder ached. Why didn't she just leave him alone? He was injured and exhausted. He craved sleep. Wasn't sleep the best medicine?

"What's your name?"

Sighing, Arden recited in a monotone, "Thomas Marshall Jeffries, officer, and I didn't do it. I swear. I was home in bed at the time being harassed by my wife, although at the time I did consider killing her."

"Enough with the dramatics. I don't like this any more than you do, but if you sleep too long and you're bleeding into your brain, you'll be dead by morning."

"At least then I'd be able to get some sleep."

"Not on my watch. You don't think I'd let you die on me and leave me to face a $130,000 loss. Where do you live?"

"Only $126,000."

"Where do you live?"

He tried to fall asleep. If he did, maybe she would leave him alone.

Another shove. At least she shoved his uninjured arm. His right shoulder ached as if it had been hit with a boulder.

"2222 Braddock Street, at least until I can find a quieter place to sleep, maybe under the 405 overpass on Jefferson."

"That can be arranged."

"How? Please tell me."

"Talk to you in an hour."

"Two hours?"

"One."

"Two and I'll make you breakfast." He prayed his head would stop pounding by then. Sam could help. She liked helping him in the kitchen.

"One hour. Doctor's orders."

"Any orders about skipping an interrogation session in exchange for French toast with Macdonald maple syrup, the finest?"

"Tempting, but no. I'd rather have you alive in the morning; grumpy but alive. One hour." She gently kissed his bad shoulder in the dark.

"Can't I just die in peace?"

"Nope."

"Can't we negotiate?"

"Never; you're a professional. I'd lose."

Arden felt Marisela roll over and heard her reset the alarm for another hour. He tried to allow sleep to conquer the throbbing in his head. Minutes passed. Every muscle in his body felt strained and worn. He tried to relax. He started by relaxing his toes and worked his way up his body, seeking relaxation and sleep. It didn't work.

Still facing away, Marisela asked out of the darkness, "How could we lose $126,000 in a morning?"

"Stocks go up and stocks go down."

"Brilliant analysis." She turned toward him. The bed squeaked.

"In my defense, I do have a concussion." Arden rolled onto his side to face her in the darkness, just able to discern her wonderful shape beneath the covers. He loved women's hips. "Maybe Antioch will go up $126,000 tomorrow."

"We better go back to the hospital."

"Why?"

"If you believe that, your brain *is* scrambled." After a pause, she said, "You seem to be taking it well."

"Probably still in shock from the concussion."

"Guess we can figure out what to do tomorrow."

"Not much point worrying about it now, just make us mad."

"Or keep us mad." She turned her pillow over, thumped it and settled back down. "Why'd we ever buy so much company stock?"

"Antioch's stock-matching plan was generous, and they gave me a pile of stock options when I took early retirement."

"Eleven years in a lab at Antioch and for what?"

"Twenty-two years in HR," Arden said, thinking back to all his years in human resources with the pharmaceutical giant. He and Marisela had met at Antioch.

"A lot of years to lose."

"Too many. I've been working since I was 16. We skipped vacations and fixing up the house, drove old cars, never replaced anything unless it broke, all to save for retirement and now we could be working until…until…" He did not want even to think about it.

"How long do you think?"

Forced to, he considered the question. "Five or six years to save what we lost," Arden said, forcing his aching head to function. "Assuming Antioch doesn't fall farther tomorrow."

"Will it?"

"The Devil only knows."

"What about the Las Cruces house?"

Over the July 4th weekend they had fallen in love with a white abode, Spanish-style house just below the crest of a mesa west of Las Cruces, New Mexico. The two-story living room had floor-to-ceiling windows offering sweeping views of the broad Mesilla Valley, the meandering Rio Grande river and the jagged Organ Mountains beyond. The sellers wanted a long escrow, which suited Arden and Marisela, since they planned to work in Los Angeles for one more year before retiring.

Arden said, "We should still be able to afford it, but I don't know how long we can carry two mortgages without draining our savings."

"We can replenish our savings when we sell this place."

"That's the plan."

Marisela fell silent. Arden sighed and tried to relax again, fighting to push financial worries out of his mind. He lost the fight.

"Did you check the doors and windows?"

"Yeah." Arden was discouraged and sore, but eager to fall back asleep.

"Are you sure you checked every window?"

"Certain." Arden sensed the worry in his wife's voice. Keeping his eyes shut for one more glorious minute, he steeled his nerves and with great reluctance swung his feet out of bed. The room swung, swayed and dipped, then settled down to a point where the nausea that engulfed his body receded to a manageable level.

"Where are you going?"

"To check all the doors and windows." If he went as slow as a sloth, he could do it without vomiting. He would find nothing unlocked and, even if he did, who gets robbed twice in 48 hours?

Marisela sat up and switched on her bedside lamp. Arden squinted to minimize the offending light as it assaulted his brain through his sensitive eyes. She sat rigid, her face set, deep lines radiating from the ends of her sensuous mouth and dark eyes. "I thought you said they were all locked."

"You'll worry unless I check again."

"I won't."

"You will. I can't remember much of anything since I got whacked on the head anyway. For all I know, I left the television, stereo and stove on."

"You didn't."

"How can you be so sure?"

"They stole the television and stereo."

"Maybe just the stove then."

Nervous, nauseous and hurting, Arden checked the house. He knew no one would be there, yet his aching body disagreed. He was tense, scared and had to swallow several times before stepping around the dark corner into the kitchen at the bottom of the stairs. At least the nausea was subsiding into an uneasy miasma that engulfed him, as if it was a premonition of sickness to come, soon.

Arden returned from his reconnaissance to find Marisela still sitting up in bed, clutching his pillow to her stomach. In the halo of her bedside lamp, she looked like a frightened child.

"Everything's locked, barred and bolted," he reported. "The drawbridge is up, the moat is full of crocodiles, and the watch is armed and alert." With his head pounding, he felt as if he was about to fall over and his feet were freezing. It was a warm night, but the wood floors felt like ice. Were cold feet a symptom of brain damage?

"Thanks," Marisela said with the broad warm smile that could make him do whatever she wanted. She patted his good shoulder, handed him his pillow and, turning off her light, snuggled back under the covers.

Arden slipped back into bed and felt the warmth of the covers envelope him. Waiting for his head to stop feeling as if he was at sea in a gale, he watched her in the darkness. She was worried. He had not heard the alarm when she last checked on him; apparently she had not needed it. Losing $126,000 in a day was a great boon to insomnia. Worse, she had endured a tortuously long day. She had dealt with the doctor, the police, and started the burglary claim process with the insurance company, all while shepherding his parents around the hospital to the ER, radiology, the cafeteria, and then back to the parking structure to find their car. Worried, his parents fell to bickering, which caused them to lose their sense of place, time and, it seemed, logic. Marisela had alluded to it all as she and Arden brushed their teeth and prepared for bed. In a crisis she came through, but Arden knew from long experience that she was exhausted afterward, often too exhausted to sleep. She turned over again.

Arden shifted with the utmost care over from his back onto his good, left side with as little disturbance of the bed as possible and tried to find sleep. The throbbing in his head and aching in his right arm and shoulder made it a challenge, not to mention the knowledge that in less than an hour Marisela's sweet, yet insistent voice would once again ask him his name, date of birth and address. At least she did not ask for his bank PIN number and retirement account passwords. He would never remember all of them.

The neurosurgeon who checked the CT scan of his skull found no fractures and no internal bleeding, but Arden's head still ached. It throbbed if he opened his eyes. Tentacles of pain shot through his head if he made any sudden movements with his head. The neurosurgeon told Marisela to check him every hour throughout the night and to watch for dizziness, severe or sudden headaches, double or blurred vision, dilated pupils, ringing in the ears, bad taste in his mouth, moodiness or drowsiness. Who wouldn't be drowsy after such a brutal day? Because of the concussion, the neurosurgeon had hesitated to prescribe pain killers for Arden's arm and shoulder. Drugs could worsen any possible brain damage. The bones in his right shoulder, arm and hand had no breaks, but they all ached with a dull, cold tingle that bordered on the fringes of agony. Twinges of pain coursed through them if he moved in certain ways and he could never be sure which way would cause the painful twinges. Arden could not remember what had happened when he got hit from behind, but he must have fallen against the metal shelves near the garage door as he crumpled to the floor.

The neurosurgeon said Arden had suffered a concussion that would probably have little, if any long-term affect, but warned Arden that his memory might be affected. Arden remembered most of the day: clearing his desk of three settled mediation cases, saying goodbye to colleagues at work, the stock loss, arriving home, the leaning fence, arming himself with his golf club, the burglars and....nothing. Well, nothing until he was at the ER. Had Marisela taken him to the hospital or had he gone by ambulance? The only ambulance ride of his life and he missed it? He wondered how loud the siren was inside. How comfortable was the gurney? Did it feel like you were whipping through the streets at 60 mph? How fast do ambulances actually go? Do they go faster if you are about to die and slower if it's only a broken arm? Does the driver carry charts of medical conditions and how fast to drive for each? He wondered who had found him: Sam? He hoped not, or Harry, his neighbor?

The doctor said he might lose bits and pieces of other memories besides this afternoon's gap. Arden hoped to God he could still remember enough to do his job. He had cases to mediate and he never took notes. He ran through several cases in his head. He seemed to remember everything he needed to know: parties, major and minor issues, resolution strategies, opening and most recent negotiating positions, rate of movement in positions, stage of the mediation process, and a dozen other factors crucial to each case. But how would he know if he could not remember something? If you lost your memory, did you remember that you had forgotten something?

"What was that?" Marisela asked, sitting up, tense and rigid, the bed rocking.

"What?" Arden asked, his heart beating fast and his eyes wide, trying to probe the darkness as his ears strained to hear any sounds.

"I thought I heard something outside."

"I didn't hear anything."

"I thought I did."

With her fear seeping into him, Arden decided to take precautions for his next reconnaissance. After sitting up with the utmost care to ensure his head did not rebel, he walked to his home office next door where he armed himself with a bayonet from the closet. Family lore said his grandfather brought the bayonet back from fighting the Japanese in the Pacific, although Arden had learned that the bayonet was Prussian from the 1870s. How it had ever found its way to the Pacific, if it ever really had, he would never know.

Arden protected his already damaged head with a hard hat, a gift from a construction firm in Vancouver for which he had mediated a labor dispute. Armed with 18 inches of steel in his hand and at least some protection for his battered skull, he felt at least slightly more confident searching his house for burglars in the middle of the night than he had the first time. He checked downstairs—nothing, and then silently opened Sam's door to check on her. In the half light through the blinds from a streetlight, he could see she at least was asleep. He stood and watched her with fondness recalling nights watching her sleep as a baby. At least he had not forgotten those memories. He checked her window; closed and locked. His eyes wandered over the walls, wallpapered with images of Space

Shuttles, the moon, Viking mission images of Mars' red terrain, and astronauts hanging in the blackness of space in Manned Maneuvering Units as if they were on a Hollywood set.

With the hard hat and Prussian bayonet hidden in the linen closet just outside their bedroom door so Marisela would not see them and get even more scared, Arden slipped back into the bedroom to reassure her and try to get back to sleep. She settled back under the covers. He glanced at the clock. Twenty-five minutes until her next check on him; barely worth trying to sleep, even in the unlikely event he could find sleep.

The thought of how much money they had lost leapt to the front of his mind. It would take at least six years to save that much to rebuild their retirement funds. Of course, if he was bleeding into his brain, it would not matter to him. Wealth without health was worthless, unless the wealth could buy health; sometimes it could, sometimes it couldn't, and would his heart last another six years? His father and both uncles had died young of heart disease; younger than he was now.

Putting such gloomy thoughts aside even as he told himself to ride the exercise bike tomorrow, Arden wondered if his memory had been damaged. How could he tell? He quizzed himself. Where had they married? Reno. What did they do on their first date? A movie. Which one? *Lion of the Desert*. Good movie, although Marisela had been more interested in talking than watching the film. Great scene of a sword fight on horseback. So far so good.

Crossword clues; a good test. A seven-letter word for befuddle? Flummox, bedevil, confuse, stupefy or, he searched his mind for a moment, astound. How about a nine-letter word for rescuer? Lifesaver, recoverer, deliverer or, he forced his brain to function. Yes, of course, St. Bernard. No problems with his memory there. Or was it memory? Seemed to be more analytical thinking, although he was certain he had used some of those answers before, so they must have been in his memory.

Strictly memory; what is a Pareto optimal solution? In a negotiation, the point at which nothing can be added to one party's position without making the other party worse off. In one sense, the fairest possible negotiated outcome.

Nash equilibrium? In a game in which the players know each other's strategies, if each player has chosen a strategy and no player can benefit by changing their strategy, then the current set of strategy choices and the corresponding payoffs constitute a Nash equilibrium. It was named for the mathematician featured in *A Beautiful Mind*, John Nash. But who played him? Arden trolled through his memory. Cameron Crowe? No, he did *Fast Times at Ridgemont High*, *Jerry McGuire* and *Almost Famous*. John Nash was played by the other Crowe, the *Gladiator* guy...Russell Crowe. Nothing wrong with his memory there.

Old mediation cases? At Antioch he had handled a plethora of HR cases. Only a handful were memorable, although a few were funny. A female lab tech sued Antioch because, as far as Arden could determine from his investigation, the handsome principal investigator in the lab was sexually harassing every other female tech, but not her. Arden grinned. The old proverb was true; people wanted what they did not have.

Arden's most interesting cases had been in the past couple of years after he took early retirement from Antioch and accepted a position at Equitable Mediation. His mind flooded with memories of a movie star's divorce of a Manhattan cocktail waitress who had signed a pre-nup. The ex-waitress appeared to be destined to get not a single dollar of the star's millions since the pre-nup ruled out any compensation until after five years of wedded bliss. They were married four years. Arden liked the ex-waitress and loathed the star, so he was overjoyed when he discovered that the star signed the pre-nup using his stage name, not his real name, voiding the agreement.

Arden recalled a case in Borneo he settled for a mining company that resulted in the gift on his final night of an entire roast pig, from snout to curly tail; hard to get that through customs. At least Jerry Goldstein had not taken that case; what would he do with a roast pig?

Arden smiled. At least those parts of his memory were fine.

Law school? Arden thought for a moment. It had been more than 20 years since he had practiced law. How much could he have remembered even before getting hit on the head? Not much.

History. US history. The Constitution: "We the People of the United States, in Order to form a more perfect Union, establish Justice...." Too easy.

Fifth Amendment? "No person shall be held to answer for any capital, or otherwise infamous crime, unless on a presentment or indictment of a grand jury, except in cases arising in the land or naval forces, or in the Militia, when in actual service in time of War or public danger; nor shall any person be subject for the same offence to be twice put in jeopardy of life or limb; nor shall be compelled in any criminal case to be a witness against himself, nor be deprived of life, liberty, or property, without due process of law; nor shall private property be taken for public use, without just compensation." Memory like a computer.

What was that girl's name in elementary school for whom he had harbored a deep and abiding crush, at least until they were freshman in high school? He frowned in the dark. He had to remember her name. He had loved her, or at least lusted after her. He just had to remember. He squinted in the dark, forcing his mind to remember. He could not remember. He could remember his parents arguing about where to spend Christmas Eve dinner when he was seven, at which of their parents' homes, but he could not remember the love of his life—at least she had been in elementary school. Why not? He had to have known her name before he got smacked on the head. What was her name? Colleen, Karen, Kira? Shannon, Sharon, Susan? Not even a glimmer of a memory.

Giving up, he tried to remember the name of the movie he loved centered on a lawsuit against a company dumping toxic chemicals in the Northeast. John Travolta was excellent in it as the driven, uncompromising lead attorney. It was far better than most of the movies based on Grisham's legal thrillers but, Arden remembered, it was not based on a novel by Grisham. Arden dredged through his mind, but could not remember. He knew he must have known the title. He remembered *Gladiator*, which wasn't bad, but he loved the other movie. What was it called?

Would he have remembered the name of the girl and of the movie if he had not been whacked on the head? Doubt entered his mind. He did remember reading that a high percentage of facts that people are 100 percent certain about knowing, they actually do not remember correctly. But he wasn't even remembering incorrectly. He just could not remember, period. Was that due to the concussion or just normal forgetting? How would he know? Most of everything you see, hear or read you forget anyway. How can you tell what you should have remembered?

This was ridiculous. He rolled over, forced his eyes shut and tried to sleep.

"What's your name?"

Chapter 6

Tuesday, August 5, 2008

"Media's reporting it as an investigation," Antioch CEO Richard Sloane said as he swiveled in his high-backed, tan leather chair. The hum of the Falcon 7X's three Pratt and Whitney turbofans was faintly audible in the plush cabin as the jet cruised at 550 mph 35,000 feet above the Atlantic on its way west. "Couldn't even be bothered to say it was an informal investigation. Not like the SEC's issued a Wells Notice or anything."

"You're assuming they even know the difference between an informal investigation and a formal order of investigation," silver-haired Lincoln Avery said. Seated in another leather chair across a cherry-topped table from Sloane, Lincoln was Antioch Pharmaceutical's Chief Legal Counsel and Vice President for Legal Affairs. "Going to the Olympics?"

"Supposed to, but who knows now?" Sloane had been looking forward to the games in Beijing. "Maddy and Britney will probably end up going by themselves. Antioch has a stack of tickets; boxes at most of the venues." Sloane took a long swallow of his Royal Brackla whisky and soda. His mind returned to what was uppermost amongst his worries. "No way in hell this is going to turn into a formal investigation," he vowed, slamming a fist down on the table. "What's dropped me dead center in their crosshairs?"

Lincoln sipped an ice tea from an etched crystal Collins glass and glanced over Sloane's shoulder at Jennifer DeCarlo.

"Go ahead," Sloane said, answering Lincoln's unspoken question. Jennifer knew more about Sloane's business than his wife did.

"I have not had much time to research the issues involved," Lincoln began in his precise, measured voice, "but basically it appears they fall into the areas of misstatements and omissions, misrepresentations to customers, and insider trading."

"Sounds like bullshit," Sloane said, glancing up as one of the three flight attendants—the busty redhead—approached. He waved her away without a smile. He would make it up to her next time he flew alone.

"It may be," Lincoln agreed. "At this stage, basically they are just informally investigating, requesting documents and our cooperation in arranging interviews with key executives, directors and managers."

"Not me?"

"Not yet."

"Bastards." Sloane took another drink and glanced out a window at the long, white, wind-driven clouds.

"They will get to you or they may not, depending on how much and what they learn from the documents and the interviews."

"I'm just pissed they think they can investigate my firm, send the stock into the crapper, cost me and the firm a fortune in stock value, and then, when all the shouting's over and they discover not a damn thing, say they were just doing their god-damn job."

"This your first dealing with an SEC investigation?"

Sloane shook his head. "First as CEO."

"Relax," Lincoln advised, taking another drink of ice tea. "It is relatively common."

"The stock falling 35 percent in a day isn't." It could cost him his job, if not his wealth. He had been lightening his exposure to Antioch stock.

"Bad timing with the investigation and the clinical trial issues hitting Wall Street the same day, but the stock is already coming back."

"Crawling back."

"It is headed in the right direction. Maybe the Dow will top 40,000 like that book predicted."

Ignoring Lincoln's optimistic hopes, Sloane asked, "Are the FBI or US Attorney involved?" If they were, Sloane knew, it was much more serious. They investigated behavior that was clearly criminal and, unlike the SEC, were far less amenable to reasonable negotiation.

"Not that I know of, but I am obligated to warn you that the SEC never confirms or denies whether any other government bodies are investigating the same areas of concern."

Sloane snorted and looked at Lincoln with an expectant stare.

"One of my staff used to be with the US Attorney's Office, so I am certain on that count, but my contacts at the FBI were harder to reach," Lincoln said, lowering his voice, even if Sloane had vouched for Jennifer. "I had not heard back before I had to board the aircraft. Even if they are involved, the government is bared from using information from the SEC investigation to build a criminal case."

"At least not officially," Sloane said. "Chinese walls are about as porous as a torn screen door."

"I recommend hiring an outside law firm to investigate everything in which the SEC might even remotely be interested."

"They won't find a damn thing. There's nothing to find."

"Even so, the appearance of cooperating and investigating ourselves will enable us to negotiate a better deal with the SEC if it ever comes to a Wells Notice."

"That'll never happen."

"It might."

Sloane glared at Lincoln, then backed off. Lincoln might be right. "Who?"

Lincoln considered, swishing the ice around in his tea. "Ken Lim of Arnold, Birch, Boardman and Epstein would be a fine choice."

"Set it up."

"I also recommend, strongly, that you instruct everyone on your executive team to cooperate fully."

"Done. I'll draft an email before we land and set up some face time with each VP to hammer home the importance of cooperation." He could also use the face time to ensure that each executive still supported him.

"I further recommend that you instruct the board and your executive team that they should not alter or destroy any documents, even if they are as incriminating as a confession. A single altered, let alone destroyed document can mean 20 years in prison and up to a $10 million fine; far worse than if the SEC finds evidence supporting every single issue."

"They'll cooperate." Sloane fiddled with the emerald cufflinks Maddy had given him when they arrived at Cowes. She had seen them at Tiffany's in New York and thought they were perfect for him. She had a weakness for cufflinks, watches, ties, shoes, and just about anything else that caught her eye, for him or her, up to and including cars, houses and a private garden she had bought in Belgravia one weekend in London on a whim.

"Excellent," Lincoln said, beaming at his client. "If you fully cooperate, the odds of being sanctioned are zero."

"Potential damage?"

"For misstatements, the largest settlements for a company can run up to $50 million, for individuals up to $225,000."

"Peanuts."

"Fines are not really something we need consider. For all types of charges, if you head them off at the administrative proceeding stage, only about 18 percent pay any fine at all," Lincoln explained with his cultured, well-modulated voice. Sloane sometimes thought he sounded like a Shakespearean actor playing an attorney. "If a case reaches the courts, about 80 percent pay a fine. Jail time is never imposed."

"Jail's out of the question. Antioch's done nothing wrong and neither has anyone on the Antioch team," Sloane said, his indignation growing.

"Of course," Lincoln nodded, serene and completely at ease.

"Our D&O insurance will cover any fines and costs?"

Lincoln nodded about the directors and officers insurance. "In most cases."

"Civil penalties?"

"In 2006 AIG paid $800 million," Lincoln said, his ice tea half way to his mouth as he stared at Sloane, letting the figure sink in.

"That's gotta hurt," Sloane said, working out how much such a penalty would hurt the company's bottom line; significantly, but far from crippling with $5 billion a year in net income.

"It was the largest penalty they have ever imposed. A $100 million civil penalty and a $700 million disgorgement, so in essence they had to give back their ill-gotten gains and pay a $100 million fine."

"I'm sure their gains were a damn sight more than what the SEC uncovered."

"Undoubtedly."

"What was the fine for?"

"Securities fraud."

"Let's hope to God no one at Antioch's done that," Sloane said, before vowing, "If they have, they're gone."

"Of course." Lincoln smiled.

"I will not allow such behavior on my watch."

"Of course not."

"Never."

"If it happened, it would be no reflection on you; one bad apple among 12,000 employees," Lincoln said. "Not your fault at all. Only a vile person would let such a thought even cross their mind, let alone ever voice it."

Half an hour later, Sloane stalked from bulkhead to bulkhead in his bare feet on the plush flock-dyed wool carpet in the jet's master cabin. The suite contained a Queen-sized bed, a full bathroom and big-screen plasma television built into a bulkhead. Andre Bocelli's tenor filled the cabin from the built-in stereo system. His singing usually soothed Sloane.

"I don't know why you bothered to have me rush from Portsmouth to Heathrow, fly to Laussane and then all the way across the Atlantic just to hear you rant about the SEC," Jennifer DeCarlo said. She lounged on the bed, sitting atop the rose red coverlet, a Riesling-filled goblet in her right hand. Her long-fingered left hand was draped over a pillow, displaying a ring with a yellow diamond the size of a kernel of corn.

Sloane stopped, drank down the last of the whiskey in his crystal tumbler and glared at Jennifer. "The SEC has no God-damn right to investigate Antioch. We've done nothing wrong. They'll owe me and every Antioch employee an apology before this is over."

"When will we be in Boston?" Jennifer asked, yawning and not even bothering to hide it. A mistress, Sloane thought, could behave in ways he would never let a wife even consider.

"We're stopping in Washington first. Andrea's juggling my calendar." His calendar was often booked a year in advance.

"Washington?" Jennifer asked with a frown. He knew she hated the capital; far too few people she knew with whom to socialize, shop or gossip.

"I have to talk to some people I know at the SEC." Sloane set his tumbler on a teak bedside table. "I have to head this off before it gathers any steam."

"Are you in trouble?"

Sloane sniffed. At least Maddy had asked, "Are *we* in trouble?"

"Who knows?" He could smell Jennifer's perfume, reminding him of illicit rendezvous from Paris to Shanghai, London to Johannesburg, and a dozen less-exotic locations in between. Visions of her lovely breasts bouncing over him as they had sex flitted across his mind. She loved being on top and he was far from against such a position.

Jennifer frowned, which only increased the allure of her cute features. She looked 21, with a turned-up nose and mischievous eyes that promised to take you to Heaven or Hell; you just never knew which.

"Don't you know if you've broken the law?" she asked.

"Course not. The IRS code and the SEC regulations are tens of thousands of pages long. No one knows them all and even for the parts that are well known, I could ask seven different experts the same question and if I showed you the answers, you'd swear I'd asked each one a completely different question."

"But one of them would be right."

"Maybe, but damned if I'd know which one."

"You could call the SEC or the IRS."

"And get a different answer every day of the week from them, too. There's enough gray area in their rules to cast a shadow from Washington to Boston."

"Sounds like a nightmare."

"We make money and let the lawyers make sure we don't bend any laws too far. If we make money, everyone benefits anyway." He leaned against the wood-paneled bulkhead by the bed and added,

"Everything my team's done, we've checked with our attorneys up and down the line, and the board approved it all. Antioch is spotless as a choir boy scrubbed clean for Sunday mass."

"Good." Jennifer set her empty wine goblet down on the teak side-table. Looking up at him through the tops of her enormous eyes, she asked, "So, are we going to fuck or not?"

Chapter 7

"Dow's up," Arden told Marisela as she tore a toasted bagel in two. "Antioch's meandering up and down, like it can't decide whether to plummet even more or roar back up."

Sam munched Cheerios and flipped through a glossy *Aviation Week & Space Technology*.

Marisela nodded and asked. "How's your head?"

"Fine, but it feels odd, probably more from lack of sleep than anything else." Arden was unshaven and his teeth were encased in a layer of gummy grime. The thieves had stolen his razor and electric toothbrush. Who steals a toothbrush? Would they bother to change the head before they used it?

His head had an odd sensitive sensation. He feared that if he moved too fast, his skull might come apart like a violently shaken 3D puzzle. His shoulder and arm were still sore, but had ceased throbbing, settling into dull, constant aches that distracted his thoughts. He took a bite of cereal and got a rather nice blueberry in the spoonful. At least his sense of taste had not been affected. Glancing over at the mess left by the burglars in the family room, he thought about doing some cleaning up after breakfast.

Neither Marisela nor Sam looked like they wanted to talk. Marisela hunched over her food, her face slack and body in languid repose. She appeared to be engulfed in her own thoughts. Sam flipped through images of aircraft, engines and rockets. Guidebooks for Atlanta, Boston and Indiana sat stacked beside her bowl.

She had her heart set on going to Georgia Tech, MIT or Purdue next fall in pursuit of her dream of becoming an astronaut.

Arden asked, "Done your homework?"

Sam nodded without looking up from an image of the Space X Dragon rocket.

"Mom check it?"

Sam nodded.

"Not that I remember much calculus," Marisela warned.

"Don't look at me," Arden said. "I've never used calculus in a case."

Arden stared down at his breakfast. Beside his bowl sat a blank crossword from *The Globe and Mail*. Equitable Mediations subscribed to dozens of newspapers. Arden and the other mediators used the newspapers to stay abreast of any disputes they might have to mediate, although Arden used them mainly as a bountiful supply of crosswords. He hoped the Canadian paper of record would offer a challenging crossword, especially since he knew little about beavers, igloos or ice hockey. If the concussion had indeed affected his memory, instead of doing it in his head, he just might have to use a pen. But right now he did not feel like tackling the puzzle.

"Except for Antioch, the market was way up yesterday," he said, "even with all the doom and gloom news about housing, subprime mortgages and the banks."

"Did you lose a lot?" Sam asked, taking a drink of milk. She pushed her long black hair behind her right ear just as her mother did at times.

"Too much," Arden said with a reassuring grin for his daughter. Arden glanced at Marisela, who yawned. He said, "They took the microwave and the coffeemaker." He usually had coffee ready for his night-owl wife when she crawled downstairs.

"Did you add them to the list of stolen things?" Marisela asked.

Arden nodded. Marisela had talked with a Detective Ranjan the night before at the hospital. The detective had requested a list of the stolen property.

"Guess I could heat some water for coffee in a saucepan," Marisela said as she looked doubtfully over at the stove. "At least they didn't steal the stove, and I assume they didn't steal our pots and pans."

"I wouldn't put it past the bastards."

"Arden," Marisela said, tilting her head to the side with a look of displeasure before her gaze flicked over to Sam and then back to Arden.

"I've heard people swear, Mom," Sam said with a giggle. "Your car's got a mega dent in the front, Dad."

The thieves had knocked out Arden, loaded up their pilfered goods and sped out of the garage, smashing into the front driver's side of Arden's ancient Karmann Ghia in the driveway as they escaped.

"Detective Ranjan said it might make it easier to find them," Marisela said.

Sam giggled and said, "Look for a truck with a Kharman Ghia-shaped dent in the front."

Marisela laughed too, then sighed and stretched her neck back as she closed her eyes. "At least tonight I don't have to wake you every hour. I barely slept at all."

"Me neither," Sam chipped in, finishing her breakfast and taking the dishes over to the dishwasher. "I kept waking up."

"Scared?" Arden asked.

"It's freaky to think of someone, some stranger or, worse, strangers in our house. Weird and scary."

"It won't happen again," Arden said. "It's a once-in-a-lifetime thing."

"It scared me," Marisela said. "Everything seems..." Her dark eyes flitted around the room over the spots where the missing appliances had resided just the day before. "Dirty and dusty and messy."

"We'll clean it up, replace everything and get it all back to normal as soon as the insurance company settles with us." Arden hoped the insurance would cover most, if not all of the cost.

Sam trotted upstairs to her room while Marisela continued lethargically eating.

Foregoing his crossword and with little interest in breakfast, Arden took the *Los Angeles Times* off the counter and pulled out the business section. He found a story about Antioch's failing clinical trial for a laboratory-grown heart valve at the bottom of the front page beside a story about the SEC investigation into Antioch that contained a photo of a smiling, confident Richard Sloane. Arden disliked the way Sloane looked: commandingly tall; a touch of gray hair to give a hint of vast experience; a tanned lean face that suggested rugged toughness balanced by a measured smile; and a dark-blue suit and red tie that made him look like every other CEO or politician. Did they all use the same media consultant?

Arden asked Marisela, "Should we sell our Antioch shares?"

"Wouldn't that just lock in our losses?" She munched on her bagel. "I think it'll come back. My parents just bought and held."

Arden nodded. Marisela's implication was clear. Her parents had retired well off, so selling at a loss was a dumb move. He agreed, but he could not help worrying. He wished he had her great faith in the long-term upward trend of the market, even after 10 months of a bear market. What if they were living in a 30-year period of economic contraction? "It could fall a lot more."

"Don't they say you can never time the top or the bottom of the market?"

Arden nodded without enthusiasm.

As she tore her bagel into even smaller pieces, Marisela's tongue poked out from the corner of her mouth, as it did whenever she was deep in thought. "Do you really think we should? If we sell and miss the start of a bull market, we'll miss out on most of the increase. I read that if you missed the few best months in the stock market's history, your return over 20 years went from averaging 8 percent a year to about 2 percent."

"We don't have 20 years." This was not getting them anywhere. No one knew where Antioch, let alone the market, was headed and Marisela was right; if they sold now, they were locking in their losses. Arden watched her for a moment and, guessing the true cause of her worry, said, "Maybe we should get an alarm."

"Or a dog," Marisela said, perking up at the suggestion and stopping her assault on her defenseless bagel. "Or a gun?"

Arden frowned. "I'd go with the alarm," he said, seizing on the least objectionable of the options. "We aren't around enough to give a dog a good home."

"All the more reason to have a dog at home when we aren't."

"It'd chew the furniture, scratch the doors and pee on the carpet."

"They can be trained, you know."

"When are we going to have time to train a dog?"

"Then an alarm."

Arden nodded and Marisela turned her attention back to her bagel.

A few moments later, paraphrasing the news story, Arden said, "Antioch's CEO, Richard Sloane, said the six deaths in the trial were unfortunate, but not directly related to the new heart valve."

"May not have been," Marisela said.

"Some analyst says this could cripple Antioch in the short run, if the trial fails."

"Do you think it will cripple the whole company?" Marisela ate some more of her blueberry bagel. "Antioch's a huge multi-national."

"Sloane agrees. He says it's just one of several of the company's major clinical trials; nothing to worry about. Antioch is strong, will continue to innovate and will recover. Blames it on a personnel problem. A VP was fired over it; oh, sorry, resigned to spend more time with his family and pursue other interests. But the SEC's investigating Sloane and Antioch."

"What for?"

"Misstatements to investors, for one thing."

"I've kept in touch with some of the researchers over there and they're confident this will blow over."

"Any insider information?"

"Nothing to make us a fortune, but it might be best to hold on, don't you think? In the long run, the market will go back up."

"In the long run, we're all dead," Arden said, even though he grinned as he said it. His eyes wandered over to the empty space on the bureau in the family room where their flat-screen television had been until yesterday. He should clean it up. Shards from the garage door still lay scattered in a triangle pattern on the carpet.

Finishing her bagel, Marisela asked, "Can you look into getting an alarm today?"

"Okay, and I'll keep an eye on Antioch. We're down four or five year's worth of savings already just on Antioch alone."

"I guess we should try to save more."

Arden nodded.

Marisela hesitated and said, "Yesterday at work four people were laid off."

Arden shut his eyes and sighed. Opening them, he met her gaze and said, "You had one hell of day."

"Yours wasn't much better." She reached over, took his left wrist and felt for his pulse.

"It isn't off."

She nodded, but still concentrated on taking his pulse.

"I'm fine."

She nodded again. Resigned, he waited for the verdict.

Marisela nodded a minute later. "Sounds steady and even." She rose and walked over to the counter between the kitchen and dining area. "I think I should be okay. I have seniority and my team is pretty lean. We've had some promising results recently." She sounded braver than she looked.

Arden nodded. "Maybe we should stop using the gardener. Sam and I can keep the yard looking alright."

"And maybe the cleaning lady."

Arden nodded.

"Aurora's been with us for years; maybe give her a month's severance?"

Arden loathed the sound of such a severance package, but nodded. It would save them money in the long run. "Stop the magazine subscriptions?" Arden pushed Sam's aviation magazine across the kitchen table toward Marisela, who nodded with a sad, reluctant look.

"And the newspaper," she said.

"I can read it online for nothing or get a copy from work. I can ask for more cases."

"There's often piece work other labs need done, nights and weekends."

Arden hated the sound of that. She already worked long hours. "Are you sure?"

"We've been planning to retire early since we got married. I don't want all those years of saving to have been for nothing. If I have to miss a few evenings and weekends with you and Sam in the short run, so be it."

"What about Sam's college-scouting trip?"

"We paid for half already."

Arden nodded. "Retire to a cheaper place?"

"We both love Las Cruces and that house."

"Carrying two mortgages will be tougher now. If we put off buying the Cruces house, it'd be less risky."

"Don't we have other investments?"

"We do, but we just lost $130,000."

"$126,000." Marisela smiled for a moment.

"With the housing market falling," Arden said, "this place isn't worth what it used to be so we won't have as much left over after we sell it and pay off the Las Cruces house. That means less to live on when we retire."

"Can we even afford the Cruces house now?" She ran a hand through her hair, twitching the ends of her dark tresses.

Arden noticed the angry, red chewed part of her right thumb just above her nail. "We probably can, but the stocks we were going to sell for the down payment are worth less than they were, so we'll have to sell more of them."

"When's the down payment due?"

"Closing day: October 18."

"At least the sellers wanted a long escrow. Better chance stocks will be up again by then."

"I hope so." The plan to buy the house in New Mexico and then sell their Los Angeles home in a year or so to pay off the New Mexico house, which had seemed so safe and simple to Arden, now seemed far more risky. "We're cutting it tight, but I think we can still manage it." Arden rose and walked over to the counter beside Marisela.

"Sounds like we should work a few more years," she said. "Maybe you could take a consulting job."

Arden did not answer. He hated when his colleagues took consulting positions with companies that had just been involved in mediation cases with his firm. Even if there was no impropriety, such behavior reeked of a conflict of interest.

"Just a short-term position," Marisela suggested.

"We should be alright," Arden said. He sighed. He felt tired, worn out and powerless in the face of the recent devastating changes in their lives. "It's only a couple more years of working. What difference can it make?" He swallowed, wondering.

Marisela looked at him and their eyes met. She said, "You aren't your father or uncle."

Arden nodded.

"I want you alive to enjoy a long retirement with me."

"So do I."

"How long will we need to work?"

"I won't know until Antioch settles down. The market's been trending down. Hard to know how much money we have, let alone how much we'll need."

"At least Sam's college fund is alright."

"She's lost some, but she should still be able to go to any college she wants."

"She wants Georgia Tech, MIT or Purdue."

"Our daughter the aeronautical engineer. Where did that come from? Did I toss her up in the air a lot when she was a baby?"

"She doesn't own any Antioch stock, does she?"

"No." Arden shook his head. "She's safe."

Chapter 8

After calling their bosses to say they would be in late, Arden and Marisela went through every room in the house, making a list of everything they could remember that was missing. Sam tagged along, having already made a list for her room the night before.

It took them more than an hour to go through the house. Every room was like some demented game of reverse concentration: match the image of the room in your memory with what you are seeing now. What's missing?

"The Ethiopian sword's gone," Marisela said, pointing at the space above the stairs where a scimitar had hung from a red velvet lanyard.

"Why'd they have to take that?" As a boy, Arden had admired the ornate, ivory-handled sword, which his great grandfather, a Canadian, had brought back in 1924 from Ethiopia where he had served in a League of Nations mission to end slavery in the African nation.

After making an inventory of everything they could remember that was missing, Arden and Marisela searched their financial files for receipts for the missing items. They found one for the flatscreen television from the family room, which they had bought as a present to each other the previous Christmas. They found no other receipts. Who keeps a receipt for an electric razor or a coffeemaker?

Next they dove into their photographs, which an agent had suggested doing when Marisela called their insurance company's

24/7 claim line the previous night. Most of their photos had been on their home computer, which the burglars had taken, but by using Arden's work laptop they accessed the website from which they printed their photos. Most of the pictures except for the most recent were on the site. They found a few photos that showed Sam's television in the background, but other than that, all were of trips, outings, Sam's school events or backyard barbecues. None showed anything that had been stolen.

"Not exactly a mountain of evidence," Arden said, eyeing the long list of stolen goods and the lone receipt and single photograph. "Sure wish I'd photographed my electric toothbrush," he added with a grin.

Even though it was past 11, before she left for work Marisela started to dust the television room.

"I'll do that later," Arden assured her.

"I'd rather have it cleaned up now."

"I'm usually the neat freak." She didn't even smile. Arden sighed and helped pick up the splinters from the garage door as Marisela dusted.

After they finished, Marisela asked, "Can you get the door replaced today? I don't want to spend another night with it broken." Marisela looked at him with a look that pleaded for understanding.

"I'll do my best." Arden hugged her. "With the garage door closed, no one will know the door's broken."

"I'll know."

Later that morning, Arden sat on the sofa and opened yesterday's mail as he listened to a transistor radio he had found, which the burglars had not.

"President Bush's personal envoy to the Middle East is meeting today with the President of the Palestinian National Authority, Mahmoud Abbas," the announcer said. "US envoy Jason Sardina said prospects for a comprehensive settlement remained remote, but that progress is being made."

"Give me a call Sardina, we can reach a fair agreement in one long weekend of talks, no problem," Arden told the radio. "Then we can tackle Northern Ireland and get that little disagreement solved by the end of the month."

Arden sighed and tried to relax. He felt a vague all-encompassing nervousness about the Antioch stock, retirement, the Las Cruces house, repairing his smashed car, Marisela's and Sam's fears about another burglary, and replacing everything that had been stolen. It seemed like too much to worry about and too much to do. He felt as if he should be doing something every second. His body just would not relax. His innards were vibrating, unable to remain still no matter what he tried.

He glanced down at the mail in his lap from the World Wildlife Fund, Amnesty International, three bills, *Drug Discovery Today* for Marisela, the *Aeronautical Journal* for Sam, and the Peace Corps alumni magazine for him. None of it seemed of much importance at the moment.

Someone rang the doorbell. Rusty, Harry's coon dog next door, woofed.

Arden's other neighbor, Buell, was at the door in shorts and a Napa Valley winery T-shirt. "When are you going to fix your fence?"

Arden scratched his head to buy time. He was not prepared. Preparation was crucial to a successful negotiation. Without it, you could find yourself in worse shape after reaching a deal than if you had not negotiated at all.

"We both use the fence, so maybe we can both chip in to cover the repairs," Arden proposed with a neighborly grin. A headache lurked just behind his eyes, threatening to engulf his head.

"It's on your property; your fence, your bill."

Arden was about to dispute the point, when Buell added, "If it falls against my house, you'll be paying the cost to repair the damage."

The thought that Buell was a jackass crossed Arden's mind, but he realized he would have to negotiate with Buell, just not now. Time to reset the process. "I know the fence issue needs to be resolved and I agree it's important, but I'm a little busy right now. We were robbed yesterday."

"Robbed? You leave a door unlocked or something?"

Arden had just finished a light lunch while reading David McCullough's *John Adams*, when Detective Sadhir Ranjan arrived. Ranjan looked to be an exotic mix of Hispanic, Asian and Indian, and about 25 years old or 50. He had the type of skin that aged well, never showing a line until old age was reached, Arden thought, probably sometime in the ninth decade. Once seated in the living room, Arden did his best to describe the burglars.

After noting the description, Ranjan asked, "Had you consumed any alcohol yesterday?"

"Wish I had, would have made the conk on the head hurt less."

"Had you taken any drugs, prescription or otherwise?"

"Not even after the conk on the head."

Arden gave Ranjan the list of stolen property, the sole receipt and the single photograph of the television. The detective started down the list, asking if Arden had any information about the model, size, color, condition or serial number of each stolen item. As he struggled to remember and describe the myriad possessions that had been stolen, Arden grew tired and confused. He wished Marisela and Sam were home to help. He felt as if he was the criminal being grilled, albeit in the nicest way. Wasn't he the victim?

Ranjan asked for the names of anyone who could verify that Arden owned what had been taken. After retrieving their address book, Arden gave Ranjan the names and contact information of friends and family who might be able to support Arden's claims. Did anyone notice a toaster?

Ranjan took scrapings of paint from the bumper of Arden's car where the burglar's truck had smashed into it. Then he went into the garage and found the dented spot where a crowbar had been used to lever up the door. Sighing, Arden realized that was one more thing to fix or replace.

Walking through the garage and into the house, Ranjan checked each room, deep in thought as he inspected everything on each wall from floor to ceiling in careful order from left to right. Arden thought it was nothing like on television dramas in which the police stalked into a room and randomly rutted around, finding the key piece of evidence in seconds. The relentless precision of the inspection made Ranjan seem robotic.

His inspection complete, Ranjan gave Arden his card.

"Any chance we'll see our stuff again?" Arden asked, afraid to have his fears confirmed.

"The more information you can provide about what was taken—serial numbers and makes and models—the better the chances. I wrote the case number on my card. You'll need it for your insurance claim."

"Guess I should have made a list, like they tell you," Arden said lightheartedly, but feeling like an idiot. "Do you know why they targeted our house?"

Ranjan glanced around. "Looks like you tend to leave your blinds open."

"My wife likes the plants to have light."

"Means the burglars can see everything you own. Garage doors are easy to open and the door into the house is an interior door, hollow core. My seven-year-old daughter could kick it in. It doesn't even have a deadbolt."

Arden nodded as he tried to hide his embarrassment.

After Ranjan left, Arden called three alarm companies to make appointments for estimates. Then he called Danny Flores, who did odd jobs for them. Danny had another job lined up for the day, but promised to pick up a solid-core door and deadbolt after work and install it that evening.

Then the loss adjustor from All Risk Insurance arrived. The adjustor used a digital camera to photograph each room and then filled out a loss form on his laptop, listing all of the missing property.

"Do you have receipts for any of the stolen property?"

"One," Arden said, feeling like a fool.

The adjustor smiled. "That's one more than most people have. Don't worry. If we insisted on receipts and proof of all losses, we'd never pay out."

The agent asked Arden a long series of questions about what had happened while he recorded their 30-minute conversation with Arden's permission. Again, Arden felt as if he was on the stand testifying in his own defense and doing a piss-poor job of it.

The agent said as he closed his laptop, "Our goal is to compensate owners for their losses as promptly as possible. You have uninsured motorist coverage, so we'll cover the cost of repairing or, if required, replacing your vehicle. For everything else, with your $43,000 loss limit, I think you should be able to replace everything you've lost. Your deductible is $500."

"Buying all that stuff new will cost more than the value of the old stuff, though," Arden said.

"True, but All Risk, unlike most insurance companies, offers replacement value on stolen and damaged property, not actual value."

"What happens if the police find our property after we've replaced it?"

"In most such cases, we let you decide whether to return the item you purchased and keep the old one or let us dispose of the old item." The adjustor added with a grin, "But this time, please keep your receipts."

That evening the handyman Danny Flores removed the shattered hollow garage door and replaced it with a solid-core door with a heavy duty, 1.5-inch deadbolt. When he was done, Marisela said, "Now maybe I can get some sleep."

After dinner, Arden decided to try to settle the fence issue.

"I'm willing to split the cost of the supplies to repair the fence and we can repair it ourselves together," Arden offered his neighbor, Buell, as fond memories of working with his father building fences filled his mind. "We can both save a little money."

"No," Buell said as he stood in his doorway like an immovable object.

Arden stood on Buell's front steps in the warm evening air. "We'll even get some exercise in the bargain," Arden said. The thought of Tom Sawyer convincing the neighborhood kids to pay him to whitewash a fence flashed through Arden's mind, even though the cases were completely different. Even so, Tom would have handled Buell easily.

"I don't do manual labor," Buell said, his muscular arms crossed over his chest as his face hardened into a severe look of displeasure. "I've never done manual labor in my life."

"I didn't mean to offend you." Arden was beginning to regret having come over to settle what he had thought would be a simple issue. "It wouldn't take long."

"It's your fence, you fix it."

"It's a shared-use fence."

"It's your fence."

"We both use it and if it's falling over, both our properties suffer."

"If you don't paint your house, the neighborhood looks crappy and my property suffers; still doesn't mean I have to split the cost of painting it with you."

"I'd even be willing to go fifty-fifty on the materials and do all the work myself." Arden enjoyed working with Sam.

Buell took a step back, said, "No, it's your fence, you fix it," and slammed the door.

The scream hauled Arden out of a deep sleep. His eyes shot open. His brain scrambled to figure out what was happening. He could just discern Marisela sitting up in bed beside him in the dark. He checked the clock, 3:36 a.m., and reached out toward his wife. His hand had just touched her left arm when she screamed again. Arden recoiled, whipping his hand back as if he had touched a flame.

"Marisela," he whispered, afraid to touch her again.

She did not respond. She sat staring straight ahead into the darkness.

He whispered, "What's wrong?"

Nothing.

Arden swallowed, anxious, afraid and wondering what to do.

"You got them?" Marisela asked, her voice calm.

Arden frowned. He tried to figure out what was happening. His eyes scanned the dark room. He saw no one.

"Did they take anything?" Marisela's tone was clear and precise.

Arden sat up, careful not to touch his wife. Another scream might stop his heart.

"Well, then it's alright," Marisela said, her voice light. "Thank you so much."

With that Marisela rolled back onto her side, pulled up the blankets to her neck and settled in to sleep.

As she fell back asleep, Arden sat staring down at her, bewildered.

Chapter 9

Homeboy, burglar and would-be electrician Angel Morales strode over to a rotating baggage carousel in LAX's Terminal 3. He smiled as he watched the luggage pass before him like candy on a lazy-Susan. He slipped through the cluster of recent arrivals from—he noticed on the board above the carousel—Flight 2301 from Vancouver and stood at the edge of the machine, his right shin against its metal side. Lot of Asians and Indians on this flight.

If Diego or Cesar had been with him, Angel would have used them to shield him, but instead he waited until a tall, blond *bolillo* in a suit next to him started to lift a black suitcase off the carousel. In one smooth motion Angel swung the next bag off the carousel and was walking away before the passenger in the suit had even set his bag down. Angel's new possession looked like a hundred other bags: black and rectangular with built-in wheels and a collapsible handle. As Angel passed a trashcan he tore off the airline baggage tag and tossed it into the can without breaking stride.

Outside as he waited for a light to change to cross the street to the shuttle stop, Angel reached down and opened the bag's identification holder. He slid out the little card with the owner's information neatly penned on it. As the light changed and he started across the street amidst a dozen other travelers, he dropped the white card in the gutter between a chip bag and a crumpled airline boarding pass. In less than three minutes he was back on a bus leaving the airport, his new bag resting against his shins, a contented smile on his face. It was hot out, but the bus was air conditioned, cooling Angel after his brief stint of work.

Angel hoped he would do better this time. In the last bag he lifted he had found a bunch of men's clothes and shoes—too small for him—and a cheap electric razor. A year before in June he had taken a bag and found a treasure trove: a camera, a portable DVD player and a purse with $250 within its leather folds. That lick had put him close to paying for electrician's school in Phoenix, at least until Gabriela, his previous girl, had wanted new shoes. He glanced down at his new sneakers from the most recent house burglary and fondly recalled the fine ones he had bought after snaring that suitcase: $120 and worth every penny.

What some people checked at the airport amazed him. Didn't they know thieves love to get jobs as luggage handlers? It was as good a job as a valet. Cesar had been a valet at a dozen restaurants and made some nice licks before he got his ass fired. It was amazing what people left in their cars and didn't remember until days or even weeks later. Many even left their house keys on their car key rings. The mall parking lot was also a good spot, but smashing a window with the top of an old spark plug could draw attention and rent-a-cops were far more common at the malls than at the airport baggage carousels. Airport security centered on the planes and baggage going out, not bags coming in. A golf course was also an easy place to make some cash. Thousand-dollar sets of golf clubs sitting around like litter. Just had to dress right to fit in.

Later that warm clear day, the stolen bag and its contents disposed of at *El Tigre*'s, Angel strode past a liquor store, its stucco walls adorned with graffiti from end to end and from sidewalk to roof. Feeling content, Angel strolled on past a two-story apartment building with a wide-open front door through which he spotted a row of mailboxes, most with missing or broken doors. He considered scooting in to see if there was anything worth taking, but could see that the boxes were empty. The mail had not yet come today or someone else had beaten him to cleaning out the boxes on the off chance of finding a birthday card with cash or a check to try cashing.

Angel walked on past a row of bungalows, their front yards adorned with tufts of dry, dead grass after the hot summer. Pollen assaulted his dry nose. Rusted cars spotted with Bondo were visible in several backyards. Grease-stained fast-food paper bags, crumpled and yellowed *La Opinion* newspapers, and discarded chip bags rustled and crinkled in the breeze against rusted, four-foot high chain-link fences at the front of several properties. The brilliant sun glinted off shattered soda bottles in the gutters. At one time Angel had collected empties. Not now; too hot, too dirty, and too much work for far too little cash.

Before a two-story wood-frame house with faded and rain-stained white stucco walls, Angel stopped to scan up and down the street. A tan mongrel trotted along behind a street peddler selling mango on a stick, *elotes con chile* and *churros*. Bells on the vendor's cart jingled and jangled as he trundled along the uneven sidewalk, sweat plastering his purple and gold Lakers T-shirt to his back and chest. Angel thought he heard the crow of a cock; someone was raising birds for the fighting ring. He would have to find out who and maybe get into that action. Completing his survey of the area, Angel decided all was well. It never hurt to be too careful. You never new when misery would come your way.

"*Mami*," Angel called as he held the rust-streaked, white security door of his *mami's* bungalow open with one foot and pushed open the front door with his hand still on the key. The yellow and pale blue cockatoos in a cage hanging from a hook on the veranda chirped a welcome. "I'm home."

It wasn't really his home. His *mami* had bought it after an enticing mailer arrived announcing zero-interest mortgages for those with less than optimal credit scores. For two years his *mami* had been the proud owner of a two-bedroom, one-bath 1932 bungalow in Boyle Heights. Even though he had never lived there, Angel was happy to have somewhere to crash whenever he wanted. After his father disappeared, he and his mom had moved 16 times in 10 years.

"Shoes off," his *mami* ordered as she bustled out of the kitchen. Short, broad and solid, Angel's *mami* wiped her hands on a white dishtowel that had been worn thin. She straightened a dark painting of Jesus on the wall in the living room before rushing over to give her youngest son a hug and kiss on the cheek.

"*Mami*," Angel protested, struggling to break free of her steel-like arms.

"Your shoes," she said as she released him and hurried back into the kitchen. "No dirt in my home."

"They're brand new." His nose detected the tantalizing aroma of frying empanadas, his ears the crackle and pop of bubbling oil. Smelled like chicken empanadas, his favorite. Angel hurried through the tiny, dark, yet cool living room with its rabbit-eared television, the simple wood cross on the wall, and the pair of barred windows either side of the fireplace, which did not work. Well, it worked, if you did not mind risking burning down the house. Angel wondered if his *mami* had fire insurance; might be an easy few grand.

"New shoes?" His *mami*'s dark eyes narrowed as he strode into the kitchen and sniffed at the cast-iron pan filled with frying golden empanadas.

He nodded, lifting his right foot to show off the gleaming white Nikes with black laces. "*Dulce*, huh?"

She nodded as she transferred the empanadas from the bubbling oil in the pan onto a burnished metal tray covered with paper towels. She stood on tiptoes to better see into the pan. As he reached for one of her golden creations, she slapped his hand. "Later. For dinner. Are you staying?"

He shook his head. "Going out to eat later."

"With that Tiffany?" She said it so that the disapproval came through as clearly as if she had said, 'With that whore?'

Wanting to avoid a battle and having already seen the opened envelope displayed prominently on the table, Angel shook his head and said, "Diego and Cesar."

"I do not like you being with them." She had stopped her transfer operation and stared hard at her son. "They have no jobs. They lead you into trouble."

"Diego works."

"Where?"

"Packing sandwiches. Catering place. Graveyard. Good sandwiches."

"You should eat tortillas."

"They don't do tortillas."

"You should not be with the two of them."

"I'm careful."

"Careful and not being in trouble are two different things."

"I'll stay safe, *Mami*, I promise."

"When you were a *nino*, you promised me you would not drown when you went to the beach on a school field trip. Now you promise me you will be careful." She pursed her lips and shook her head, before starting another batch of empanadas frying.

Angel remembered that trip: the beach, the sun, the ocean, and the massive waves. It was the first time he had ever left the *barrio*. "I didn't drown."

His mother glared at him. "How is your job?"

"Hot and dirty." Angel worked part-time at a metal fabrication shop just off Slauson. "They should only hire Cocoa Puffs and Brazers."

"Do not call them that." She glared at him. "You should take pride in your work."

"Why?"

"Every job is important."

"Then why's it pay minimum wage? I deserve better."

"You deserve what God gives you."

"God should do better."

Her slap stung his cheek. "Your father would never have let you speak such blasphemy." As the sting faded, she said, "Maybe you could join the Army, like Ernesto."

"And get my ass shot off in Iraq?"

"Do not swear, Angel."

"Ass isn't a swearword, *Mami*." Angel took a Spanish cookie out of a pink, pig-shaped jar on the counter and ate it in one bite.

"You used to fix cars on the street." His *mami* finished adding another batch of empanadas to the bubbling, spitting oil.

"Cops kept shutting us down."

"If you had done better at school, you could have a better job. I always thought you could do better."

"And work at the meatpackers, like Pony?"

"Who?"

"Daniel."

"He finished high school and two years at community college." Angel's *mami* was proud of her cousin's son.

"Now he guts steers and hogs, pulls out the organs, and washes the blood and guts down a hole with a big hose." Angel felt disgusted at the very thought of such a job.

"Maybe if your father had never left, maybe…" his *mami* said, her voice trailing off into possibilities that would never be.

"Maybe I'll apply to that trade school in Phoenix." Angel grabbed a hot empanada from the tray and juggled it from hand to hand as it cooled. "Be an electrician. Real money."

"Save your money, then, for school. No new sneakers."

"Just need a little money to get there and to live on."

After focusing on her empenadas for a few moments, she said, "Marisol's *quincinero* is next month. We should give her something nice."

"We will."

"The mortgage is due again," his *mami* said, as if discussing one of their distant relations in El Salvador. "Could you help out a little?"

"Sure, *Mami*." Angel glanced at the opened envelope displayed on the table from the bank with, he knew, the mortgage statement inside. He pulled his black leather wallet out of the back pocket of his new baggy blue jeans and extracted $40.

His mother pursed her lips and frowned. She eyed the $40 with disdain. "The mortgage is $1,491 a month." His *mami* cleaned houses for $19,000 a year, but had a $400,000 mortgage at 3 percent for two years. The two years were almost up.

"It's all I got," Angel said. Felicity's party had been great; lots of beer, weed and with Tiffany not there, Angel had spent an hour in Danny's car with Jennifer. She had amazing tits and the most agile tongue around.

"I will lose my house, my home," his *mami* said, "our home, Angel."

"The rate goes up, is it next month?"

"God will take care of me….with a little help from my youngest son."

"It's all I got," Angel repeated, shrugging. Tiffany had smothered him with kisses, with tongue, and gave him a nice blowjob when he gave her the $40 gold necklace he had bought her. She thought it was a $400 necklace she had been eyeing at the mall. The sex had been worth about $400 for all her enthusiasm, but what difference did it make if she thought it was the $400 necklace?

His *mami's* eyes went to his sneakers.

He said, "Old ones wore out."

"You have never worn out a pair of shoes in your life. New jacket?" She grabbed at the leather coat that had caught his eye on a buying spree to the garment district downtown after the lick with Diego and Cesar.

"Patel's mom said you went to Las Vegas again." His *mami* said it as though she would have to wash her mouth out with bleach after speaking two such vile words.

"You play bingo."

"At the church," she said, appalled at the comparison. Her eyes were wet and he heard the sniffle in her voice as she fought back tears. "My home, Angel. You waste your money. You should save. Save for the future, for electrician school, for a wife, for a family, for a house. That is how I could buy a house. Save, save, save; then one day you can have a house and a nice home of your own."

"And a nice big mortgage?"

Angel didn't even see the slap coming.

Chapter 10

"I was wondering if there was any chance of getting a few extra cases?" Arden asked as he sat forward in a chair across from his new young boss.

Keith Kennelwhite's blue eyes narrowed as he took on a pained expression. "With the economy the way it is, we're getting fewer cases." He shook his head with a sad look. "Strange, you'd think people would want to avoid court costs and use our services more in such tough financial times. As much as I hate to admit it, Never-Fail, I think everyone agrees the trend in our caseload is down."

"I'm sorry to hear that." Arden hated Kennelwhite's use of his nickname. Friends and colleagues could use it, not some pompous kid of a boss. Worse, Kennelwhite said it in a way that made it sound like a put-down or at best a challenge.

"Maybe you could do some consulting on the side," Kennelwhite suggested.

"I'm happy just focusing on the cases we have."

"The firm encourages it now, helps cement relationships with firms that might need our services in the future." Kennelwhite gave an encouraging smile, tinged, Arden thought, with just a touch of condescension, as if Kennelwhite was his elder.

Arden asked, "You don't think it makes it appear we might be closer to some parties to a mediation than to others?"

"Of course not," Kennelwhite said, leaning back in his chair with a big grin. "Our reputation is for unbiased, impartial and cost-effective mediation services. No one would ever question that. That's why we're the largest mediation firm west of the Mississippi."

Arden wondered if anyone had ever questioned the dominance of General Motors, IBM or Xerox in their heydays. "Nothing extra on anyone's plate they'd like to pass along?"

Kennelwhite shook his head, leaning forward to rest his elbows on his desk. "In fact, we're getting fewer cases in the area, so we'll all have to travel more to cover the ones that are coming over the transom."

Arden assumed it was a royal 'we,' since from what Arden had heard Kennelwhite had never mediated a case in his life. He had an MBA and came from the business development part of the firm, not from mediation.

Arden hoped he would not have to travel too much more. He was away from Marisela and Sam enough as it was and since the burglary he hated the idea of leaving them home alone at all.

"Kelly is off to Singapore tomorrow, Donna is doing an oil case in Louisiana," Kennelwhite said, glancing down at a printed list on his desk. "And you're off to Reno early tomorrow to meet with CSM International, right? Do you have your pre-negotiation report prepared yet?"

Chapter 11

"If Peru's Congress passes the nationalization law next month, we stand to lose our shirts; at least $700 million on the Sierra Verde mine alone," CSM International's representative, Gordon Hayes said. Some of his minions were still booting up their laptops or plugging their black machines into outlets hidden beneath sleek recessed doors on the top of the conference table. "For our four mines in Peru, the total balloons to more than a billion. I was assured you could avoid that."

"Minimize, not avoid," Arden corrected the intense, bald young man across from him.

Hayes scowled over at a blank *The Times* of London crossword puzzle, several other blank crosswords, and the scuffed John Adams biography sitting on the conference table beside Arden. An expectant half-smile spread across Hayes's face, as if he was about to watch a daredevil attempt a death-defying feat, and fail.

"How minimal a loss?" Hayes demanded. "An arm or an arm, a leg and a butt cheek?"

Arden smiled thinly. "A tenth of your projected loss."

The AC made the room dry and cold. It beat Reno's temperatures outside, which topped 90 degrees, but Arden was glad he had worn his suit today. The 10-year-old jacket kept the chill out, although his hands felt as if they were immersed in ice water. He hated AC; he was always too hot or too cold.

"A tenth? More than a hundred million's still a major-league hit," Hayes said. Arden guessed that $100 million was far more of a hit to young Mr. Hayes's rising reputation than to the overflowing coffers of CSM International. According to the conglomerate's reports, commodity prices had been rising as money fled mortgage-backed securities, which appeared increasingly risky, into commodities. Asian demand for raw materials had exploded, pushing prices even higher. With their rise, the profits of the multinational mining corporation were skyrocketing faster than a Space Shuttle liftoff.

Arden rose and strode across to a thermostat near the door, earning raised eyebrows from Hayes at the interruption. Arden punched a button and increased the temperature a couple of degrees before returning at a carefully measured pace to his chair. As he went, he returned the appraising look of a cute brunette tapping on her laptop on Hayes's side of the table. Arden lingered for a moment on the thought that if he was unmarried and a few years younger....

With a look of disgust Hayes said, "For a hundred million, we might as well fold and sic the lawyers on 'em right away."

"A bad deal is better than a good lawsuit," Arden recited an old saying.

"The whole thing reeks of socialism."

"Nationalization is legal under Peruvian law."

"Hell, they can pass a law repealing the law of gravity, but the rain will still fall."

"Peru's Congress determines what the law is in Peru, Mr. Hayes."

"We spent more than $100 million developing mines in Peru, everything from exploration and the mines themselves to carving out roads, building smelters, enlarging ports and training thousands of personnel. They can't just take all that away for nothing."

"Compensation is on the table."

"Peanuts."

"In any case, the nationalization hasn't passed yet. By the time it is, we may be able to minimize its effects."

"How?"

Arden tapped the table top with his long fingers. He believed in making others think he had memorized everything there was to know about the issues under discussion, so he sat with no notes or laptop, let alone any pre-negotiation report for his boss, Kennelwhite. It tended to worry, if not scare people, although he had been hesitant to enter this conference without any notes. Had his concussion affected his memory? He would soon find out.

"First," Arden said, "I suggest you take steps to decrease the risk of nationalization actually happening."

"The Peruvians are hell bent on it. Nothing short of an act of God is going to change their mind and I doubt Jehovah's going to come down from on high to tell *el Presidente* Giampietri not to steal our mines."

"There's always a chance for a reasonable negotiated settlement."

Hayes snorted. Arden glanced at Hayes's minions. They all either sat like cardboard cutouts or nodded agreement like bobbleheads, except for the cute brunette at the end, who risked a furtive, yet encouraging smile toward Arden.

"How?"

Arden met Hayes's demanding glare for a moment, the silence building. Arden waited for Hayes to lower his eyes before he said, "Decrease the economic and political value of nationalization to the Peruvian government."

"How?"

Arden was tiring of the single word questions. If he wasn't so desperate to get every case he could, he would have given Hayes a lesson in improving his interpersonal relations in the guise of how to deal more politely with the Peruvians. Instead, meeting Hayes's expectant glare, he said slowly, as if explaining to a child, "First announce plans to enlarge the mines in Peru."

"Enlarge?" Hayes demanded, sitting up straighter. "Sink more money into mines we may not even own next year? That's throwing good money after bad. Maybe you should leave the financial planning to the guys with the MBAs."

"I didn't say to actually do it yet," Arden clarified, keeping his voice calm and even. He needed this job. "Just announce the plans."

A grin spread across Hayes's babyish face. He nodded. "The Peruvians will know we won't invest the money if they nationalize, *quid pro quo*." Two of his underlings scribbled on legal pads, while four laptops clicked as fingers hit keys. Arden wondered why they needed so many people taking the same notes. Did anyone ever read them all?

"String them along like a donkey with a carrot," Hayes said with glee. "We could hold the promise of enlarging the mines out to them for years. We may never need to invest another dime in the damn country."

"If you don't, the next time you try the same tactic, no one will believe you."

"Maybe."

Arden already knew Hayes was counting on the fact that it would be someone else facing the next nationalization.

Hayes barked, "What else?"

Arden hesitated long enough to be just shy of insolent. "Borrow the money for the further development of the mines."

"That's standard operating procedure."

"Borrow from as many different banks in as many different countries as possible, especially countries with strong economic and/or political ties to Peru."

Hayes frowned for a moment, but the confusion passed. "So if the Peruvian's nationalize, the foreign banks lose a juicy profit on a major loan. They'll all go screaming like little girls to their own government to put pressure on the Peruvians not to nationalize."

The minions took more notes. Maybe each one reported back to a different boss.

"What else?"

Arden ignored the bark-like nature of the question. If Hayes wanted to play the big boss for his flunkies, so be it. "Sign long-term contracts with the labor unions for the mine workers and with whoever supplies the mines with everything from coffee and staplers to security and garbage disposal."

"The miners aren't unionized."

"Let them unionize, encourage them to, fund it at first if you have to."

Hayes's eyes narrowed and his subordinates stopped taking notes. "That'll cost a pile of money: higher wages, shorter work days, maybe even sick time and pensions if it gets completely out of hand, not to mention safety and environmental improvements."

"A pittance compared to losing the mines."

Hayes stared at Arden, thinking.

"With long-term contracts and just a little more pay each year, especialy if you pay more than any other mine in the area, the workers will oppose nationalization."

Hayes nodded. The peons resumed their note taking. "What else?"

"Most of your copper and zinc goes to European, American and Asian smelters, and your sales have been stable for years. Offer long-term contracts at current prices to all your major customers."

"Haven't you read the news? Commodity prices are shooting through the roof. We'll lose a fortune."

"You'll lose little relative to what you'll lose if the Peruvians nationalize. If you sign long-term contracts and Peru nationalizes, they'll have companies in a dozen countries lobbying their governments to oppose nationalization in order to keep their favorable long-term contracts, not to mention threatening to reduce their business presence in Peru."

Hayes nodded. Pens scribbled. Fingers tapped keys.

Arden said, "Instead of paying taxes to Peru—"

"We only pay about a *centimo* per million income."

"However much it is, it might be prudent to make Peru an offer. Instead of cash, offer them CSM shares. Make it a long-term deal; the government gets more shares the longer the deal remains in place."

Hayes snorted as a sly smile spread across his youthful face. "Give away one of the cow's teats to keep the milk flowing; brilliant." He patted the edge of the table, unable to contain his excitement at the idea.

"Nationalization has economic and political motives, so I would also recommend making some moves to improve the company's image in Peru."

"We have excellent PR people who handle our image globally."

"Americans?"

Hayes looked wary for a moment but nodded, his eyes narrow, his body tensing for the riposte.

"Hire a Peruvian firm to handle a campaign in Peru for you."

"I'm sure our people are far more experienced with that sort of thing."

"Not with Peruvian culture, mores and beliefs."

Hayes tilted his head to the side. His minions sat silent in their dark business suits. "Does Peru even have PR firms?"

"When the Chinese, Saudis or the Indians want to lobby Washington, they hire an American firm."

"I'm sure they're the best."

"For an American audience."

"They're the best."

"They're the best because American firms know Americans. Americans don't know Peru. Hire a Peruvian firm. They'll know Peruvians and how best to convince them that CSM is the finest company Peru has ever been involved with. You can even play it up as returning some of your profits back to Peru."

Hayes nodded. His assistants took notes.

"One other thing, create a subsidiary company to run your operations in Peru and put some popular, well-known Peruvians on the board."

"I love it. It doesn't even have to have any real power," Hayes said with a malicious smile. More flunky note-taking.

"You have to give it some power."

"Why?"

"The Peruvians aren't stupid. They'll soon figure out the subsidiary is just a front. Then your company will be lucky to escape with just losing your mines."

"The Peruvians won't figure it out, no one will. Our lawyers can create such a myriad of companies and subsidiaries it'd take a dozen Harvard PhDs to sort out who controls what."

"I recommend in the strongest terms against any fraudulent activities."

"Relax," Hayes said holding up his hands in a conciliatory gesture, "I'm taking your advice."

"But far from in the right way." Arden did not need the job this much.

Hayes eyed Arden, leaning forward on his elbows, which rested on the table. His eyes cold and hard, his voice like ice, Hayes said, "You advise, I'll draft our company's plan and our CEO will decide on the most...appropriate course. What else?"

Arden hated it, but he never could control how the parties he advised used his suggestions. Few, however, were as open about distorting his advice as Hayes appeared to be. Why couldn't he be a day away from retirement instead of what was now six or more years away from that golden day? As Dostoyevsky wrote, "Money is coined liberty." With money you could say anything you wanted; without it, you might as well be a slave. Arden wondered whether he could find some consulting work and drop this job. If only he did not have a mortgage, Sam to send to college and so many other bills.

"My CEO said you're the best," Hayes prompted. He leaned across the table and *sotto voce* said, "I heard his son married an Atlantic City cocktail waitress on Saturday and you had it annulled the same day you arrived."

"She was reasonable."

"That's not what the first five fixers CSM sent out to solve the problem said."

"There's always an equitable solution, if you can find the right approach."

"My CEO said you've never lost a case. He said they call you Never-Fail Jeffries."

"Mediators don't win or lose."

"Never left one unresolved then."

Arden detested the cunning look on the younger man's face, but the challenge was clear.

"What else?"

Arden hesitated. It was his job to advise and provide counsel. Hayes's CEO would not do anything illegal. Why bother breaking the law for a few mines in Peru when the firm had global interests that dwarfed their Peruvian operations?

Arden suppressed a sigh and said, "You should support the biggest Peruvian proponents of nationalization."

"The biggest *opponents*," Hayes corrected.

"No, *proponents*, the supporters."

"Of nationalization?" His face wrinkling in confusion, Hayes sounded and looked as if he thought Arden was insane.

"Yes."

Hayes was about to say something, but waited. Arden's respect for him increased an iota. Hayes was learning patience.

"If you spend money supporting those who oppose the nationalization, you gain little," Arden said. "They're already on your side. But if you aid those who support nationalization and win them over, you not only gain a friend, you lose an enemy."

"There's no fucking way on this earth *el Presidente* Javier Giampietri and his crew are going to take money from us to oppose nationalization, not if we gift wrapped it and had it delivered by Santa Claus with the Easter Bunny and Jesus Christ riding shotgun."

"I'm sure he'd be happy to have some of his pet projects, such as his plan for a solar energy farm in the Sechura Desert, handsomely funded."

Hayes chuckled, pens scribbled notes and fingers tapped keys.

With the major points covered, Arden wrapped up his presentation. Hayes rose and, with some reluctance, extended his hand. Arden stood to shake hands. With a faint look of distaste, Hayes said, his voice low, "Thank you. I'll take your suggestions under careful consideration." He looked straight at Arden and after a moment's hesitation, added, "Makes this whole thing look less bleak. We were planning on taking them to court. Legal is already researching the most favorable venues for us."

"I'm certain you can reach an equitable arrangement with the Peruvians."

Hayes's eyes fell on the blank crossword. "Good luck with the puzzle; must be a tough one."

Arden noted the condescension in Hayes's voice. Arden patted his suit jacket's pockets; no pen. He glanced across the table. The cute brunette caught his eye and slid a silver pen toward him. Arden picked it up and without any hesitation wrote in all the answers to the puzzle. Finished, he realized everyone in the room was staring at him. He slid the pen back across the table to the cute brunette and as he turned to leave, said, "No harder than dealing with a nationalization."

Chapter 12

"We at Antioch are fully confident that the SEC investigation will be resolved in a reasonable and timely fashion," CEO Richard Sloane said, facing the camera as he appeared on a business news channel. "Our management team at Antioch believes in the highest principles, is fully aware of all relevant government regulations, and our entire global team's constant goal is to help our customers, many of whom are seriously ill, regain their health and lead healthy, productive and fulfilling lives."

"So the SEC investigation is groundless?" the earnest, tanned anchor asked.

Sloane shook his head as if asked about an ancient misunderstanding between old friends. "We at Antioch pride ourselves on abiding by all the applicable laws for the good of the millions of patients who have been helped by our wide range of medical treatments and products." Sloane gave the camera his long-practiced reassuring smile. "We look forward to working closely with the SEC to ensure that Antioch continues to set the standard in the industry for compliance wherever any one of our 21,000 employees conduct business in their quest to advance medicine around the globe."

"Your stock's recent decline was also attributed to reports about your lab-grown heart valve clinical trial. Are you confident the cause of the difficulties will be remedied?"

"We most certainly are," Sloane said, leaning forward toward the camera to give added force to his words. "We are confident our researchers are the best in the world. We continue to produce the finest products that help improve the lives of countless ill and suffering people the world over."

"Have you met with the families of the six patients who died?"

Sloane paused, looked down and even closed his eyes for a moment, making it look as if the subject was too painful to discuss. Opening his eyes and peering into the camera with his head tilted to one side, he said slowly with pauses between each phrase to add weight and emotion to each word, "We at Antioch, are forever saddened, by their loss, and our deepest, most heartfelt, sympathy, goes out, to their families." Then he sped up, raising his voice, as if making a vow. "We are bound and determined that their lives will not have been so grievously lost in vain. We are fully and completely dedicated to ensuring that their participation in this promising and innovative clinical trial will lead to vastly improved treatment for patients suffering from conditions affecting the heart's valves. We are optimistic that the issues can be resolved, and an effective and life-saving laboratory-grown heart valve can be produced safely and efficiently to benefit hundreds of thousands of patients around the world."

A half-hour later as the news shifted to Beijing's rebuff of President Bush's comments about China's human rights record just days before the opening of the Beijing Olympics, Sloane sat in the back of an air-conditioned Antioch limousine speeding through humid Manhattan toward a private heliport on the East River. Even though he had just completed his ninth interview of the day, Sloane answered emails on his Blackberry at a speed that would have impressed even his texting-addicted daughter.

Sitting beside him, Antioch's VP of Marketing and Communications Lester Eastbrook asked, "You truly believe Yu will be able to fix the valve trial?"

"Of course."

"I've studied some of the reports," Lester began, glancing forward at the raised tinted partition between them and the gray-haired driver.

"So have I," Sloane said, his attention still focused on the ream of emails clogging his inbox.

Eastbrook pushed his stylish glasses back up his narrow nose and tried again. "Some of the researchers aren't so sure."

Sloane replied affirmatively to a question from the VP of Operations about a negotiation to purchase a large supply of drugs from India for the United States and stopped mid-reply to an email from a VP requesting increased lobbying efforts to block the importation of potentially lower quality Canadian pharmaceuticals by a rival firm into the United States. His eyes narrowing and his brow furrowing, Sloane stared at Eastbrook. "Who are the doubting Thomases?"

Eastbrook sniffed, wiped a hand over his lips and said, "No one in particular; it's just what I've heard."

"Everyone I've talked to is sure Yu and his team can figure out what went wrong, fix it and get the heart valve approved post haste."

Eastbrook nodded, but still looked as worried as a hen with a ravenous fox at the coop door. His voice low and cautious, Eastbrook said, "I thought you were going to go a little easy in the interviews."

Sloane deleted two emails and forwarded one from a manager to that manager's director with a note that managers must go through directors before contacting the CEO. He had enough emails as it was. "I did go easy," he said, biting off the words as a warning.

"I thought we agreed that you were going to stick to the talking points; that we're analyzing the data from the trial, but that it's too soon to tell what we'll find. I thought we agreed that the focus was going to be on how we were moving Heaven and earth to find out what happened in an attempt to try to help the families of those who died; to help them find closure."

"Never, ever focus on the negative, Lester. Dead trial subjects are about as negative as it gets."

Eastbrook still looked like a puppy who had just lost a long-cherished bone.

Sloane would have liked to have jettisoned Eastbrook months ago, but lacked the votes on the board to do so. Even if he had the votes, with the SEC investigation and the stock slump it was not the time to oust another VP, which would make it look like Antioch was in the midst of a purge that would devastate the stock price even more.

Eastbrook said, "We may want to shift attention away from that trial."

"Why?"

"If it fails and the media and Wall Street are focused on it—"

"It won't."

"Several researchers have confided to me that they think it might not work."

Sloane sighed as he made a mental note to identify those particular researchers. He loathed pessimists, especially ones who spoke to his VPs confidentially. "Lester, let me tell you a story." Sloane set his Blackberry down precisely on the tan leather seat between them. "In October 2000, Ann Mulcahy, CEO of Xerox, said that Xerox's business model was 'unsustainable.' The stock fell 26 percent that day. Not a damn thing had changed in the company; not its sales, not its revenue and not its projections—nothing."

"I don't see," Lester began, leaning forward in his seat and turning to face Sloane.

"No, you don't. Let me tell you something, Lester, a part of being a CEO, a big part, is confidence. You have to project an aura of confidence or Wall Street will eat you alive and so will every other company in your sector. I know that Yu and his team will figure out what the hell happened to those poor bastards who died. They'll figure it out and fix it. I have no doubt."

"How can you be so sure? If you're wrong, the media will skewer us."

Sloane sighed and, tilting his head to one side, said, "To be perfectly honest, I'm not. But I'm pretty damn sure they can. If they do, I'll be right, the heart valve will benefit thousands of people, we'll make a nice pile of cash, the stock will recover nicely, and you and I will still be in our current positions to celebrate the New Year."

"And if they don't?"

"The media will know it soon enough and they'll be trumpeting that news."

"Which will kill us."

"And what I said today won't be worth a pound of shit because the stock will be trading at about a dime, and you and I will be looking for a new line of work."

Sloane returned to his emails. He approved a meeting to discuss plans for a new drug lab in Shanghai and added two of his favorite directors to a meeting analyzing plans for a manufacturing plant in Haryana, India. He would have to incorporate a loophole for such plans in any legislation their lobbyists were supporting banning the importation of pharmaceuticals from overseas.

A glance told Sloane that Eastbrook was still far from pleased. The VP tapped his fingers on the leather armrest beside him, gazing out the window at the busy Manhattan streets with a look of intense thought. Sloane spotted a hot chestnut vendor and made a mental note to see about buying one for his Boston house. It would be nice to have hot chestnuts whenever he wanted them.

"Lester," Sloane said, "I should mention that Anne Mulcahy probably believed 100 percent that what she said was right. Maybe she was at the time, but it's neither here nor there. She cost the company a bundle in value in the short term. If she'd kept her mouth shut, the stock would have continued on its merry way up. Even now Xerox is still an $18-billion-a-year company." Sloane decided not to mention that Mulcahy kept her job; made the story less powerful. "A CEO, regardless of what's happening, has to be optimistic."

"Even if the company's suffering a setback?"

"Especially if the company's suffering a setback; not that we are. John Madden, the football coach, once said that when his team won, it was his job to point out what they did wrong, and when they lost, it was his job to restore their confidence and focus on what they did right, since the media, their families and everyone they knew would point out in the minutest detail how they screwed the pooch."

Eastbrook nodded, but looked far from convinced. "I think we should still stick with a more prudent communications approach in relation to the heart valve trial, at least until Yu figures out what went wrong. Maybe we can add some more researchers to his team to help him."

Sloane turned to face Eastbrook, closing the distance between them. "What's your title?"

A frown mixed with a trace of fear flitted across Eastbrook's face. "Vice President of Marketing and Public Relations."

"Any part of that title include the words research, heart valve or principal investigator?"

Eastbrook stiffened, swallowed and shook his head. He looked as if someone had slugged him in the gut.

"CEO in your title anywhere?"

"No."

"Then stick to your department and let me worry about the valve trial. You stick to squashing ain't-worth-a-shit rumors and telling the public what I tell you to tell them. Understood?"

Chapter 13

Friday, August 8, 2008

"More travel?" Marisela asked over breakfast. Her cold voice and rigid body betrayed her opposition when Arden mentioned that he was going on yet another business trip.

"Not until next week." She still looked mad. "I don't have any choice." Arden was tired. His flight home from Reno the night before had been delayed. His head ached; from the concussion or the late night?

He ate a mouthful of Life cereal, regretting that they had cut out blueberries from their weekly shopping trip to save money.

Marisela said, "A consulting job would keep you home."

Arden pursed his lips and said, "I'm not taking any consulting jobs; not that any have been offered anyway."

"Because everyone knows you don't want them. If you let people know you're interested, the offers would flood in. Everyone knows you're the best mediator there is."

"I have that reputation because I don't ever take consulting jobs, so everyone knows I'm impartial."

"I don't think taking consulting jobs would destroy your reputation. Times are getting tought, people would understand."

"I wouldn't understand."

They fell silent, munching their breakfast.

After a sour frown crossed her face, Marisela asked, "How'd Antioch do yesterday?"

"Up a nickel."

Marisela shook her head, a look of dejection on her face.

Sam flipped through a glossy booklet from Georgia Tech as she ate her cereal.

Marisela took several bites of her toasted egg bagel and asked, "Remember Andy Lau, from my lab at Antioch? He works for a drug company in Shanghai now. He emailed me. They have a lab in Van Nuys and need some bench work done."

"Another job?" Arden saw a light on the horizon, a faint, wavering glimmer, but at least a light.

"Two nights a week and one weekend day for as long as it lasts."

"That's great." Arden paused. He did not want to appear too eager. "If you're sure." He did not want Marisela to think that she had to work extra while he refused any consulting work. His voice neutral, he asked, "How much does it pay?"

"About a third less than I made, but we need the money."

"That'll mean some long days. We'd miss you at dinner."

"I can make things Sunday to last us through the week," Marisela said. Turning to Sam, she asked, "Can you take over some of the cleaning and gardening?"

Sam looked far from excited at the prospect, but nodded. Marisela glanced at Arden and said, "Maybe we can contribute a little to her college fund for cooking and cleaning some."

Sam was suddenly far more interested. "How much?"

"Ten an hour," Arden said in a tentative tone. How much is child labor worth?

"Fifteen," Sam shot back.

"Twelve, and you sweep the driveway, clean the bathrooms and help your mom with the cooking."

"Deal."

"School comes first, though," Arden warned, wondering whether he had just been taken given how quickly Sam had agreed. He never did well negotiating with Sam; she knew all his secrets. "I don't want to see any Bs on your report card."

"Only the best and brightest get a seat on the Space Shuttle," Sam said with a confident grin.

As they stood on the neutral ground of the sidewalk at the border between their properties after breakfast, Arden told his neighbor Buell, "Arbitration would be fair."

"You're an arbitrator, aren't you?" Buell demanded.

"You can choose whoever you want to use."

"You all stick together, I'm sure. No way." Buell turned to stalk back to his house.

"We need to settle this."

"It's settled; your fence, your repairs," Buell yelled over his shoulder from his front porch. "Check the law." The door slammed.

Later that morning Arden stood, hands in his pant's pockets, leaning against the wall in his firm's main conference room. Donna Levin, a fellow mediator, stood beside him, her muscular arms folded. She was an ex-collegiate volleyball player with a national title to her name. Equitable's other mediators and staff filled the high-backed chairs around the room's 25-foot conference table and clustered along the walls in a horseshoe facing their new leader, Keith Kennelwhite.

"I was brought in to maintain this department's profitability," Kennelwhite announced from the head of the table. A notepad before him was covered with his cramped, yet precise handwriting. "One way to do that is to cut costs. Therefore," he said, looking around the assembled staff with a profound sense of gravitas, "the company will no longer subscribe to any newspapers."

"You're going to balance the books by cancelling newspaper subscriptions?" Arden asked, smiling with disbelief, but also to lesson the impertinence of his jibe.

Kennelwhite shot him a glare, which transformed into an understanding smile one might give a confused child. "No, of course not. The television in the lunch room will now only have basic cable."

"I didn't even know it still worked," Donna Levin whispered too loudly, earning her own glare from Kennelwhite.

"Parking rates will also now increase to the full amount," Kennelwhite continued. "The company has been subsidizing your parking and much as management regrets it, we can no longer afford the increasing cost of doing so."

"How much?" Arden asked.

Kennelwhite glanced down at his notes and after a long pause finally found the figures. "Ninety a month in the lot on Wilshire; $60 for the Doheny lot."

Arden paid $30 for Doheny. "A 100 percent increase?"

"We must all tighten our belts a notch or two," Kennelwhite said with a smile that sought understanding, as if they were all in this together.

"He'll still have his reserved spot in the back of the building, I'm sure," Donna whispered in Arden's ear.

"Gratis," Arden whispered back.

"Unfortunately, all office parties are cancelled until further notice and there will be no food ordered for any lunch meetings."

"Does that rule out your secret weapon?" Donna whispered.

"Never," Arden vowed. "My secret weapon is homemade."

Kennelwhite continued, "All orders for office supplies will now need to be approved by a director."

"Isn't he the only director in our department?" Donna whispered.

"In order to streamline the mediation process," Kennelwhite said, not having heard Donna, "all mediators will be required to submit to me case plans before each mediation session, as well as a post-meeting report on how the mediation progressed at each conference so we can plan strategy and tactics to more quickly and efficiently resolve cases. The goal is to increase case flow."

Donna whispered to Arden, "You've never written a report in your life."

"Never needed to." Arden tapped the side of his forehead with his index finger.

"Better than any computer, eh?"

"Never crashes," Arden said.

"Until that burglar hit you."

Arden laughed.

"You have a comment, Never Fail?" Kennelwhite asked, raising his voice, his pale eyes locked challengingly on Arden at the back of the room.

Arden frowned with disapproval at Kennelwhite's use of his nickname. "I just wondered whether that was the best use of your valuable time."

"Mediation is our business."

"You have some of the finest mediators in this room, with decades of experience," Arden said, earning nods from his colleagues. "I just thought, given that you're a director and given your background, that you'd focus more on the financial side of things: business development, client mining, budgeting, long-term planning, cost-cutting, penny-pinching, and such."

Kennelwhite choose to ignore the snickers of some of the mediators. "The two areas are intimately intertwined. If the mediation cases aren't handled efficiently, the bottom line suffers. Settled cases mean money in the till, and we need to keep them all moving along as rapidly as possible. A rapid flow is key."

"That's what my urologist says," the Old Man, Peter Johnson ,muttered, earning laughter from the room.

When the laughter subsided, Arden asked, keeping his face relaxed and open, as if he was merely trying to understand the great man and his thinking, "Won't having mediators write reports slow cases down rather than move them along faster?"

"I want to make certain cases are being handled in an expeditious manner." Kennelwhite stared at Arden, letting the silence build.

"I look forward to your input," Arden said with a slight inclination of his head, as if bowing to a king—or a dangerous fool. Arden wished he was only a day away from retirement rather than six years or more. "I'm sure your advice will greatly speed up the mediation process and turn us into a mediation factory par excellence."

Donna smirked, but Kennelwhite could not see her expression since she hid it behind a hand as she scratched her forehead.

After the meeting concluded, as they walked out Donna whispered to Arden, "You think he knows the first damn thing about mediating?"

"About as much as I know about business development," Arden said.

"The Peter Principle in action. Why'd they ever hire a guy with an MBA and a background in accounting to direct the mediation department?"

"Maybe I should look for a job as a neurosurgeon. I know nothing about medicine, should get a job right quick."

Arden stopped at the lunchroom. He took a stack of 40 news-papers that had been gathering dust for weeks after mediators had skimmed them for information about various cases with which they were involved. The crosswords in them would keep Arden busy for a while at least.

Back in his office, angry at being treated like a novice in the mediation field, Arden skimmed various websites for mediation jobs. There were fewer openings than when he had looked a few years before after taking early retirement from Antioch. At first he thought several positions looked like good possibilities, but as his anger and desperation to take leave of Kennelwhite and Equitable Mediations passed he read the job descriptions more closely. He could tell they were far worse jobs than the one he had now, even with Kennelwhite as a boss. Worse, the few that listed a salary were far below what he was making. Now was not the time to take a pay cut. Even so, the six or more years he had to work at Equitable, which had seemed onerous but far from terrible, now seemed far, far worse with the addition of Keith Kennelwhite as his boss.

"Dad, if I'm going to college next fall, I'll need a car," Sam told Arden over his cell as he stood at his office window, staring out over the tar-spotted roof of the adjacent building.

"Maybe you can go to UCLA," Arden said, forcing his mind to consider Sam's problem and not any of his own. "You can live at home and take the bus." And we can save money, not to mention get to see you every day for four more precious years.

"The bus?" Sam's disdain was clear.

"It runs straight up Overland, over on Santa Monica and then up Westwood straight into the campus; convenient."

"Dad." Sam drew out the word into at least three syllables. "UCLA?" A long four syllables. "They don't produce astronauts."

"There's been eight and even one woman." Arden had checked.

"Purdue's produced 22. Georgia Tech a dozen and three women, and MIT has 34 alumni who've been in the program."

"Eight isn't a number to sneeze at. How many astronauts have there been?"

"About 300."

"So UCLA's eight isn't bad."

"Dad." Sam stretched the word out as if it had a dozen syllables this time.

"Chicklet, don't whine."

"I want to go to Purdue, Georgia Tech or MIT. They're the best aeronautical engineering programs in the world. They've produced almost seventy astronauts."

"I thought Cal Tech was the best. You could live at home and commute to Pasadena."

"I want to go to Cal Tech for graduate school, but I want to go away for my bachelors. I thought you and Mom were retiring to New Mexico anyway."

"Not for a few years now."

"But you're buying a house there."

"We're not sure we can afford the house now. If you go to Cal Tech, we'd stay here for a while."

"I'd need a car for Cal Tech. But I don't want to go there, and if I go to an out-of-state school, I'll need a car."

"Aren't you going to live on campus?"

"It's $8,000 to live in a dorm on top of the $25,000 out-of-state tuition for Purdue. Georgia tech's $20,000 and MIT's thirty. I'd rather find a place of my own. It'd be cheaper, and I want to look around a bit on weekends so I'll need a car."

"You'll be studying weekends."

"Not all the time, Dad."

"At that price, you better be, especially if you ever want to command a Space Shuttle mission."

"A private space mission; the Shuttle program's nearing the end of its useful life."

Arden nodded, even though Sam could not see him. She went on about the winding down of the Space Shuttle program and the rise of private firms to deliver supplies and astronauts to the International Space Stationfor a push to return to the Moon and then to Mars and beyond. Sam had big dreams for private space exploration, and for herself.

Arden sat down at his desk. When Sam paused to take a much-needed breath, he said, "Let's wait until next fall to look for a car and we can decide then if you need one."

"If we get one now," Sam said, rapidly switching from rockets to cars, "I could drive to school and you wouldn't have to take me.

You wouldn't have to listen to my music in the morning instead of your news stations."

"I don't have to drive you to school, Chicklet. The music is part of our deal; we listen to your radio station on the way to school and you empty the dishwasher after school."

"If I had a car, you wouldn't have to drive me at all. I'd still empty the dishwasher."

"I barely get to see you as it is, especially with more of my cases out of town now."

After a pause, Sam asked, "When I do get a car, you're paying half, right?"

"That's our deal, but only for a decent, reliable car."

"Don't worry, Dad, I don't have that much saved up from lifeguarding anyway. You're going to cover the insurance?"

"Aren't you supposed to be in swim practice?"

"We're on break. I'm watching the crew of the Endeavor get ready for their mission in November. Cool, getting the ISS ready."

"ISS?"

"International Space Station."

"How are you watching it?"

"On Asia's laptop. Insurance?"

"Alright, alright, I'll cover it. Have you talked to your mom about this?"

"Of course."

"What'd she say?"

Samantha fell silent.

"Sam?" It was Arden's turn to draw out a word into several syllables.

"She said I'd have to pay for insurance," Sam said, then added before Arden could respond, "but if you're willing to cover it, I'm sure she'd change her mind."

His exasperation mounting at his daughter's tactics, Arden said, "I've told you before don't try to play Mom and I off against each other. An agreement will only last if all the parties involved feel they've reached an equitable arrangement after a fair and open negotiating process."

"You also always say to shape the negotiations before you sit down at the table."

Arden smiled despite himself. "I'll see you when you get home."

"What about the insurance?"

"We'll talk with Mom. See you later, and train hard."

Just after Sam rang off, Arden's phone rang again. It was an old Human Resources colleague at Antioch, Dan Overly. Arden checked his watch. He had time before he had to go to a mediation. He did not have a pre-mediation report prepared, but Kennelwhite had not been clear on when his edict was to take effect; maybe next week? Arden asked his former colleague, "How's life at Antioch?"

"A morgue would be a cheerier place to work."

"Heard anything about the SEC investigation?"

"Hell, if I was privy to anything important, I'd have played the market and be retired to southern Spain by now."

"Good luck with that," Arden said with a chuckle.

Turning serious, Dan said, "I just hope they can fix that damn valve trial."

"Is it that important to Antioch?"

"Probably not, but Wall Street thinks so, and what Wall Street thinks determines stock price, which determines whether I have a job next week."

"Is it that dire?"

"If the stock doesn't recover, Antioch's going to have layoffs. New projects are on hold, they're raising the costs of our health benefits, cutting back on matching contributions to our retirement plans, and making us pay full for parking. There's talk of pay cuts."

"At least you'll be out of there soon." Dan was in his mid-sixties. Thank God Marisela had left Antioch years ago.

Dan laughed, but it was tinged with a bitter edge. "Guess when my meeting with the retirement people was to figure out if I can retire next year?"

"I'm afraid to ask."

"The day Antioch tanked. I figure I lost two hundred and fifty grand in the market while I was sitting their talking with them about my wonderful retirement." Dan had been at Antioch far longer than Arden.

"Christ," Arden said. "I'm sorry."

"Feels like I've been cut off at the knees. We have enough company stock to wallpaper our house; might as well use it for that now."

"So do we."

After the call and still with a few minutes before his mediation case, Arden checked the Internet. He printed crosswords from several of his favorite newspaper websites—he did crosswords so fast, he never seemed to have enough, even with his purloined stack of papers from work—and then skimmed the news. A military conflict had erupted between Russia and the former Soviet Republic of Georgia, which had launched an offensive to retake the breakaway province of South Ossetia. Arden's financial worries were put in perspective as he read that fighting had devastated the capital, killing at least 1,400, as Russia sent tanks in to support Russian peacekeepers. Arden wondered what the peacekeepers were doing there in the first place, but skipped to a story about a car bomb in Iraq killing 21 people and then a story about the summer Olympics in Beijing. President Bush and 80 world leaders attended the opening ceremonies. Bush was the first sitting president to attend the ceremonies in a foreign country. Great for him, Arden thought. Now that you have had your fun, do something about the housing market and unemployment.

Arden decided to check his stocks but could not remember the passwords for his accounts. Frowning, he searched his memory: nothing. Had the concussion scrambled his memory? He had had a mild headache the night before, probably from the concussion. He tried to remember, but couldn't. Frustrated, he was on the point of calling the companies, assuming he could remember the pertinent information to convince them they were his accounts, when he remembered the rarely used list of scribbled passwords and user names he kept on the first page of his daybook. He had scribbled them for greater security so only he could read them.

As he wondered how many other gaps were lurking in his memory, he went to one of the stock sites and saw that stocks were racing up again: the Dow above 11,500. It would help cover their Antioch losses a tiny bit. He had watched Antioch's CEO, Richard Sloane, on a business channel the night before. Sloane had still sounded confident that the SEC investigation would uncover nothing and that the heart-valve trial would succeed. Arden prayed that Sloane would be proved correct on both counts. Antioch was a tad up; three cents. Wall Street appeared to be waiting to see what happened with the investigation and the trial before deciding Antioch's fate—and the futures of Arden and Marisela, Dan and Maria Overly, and a few hundred thousand other Antioch employees and investors.

"What case do you have?" Donna Levin asked Arden as he strode down the hall toward one of the company's conference rooms, a plastic container in his left hand and a folded newspaper in his right.

"Farris-Thierry," Arden replied.

"Good luck with that one," Donna said, shaking her head as she clutched her laptop, two legal pads, three pens and a pencil. She liked to be prepared. "What are you, they're fifth mediator?"

"Sixth."

"You're the last mediator they could find to take the case, so you better settle it, Mr. Never Fail."

"That's my plan. Besides, I asked for it." He needed the money.

"I hope you and Marisela don't have dinner plans. Did you draft a pre-mediation strategic and tactical plan for young Prince Kennelwhite?"

Arden shook his head with mock sadness. "Slipped my mind."

"Nothing slips your mind."

"I *was* conked on the head."

"He won't like it."

"He will if I settle it."

"Good luck with that."

"Sixth time's the charm." Arden waggled the plastic container, which rattled.

"Even with your secret weapon, you're going to need a lot of luck reaching an equitable arrangement with those two Gila monsters," Donna called back. "Hope you have the SWAT team on speed dial."

"Perish the thought. I never miss making a deal when a fair. equitable arrangement is offered."

"What if there isn't one?"

"How'd you do it, Never Fail?" Donna asked as she stuck her head through the open doorway of Arden's office late that afternoon.

"You can read it all in Kennelwhite's post-mediation report when I'm finished writing it in a minute or two," Arden said, pausing as he typed on his computer keyboard. "What else can I say?"

"That you're working on your *pre*-negotiation report?" she asked with a smirk.

"No point now, it's settled. Conciseness counts, right? Five lines outlining the settlement and done."

"I'm impressed."

Arden picked up the empty plastic container from his desk and held it up. "My secret weapon always works; gets them talking."

"It took more than Marisela's shortbread, I'm sure," Donna said, leaning her six-foot frame against the doorframe.

"I also offered a fair and equitable settlement."

"I've offered those before and been shot down faster than a brick falls."

"A fair deal will always be accepted."

"Bull," Donna said with a broad grin.

"A fair deal with shortbread always works."

Arden arrived home and Harry, his retired neighbor, called out, "You hear the city's trying to get another football stadium built to lure a team here?"

"Yeah," Arden said as Rusty woofed a greeting from his perennial perch on Harry's shaded front porch. The old coon dog knew how to enjoy life. "Given the way the city's make-up is changing, a new soccer stadium would be more popular. Chivas draws more soccer fans than the Kings or Clippers, let alone how many a football team would draw."

"Some owner will come after they offer him a nice sweet deal," Harry said as he pruned a rose bush on the edge of his immaculate property. "He'll field a decent team for a few years, then trade all his best players for cash, win three games all season and complain no one's coming because the stadium's old and guess who'll be on the hook for another new stadium? Me and you, Arden, me and you, and every other damn taxpayer."

"I haven't watched a game in years; officiating's unfair."

"Has been since the days of Bronko Nagurski."

"But now everyone sees it on the TV replay." Arden paused and added, "Maybe I'll be able to take Sam to a game. She's never seen one. Maybe even see my Chicago Bears."

"If you can ever get decent seats." Harry wiped a bulging forearm across his sweaty forehead. "The rich and the corporations get all the best seats. You're lucky to get one in row three-hundred and twenty in the end zone, and if you do, it'll cost you $400 to take the family, assuming you want a beer and a hot dog."

"Luckily Sam doesn't drink beer."

"She'll be out the door soon. You retiring next year?"

Arden shrugged. "I doubt it."

"Sorry to hear that; thought you were. Not a good time to be selling your house anyway. Roy, down the street there, just sold his; got $100,000 less than he would have got last year. He's bitching no end. Only got madder when I asked him why he sold if he was so angry at the price. Turns out his wife got a new job in Diamond Bar and hates the commute. Roy's been commuting to hell and gone down to Irvine for 15 years."

Things were getting worse. If Arden's house was worth less, it would cover even less of the cost of the Las Cruces house. Arden might have to work not just six more years, but another ten or more. As Harry pruned his roses, Arden felt for his pulse in his neck and listened. After a minute he had heard no jumps, misses or off beats.

Glancing over at the sagging fence on the other side of his property, Arden asked, "Seen Buell around?"

Harry shook his head.

"I stuck a letter in his door this morning."

"Why didn't you just talk to him?"

"Afraid I might end up in the mother of all arguments with him again." Arden was a professional mediator and here he was afraid he would lose his cool over a puny fence dispute with a neighbor. Maybe that concussion had damaged his ability to reason. "If it happens again, I might lose my temper and hit him."

Harry tilted his head and stared at Arden. "I have never even seen you irritated, let alone angry."

"I've got a temper. I just control it."

Harry shook his head in amazement.

"I used to play football, hockey, lacrosse and soccer as a kid," Arden said. "If someone pushed me, I'd go after them. My mom invited my sister to come watch me play hockey one time and my sister asked, 'Why? He spends all his time in the penalty box.'"

"You never can tell about people," Harry said, staring at his neighbor as he took in this new information. "What'd our neighborhood pest do to piss you off?"

"Buell says that fence is on my property so I have to replace it. I offered to pay half, since we both use it."

"Seems fair."

"He didn't see it that way."

Arden sat at his desk that night with a donation slip from a charity. The attendant had scribbled on the receipt "housewares: two bags, clothes: three bags, books: two bags."

"Do you remember what we gave to Goodwill last week?" Arden asked Marisela, who was editing a paper from another researcher on her laptop. Freelance editing paid $60 an hour. Good money, but there was far from enough of it.

Marisela looked up and considered. "A few pots we don't use anymore, a stack of books and half a closet's worth of clothes Sam grew out of or wouldn't wear any more because they were 'totally ancient,' to use her term."

"I need to determine the value of it all for our taxes."

"How on earth do you figure that out?"

"It's supposed to be based on comparable value in the charity's store, a consignment store or some other reasonable method of valuation. It's a guess. How much can you get for an old dress? A pot? A hardcover book? It all could be worth $20 or $200."

"Probably not $20, maybe $150?"

"No one ever seems to check." Arden sighed. "What does it matter? One-fifty it is," he said as he scribbled the figure on the slip for future reference. "Only saves us about 30 bucks on our taxes anyway." He put the receipt in a folder he kept for tax write-offs and leaned back in his chair. His head ached, but at least the headaches were diminishing, seeming to hit only when he was stressed. Unfortunately, with financial worries and a worsening job, he was stressed most of the time.

Marisela asked, "How was work today?"

"The new boss is a control freak." Arden massaged his forehead with both hands. "Wants reports before and after every mediation session."

"Seems like a waste of time. How many mediation sessions do you have in a week?"

"A dozen or so. I'll be spending more time writing reports than mediating."

As he rubbed his forehead, he felt Marisela take his wrist. He relaxed as she felt his pulse. "I'm fine."

Marisela stood beside him and listened to his pulse.

"I said I'm fine. Just a little tired."

Marisela ignored him.

Moments later she said, her voice soft, "It's off a little."

Arden sighed.

"Did you check it today?"

"Yes, it was fine."

"Bad day?"

"Looking for another job."

"Work's that bad?" Marisela frowned with concern.

Arden nodded. "Nothing out there, though."

They waited.

Marisela felt his pulse again. Arden told himself to relax.

A minute later, Marisela said, "Sounds fine now." She looked down at him as she stood beside him, concern in her eyes, and added, "Keep an eye on it."

"I'll be fine."

"I don't want to retire without you, Arden."

Late that night, Arden heard a roaring hum from downstairs. He peered through half-open eyes at the clock on the bedside table; 11:30 pm. He had been asleep an hour. After a hectic day, he was exhausted. A faint pain throbbed throughout his head. Ignoring it, he rolled over with great care, but saw that Marisela was not yet in bed. Such an occurrence was not uncommon. She was a night owl.

Cocooned in the sheet, Arden took a deep breath, closed his eyes and tried to relax so he would fall back asleep before he was fully awake. The window was open, letting in the refreshing night air that kept the temperature just below uncomfortably warm. He was relieved that Marisela had not closed it yet. They had slept with open windows in their second-floor bedroom in the summer for years, but since the burglary she had been closing and locking the window as soon as she came to bed.

Arden smelt the dry desert air coming in from the east and hoped tomorrow would not be too stifling. He did not know whether the Santa Ana winds were supposed to blow.

What was that humming noise? He waited, but it continued.

With a sigh, he swung his legs out from under the sheet and felt the cool wood floor beneath his feet as he stood. Sam should be asleep, but he staggered into the walk-in closet to don his robe anyways before tramping downstairs.

Arden found the source of the noise. Marisela was vacuuming the carpet in the living room.

"What are you doing?" he asked. They had spent part of each evening cleaning up the mess left by the burglars. To Arden's eyes, the house was in decent shape, albeit missing a bunch of stuff, and he was the neat one.

Over the vacuum she did not hear him and, her back to him, did not see him. She wore a black, thigh-length dressing gown with tiny white flowers scattered all over it. Her legs were firm and, with lustful thoughts, Arden wished that she had come up to bed if she was going to be awake so late. He would have enjoyed staying up with her having fun in bed.

"Marisela!" he called as he moved toward her.

She switched off the machine, which had been filling the house with its muffled roar. "I'm sorry, did I wake you?"

"No," he said, shaking his head and resting his hand on her upper back. He noticed the vivid red sore where she had chewed the skin above the fingernail on her right thumb. "You okay?"

"Fine." She sounded cheerful, far too cheerful for so late, let alone for someone aggressively vacuuming at such an hour.

"What are you doing?"

"Just some cleaning," she said, as if it was normal to vacuum at midnight. Abandoning the vacuum, she grabbed a dark green feather duster and attacked the top of a massive China bureau near the kitchen. It had probably been too heavy for the thieves to take, although Arden would not have been sad to see the last of it.

"Shouldn't you try to get some sleep?"

"I'm not tired." She dusted the bureau, swishing dust into a miniature cyclone captured in the light from a floor lamp.

"You have work tomorrow."

"I know," she said, an edge in her voice as her back and legs tensed.

"Let me get you some wine, help you relax."

"We don't have any."

They also were not buying any nuts, salmon or prepared salads anymore in their quest to cut spending and bring retirement back within closer reach.

Placing his hands on her shoulders from behind, Arden turned her around with great gentleness to face him. Her face inches from his, he said as he drew her to him, "You don't have to clean now."

"I should."

He felt her stiff body and saw the mask-like quality of her face. "It'll keep."

"I have to."

"Why does it matter if the place is a little messy for a few days more or less?"

"It does. You like it neat."

"It's fine the way it is."

"It isn't. I need to do some cleaning."

"Why? Who cares?"

"I do."

Arden looked down at her, forcing her to look into his eyes. "Marisela, it doesn't matter."

"It does."

"It won't make the burglary not have happened."

"It will," she snapped in one last defiant stand before her shoulders slumped and she sank into his arms, her dark head against the front of his black robe. He felt her body tense as she fought to hold back tears.

"Why us, Arden?" she asked, her voice muffled by his robe. "Why did they have to come into our home?"

"Bad luck. I doubt it'll ever happen again."

Her head shook against his shoulder as he rubbed her back, trying to draw out the fear that contorted her body.

"The detective said burglars sometimes rob the same house months later," Marisela said, "after the owners have replaced all their stolen things."

Arden nodded, struck by the elegant simplicity of such an evil idea.

"I wish...I wish.....," Marisela began, unable to put into words what she wanted.

"Just be glad you and Sam were out when they broke in."

"You weren't, and they hurt you." She looked up at him, her dark eyes glistening at the rims. She touched the back of his head, ever so tenderly, as if she was petting a day-old kitten. She lost her battle to contain her tears and began to cry. "I might have lost you. We might have lost you."

"I'll be more careful next time," Arden said and, even as he said it, knew he should not have, as Marisela's body, which had been ever so slightly relaxing, tensed as hard as iron.

"We should get an alarm system, a dog," she said through her tears, "or a gun."

"Three companies are coming to give estimates on an alarm system."

"What about a dog?"

"We aren't home enough to take care of one."

"A gun?"

"I couldn't see myself ever shooting anyone."

"I could."

Chapter 14

"Congressman Boardman," Antioch CEO Richard Sloane said, beaming, as he shook the silver-haired guest's firm hand in the expansive foyer of Sloane's primary Boston residence. Shaking ten thousand hands every campaign season had given the Congressman the hand strength of a bodybuilder. "And Tessa," Sloane added, turning to embrace the congressman's wife. An ex-political reporter for the *Washington Post*, she had switched to covering national security to avoid any potential conflict of interest with her new husband.

Ushering the power couple from the entry hall onto the balcony that overlooked the great room, Sloane pointed out the seven food stations scattered around the great room, south wing and terrace. Chefs from top local restaurants were creating their most-asked-for dishes on demand. Sloane checked his watch and mentioned that Tom Petty and the Heartbreakers would perform in about an hour. Then with a warm "enjoy yourselves" he left the politician and his inquisitive wife taking in the view out the 60-foot windows that formed the great room's south wall. The sun, its bottom rim just touching the western horizon, cast its golden rays over the lily-pad-covered surface of Hammond Pond below the Sloane's new property.

"I love the architecture in this village," one of the network television news anchors said as Sloane glided past a group at the bottom of the grand staircase. The anchor had interviewed Sloane more times than he could remember. Sloane had also taken the anchor as a guest to Liberty National Golf Club and sailing on one of Sloane's prized racing yachts. "It's on the National Register of Historic Places," the anchor reported to the group around him. "Chestnut Hill has a splendid array of Colonial, Italianate, Shingle, Tudor and Victorian architectural styles." Sloane smiled. Like him, the anchor had been briefed for the party.

Sloane's new Boston home—his fifth, joining a beach house in Newport, Rhode Island, a ski chalet in Vail, Colorado, a gentleman's farm in Fairfax, Virginia, and a chateau in Nice, France—was far from a historic design. Built in 2002, the four-bedroom, five-bath, 8,200-square-foot modern home offered unparalleled water views from every room, including all five bedrooms and a fantastic view from the massive whirlpool tub in the master bathroom. Terraces, patios and an outdoor kitchen set amidst the landscaped property reminded Sloane of the country estates he and Maddy had visited in the Wiltshires during their last trip to England, albeit on a much smaller scale. English homes built before 1900 were paid for by owners who paid no income taxes and therefore had mountains of pounds sterling to lavish on their palatial country seats.

"Lovely, it's just lovely," Sonia Gershon gushed. She and her husband, Bill, whom Sloane considered a key friend, stood just inside the great room admiring the view with Sloane's wife, Madison; "Maddy" to everyone worth knowing. Sloane admired Maddy and Sonia as he approached. Both women were tall, thin and had the most flawless bodies diligent exercise, a nutritionist-controlled diet and near-perfect genetics only slightly augmented by the latest plastic surgery could provide.

"A fantastic view of the gorgeous pond, and a wonderful house." Sonia cast her pale blue eyes up to the cathedral ceiling four stories above and exclaimed, "Such a spacious home. A splendid sense of space; airy and yet so terribly homey, Maddy."

Sloane agreed. It still seemed spacious and airy even with 250 guests in attendance. He had not needed the house. They had owned a nice 5,200-square-foot, four-story apartment on Arlington in the Back Bay before Sloane drove past this house one morning on his way to Worcester to play golf at one of his clubs. He stopped the second he spotted the soaring house across Hammond's Pond. On a whim, he decided he had to have it, and he did within the month.

"It is rather nice," Maddy agreed, displaying her perfect, capped white teeth. "Although it is one of the smaller houses in the area. If you look over there," she said, pointing a long, elegant arm adorned with a gold-and-diamond bracelet, "You can see the home of the owner of the Red Sox; such a nice man and so generous."

"Maybe you can get some tickets from him," Bill told Sloane as the CEO joined the group. "But not for the World Series this year."

"I'll be happy if it just isn't the Yankees," Sloane vowed as he accepted a Riesling from a passing waiter. "Maddy and I were there last year. Antioch has a box at Fenway." Sloane put his free arm around Maddy's 26-inch waist, feeling her warmth through her tight, silk designer gown.

"And you didn't invite me?" Bill asked, with feigned horror.

"You didn't miss much. First game was 13-1. Rockies couldn't do a damn thing right. Boston scored three in the first and never looked back. Maddy spent the last two-thirds of the game on a call to her mother. Game two was closer, 2-1."

"Yet the question remains, you didn't invite me?"

"I figured you'd like playing Augusta more than watching Beckett strike out nine Rockies, including the first four."

"Maybe," Bill conceded, "but the World Series *and* playing Augusta would have been perfectly acceptable."

Sloane laughed.

"Fantastic home," Bill said, taking in the expansive room, the guests, the food stations, and the giant ice sculpture on the central, massive natural onyx table. The sculpture combined the logo for Antioch Pharmaceuticals, which was picking up the tab for the party, and the multi-colored Olympic rings. The Olympics, just beginning in Beijing, were the theme of the party, with a healthy smattering of athletes amongst the usual businesspeople, politicians, movie stars, musicians, and people famous for being famous Sloane invited to such events. Bill said, "Good time to buy a house, too, I'd wager."

"Prices are down a tad," Sloane agreed.

Bill was the head of the Security and Exchange Commission's Division of Enforcement. Regal with graying straight hair, he put a hand on Sloane's shoulder and asked, "Subprime market not hurting you, is it, Richard?"

Sloane chuckled. "Of course not. Antioch isn't one of those damn fool banks who gladly loan money to the homeless for a signature and a handshake."

"Can't be all that bad. Bernanke promised last year that the sub-prime mortgage problem will be contained."

"Right, like a plague in a prison."

Bill laughed. "Given I missed the World Series, am I going to have the pleasure of playing down at Augusta next spring?"

"Lobbying early, aren't you?"

"Last year was a once-in-a-lifetime experience."

"Then it stands to reason it won't happen again," Sloane said with a laugh. Maddy cast him a warning look, but he knew how to handle Bill. "Don't worry. You're down on my short list to invite. But promise me you'll avoid Rae's Creek this time."

"If you invited me more often, I'd have a better chance of knowing which club to hit on 11."

"You always under-club. Maybe one day when you're a member you'll learn what club to hit."

"Me? A member?" Bill asked, shocked. "I could never afford the fees, even if I was ever asked."

Sloane leaned in close and whispered in Bill's ear, "To be honest, the fees are far lower than at any of my other clubs."

Bill guffawed. "Says the man with the new $8 million home."

"I'm not one of those Wall Street fund managers bringing in $150 million a year. That's what I should have gone into; fund management, not scrimping along in biotech like some Peruvian peon."

Glancing at their wives, deep in conversation about an upcoming shopping trip to Paris and Milan, Bill asked, "How about showing me the gardens?"

"It's 81 degrees and humid as a sauna out there," Sloane warned, wondering why Bill would want to even consider stepping outside beyond the terrace, where the draft from the industrial AC through the open towering 60-foot patio doors helped alleviate the humidity and the heat.

"A little crowded in here," Bill said, even though there was still ample space in the great room for at least another 100 guests and their dates.

"If you think you can stand the humidity," Sloane said, "I can."

"Better than Washington this time of year."

As Sloane led his guest outside, a slim Asian man in his forties with a plate heaped with Korean BBQ beef brisket caught his arm. "Richard, how's that clinical trial going?"

Sloane stopped and, recognizing the man, a fund manager from New York, smiled and said, "Terry, we have the finest researchers in the world and we're confident they'll figure out what happened. Nothing serious, they tell me."

"Six dead isn't serious?" Terry asked, raising his eyebrows. "Next you'll be telling me 9/11 was a hoax, and Iraq and healthcare aren't going to be major issues in the election."

Sloane chuckled, glanced at Bill to let him know this would take just a moment, and turned to put a friendly hand on the fund manager's shoulder. Sloane could smell the Korean BBQ and the thought crossed his mind that he had not had time to eat beyond a couple of *hors d'oeuvres* since breakfast. He should have eaten before the event, as he usually did, but there had been far too much to do. "Terry, sometimes luck runs against you; sometimes it runs with you. We've had clinical trials that lost no patients and the drug failed miserably. Others lost a dozen patients and proved wonderfully therapeutic."

"Which type of trial is this one?" Terry asked, emphasizing his question by gesturing with his silver fork.

"As I said, we are confident we will find the solution. A month, maybe two and we'll be right back on track. Doctor Yu, the PI, emailed me just this morning to say he has a strong possibility he's investigating."

"Let me know what he finds out," Terry urged as Sloane turned to walk toward the gardens with Bill.

After a fifteen-minute tour of the extensive gardens overlooking Hammond's Pond, the pair of men, their drinks drained, their shirts darkened with perspiration, meandered back toward the glass-fronted mansion. The gentle burble of conversations rose as the Heartbreakers started to warm up on the stage that had been constructed on the main terrace. Sloane smelt roses, camellias and a profusion of other flowers, their scents wafting to his nose on a gentle, welcome breeze that had arisen with the setting sun.

Bill stopped at a curve in the path but instead of admiring the view, he looked down to peer at the intricate geometric pattern of the pavers at his feet. "Richard," he said, stopping his host who had continued walking. "Before we rejoin the wives, I wanted to make a suggestion."

"You don't like the house?"

Bill chuckled and, waving his empty Waterford tumbler toward the expansive house, said, "Of course I do. It's perfect. No," he said, looking down again, "I wanted to suggest, just between you and me, that you might want to look into some of your...recent actions."

Richard frowned. He did not have a clue what Bill was referring to.

Bill sighed, pursed his lips and, looking with a worried expression up at the crowd in the house and on the broad terrace, said, "We've come into some information."

"I'm aware you're investigating Antioch."

"Richard," Bill said, paused, then rushed on, as if he was going over a waterfall and wanted to finish speaking before he hit bottom. "We have received complaints that you personally sold stock even while you were pushing the stock in the press, that you took a significant loan from the company in exchange for not selling a large block of stock, used company funds for your personal use, and that you pressured researchers to alter the results of a clinical trial, one in which a number of subjects succumbed."

Sloane stood stock still, holding his glass at his side, stunned. At first his mind was filled with a furious anger at the temerity of the accusations and their falsity. Then his mind shifted to another matter which, if anything, angered him far more. "This is the first I'm hearing of this," he said, his lips tight and his words clipped as he peered at his guest. "We spoke in Washington at Komi's no less and you did not mention any of this over the sushi, sashimi and that fine Kimura sake."

Bill wiped the back of his hand over his dry lips and, looking out at the low, wooded hills across Hammond Pond with the occasional mansion, estate or cottage peeking out of the fully leafed trees, said, "I didn't know then." He looked back at Sloane. "The investigation was focused on Antioch, but information is now surfacing that points at you personally."

Sloane met Bill's gaze. He had taken ample, extensive and expensive care of Bill, made contributions to his political party up to the limit, and was close friends with Bill and several other key SEC officers, yet it was all for naught. Here he stood in his garden at his housewarming party/Antioch Pharmaceuticals August Summer Olympic Fling being told the SEC was investigating not only his company but him personally. This was not how things were supposed to work.

"I'm sorry, Richard," Bill said, glancing at a Boston Celtic guard and his wife who strolled along a paved path twenty feet up the hill. "I don't have any choice in this, none at all. My investigators are still gathering information, but I wanted...I wanted to let you know this isn't just about Antioch, it's about you now."

Sloane nodded, went to sip his drink and, realizing it was empty, looked back at Bill. He placed a hand on the damp shoulder of Bill's Egyptian cotton dress shirt and, controlling his anger, said with a reassuring smile as if Bill was the one under investigation, "I understand, Bill. These things happen. I've done absolutely nothing wrong, so we'll get this all cleared up. My firm and I are fully cooperating." Sloane would need Bill in the future, even more now. "Few months, it'll be settled and it'll all be in the past like a summer squall."

"I'm sure we won't find anything or I wouldn't have warned you," Bill said, the words rushing out.

"We'll get it taken care of, Bill, and all will be well, just as it's always been between us, old friend," Richard said, forcing himself to grin. "I'd hate for you to miss out on Augusta in the spring."

"The Howards settled in?" Maddy asked as Sloane dragged into their bedroom at 3:35 a.m.

"As cozy as if they were at home," Sloane assured his wife as she changed into an ivory chemise night dress. "Beverly's bitching about the humidity. Stan seems happy enough, drunk as an Irish Navvy on St. Patrick's Day, but happy."

"Beverly would complain about the snow at Chamonix, the beaches on Anguilla and the wine in Burgundy," Maddy said with a wicked grin, which highlighted her high, tanned cheekbones.

Sloane went into his Cedar-lined dressing annex just off the bedroom and changed into his pajamas. The caterers, band, servers, sprinkling of stunning hired hostesses, and clean-up crew had all finally departed. The couple who served the Sloane's as live-in servants were finishing the clean-up.

"Learn anything more about the investigation from Bill?" Maddy asked when he emerged from his annex.

"It's aimed at me, as well as at the company; insider trading, pressuring a PI to change a report, misstatements to the public, and misuse of company funds for my personal use."

Maddy pursed her lips as her brow wrinkled with displeasure. "Everything you've done has been for the company, for the shareholders and for all the patients Antioch's products have helped. How could they possibly think anything different?"

"God only knows." Sloane set his Maurice Lacroix 18k watch down on his chrome-and-glass bedside table.

"Apart from finding out who slandered you with such vile accusations, the only question is whether the SEC will see the truth behind such baseless allegations," Maddy said, folding down the comforter and sliding into bed. Sitting up against the pillows in the king-sized bed, she looked regal with her carefully coiffed black hair, not a single gray strand in sight, and her ivory chemise cut low, but not too low on her surgically-enhanced breasts.

"I thought I could rely on Bill, Stan and the others, but now, who knows?" Sloane said, anger seeping into his rigorously controlled voice. He was tired after a long afternoon and night of shaking hands, making small talk and ensuring that he spoke with all of the people he had been briefed to speak with about topics of concern to Antioch's future—and his.

"All the time and resources you spend on them, they should be good to us," Maddy said, then added as an afterthought, "and Antioch."

"Politicians are about as reliable as a paper umbrella, just when you need them, they melt away in your hands."

"You are doing everything Lincoln advised?"

"Of course."

"He's the best; everyone says so."

Sloane nodded. "He knows the SEC inside out." Lincoln had held various top-level positions at the SEC for a decade before becoming Antioch's chief legal counsel.

"Well, I am sure you can handle the SEC. What about the clinical trial? I cannot believe how much it hurt the stock price. You would think you had died, not some silly trial subject who already had both feet in the grave."

"I've been emailing Yu every day, but he and his team have nothing yet."

"They will figure it out and if he does not, we will find someone who can."

"Right." His anger dissipating, Sloane said, "There are some fine researchers coming out of India and China these days; loyal, American trained, smart, dogged workers, and cheap. A dream."

"Isn't Yu Chinese?"

"Yes and no. He's a Canuck, Westernized. Doesn't understand how things work."

"You should only hire researchers direct from China or India. They're more grateful, and they do what they are told."

Sloane nodded as he slid into bed beside her. "We have other trials," Sloane said, "so if Yu can't fix it, we'll find another PI and start playing up our other trials to the Street and in the media. Already have. Les Eastbrook at least has a handle on that."

"Are you really unable to get rid of him?"

"Not now."

"And the board? Do you still have enough votes?"

"From my last round of calls and meetings, six are rock-solid supportive, three moderately so and two are sitting with the fence firmly wedged up their asses."

"Leaving four against you," Maddy said, nodding as she analyzed the information. "O'Keeffe, Short," she counted on her manicured fingers.

"Larson and Pearson," Sloane completed her thought. "They think the stock is going to stay in the basement, the SEC will hang me, the valve trial's a fiasco and a new leader is needed to convince Wall Street the company can stage a comeback."

Maddy nodded, her lips set in a grim line.

"Of course, all the others agree that the stock might not come back, the SEC may find something, the valve trial may be a failure and another CEO is needed, but don't think right now's the time to dump me," Sloane said. "They want to wait until they've built support for their chosen replacement."

"How long do we have?"

We? Sloane wondered how his job had ever become their job? He scratched the side of his head. "Couple of months."

"What then?"

"By then, if we cooperate fully, the SEC investigation might be completed and the stock should recover. Then it'll be hard as hell for them to oust me. Maybe the trial will even be back on track."

"Even if the SEC finds something?"

"They always find something. As Vanderbilt said, 'You don't suppose you can run a railroad in accordance with the statutes, do you?'"

"You better be the soul of helpfulness then," Maddy instructed. She plumped her pillow and settled more comfortably under the covers. "Did you hear Tony D'Angelo trying to convince that civil engineer...oh, what was his name?"

"Liam Shay?"

Maddy nodded, looking as if she was speaking about a child molester. "Shay actually said—I swear I heard him—that he does not want to expand. Tony offered to bankroll the whole thing; new offices in 16 cities."

"Liam's already senior partner in the largest engineering firm in Massachusetts," Sloane said, "and the youngest partner in the state's history."

"Tony would make him the senior partner in the largest engineering firm in the country, and then the world. I swear as God is my witness that I heard Shay say that he has enough work and—do you believe this?—enough money."

Sloane shook his head in amazement.

"By the way, how much did we raise for that charity tonight?"

Sloane shrugged and shook his head.

"More than they will see in a year of their usual puissant little fundraising efforts," Maddy said, settling well down into the king-sized bed to sleep. "I hope they send us a nice thank you card and at least some flowers. Make sure Sandy gives all the receipts to Dan for our taxes."

"Antioch paid for everything."

"We paid and Antioch will reimburse us," Maddy corrected him with a gentle, if condescending smile. "We will claim the costs and if the IRS says anything, we will say Dan forgot that we had been reimbursed."

Sloane frowned. All he needed was an IRS investigation on top of the SEC investigation.

"Don't worry, dear," Maddy said, patting his hand, "the IRS never investigates little things like that, especially for people like us who do charity work, any more than the SEC ever sends anyone like us to jail."

Chapter 15

Saturday, August 9, 2008

"I'm on the red line beside this rich *gringa*," Angel Morales told Diego as they squeezed out dirty rags in buckets of cold, oil-filmed water. "Niemen Marcus bag at her feet."

"*Chido*," Diego said around the chocolate bar that protruded from his mouth like a fat cigar.

"Grabbed the bag, stepped out, the doors closed," Angel said. "Her face against the glass door screaming at me like I stole her kid or somethin'."

"Rent-a-cops chase you?"

"Big crowd. Had my windbreaker off quick. No one recognized me."

"Anything good?"

"Bunch of *joder* women's shoes."

"Not your size?"

Angel shot Diego a warning glare, then grinned. "Not my style."

"Fit Tiffany?"

"Spoiled her enough. *El Tigre* gave me seventy-five." Barely make a dent in what he needed to get to electrician's school in Phoenix, but it bought a nice watch in an alley in the garment district.

Angel half-heartedly scrubbed the silver rim of a 1976 blood-red Riviera sedan. His eyes constantly moving, he scanned the long line of low-riders and customized classic American cars led by a Lincoln Mark IV waiting to be washed. Many of the cars had stickers on the rear window proclaiming "In memory of" a fallen son, brother, father or cousin in white lettering with dates of birth and death, and a cross, Virgin Mary or portrait of the dead. Music blared from many of the cars. Latin American *rockero* bands competed for predominance with Mexicans Ana Gabriel, *Los Tigres del Nortes* and Vicente Fernandez.

Always watchful, Angel's eyes checked all the homeboys as they washed cars in their black jeans and sneakers, white socks and T-shirts, and their black hair shorn to the skull. Many sported thin mustaches. His eyes flitted over the girls in tank tops, short skirts or shorts, and sandals, with a few seductively barefoot, who helped scrub, wash and polish the cars. Many of both sexes wore gold crosses around their necks, and many of the young men had tattoos of the Virgin Mary on their forearms, while Aztec motifs and intricate gang names adorned necks, backs and some foreheads and cheeks.

Across the parking lot Angel spotted two of his young cousins smoking Marlboro Reds and checking out each other's tricked-out bicycles. Each bike had enough chrome to cover a house. One cousin, Chaco, was shirtless to better show off his oversized muscles, as well as the nine-inch scar that snaked across his abdomen where he had been shot last summer. Chaco had not kept his eyes roving for one crucial moment and had paid for the lapse with a bullet in the gut.

Near the street corner, Angel eyed several girls, looking like a murder of crows with their long black hair, huddling with two of their babies. For a second Angel wondered where his son and daughter were, or their mothers, but the thought passed and was forgotten as quickly as it had flitted into his mind.

As he washed one of the Riviera's rims, Angel watched Vincent Villa stagger past the young mothers, his eyes sunken as he begged for $10 to score yet another hit. Vincent appeared to be sleepwalking, harmless, but Angel found addicts sinister. His mother said they were possessed. Angel agreed. No way he would ever become an addict. He could handle drugs.

Cesar swaggered over and started shining the Riviera's front bumper, although he was far from attentive to his task. "You think Mrs. Rolinson would give me a shot?" he mused about an English teacher at school.

"If she was completely wasted," Diego shot back, his latest chocolate bar inhaled.

"She wants me," Cesar insisted.

"She's *loco* for her husband," Diego said. "Got her a black Beemer for her birthday. Probably sucks him off every night and twice every morning before they get into the shower together and she lets him do her any way he wants."

Angel chuckled.

"Nice rims," Cesar said, eyeing the car's wide, chrome rims. "You hear Pedro stuck up the liquor store on 9th?"

"Pedro Cristiano?" Diego asked in disbelief. "He's ten."

"Twelve," Cesar said. "Got $13 using his brother's three-eight. Korean owner gave him the money, then came after him with a knife. Pedro didn't have no bullets or he'd have popped him. Cops brought out a helo and the dogs. Told Manny's *mami* they were searching for a dangerous, violent criminal."

Diego and Angel laughed.

Angel asked, "Nab his ass?"

"Nah, hid under his cousin's van," Cesar said. "Got hell from his *mami* for getting oil all over his jeans, but the cops never found him."

"We should *vamos*." Angel's thighs were sore, his sneaker-clad feet were soaked and, even with a bandana tied over his buzz-cut head, he felt as if the August sun was burning a hole through his skull. There was plenty of Modelos around, but he had already downed three and wanted a drink of water more than anything else.

"Never liked Bullet anyway," Angel muttered, flexing his water-wrinkled hands. The smell of exhaust fumes, soapy water and fried food from a taco wagon at the curb assaulted his nostrils.

As he scrubbed a front tire rim, Diego asked, "Remember that time you and him got into it over Tiffany?"

"*Calloso cabron* fondled her ass," Angel said, his rage rising at the memory. He straightened, threw the sopping rag he had been using into a black pail of water beside him and stretched his back.

"She didn't seem to mind," Cesar said with a grin.

"*Jode a tu madre,*" Angel said. "Let's *vamos.*" He eyed the others washing cars in the garage's parking lot, which was owned by a *veterano*, an older ex-gang member. Large homemade signs proclaimed the carwash was to raise money for Manny "Bullet" Ramirez; dead at 19. He had been knifed in prison by a gang member from the rival 32nd Street gang.

"I like it here," Diego said, casting a leering eye at Felicity Ortega.

"Nice view," Cesar agreed.

Angel's eyes took in Felicity's tight ass encased in wet jean-shorts that just failed to cover the bottom of her ass cheeks. She was barefoot and her T-shirt, wet in enticing places, barely concealed her magnificent breasts and did nothing to mask their wonderful shape.

As Diego and Cesar eyed their vision of lust, Angel grabbed a rag and wiped down the side of the car, leaving streaks. He said, "Should be doing this for Pony."

"What for?" Diego's eyes were still locked on Felicity's ass.

"Needs a new kidney."

"Why?"

"His tattoos are like a big scar."

"So?"

"Keeps his skin from letting poison out. Doc told him his kidney's work too hard," Angel explained, then warned, "Watch for Rafael."

"Fuck Rafael," Diego said. "Little shit couldn't keep a girl like Felicity happy for more than a second."

"And you last longer?" Angel asked as the Riviera they had been washing drove away and another arrived; a metallic green 1970 Plymouth Roadrunner.

Felicity finished scrubbing the hood of a dark blue Chevelle SS 454, depriving Angel and Diego of the splendid view of her rear. She glanced over at them and offered them a flashing coquettish smile.

"That's my signal," Diego announced, tossing his rag in a bucket and wiping his wet hands on his already damp jeans. He started to dig in one of his pockets.

"She's mine," Cesar said.

"No way, that's my signal." Diego shoved Cesar out of the way.

"Your signal to get your head knocked off," Cesar said as Diego swaggered over toward Felicity.

Angel kept an eye on Diego, who was so engrossed in his attempted seduction that he did not see Rafael stride over in behind him, like a hawk diving on a pigeon.

Angel cursed. Everyone knew he and Diego were tight, even if the *cabrón* always wanted to fight over the split. If anyone beat on Diego, it would reflect poorly on Angel.

"It's hers now," Angel heard Diego assert as he and Cesar, who had tagged along, reached the lust triangle. Felicity was holding an iPod, while Diego, short, stocky and broad, faced down the wiry Rafael with a look that could have froze a flame.

"Give it back," Rafael ordered his girl.

"He gave it to me," Felicity spat back. "I'll keep it if I want to."

The sounds of hoses spraying water, sponges being squeezed out and cars being scrubbed receded and then ceased as all eyes fell on the rapidly developing situation.

Rafael's dark eyes glanced from Diego to his 17-year-old girlfriend. "Give it back, Felicity. You don't accept gifts from this *mariposa*."

Diego threw a punch at Rafael's face. Rafael dodged left. The punch brushed past his right ear. Felicity screamed as she scrambled back along a red Charger to get out of the way. Rafael threw a short, sharp hook into the side of Diego's head. It would have stunned most men, but Diego was built like a fire hydrant; short and sturdy. He hit Rafael back.

In seconds Angel saw that Rafael was losing the fight. He had got in some good punches, but Diego was too tough. Diego could take an awesome amount of punishment, while dishing out plenty.

Rafael stepped back against the irregular ring that the crowd had formed around the fighters. Rafael lowered his head to snort blood out of his bleeding nose. Squinting through a blackening half-closed eye, he slipped a knife out of his jeans pocket. He swung at Diego, who jumped back to avoid the six-inch blade.

As Rafael advanced to carve Diego into bloody pieces, Angel grabbed his knife arm from behind. In one smooth motion, Angel brought his other fist down hard on Rafael's hand. The blade clattered to the ground. Angel kicked it away.

Rafael hit Angel awkwardly in the back of the head with his free hand. Angel punched him in the nose. Pain shot up Angel's arm but he felt the satisfying crunch of bone breaking.

"*Basta! Basta!*" the garage owner yelled, forcing his way through the crowd. "Now! It's over! Now!"

Angel knew that Rafael disagreed.

Arden and Marisela spent Saturday morning meeting alarm salesmen. Arden finished seven crosswords in his head while they waited for each salesman to evaluate the house. Marisela asked each salesman for their most comprehensive system. Arden asked for their most basic system.

"I thought we were trying to save money to retire," Arden said after the third salesman left.

"We'll never retire if someone breaks in and kills us in our sleep."

Arden met her set eyes. He knew when not to argue. He also knew when to negotiate. In a gentle voice he said, "I don't think we need sensors in every single room. The system with the perimeter sensors should be enough, don't you think?"

Marisela met his eyes, gauging his opposition. "I guess that'll be alright. But I want the 24/7 monitoring and the armed response with the panic button."

That afternoon Arden pushed a red, oversized plastic shopping cart through a big-box store as if he was pushing it through molasses. His forearms rested on the handle and he took slow measured steps as he tracked Marisela through the endless store. She led the way with a degree of uncertainty, peering right, left, back and forward trying to get her bearings. Arden would have helped her find what she was looking for, but he had long since written off any time savings gained from helping. Whatever he did, this was going to be a day-long expedition. Besides, Marisela found various things on her too-long shopping list while she was lost looking for something else entirely.

Arden wished he had brought some crosswords from the stack of newspapers he had taken from work before Keith Kennelwhite canceled the subscriptions. They would have helped pass the time. He looked down at the cart. It was heartbreakingly barren when he considered all the things they had set out to replace. A coffeemaker and a microwave sat in the cart, as did a digital camera, although only one. The burglars had taken Arden's and Sam's, but Marisela had balked at buying two of the same camera.

"I'm not sure which one Sam will want," Marisela said as her dark eyes shifted from one possibility to another at the long, glass camera counter.

At least, Arden thought with a wry grin, the lawnmower and weed-whacker could wait. Watering restrictions meant they could only water once a week and in the race between the sun's attempts to scorch the grass and the watering system's attempt to keep the grass green, the August sun was the clear winner.

Arden followed Marisela into the television section of the store.

He calculated the price of what they had purchased so far; too much. The insurance company had seemed amenable to replacing everything, but for all their niceness, it did not settle the issue of which model of anything to buy. Microwaves, coffeemakers and everything else they looked at all had huge price differences between models. Should they buy the least expensive model to ensure that All Risk Insurance covered the cost, a model that resembled what they had bought years before or a more expensive model that would be nicer to have? Arden realized that his preference was for the lowest priced, while Marisela liked models in the upper-middle part of the price range.

Arden wished he had just let Marisela do all the replacement shopping, but the red welt above her thumbnail reminded him with sudden clarity that he had to take care of her. She was scared and worried, even if she hid it well, except for her gnawed thumb. Besides, he did not want her spending thousands more than the insurance company would pay.

"Should we get the 32 or the 40 inch for the living room?"

Marisela's question pulled Arden out of his thoughts. "What?"

"For the living room, should we get a 32 or a 40 inch, or maybe a bigger one?" Marisela strode before a row of flat-screen televisions, considering her options.

"What size did we have before?" Did he know that bit of information before he got hit on the head? Probably not. Television was not one of his major interests.

"It was 40, but maybe we should get a 50 inch." Marisela glanced down at her shopping bible, *Consumer Reports*. "LCD, LED-

LCD or plasma," she said, deep in thought as she tapped her long fingers on her thigh and skimmed the magazine's article on televisions. "Plasma is good for dark or dim rooms."

"Our living room is bright."

"LCD works well in bright rooms and uses less energy than a plasma."

"And LED-LCD?" Arden tried to appear interested.

"Ultra thin, good for all lighting conditions. What do you think?"

"What'd we have before?"

"The models have changed since then. I think either an LCD or LED-LCD."

Arden forced himself to ask, "Don't we need one for our bedroom and one for Sam?" He kept telling himself that the insurance company would reimburse them, but he was still nervous spending so much money so fast.

"Maybe a 50-inch LCD for the living room, a 40 inch for our bedroom and a 30 for Sam."

"Or a 26 inch for Sam and we put the price difference into her college fund," Arden said with a grin.

"I don't think the insurance company will cover the difference."

"We don't know what they'll cover."

"Even if they cover 90 percent of what we spend, we'll have all new stuff for 10 percent of the full price."

"That's still a lot of money."

Marisela eyed him with a look of warning. "You didn't have to come, Arden."

"Who else would barter for you?"

"Americans don't barter."

"Maybe we should go down to Tijuana and buy all this stuff. I could get us great prices."

"I'm not going to Tijuana." Marisela stopped, looked around to ensure there was no one within hearing and whispered, "I don't like this either, Arden, but we need to replace everything and get our lives back."

"We could wait until the insurance company sends us a check. Then we'll know how much we can spend. With our retirement accounts so far down—"

"I'm not living without coffee, a microwave or a television for a month while they decide how much those…those men stole from us."

"The adjuster said it wouldn't take long."

"He said it could be a month and it'd be better if we just sent them receipts anyway."

"Or a few weeks."

Marisela eyed him, her body rigid. "I'm not waiting, Arden." Her face hardened.

"It wouldn't be long."

"No."

"We could get the essential stuff now: microwave, computer and maybe the televisions. Then, if they don't give us enough to cover everything, we can skip replacing some of the stuff we never used anyway, like the crock pot and the deep fryer. We probably don't have time to buy everything now anyway."

Marisela still stared at him, daring him to continue.

Seeing defeat looming nearby, Arden asked, "How about a 50 inch, a 40 and a 30 then?"

"LCD?"

"LCD sounds wonderful." Arden was lucky; Marisela did not notice his undertone of sarcasm as she turned to begin her evaluation of the multitude of makes and models of each size of LCD television. This was going to be a long day.

Arden asked, "Can we stop at the library on the way home? I need some books to read." He certainly was not going to buy any.

"At least the thieves didn't take any of our books."

"Not a lot of literate thieves in the world."

As Arden pulled into the driveway with the car laden with their replacement purchases, he spotted Buell and his young daughter playing in a sprinkler in their bathing suits in their front yard. Arden helped Marisela unload the car to the accompaniment of Rusty's woofs from next door. Once everything was inside, Arden walked over to talk to Buell.

"I checked the law on the Internet," Arden said, hoping the presence of Buell's daughter would soften his neighbor's attitude. He would have checked the law sooner, but as a mediator he was usually brought into cases where the law had already failed to settle the issue. "The law states that a shared-use fence that is between two properties should be maintained with the cost shared equally between the owners of the two properties."

"Right," Buell said, smug as ever.

"So you agree to split the cost of repairing the fence?"

"No way."

"But the law is clear."

"I agree," Buell said, still grinning.

"I don't see—"

"If the fence was *between* our properties we would share the cost of repairing it, but it isn't between our properties. It's completely and totally on your property."

Arden peered at the offending fence from the shade of Buell's ficus, which provided a dense canopy over a large portion of Arden's front yard. "By an inch?"

"By 6 inches."

"Six inches?" Arden could not believe Buell was being such a jackass.

"Six inches, six feet, it's still on your property."

"I don't even accept that it's on my land six-tenths of an inch."

"So check it."

Chapter 16

Arden detested having to write an opening position paper for Keith Kennelwhite. Arden could remember it all in his head, but he had no choice. Kennelwhite had emailed every mediator that no new cases would be assigned to anyone who was behind on submitting their pre-mediation, in-process and post-mediation reports for every single one of their current cases.

Arden had two cases for which he had not submitted reports. One was between a home owners association and a homeowner over mold caused by water damage and the other involved the winner of a contest who claimed that advertising for the contest, which promised "Free use of a car of your choice from our lot for one full month—30 full days," meant he could use a car for 30 individual days, not for just one continuous month. Small cases, but Equitable handled everything from the largest billion-dollar disputes to the smallest disagreements where emotion, reputation and face were far more involved than money.

Loathing having to write such elementary information down, Arden avoided the task and pulled up a news website he frequented. Russia had vowed to stand by South Ossetia against Georgia, defying a ceasefire. Some 100,000 Georgians had been displaced by the conflict. In Iraq, a female suicide bomber killed 17 and wounded 75. In the Beijing Olympics, the American team rejoiced when

James Black upset the great Swiss tennis star Roger Federer, but mourned when sisters Serena and Venus Williams each lost in their singles matches.

Surfing to his favorite business sites, Arden skimmed several news pages to learn that inflation had soared to a 17-year high and foreclosures had skyrocketed 55 percent since a year ago. He was happy to see that the Dow was up a little, topping 11,600. Antioch, however, was still down, way down. Why had he ever bought so much of it?

Interrupting his stalling, Sam called to ask if he could pick her up from the library, where she was participating in a Save Darfur Day.

"Why?" Arden glanced at the time on his computer: just past 3. Sam's event was scheduled to end at 9 after a dinner that would replicate what those suffering in Darfur got to eat for a day, if they were lucky.

"I'm just tired and have a stack of books to carry." She sounded timid and frail, far from a young woman bound for college in the fall with astronautical ambitions.

Arden frowned and bit his lip. He was relieved that he had passed on a mediation case between two resorts in Bermuda locked in a heated debate over the location of their mutual property line. This was no time to be away from Sam and Marisela, even if it meant missing a lucrative case, not to mention a trip to Bermuda. Without him at home, neither of them would get any sleep and Marisela would chew her thumb off. "I'll be there in 30 minutes."

Just as he was leaving, Arden's real estate agent, Roxanna, called about the closing of the Las Cruces house.

"I'm not sure if we're going to be able to buy it." Arden glanced at his calendar to see how long it was until the October 18 close. "If the market goes down much more, we might have to postpone buying anything."

"I'm very sorry to hear that. With prices down and interest rates low, there's no better time to buy."

"How much do you think our house in Santa Maria's worth now?"

"Most of LA's Westside is down about 20 percent, some more, some less. Let me pull some comparables."

Arden shuddered as he realized that they would be lucky to get only $120,000 less than he had planned from selling their house. Worse, houses were taking far longer to sell. That meant carrying two mortgages longer, with less money after their Antioch loss to do it with.

"We have until the October close," Roxanna said, "so we can give it some time. Maybe things will improve."

Arden found Sam slumped against a bike rack in front of the library with three thin books under her arm. He did not comment on their heft. They went back inside so he could pick up a couple of US history books to read. When they arrived home, Sam slogged from the car to the house as if she was not going to make it.

"Are you sure you're alright?" Arden asked for the third time as he opened the front door.

"Just tired." Sam trudged up the stairs. "I'm going to take a nap," her voice drifted back down to Arden, who stood at the bottom of the stairs staring up after her.

He knew she had been having trouble sleeping. He hoped the installation of an alarm, scheduled for Monday, would banish her nightmares about another burglary.

Arden went into the spare bedroom, once intended for a second child, where he and Marisela had a home office. The computer had been stolen, but Arden had brought his work laptop home to check their investments to try to make a final decision on the Las Cruces house. Before he got far, Detective Ranjan called and asked if Sam was home and whether he could stop by. In 20 minutes, Ranjan stood on Arden's doorstep.

"We found a couple of things that may be from the burglary of your home," Ranjan said as Arden led the detective into the living room.

Arden peered down at the iPod and wallet the young detective held out in sealed clear plastic evidence bags.

"The iPod might be Samantha's," Arden said. "They all look alike, don't they?"

"They come in different colors, but there are millions of each color. The key to identification is the songs."

"The wallet might be mine. I had an old one in a drawer by the bed. I kept some old money in it."

"Old money?" Ranjan asked as they sat down in the living room.

"Two-dollar bills," Arden said with a sheepish grin. "They're a tad rare and I like the painting of the signing of the Declaration of Independence on the back."

"Nothing in it when we found it."

"Where'd you find it?" he asked Ranjan, who sat on the tan sofa that ran along a wall opposite where the new flat-screen television now hung.

"A *cholo* told his parole officer he thought the iPod might be hot," Ranjan explained as Arden sat in a fabric-covered swivel chair, which clicked as he turned to face Ranjan.

Arden frowned in disbelief. "Did he just give it to you?"

Ranjan shook his head. "Someone gave it to his girlfriend. *Cholo* was pissed some other guy was giving his girl gifts. He thought it might be hot, so he came to us."

"Bizarre."

"Sometimes we get lucky, especially when love and hate are involved. We picked up the suspect who gave the girlfriend the iPod and found the wallet in his pocket."

"Why'd you think it might be mine?"

"It was in his pocket, but it was empty. Not many people carry around an empty wallet." Ranjan unzipped the bag and handed Arden the wallet.

Arden opened the wallet, which felt dry and brittle, and tried to remember the one he had owned. "Might be mine." The main compartments were empty, but he pushed on the top and bottom of the wallet and one end popped open. The sewing had long since given way. He stuck his fingers in and withdrew a two-dollar bill. He unfolded it and displayed to Ranjan the image of the painting of the Declaration of Independence on the back.

"Yours?" Ranjan asked.

"Mine." Arden handed the wallet and bill back to Ranjan. "I used to use the wallet, but wanted to make sure I didn't spend the two-dollar bill, so I hid it. You've got him then."

Ranjun grinned, but shook his head. "I can place the stolen property with the suspect, but now I have to prove the suspect knew the items were stolen and that he took them."

"Sounds tough."

"The law's tilted in favor of the criminals."

"And citizens," Arden said with a measured look at the detective.

Ranjan's gaze met Arden's and the detective's eyes hardened. In a formal tone he said, "I'd like to see if your daughter can identify the iPod."

Arden excused himself and went upstairs to wake Sam. She lay on her bed reading her prized copy of *Breaking Dawn*, the fourth and final installment in the Twilight series about a teenaged girl who falls in love with a vampire. Arden asked, "Couldn't get to sleep?"

Sam shook her head.

"Detective Ranjan's here. He might have found your iPod."

A smile transformed Sam's drawn face as she bounced off the bed and bolted down the stairs two at a time. She spotted the iPod in Ranjan's hand and screamed, "You found my iPod."

"Maybe," Ranjan cautioned, taking the machine out of the plastic bag. "Can you tell me some of the songs that were on yours?" Ranjan switched the iPod on.

"What about fingerprints?"

Ranjan chuckled. "If thieves never wore gloves and left clear prints on everything they stole, my clearance rate would be 100 percent instead of 23 percent. That's assuming I could convince the department to pay for a crime scene unit for every burglary."

"You solve less than a quarter of the crimes you investigate?" Arden asked, shocked.

"Better than the national average of 18 percent. I miss the days when I was in the auto division. I had a 62 percent recovery rate; of course many of the cars I recovered were stripped down to the frames, but I still got the clearance credit."

"I thought the police caught most crooks," Sam said.

"Burglars are careful about when and where they operate," Ranjan said. "I spend 50 hours a week figuring out how to catch them. They spend 24 hours a day, seven days a week looking for an easy way to steal something where they won't have to work too hard to pick up some easy cash and won't get caught."

"Do you think the burglars cased our house before they robbed it?" Sam asked, her eyes wide with excitement—or was it fear?—at the thought.

"I doubt it," Ranjan explained. "Even with bank robbers, only a few have ever even been in the bank they rob. Burglars drive around looking for an empty house. Many walk up and knock to see if anyone's home. If someone is, they ask for directions and move on to try another house. Others rob the homes of people they work with, since they know their co-workers' hours and when their houses will be empty."

"That's terrible," Arden said, picturing his colleague Donna Levin clambering through his kitchen window to snatch the glass paperweight from Scotland she had often admired.

"No honor among thieves or their friends," Ranjan said. "Burglaries are hard to solve because homeowners often don't even know they've been burgled for hours or even days, and usually have trouble telling us what was stolen. Even if we catch someone and recover the property, proving it was the homeowner's is often next to impossible." Seeing the effect of his words on Arden and Samantha, Ranjan added, "Sorry to be blunt, but in most cases there's little we can do. In this case, we just might have got lucky. Can you tell me what songs were on your iPod?"

As Arden turned to his daughter, Sam stuck the tip of her tongue out the corner of her mouth as she thought, just like her mom. "Pink, 'Who Knew'; Daughtry, 'It's Not Over'; Gwen Stefani, 'Great Escape'; Maroon 5, 'Makes Me Wonder'; Avril Lavigne, 'Girlfriend'; Nickelback, 'Rockstar'; and of course the classics, U-2 'Mysterious Ways'; and—"

"Hold on, please," Ranjan said, as he used the distinctive click wheel to sort through the songs on the iPod. "Let me catch up."

"You can remember all that, but you can't remember the capital of Switzerland," Arden chided his daughter, shaking his head.

"If you took me to Europe next summer, then maybe I would." Sam's large brown eyes turned up at her father as she added, "Please." She drew out the word so long that by the time she fell silent Ranjan had caught up.

"I thought we might, but not with the way our finances are now," Arden said, regretting the missed opportunity to see Europe with his daughter before she left home for college. Maybe he could take her on one of his mediation trips. As soon as he thought of it, he dropped the idea. He frowned on turning business trips into pleasure jaunts. The temptation to take advantage of the company expense account was too great and, even if he did not, the appearance of traveling on the company's dime would damage his reputation.

Ranjan said, "Looks like it is your iPod."

"I also modified the software, so the shuffle will play my favorite songs more often."

"I'm impressed," Ranjan said. "Could you just verify that it's yours by looking over the rest of the playlist?"

Samantha took the iPod and scrolled through the list of songs on the device, maneuvering the click wheel far faster than Ranjan had.

"It's mine," she squealed. "I thought I was going to have to download all my songs again. Thank you, thank you, thank you."

"You're welcome, you're welcome, you're welcome," Ranjan grinned. "But I need it back."

Sam's face fell. Framed with long, black hair, she looked the picture of despair.

"I need it for any court case that may arise from the burglary," Ranjan explained as he pried the device from Sam's clenched fingers and slid it into the plastic evidence bag. "You should be able to get it back when the DA is done with it."

"When will that be?" Samantha asked, shoulders sagging, her voice a whine.

"A few months." Ranjan turned back toward Arden. "This should help get a search warrant and move us a step closer to nailing these guys. Maybe you'll get a chance soon to see the burglars again face to face."

Passing a hand over the back of his head with gentle care, Arden said, "Hopefully under more favorable circumstances than last time."

"Detective Ranjan found a guy who had Sam's iPod," Arden said as Marisela arrived home from work. He was about to add the good news that it might lead Ranjan to the burglars, when he noticed the cardboard box full of office files and knickknacks in her arms. "What happened?"

"I went to see Ben to ask for more hours," Marisela said, setting the box down heavily on the hall table. "He said they didn't have any extra hours for anyone. In fact, they needed to cut back some personnel and, since he'd heard I had a second job, he questioned my dedication."

"That's ridiculous."

"Then he laid me off."

Chapter 17

Saturday, August 16, 2008

"He says the fence is on my property," Arden told his neighbor Harry as they strode across Arden's front yard toward the leaning fence between Arden's and Buell's properties.

After a late night consoling Marisela, telling each other they would survive, brainstorming ways to further reduce their bills, and ways for Marisela to find a job, Arden was letting her sleep in. He could do little about Marisela's lost job, their lost $126,000, or the declining stock and housing markets, but he could at least settle the great Santa Maria fence dispute.

"I offer an equitable arrangement," Arden said, "and he's stuck on whose property the fence is actually on; as if it matters."

"Guy has balls," Harry agreed as he and Arden stopped on the sidewalk to peer along the leaning fence. Rusty, Harry's coon dog, kept an eye on them from Harry's front stoop, although nothing interesting enough had occurred yet to cause him to rise from his well-worn cushion. Harry asked, "If you share the fence, shouldn't you both fix it?"

"Sure, but if I take him to court, it'll cost me more in time and fees than if I just fix the damn fence myself."

On Buell's front lawn, a nine-year-old girl in a bright yellow dress with a pink bow at the front sat at a folding card table covered with a pink plastic tablecloth. On top of the table sat a sweating, clear plastic pitcher of lemonade as large as her head. Taped to the front edge of the table was a homemade cardboard sign in pink crayon proclaiming "Lemonate Fer Sale."

"How's business, Lisa?" Arden asked, smiling down at his neighbor's daughter.

A grin spread across her face as she rattled a shoebox, which Arden noticed had "Safe" scrawled across it in red crayon. "Three quarters and two dimes already. I'm rich. Would you like some lemonade? It's really, really awesome. The most tasty-ish."

"Maybe in a minute," Arden said. As they stepped away, Arden whispered to Harry, "She's doing better than Merrill." The government had engineered the sale of Merrill Lynch to Bank of America at a greatly reduced price amidst fears of a liquidity crisis. Arden was uncertain what a liquidity crisis was, but he was becoming certain that Lisa could handle the economy far better than the Wall Street experts who populated the Fed and the Treasury Department. Turning back to more important business, he asked, "Where's the property marker?"

"Most cases there's a piece of rebar, metal or galvanized pipe with a tag at the corner of the lot," Harry said, kneeling down with great care at the end of the leaning fence where it met the sidewalk. He felt with his stubby fingers in the dry grass while Arden stood beside him feeling useless.

Harry said, "Might need a shovel to find her."

Arden seized the chance to do something. He rushed back into his house and out the back to the metal shed where they kept gardening equipment. He unlocked the rusty padlock, grabbed a dirt-marred shovel and sprinted back around the house to Harry. "Any luck?"

"None yet."

"What if we can't find it?" Arden probed the grass with the shovel. "Search the city records back to the old Spanish *ranchos*?"

"No, but you might have to pay for a survey." Harry stood as Arden took over the quest for the property marker. Harry grimaced as he stretched his old back. "Course, the survey may cost more than repairing the fence."

Arden froze as he saw the front door to his neighbor's house open. Buell peered out. Seeing Arden and Harry, Buell strode out the front door. His long legs covered the distance quickly. Arden nodded to Buell with as much neighborly camaraderie as he could muster and returned to his probing with the shovel.

"I sold three glasses already, Daddy," Lisa reported with a gleeful smile.

"Great, Lisa. That's wonderful." Buell turned his attention to Arden. "It's on your property." Buell's arms were across his muscular chest, which strained his fitted, dark blue dress shirt.

"We'll see," Arden said with an amiable grin.

"Got some searching to do," Harry said with relish. Since his retirement, he loved finding projects to fill his days.

"I wouldn't bother," Buell said.

Arden stopped and looked at Buell with a questioning look.

Buell savored the moment, a cunning smile spreading across his broad, flat face. "I had a survey done when we moved in. I have the paperwork inside, if you want to look it over."

Against his preferences, Arden decided he would have to accept Buell's offer to see the survey. He stood and thrust the shovel into the grass to stand it up while he went into Buell's house. The shovel clanged against something metallic in the soil.

"I think you found her," Harry exclaimed with glee.

Arden wrenched the shovel out, got down on his knees and felt in the gash in the turf left by the shovel. He peered down and announced, "It's here. You can see the metal post and a survey tag."

Keeping his hand on the bar just beneath the surface of the soil, he peered along the property line.

"See the fence is on your property," Buell said, making it sound as certain as the law of gravity.

"This doesn't tell us anything," Arden said, rising, his excitement at finding the marker gone. "We need to find the marker at the back of the property to know exactly where the property line runs."

"It runs straight back from the street," Buell said as he gestured along the fence.

Arden shook his head. "I've handled cases where property owners thought their property lines ran perpendicular to the street and it turned out the lots were laid out north-south or at some other angle in relation to a river, another street or who knows what. Had one where a quarter of each lot's front yard was in the next property and a quarter of the backyards fell in the other lot. Come on."

In his backyard, Arden probed the grass with the shovel right beside the fence.

"What you doing?" Will Leesing called, just his head showing above the back wood fence.

"Looking for the property line," Harry said. "Fence is sagging, so they're figuring who should pay to fix it."

Will nodded. He continued to peer over the fence as Arden and Harry searched for the marker. After several minutes, as Buell's grin grew and grew, Arden realized he was not going to find the marker. Admitting defeat, he said, "We'll have to look in your yard."

Buell led the way and they found the survey marker in the back corner of Buell's lot, right beside the fence.

"I told you; the fence is on your property."

Arden realized that Buell had already known that the property marker was on his side of the fence. Buell had been playing with him, the bastard.

Arden leaned on his shovel and glared at the decrepit, wood fence. "We both use the fence. Why don't we just split the cost. It is the law."

"So sue me."

"It'd be fair to share the cost."

"No way," Buell said, shaking his close-cropped head.

"Seems fair to split the cost," Harry chipped in, giving the fence a cautious push to straighten it. The fence creaked. As soon as Harry let go it groaned and moaned as the fence swayed back and forth. After a few moments, it came to rest in the same position as before, leaning well over.

"It's your fence," Buell insisted. "It's on your land. You want to follow the law, you fix it. If it falls over against my house, you pay for all damages. So I suggest you fix your fence before it falls over on somebody or something and I have to take you to court. Costs a lot to repair that adobe stucco I've got on my place."

"Can't we negotiate?"

"Nothing to negotiate."

"The fence."

"*Your* fence. Case closed. And I suggest you get off my land."

Arden seethed but decided that a break from negotiations might be the best course before he said or did something that would scuttle negotiations forever. Arden stalked back toward the front yard with Harry close behind. Arden stopped at Lisa's lemonade stand and, casting a glare back at Buell standing, arms crossed and guard-like on his front steps, said, "I'll take a glass of lemonade, please, Lisa."

"Me, too, please," Harry said, beaming down at the budding entrepreneur.

Lisa rose from her red plastic chair, picked up the pitcher with care and, her face the picture of intense concentration as her eyes narrowed to slits, poured lemonade into two plastic cups: one blue and one purple.

Arden and Harry picked up their cups and drank the cold, refreshing lemonade in long, thirsty gulps.

"Wonderful," Arden said. He set the empty cup down on the table, fished his wallet out of his pocket and pulled out a five-dollar bill. "Here," he said, handing the cash over into Lisa's tiny hand, "You're going to need this."

Lisa squealed with delight.

Arden glanced over at Buell, who still eyed them from the front steps, and added, raising his voice, "You'll never get any money from your father." As soon as he said it, he regretted it. Here he was, a professional mediator, losing his temper over a fence dispute. He needed some new tactics in this war, and soon.

Chapter 18

Monday, August 18, 2008

The alarm installers appeared at 8 am just after Marisela left to take Sam to a swim team workout at the Santa Maria Municipal Plunge. Then Marisela planned to go to the lab where she had been moonlighting to ask for more hours; hopefully with a better result than when she had asked the same question at her old job. She would also continue looking for a new full-time job, not that there seemed to be many based on her Internet search over the weekend.

Arden did a couple of the remaining crosswords from work in his head as workmen installed the alarm: sensors on all the doors and windows; motion sensors high in a corner of each room; and control pads in the master bedroom, the front door closet and next to the back door. Arden hoped that Sam and Marisela would get some sleep tonight, even if he probably would not: Antioch was still down and stocks in general showed little sign of returning to a bull market, let alone a rampant one. Now with Marisela laid off, he wondered how they were going to pay their mortgage. They had her severance pay and savings that would last six months if they were careful, but it could take a year or more for Marisela to find another job.

The alarm installed, the workmen gone, Arden hurried off to work, but on his front step he bumped into his neighbor from the back of his property, Will Leesing.

"Your fence is on my property," Leesing said.

This was beginning to sound like a *Groundhog Day* bad dream.

Leesing explained, "I noticed you found the property marker well inside Buell's property, so I checked our property line."

"Isn't it our fence?" Arden asked, wondering why it mattered anyway. The fence at the back of his property was in decent shape.

"The guy who owned your house before you built it, so it's yours."

"But it's on your property? It's not falling down, is it?"

"No."

"Then what's the problem?" Arden had called to say he would be late for work, but the last thing he could afford was to lose his job now. "I'm in a bit of a hurry."

"I want it off my land."

"I don't understand."

"I want my 18 inches of property back."

"Eighteen inches?"

"Yeah, I checked the property marker. Your fence is about a foot and a half on my land."

"You've got to be kidding. It's been there for years, can't it just stay there?"

"No. I want my land back. You've been using it for years."

"Eighteen inches?"

"Please move the fence or I'm going to have to tear it down."

"And then what? Have no fence between our yards?"

"If that's the way it has to be, so be it. I want my land back."

"*Eighteen inches?*"

When Arden arrived home from work that afternoon, he ignored Rusty's barking next door even as thoughts of Marisela's suggestion about getting a dog crossed his mind. Even if someone paid attention to a barking dog, who would risk their head to investigate a break-in at someone else's house? Maybe Marisela was right, a gun was the way to go. Arden disliked the idea, but if it would help settle her and Sam's nerves, maybe they should get one. Marisela's thumb looked ready for amputation from all her nervous chewing.

Maybe a dog would be better. A dog never killed anyone by accident. Then again, getting up early to feed and walk a dog, and having to walk it after work every day would get old fast. Although

Los Angeles was a moderate climate, it could get hot in the summer even on the Westside, and Arden could do without trudging through the rain after work in February picking up dog shit with a scoop, while icy water trickled under his collar and down his back. Hopefully the alarm would be enough.

"Is the alarm on?" Marisela called as she hurried in the front door later that afternoon.

"No," Arden yelled back from the kitchen, where he and Sam were preparing dinner.

Marisela appeared in the kitchen doorway and set her bag down on the counter. She had called Arden to say she had been networking with several colleagues as she scrambled to find a new job. Her face was drawn and her shoulders slumped with fatigue.

Arden said, "I'll have to show you how to arm and disarm it before we use it."

"I'm just happy it's installed," Marisela said, brightening for a moment before she turned worried again. "I mentioned to Brian Bannerjee—he used to work at Antioch, now he's with a start-up in Irvine, so I called him about any openings—that we're getting an alarm. He said he has an alarm and his house was broken into anyway."

"The alarm didn't work?" Sam asked as she snapped spaghetti in half to add to a pot of boiling water on the stove.

"I thought we were having salmon," Marisela said.

"Not on our new budget," Arden said. "You're lucky it's not bologna sandwiches on white bread, a head of iceberg lettuce for salad and water to drink."

"Maybe you should get a consulting job," Marisela said.

"Did the alarm malfunction?" Sam asked.

Arden did not respond to Marisela. She knew how he felt about accepting consulting positions. Marisela accepted a glass of cranberry juice from Arden.

"Brian's teenaged son was out and he often forgets the code," Marisela said. "Brian was tired of the alarm going off at 2 am, waking everyone up, so he left it off."

"The thieves broke in when they were home?" Sam asked, stopping as she tossed a green salad to look worriedly over at her mother.

"Sound asleep." Marisela let the words hang in the air overpowering the enticing aromas of the bubbling basil spaghetti sauce on the stove.

"An alarm system isn't designed to protect idiots who leave it turned off," Arden said, trying to reassure his wife and daughter before he ended up having to hire a full-time security guard, even if it pushed retirement off into their nineties.

As Marisela stepped over to watch Sam finish tossing the salad with a thoughtful look that told Arden she had much on her mind, Arden tried to change the subject.

"Antioch is still way down," he said. "All our stocks are way down from the high last year."

"They'll come back," Marisela said, barely paying attention to Arden's worries as she pitched in to help finish preparing dinner. She put plates on the stove's warming element. "The Fed and some analyst I heard on NPR said the housing market is stabilizing and that stocks should bounce back soon."

"And if they don't?"

"We'll work till we die," Marisela said with a wry grin, "assuming I can find a job."

"You will, Mom," Sam said with teenaged confidence.

"They gave me a few more hours a week at the lab, and I got sent another two papers to edit."

"Any full-time possibilities?" Arden asked.

"A few I'll follow-up on tomorrow, but mostly potential openings someone vaguely heard about. I'm not even sure they're real jobs."

Arden hesitated and said, "We should probably kill the Las Cruces house deal."

Marisela sighed and nodded. They had both known it would have to happen.

"You're final resting place?" Sam asked with a serious expression and then broke into a grin.

"It's pretty academic anyway," Marisela said, ignoring Sam's irreverent name for their retirement home. "If I don't get a job, we won't be able to get a mortgage to buy it anyway. Can we wait? Maybe I'll find another job before October 18."

Arden knew that was about as likely as Kennelwhite giving him a dozen new cases. "I'll talk to Roxanna. I don't think it costs us any more if we wait until October to kill the deal."

"Could we buy it and rent it for a while?" Marisela asked.

"Might be possible, if you can find a job."

Marisela waited until they were eating their salad before she broached the topic Arden knew had been on her mind since hearing about the burglary of her colleague's house.

"What about getting a dog?" she asked, slipping it into the conversation just after Sam had enlightened them about the horrors of Darfur.

"With Sam busy with all her activities and at school, and you and me working," Arden said, "I don't see when we'd have time to take care of a dog."

"I don't have a job."

"Then we don't have the money to feed a dog."

"We could get a nice little cute one," Sam said, smiling with delight, Darfur forgotten. "It wouldn't eat much."

"I doubt that's what your mom had in mind as a guard dog," Arden said with a grin at his daughter.

"Maybe a killer Chihuahua," Sam suggested, giggling. "Deadly for any burglar's ankles, unless he's wearing thick socks."

"Maybe a German shepherd or an Akita or something big," Marisela said, ignoring Sam's levity.

"Yeah, a nice cute puppy," Sam continued. "Next year I could take it to school with me. Take it for nice long walks in West Lafayette or along the Charles in Boston or out to Stone Mountain Park between classes at Georgia Tech."

"No pets in dorms," Marisela said. "And if it's with you, it wouldn't protect us any."

"A puppy?" Arden eyed the kitchen cabinets, the carpet and the yard still lit by the evening sun through the dining room's French doors. "We had a German shepherd puppy when I was a kid and it chewed the kitchen cabinets, destroyed the rugs, tore a hole through the back of the sofa, and dug up the yard and turned it into a quagmire."

"Maybe a year-old dog or a two year old," Marisela suggested as she forked romaine into her mouth.

"I think the alarm will keep us safe," Arden said. "Besides, we've had our bad luck. It won't happen again."

Marisela looked far from convinced. "Did you get a chance to cut back the shrubs near the windows?" She had pored over dozens of websites on ways to decrease your risk of being burgled.

"I should get to it tomorrow after work," Arden said. "I've been closing the blinds, making sure everything is locked up and leaving a radio on when I leave." He hoped to avoid having to get a dog. How much did a 140-pound Akita eat? An alarm was costly enough.

Marisela said, "Maybe you're right; we aren't home enough for a dog."

Arden was relieved to have avoided that added cost and responsibility.

Marisela added, "Maybe we should buy a gun."

Chapter 19

As the moon set over the jagged urban horizon to the east, Angel, Tiffany and Diego boisterously meandered along Third Avenue passing clothing stores, a sporting goods outlet, a bail bondsman, and a pair of well-lit but shuttered and bared liquor stores.

"Nice," Angel said, stopping to admire a leather jacket in a storefront. The store was a new one, its opening, a sign lit by one of the few working streetlights proclaimed, aided by a federal community redevelopment grant.

"You'd look wonderful in that," Tiffany gushed, hanging off Angel's thick neck, her breasts pressed against his bare arm. In the semi-darkness, he could smell the tequila on her breath mixed with the Cocoa perfume she adored.

Angel scanned the area around the store. His eyes lit upon a cantaloupe-sized rock in a planter in front of an adjacent store. He stalked over and picked up the rock. Striding back to the clothing store window, he eyed the padlock that secured the metal, scissor-like security grate protecting the display window. Looking up and down the street and seeing only a rusted white pickup speeding past, he raised the rock in one hand and slammed it down on the lock. The padlock bounced and rattled, but did not give way.

"Not that easy, Chico," Diego chortled. He took a swig from their remaining tequila bottle and then an enormous bite out of a Mars bar.

His anger increasing, Angel raised the rock again, this time much higher. He brought it down on the padlock with an alarming force. The metal grate rattled from end to end.

The lock held.

"That's," Diego began.

Angel raised the rock again.

"—never—"

Angel smashed the rock down toward the lock once more.

"—going—"

The rock connected with the lock. A shocking crash and rattle reverberated through the night as the grate absorbed the tremendous force of the blow.

"—to work."

The rock flew out of Angel's hand. It crashed onto the sidewalk near his feet. A shard spun off through the air past his right ear. The padlock, its hasp broken, bounced across the sidewalk away from him as if it feared another blow. Diego recovered from his shock and whooped with joy at the effect of the tremendous strike.

His body boiling with adrenaline, Angel wrenched the metal security screen open. Looking around, his gaze fell on three metal newspaper racks along the edge of the street. He advanced on the racks. With Diego and Tiffany giggling with excitement and glee behind him, Angel reached around one of the racks with both arms. He could feel his muscles bulge through his white T-shirt. He wrestled the rack off its stand as the metal bolts securing the stand groaned, screeched and whined. Finally they gave way.

With Tiffany giggling and Diego encouraging him, Angel lugged the metal box full of newspapers down the sidewalk toward the clothing store's picture window. From 15 feet away he rushed toward the window and at the last second heaved the newspaper rack through the window with a tremendous crash. Glass shattered and fell into the store, muffled by the carpeting inside. The coin box on the rack broke open, spewing coins all over the carpet, the display case and the sidewalk. Even as an alarm blared its warning, Angel kicked in some of the remaining glass shards. He jumped inside and grabbed his coveted leather jacket. Unfortunately, the jacket was secured to the mannequin displaying it with a security cable.

"*Joder!*" Angel picked up the mannequin with the jacket. He thrust it through the broken window, sending glass shards everywhere. Tiffany and Diego scurried out of the way of the wicked splinters.

A police siren sounded in the distance. Kicking out more of the shards with his new sneakers, Angel scrambled back out onto the sidewalk. He set the mannequin upright and scrambled to gather the quarters, dimes, nickels and pennies from the sidewalk, stuffing them into his pockets.

Tiffany kept laughing, while Diego joined Angel in his mad scramble for coins. The sirens grew louder. Tiffany started to run up the street, giggling and laughing as she went. Diego gathered a few more coins before rushing after her. Finally Angel, lugging the mannequin and his new jacket, tore after them, his pants slipping as his pockets—bulging and jingling with purloined coins—tugged them down around his thighs, threatening to trip him with every step.

Chapter 20

Tuesday, August 19, 2008

Arden stared down at the check: $10,562.66.

"Maybe we can save some of it," he said. "Stocks are falling again; more mortgage trouble. Home prices are falling, banks are failing, and Antioch's still way down."

"We lost a lot of stuff," Marisela warned as she brushed margarine on chicken breasts for a blackened chicken dinner. "Will it be enough?"

Arden skimmed the accompanying letter from All Risk Insurance. "They say if we find replacing all the lost property totals more than the enclosed amount, we can submit the receipts and they will reevaluate the claim."

"That sounds fine then, doesn't it?"

"They included a rental car for a month." Arden snatched a carrot off the counter to munch as Marisela started frying the chicken. The potent mix of cayenne pepper, cumin, thyme, and white and black pepper quickly cleared Arden's sinuses.

"You said the agent said they didn't want to add to our stress," Marisela said with a smile as she glided past Arden, gave him a quick kiss and slid open the drawer to gather the silverware to set the table.

"This should help. Now all we have to do is go out and buy all of it." He looked down at the check again. "I really hope we can save some of it."

"All I want to do is get everything back that we lost, so it's like it never happened."

"With our stocks falling, we could use a little extra money."

"We need to replace the things we lost, Arden. The point isn't to come out ahead. We will anyway, getting new things, but we shouldn't make money off something like this. It wouldn't be right, and I don't want to."

Arden nodded, saddened to see the chance to recover a tiny percentage of their Antioch stock loss vanishing. "Why shouldn't we get compensated a little for the stress and inconvenience, not to mention the time it takes to replace all the stolen stuff? And I did get hit over the head."

"If you want compensation, sue the burglars."

"If the police ever find them." Arden sighed. "I hope it doesn't take too long to find everything we need."

"It won't be that bad. I can do most of it, if you want."

"I'll come along." Arden wanted to make certain they kept track of the receipts. How far would $10,562.66 go?

After dinner, as Arden rose from the table, Marisela asked, "Do you really want to face it tonight?"

"I want to get at least one of the fence messes settled."

Marisela took his wrist.

"I'm fine."

"You're angry." Marisela took his pulse.

"I am a professional mediator setting off to negotiate a fair and equitable settlement over a shared-use fence." Arden turned his head to ask Sam, "How hard can it be?"

Marisela continued to take his pulse.

"I have settled multi-million dollar, nay, multi-billion dollar disputes between corporations. This is nothing."

"Quiet."

"Being treated this way is why my heart goes off."

"Shut up."

"Rudeness, plain and simple, Sam, don't you agree? Am I ever rude to Mom?"

"Silence," Marisela ordered.

Arden fell silent, trying to relax and breathe normally.

"You're fine, but make sure if things get heated, you just come home. A silly fence isn't worth a heart attack."

"If we split the cost to move the fence, we can rebuild it nice and you can get your property back," Arden offered Leesing, his neighbor at the rear of his lot.

"It's your fence on my land," Leesing said, arms folded over his chest as he stood like a sentry in his home's doorway. Did he take lessons in how to stand from Buell? Arden could hear Leesing's two boys playing a computer game in the living room. Sounded like they were doing a whole lot of killing.

Arden asked, "How about taking the case to mediation?"

"No way."

"Why not?"

"No way I'm taking a case to one of your buddies."

"You can pick the mediator."

"No way."

Arden tried another tack. "The law says it's a common-use fence. We should both pay to move it."

"I've been talking with Buell." Arden's hopes vanished. "It's not common-use. It's on my land and you improperly put it there."

"I did not put it there."

"The couple who owned the house before you did, so when you bought the house, you also took possession of the fence."

"How could I, it wasn't even on the land I bought," Arden said. "Therefore, isn't it your fence?"

"Move it by September 30 or I'll tear it down, whoever owns it."

"And leave no fence between our yards?"

Leesing unfolded his arms and leaned toward Arden. "For years I've had a shorter yard than everyone else on the block. You've had a larger yard for years. No way am I paying to get back what's been mine and was wrongfully taken from me."

"Eighteen inches?"

"It's the principle of the thing."

"Can't you just be reasonable?"

"I am. I'm not charging you rent for using my land for the past eight years."

Chapter 21

Tuesday, September 2, 2008

"It's been a month," Arden said.

"We try to get an identification as soon as possible," Ranjan said, "but this one took time to break."

Arden sat at a faux-wood-topped table in a pale blue interview room at the police station. Detective Ranjan sat across from him, his legs crossed, leaving a knife crease in his tan slacks. Arden peered down at a cardboard frame with an oily stain on the bottom right corner. The frame held eight photographs. Each photograph was of a Hispanic male. Arden frowned and slid the frame to one side, revealing a second frame under it, which also held images of eight Hispanic males. They looked like brothers; all black haired with dark eyes, and all in their late teens or the first half of their twenties.

Arden pursed his lips and scanned the photos; 16 faces, one, two or three of whom might be the men who had burgled his house, or none of them might be. "I read somewhere that it's more effective to let witnesses see photos in succession, not all at once."

Ranjan pursed his lips, his eyes narrowing as he shrugged. "Too late now."

"I'm a little tired. Just got in from Charleston; had a case out there." Arden had flown home Friday night, but saw no reason to tell Ranjan that. "I've been trying to cut back on travel, but sometimes I have to."

Ranjan nodded. His eyes flicked down to the photo-array. Arden refocused on the images. He thought he recognized two of the photographs. He fingered first one image with his index finger and then the other. Were they the ones?

"It was a little dark in the garage," he said, feeling dumb for not being able to identify the burglars with confidence. In movies and on television the witnesses always seemed so certain, so fast.

"But the garage was lit, correct?" Ranjan half asked. "The door was open, the overhead lights were on with four 100-watt florescent lights in two fixtures, one over each parking space."

Arden nodded and drummed his fingers on the tabletop. "They hit me on the head and I don't remember all of that day. I've been forgetting some things, things I used to know."

"I understand," Ranjan said, then added, "I spoke with the doctor," as if to confirm that he believed Arden.

"What happens if I identify the wrong ones?"

"We follow it up, check on what they were doing the afternoon of August 4 and clear them probably before they even know they're suspects."

"Probably?"

Ranjan shrugged. "Someone might have been driving alone to Tijuana or napping without a witness to snuggle up to in their apartment. Who knows? Let me assure you, if you ID someone and they didn't do it, we won't find any of the other evidence we need for the DA to charge them. Don't worry. Your identification is just one piece of the puzzle. No one's going to death row on your say so, Mr. Jeffries."

Arden considered and, placing an index finger on one photo in each array said, "I think these are the two men who robbed my house."

"You never saw the one who hit you from behind?"

"No, but I saw two of them, and I think these are the burglars."

"Are you certain?"

Arden's threat to Buell that he would check the law backfired. When he returned home, in his mailbox Arden found a letter with embossed letterhead from Anthony David Buell, Attorney at Law.

Arden guessed David was Buell's brother. Mr. Buell, Esquire, stated that unless Arden fixed the fence on his property that was "threatening" brother Buell's house and property, Buell, Esquire, would contact the city to levy a $500 fine for having an "imminent" threat on his land. It even set a deadline of September 30 for Arden to repair the fence. It was the same day Leesing had set as a deadline to move the fence at the back of Arden's lot. Was September 30 National Fence Day? It certainly was not National Good Neighbor Day or maybe it was, since good neighbors require good fences.

Chapter 22

Monday, September 8, 2008

"You're fucked, Angel, that's about as clear as I can put it, *com-prende?*" Chester Means said as he leafed through a thin legal file on the dented metal table between them. Two hundred and eighty pounds of gelatinous fat, sturdy bone and mediocre brain, Chester had been far from the top of his class at Southwestern Law School, but he had carved out a nice practice for himself representing thieves, burglars, drug dealers, gangbangers, prostitutes, and grifters in East and South Central Los Angeles. He spoke Spanish, thanks to a mother who had been raised in Venezuela when her father had been an oil engineer in the South American oil patch, and who had decided that her LA-born son should learn the language.

Chester shifted his massive bulk on his metal chair, which creaked in protest. He reached for his cigarettes before glancing with a dismissive glare at the no-smoking sign on the cinder-block wall beside the reinforced metal door.

"They have the iPod that Rafael Cardera swears Diego Delgado gave his girlfriend at a carwash on Hazard Avenue, which the owner identified as being from the house the DA says you three burgled." Chester lit his Pall Mall.

"Rafael couldn't tell the truth if I screamed it in his ear." In the dark blue scrubs of the LA jail, Angel Morales slouched on the circular metal stool on his side of the table and eyed his attorney. "*Poco el cabron* ratted me out." Angel had been extra careful at

LAX, the red line and every other lick he had pulled in the past few weeks. Now this. "Why me?"

"They have three witnesses who saw Diego give the iPod to Rafael's girl at the carwash and I am beyond certain that they can find another dozen if they apply some gentle persuasion."

Angel grinned at the memory of smashing Rafael's nose at the carwash. The knuckles of his right hand still ached. He should have wrapped a rag around it first, but there had not been time.

"In any case," Chester went on, puffing on his cigarette, "they arrested Diego and now he's talked himself into a nice, quick deal. Told all about the burglary; every minute detail."

"*Puto*," Angel spat, pounding his sore fist on the metal table, which produced an ear-damaging clang in the claustrophobic room and a bolt of pain up his arm. "Diego talked because I knocked him on his ass over the split. What'd he get?"

"Two years; bad luck if he serves even six months with overcrowding."

"I'll talk."

"Diego already did."

"I'll cooperate."

"I doubt they'll care."

"What am I facing?" Angel wondered how long before he could get out to deal with Diego and his mouth.

The door opened and a gruff female guard barked, "No smoking."

Chester scowled, looked around for an ashtray in vain before stubbing his Pall Mall out on the underside of his metal chair. Satisfied, the guard slammed the door shut, causing a disheartening echo in the tiny room. Angel grimaced at the smell of Chester's chosen brand. Angel smoked Marlboro Reds.

After the echo died down, Chester said, "They're counting it as your second and third strikes."

"What?" Angel roared, astounded. "I have one strike; Beemer in Santa Monica last year."

"And the burglary and the assault this time." Chester pulled an Oh Henry chocolate bar out of his slim, leather briefcase and tore the yellow wrapper open, ignoring the sign next to the no-smoking sign that asked occupants to refrain from eating or drinking in the jail's interview rooms. "Strikes two and three," he said through a mouthful of chocolate, peanuts and tasty nugget.

"That *pinche cabrones*. He's the one who clocked that dude, not me."

Chester shrugged. "First to talk, first to walk."

"If they'd talked to me first, they'd have Diego cold for clocking that dude."

Chester again shrugged his massive shoulders. "Undoubtedly, but the past is past. They have Cesar and you instead."

"Cesar will back me up."

"Scant backing, given his record."

"You've worked it for me before."

"You didn't have three strikes before."

"I've given you a lot of favors." Angel leaned across the table. To avoid getting an overworked public defender who would see Angel for a fast five minutes just before a court appearance, Angel let Chester purchase a selection of the various goods Angel came across in his adventures at well below market prices.

"I deeply appreciate the favors. If it should come to an end, I shall greatly miss our pleasant chats together and our many and varied transactions. You've been an admirable client." Chester inclined his head as if offering a benediction to a devout and loyal friend who was about to pass.

"What am I facing?" Angel demanded.

"Twenty-five to life."

"I didn't hit him."

"You were there; same thing. The law doesn't distinguish."

"I didn't hit him."

"You could have been taking a shit in the bathroom upstairs, but if you were in the house when Diego assaulted the homeowner, you're as criminally liable as he is."

"I didn't know the *puta* was going to clock the guy."

"Does not matter."

Angel spat on the floor. "No deal? You always get me one."

"Diego's already sewn this up," Chester said, finishing his chocolate bar with a final enormous bite. "Do you have anything else to give the DA?"

"I'd give 'em Diego," Angel said with relish, "for nothing."

"They already have him."

"Not for laying out the dude."

"No," Chester agreed. "They have him for enough though. That all you have to offer?"

It went against Angel's nature to cooperate, but 25-to-life changed his views. "I know a couple of *cholos* who been boosting cars."

"How many?"

"Couple a month."

"What else?" Chester jotted a note with his chewed blue plastic pen on a dog-eared and chocolate-stained yellow legal pad.

"Not enough?"

"It's your life."

"*Cholo* who lifts laptops from college libraries."

Chester jotted down another note. "What else?"

Angel sighed, wondering what it would take. He combed his memory for crimes. "Homeboy who has a key to take money out of parking meters."

"Who cares? They're all going to credit cards anyway. What else?"

Angel sighed again. "I could talk about a liquor store that was hit a while back."

"What else?"

Chapter 23

"I hope and pray 13 isn't my unlucky number," CEO Richard Sloane announced as he strode into Antioch Pharmaceutical's executive conference room to meet the corporation's lead counsel, Lincoln Avery, and a dozen lawyers from the legal department.

"I hope not, for all of us," Lincoln said, beaming as they leaned over to shake hands across the broad polished table. "Don't worry, our D&E insurance will pay for them all, even if we need 13 more."

"Sounds dire," Sloane said with a wry grin.

"Basically that is what we are here to determine."

With a confident, relaxed smile, Sloane unbuttoned his suit jacket and sat at the mammoth conference table across from Lincoln, who smiled reassuringly in greeting. White linen napkins sat at intervals precisely aligned down the middle of the table. Crystal decanters of water and, incongruously, water-beaded cans of soda stood on each napkin around the decanters next to empty, inverted etched crystal glasses. Fresh muffins sat in wicker baskets, filling the wood-paneled room with their tantalizing aromas of blueberry, cinnamon and banana. Sloane recognized several of the attorneys, including one young attorney with a startling pair of tits with whom he had enjoyed a brief tryst a year before. What was her name?

"I thought you'd be handling the Wells submission all by your lonesome, Lincoln," Sloane said.

"Even the Lone Ranger had Tonto," Lincoln said as he withdrew a stack of papers from a pristine buff folder before him.

"But a dozen Tontos?" Sloane leaned back in his chair to try to get comfortable. His upper back ached. It had been sore ever since a round at Muirfield when he and Maddy had vacationed in Scotland in May. Trying to get out of a pot bunker had strained his lower back and he had still taken four shots to escape the damned hell hole. "Think you'll need a dozen Tontos?"

"Napoleon said, 'God is on the side of the biggest battalions'," Lincoln said, holding a slim gold pen, which matched the simple ring on his fourth finger and his watch, which just showed beneath his crisp, white shirt and charcoal suit jacket.

"Let's hope we don't have to rely on God to get us out of this one." Sloane glanced up and down the row of attentive faces across the table, recalling some names for a face here and there. He smiled at his former lover whose name he still could not recall and then gazed out the broad window at the end of the room. It offered a panoramic view of the Charles River and across the water Cambridge, with the towers of Harvard's Leverett House protruding like urban intrusions above a stand of trees.

Sloane tried to fathom what the SEC possibly could have found on Antioch and on him. Even given his concerns, he was happy. He had just closed on a rare Ferrari F-50, of which only 349 were built to commemorate Ferrari's 50th anniversary. An exquisite car; now his exquisite car. Maybe he and Maddy, he and Jennifer or he and that stacked attorney he had bedded last year could take it for a nice drive up to Maine to see the leaves turning in the fall. She—the attorney—had been one of his more enthusiastic bedmates and her breasts were wonders to behold static or in motion. What was her damn name?

Sloane asked, "Should I have my management team present?"

"I recommend starting with just you. We can branch out from there as required."

Sloane grabbed a soda from the middle of the table. He passed on the etched crystal tumbler; best to appear a man of the people. He snapped the soda open and, after a quick sip, said, "Hit me with your best shot."

"Basically," Lincoln began, "the Wells notice lists a number of issues, which after examining various documents and interviewing

47 individuals, led the SEC investigation team to believe that an enforcement proceeding might be warranted."

Sloane knew the process. After their investigation, the SEC team either recommended to their bosses an enforcement proceeding or, if they found no basis for the complaints, recommended no action. If they were recommending an enforcement proceeding, they had found something; the something could be minor, major or anywhere in the vast region in between.

"Basically, this meeting is to go over the Wells notice to ensure you fully understand the contents," Lincoln said. "We have a month to respond with a Wells submission to present our case for why the SEC should not proceed with the enforcement proceeding. If we do not handle this well we could face various charges including any and all of the charges outlined in the notice."

"Let's make damn sure we handle it well then." Sloane had attended one such session before, when he was a VP at Glencoe Pharmaceuticals. That investigation led to a settlement: a $525,000 fine, internal policy changes, and 15 employees terminated. No big deal.

"I should mention before we begin that anything said in this meeting is confidential," Lincoln said, glancing at all his minions in case his younger lawyers had any thought of talking about the meeting to spouses, lovers or—God, Sloane and Lincoln forbid— the media. Lincoln's tone and stare strongly suggested that if they did, it would be the last thing they would ever do.

Turning back to Sloane, Lincoln flashed a reassuring smile for a tenth of second and looked down at the top paper in the stack before him. "Are you comfortable? Shall we begin?"

Sloane nodded.

"On or about March 7 of this year, a 60-inch flat screen television from your personal conference room was transported to your private residence in Boston."

Sloane snorted. "The SEC's investigating a television set? Next they'll be investigating how much candy I gave away last Halloween."

Lincoln said, "Only if you charged it to Antioch."

The well endowed attorney stifled a chuckle. Sloane recalled that she had an excellent sense of humor, and of adventure.

Lincoln continued, "I thought we would start with the minor charges first, just to warm up, so to speak. Was the television for the personal use of you or your family?"

Sloane's mouth hung open as he shook his head in disbelief. "It was old. The remote control didn't work. I had the television in my office replaced, but when they installed the new one, they left the old one on the floor in a corner of my conference room. It sat there for more than a month, even though I asked several times to have it removed. Rather bad form to have a broken television in your conference room. Problem was, no one knew what to do with it, something to do with environmental rules about disposing of a plasma. Finally, I just had it taken to my house here in Boston."

"Did you pay for transporting it or reimburse the company for its transport?"

Sloane sighed and shook his head. Lincoln could not be serious. If this was all the SEC had, it was less than nothing. Why even bother with a meeting?

Lincoln's minions started typing on their laptops. A few Luddites took notes on yellow legal pads.

"What happened to the television when it reached your home; the one in Chestnut Hill, I presume?" Lincoln asked, his voice even and emotionless.

"That was when we lived in the Back Bay. I had it put in my daughter's room."

"Did you reimburse Antioch for the television in any way, monetary or otherwise?"

Sloane stared across at Lincoln. This was silly. "No." More typing and note taking by the attorneys. Sloane added slowly and with precision, emphasizing each word, "It was broken. No one wanted it."

"Your daughter attends Stanford?" Lincoln asked, not missing a beat.

Sloane nodded.

"Where does she reside?"

"In an apartment just off campus."

"In Menlo Park on Maple Leaf Way?"

"Yes."

"It's a house, isn't it?"

"She lives in a house that's been converted into apartments." What the hell was Lincoln talking about?

"Who owns the apartment?"

"Antioch."

"Does she pay rent?"

"Yes, of course."

"How much?"

Sloane's anger was rising even as he hid it well, keeping his voice calm and even. "I really don't see—"

Lincoln raised a manicured hand. "We have to get to the core of each issue if we wish to avoid an enforcement proceeding. Let us just go over each issue in depth to ensure we do not miss a single pertinent fact in our reply. I want to ensure that our submission is airtight and does not miss a single relevant fact. We certainly do not wish to leave ourselves open to any hint of perjury, obstruction of justice or fraud charges."

"That's ridiculous."

"Then we should proceed carefully and thoroughly."

Sloane blew the air out of his mouth and nodded. He did not have time for this. He was far from used to being questioned in such a way and he fought to maintain his usual calm demeanor. "I think she pays about $250 a month, but I would need to check."

Lincoln pursed his lips. Sloane thought he detected a hint of distaste in the look, but only for a second and he may have been mistaken.

"The average rent for a one-bedroom in that area is $1,250," Lincoln said, glancing at one of his assistants, who nodded.

"The apartment was empty," Sloane said. "Had been for years."

"Why did Antioch own it?"

Sloane shook his head. "I'm far from certain. My predecessor acquired it. I believe the plan was for our researchers to stay there when they were out there meeting with researchers from Stanford. We do some research with the university, but it never seemed to work out. Most of the researchers prefer to stay in hotels. They don't want to cook their own meals, and some of them bring their spouses along and they prefer a hotel."

"Who set your daughter's rent?"

"I don't recall."

Sloane jotted something down with his gold pen. "I believe we can resolve those two issues easily, if you are amenable. I recommend that you pay fair market value for the television—"

"Broken television," Sloane interrupted, not bothering to hide his contempt for the issue.

"Broken television, and your daughter should reimburse the company for back rent up to the going rate for the area."

"Fine, fine." Sloane chugged down a long gulp of soda as he wondered how petty the SEC could get: who cared about a crummy, little $1,600 plasma television with a broken remote?

"Moving on, you have memberships at 11 country clubs, you order meals from a range of restaurants, you have an executive medical plan with Mount Herman Medical Center, and the use of two cars, as well as vehicles when outside Boston, subsidized housing and various other compensation," Lincoln said, reading from a list before him.

"All outlined in my contract with Antioch and approved annually by the board's Compensation Committee."

"True," Lincoln said, glancing up from his papers and looking the soul of helpfulness, "but basically I wanted to make certain that you abided strictly by the terms for each and every aspect of the contract."

"I did. I do."

"The SEC may disagree."

"I don't see how."

"You charged Antioch on May 6 of last year for the health insurance co-pay for a visit to a cardiologist at New York Presbyterian."

"My GP wanted a specialist to check out a heart murmur. He was worried about my long days; 6 to 9 or later most days without a break and constant emails, phone calls and meetings. I hadn't had a vacation longer than a long weekend in two years. Maddy was worried, too." So was his mistress, Jennifer, Sloane recalled; sweet of her.

"I pray nothing was wrong with your heart."

"Fine, nothing really. It's just missing a tiny piece, something on a valve that led to the murmur. Nothing dangerous, as long as I take care of myself, but the cardiologist was out of group."

"From my reading of your contract, Antioch should not have paid that co-pay."

"Fine. I'll reimburse the company the twenty bucks," Sloane shot back.

"Records show it was $940."

"I would have thought having a healthy CEO was worth something."

"It is. It undoubtedly is."

Sloane hoped the meeting would end soon, but it only got worse.

"Your wife and daughter often accompany you on overseas trips, including seven last year to Rio de Janeiro, Canberra, Tokyo, Geneva, London, Tel Aviv, and Rome."

Sloane was about to reach for another soda, but stopped. "They did, but it didn't cost the company a penny."

"They flew on one of the company's jets?"

"What difference does it make? The jet was taking me to various meetings and site visits. Didn't cost any more to take three people instead of one."

"They should have reimbursed the company."

"How can they reimburse the company for something that didn't cost Antioch a dime?"

"Meals, drinks, extra fuel for the weight of the additional passengers and their baggage."

"You brave enough to ask Maddy how much she weights?"

Several attorneys chuckled. Lincoln smiled for a moment. "Basically, I recommend paying the standard coach fare for a return flight to those destinations."

Sloane grabbed a new soda and took a long drink. "I believe you will find in my contract that I am authorized to take assistants with me on trips at my sole discretion."

"True."

"My wife and daughter assist me."

"In what way?"

"My wife is an excellent advisor with extensive experience with negotiations, business strategy and social arrangements."

"And your daughter?"

"Brings the youth perspective to our marketing and social media efforts."

"Have they ever drawn a salary or signed a contract with Antioch?"

"My daughter was an intern in our marketing department last summer."

Lincoln tapped his gold pen on his pad. "I tend to agree that you followed the letter of your contract."

Sloane started to smile, but it disappeared as Lincoln continued, "But the SEC may take a somewhat narrower view. I recommend that you reimburse the company for the flights by your daughter and your wife."

"I did nothing wrong."

"Consider it a PR gesture."

"It certainly isn't a legal gesture."

"Agreed, one-hundred percent agreed."

Sloane suppressed a sigh and said, "It will be done."

"Excellent. Moving on to the more potentially damaging issues," Lincoln said, his voice as calm and even as when they had started. Sloane wondered if the man ever got mad, sweated or, God forbid, lost his temper.

"In June 2007, you secured a $560,000 loan from Antioch at zero percent interest for 15 years," Lincoln read from a paper on the table before him.

Sloane nodded.

Lincoln paused and set his pen down on the wad of papers before him. "Those seem extremely favorable terms, for you."

"The board offered, I accepted."

"Why?"

"I suggest you ask them."

"The SEC did, but I would like to hear your perspective on the incident."

Sloane sipped his soda and set it down on the table. Incident? Made it sound like a purse snatching. He had done nothing wrong. The board approved, urged, almost forced him to take the loan. From long practice his demeanor and voice remained unchanged. "Maddy and I had just purchased our home in Newport and she wanted to renovate. I happened to mention to Chance Stafford that I was planning to sell some Antioch stock to pay for the remodel. He was of the opinion that my doing so would send the wrong signal to Wall Street, not to mention shareholders, about the future of the stock. He asked me to wait a few days and before I knew it the board had made the offer of a loan."

Lincoln nodded, jotting down notes. "You may need to repay that loan, immediately."

"I don't see why."

"The board may have exceeded its authority by proffering the loan."

"They broke no rules."

"Shall we call it a breaking of the spirit of the rules?"

"Barely that."

"The shareholders might disagree."

"Selling the stock would have forced the share price down, hurting the shareholders. The loan avoided that eventuality."

"Granted, but the board should not make loans to the CEO. Neither they nor Antioch is a bank. I would hate for the SEC to investigate Antioch based on the banking regulations."

Sloane sipped his soda again and nodded. He loathed this. "I'll repay the loan."

"At a somewhat higher interest rate."

"That wasn't the agreement." Sloane's voice flared.

"The agreement may have been flawed. A mistake on the part of the board, not yours, of course."

Regaining control of his voice, Sloane said, "Hardly seems fair or equitable for me to pay for their mistake."

"That is what I recommend."

With just a hint of sarcasm in his voice Sloane asked, "Can I sell some stock to repay the loan?"

Lincoln grinned for an instant, before he was back to all business. "If you need to, that would be entirely your decision."

"I hope the board and our shareholders don't mind."

"Moving on, in January of this year, just as Antioch stock was falling, you sold 100,000 shares on the eighth."

"That was entirely my decision," Sloane said with a wry smile.

"The following day on CNBC you were interviewed and said that the stock, although dipping, was strong and would recover to reach new highs."

"I believed it would and it did."

"Had you not received the day before, the seventh, an email from the PI of the laboratory-grown heart valve clinical trial that several rats had died in the animal modeling for the valve?"

"I may have."

"The SEC appears to have found records that you did."

Sloane paused, meeting Lincoln's level stare. "Even if I did—which I do not recall one way or the other—CEOs have an obligation to keep certain information secret: layoffs, plant closure and plant opening plans, new drug trials, and the progress of the clinical trials."

"It would be right and proper to mention such information to legal staff, especially after the fact, as is the case now."

"I would, but I don't recall."

"Would you like to see the email?"

Sloane shook his head. "If there was such an email, it had no impact on my decision to sell Antioch stock."

"The SEC will undoubtedly ask why you sold the day after receiving such disturbing news?"

"It wasn't disturbing. I don't even remember it. I get hundreds of emails a day."

"Your emailed reply appears to show that you believed it was extremely disturbing, even dire. Would you like to see it?"

"I seem to recall that the PI said the rodent deaths were well within the scope of random chance for the size of the trial."

"He also said in the email that all of the deaths appeared to be caused by the same thing, although he was uncertain of the cause. He said such deaths were, and I quote, 'worrying and potentially dire.'"

Sloane sipped his soda. Yu was such a worrier every second report from the PI contained the word "dire" at least once. This was not going as he had imagined, let alone planned. Never let them get you angry, never. "Brittany, my daughter, needed to pay her tuition, my wife had gone overboard with the remodel of the Newport house, and we were looking into purchasing a retreat in Montana, all of which required cash, so I sold some stock. Hardly any, really."

"One hundred thousand shares."

Sloane nodded.

"Yet you did not buy the Montana house?"

"We bought in Chestnut Hill instead. Other board members sold at the same time, and my financial advisor recommended selling at that time."

Lincoln nodded. "We will have to investigate that issue further."

"Fine. The stock did go up."

"Briefly, before falling grievously when the trial's fate became public knowledge."

"Still, after I sold, the stock rose."

"As I said, we will have to investigate that issue further. My team will look into it. Just three more issues to cover. Would you care to take a break?"

Sloane shook his head; may as well get the root canal over with. Besides, he had done nothing wrong. This was ridiculous and would soon be shown to be so.

"Did you and Antioch's Chief Financial Officer, Sandy Bohlen, disagree over whether to expense or capitalize the drug inventory for several clinical trials, including trials to grow human livers from stem cells, treat brain tumors with a vaccine made from a patient's own tumor cells, and grow hair from stem cells?"

"Yes," Sloane said as he struggled to recall the incident from the myriad of meetings, discussions and decisions he had participated in over the years. "If I recall correctly, he argued for treating the drugs as a cost for the trials, which should be expensed. I disagreed."

"On what basis?"

"On the basis that the drugs were being used in clinical trials, which, if successful, would create immense value for the company," Sloane explained as if it was the simplest of things. "Therefore, their cost should be amortized, just like any other piece of lab equipment."

"But the drugs would be consumed, as it were, in the trails. They would not last forever."

"Neither would the cyclotrons, MRIs or other equipment we purchased for the trials, all of which are capitalized."

"Yet certainly drugs have a far shorter useful life in which they are of use than the equipment you just mentioned."

"Nevertheless, the drugs add value to the company, especially if a clinical trial succeeds."

Lincoln hunched forward for a moment to peer at a young, red-haired attorney down the table.

The young attorney hesitated, met Lincoln's gaze and then looked over at Sloane. Licking his lips, the red-head pushed his glasses up his nose and said, "The legal department's analysis of the case shows that the position you choose to assume, Mr. Sloane, was a creative one, but also somewhat questionable, if our analysis is correct."

"Made perfect sense to me, and Sandy and her people approved it."

"I am certain they did," Lincoln said with a smile that bordered on patronizing.

"You know how these things work, Lincoln," Sloane said. "Our Audit Committee meets with the outside committee and negotiates every line of the financials, revenues, profits, capital costs, amortizations, and every other financial figure from A to Z."

"We may need to adjust the books on that particular issue."

"Why? It was all done properly, above board, legal, and meeting every accounting rule and principle."

"The SEC appears to question and possibly even disagree with your decision."

"It wasn't mine," Sloane said, leaning forward to emphasize his point. "The board, Sandy's people, the Audit Committee, and the external auditors all were in on the decision."

"They acceded to it."

"They were part of the decision-making process," Sloane insisted.

"However they were involved, Antioch will need to adjust the financials to reflect what the SEC believes is the correct position on the issue, as well as several other items that were capitalized instead of expensed."

Sloane sighed. "It would hurt our P and L a few million, but so be it. We did nothing wrong."

"Agreed, and we will admit no wrongdoing; you or the company." Licoln turned a new page over on his stack. "Turning to the clinical trial of Celestian."

"That was years ago," Sloane said, frowning. "It was handled by Celeste."

"An Antioch subsidiary created in 2001, correct?"

Sloane nodded.

"Why?"

Sloane leaned back, appearing as relaxed as if he was on his sofa at home in Chestnut Hill enjoying the view across Hammond's Pond. "Celestian treated diabetes, and a decision was made that it was tangential to our core business, unrelated to heart and neuro conditions, so we created Celeste to handle the new drug."

"Created the new firm a year into the production of Celestian after a seven-year development phase."

"Similar to the time frame for other drugs we've developed."

"Why create the subsidiary at that particular point in time?" Before Sloane could reply, Lincoln continued, "In the three months before the subsidiary was created, researchers working on a study of the long-term effects of Celestian reported an increased incidence of seizures and strokes, among other troubling medical issues among trial participants."

"I believe that may be true."

"When the results were made public, Celestian was taken off the market, the company, Celeste, was sued in a class action suit, and after several years of litigation filed for bankruptcy protection."

"Unfortunately. It was a sad day for all of us."

"Yes, no doubt, although Antioch was able to shield itself from any financial loss, save for the dissolution of Celeste, Incorporated."

"Thanks to your energetic efforts," Sloane said with an appreciative smile.

Lincoln acknowledged the compliment with a courtly nod. "The losses from Celeste were not counted on Antioch's financials?"

"How could they be? Celeste was a completely independent subsidiary, some might even say it was a different company."

"Yet the boards of the two companies overlapped, you owned several hundred thousand shares in Celeste, and you met with Quint MacPherson regularly."

"Many of our board members decided to invest in Celeste, true. All of us had a great deal of belief in the growth potential of the new company."

"Yet you all divested yourself of Celeste stock soon after the company was created."

Sloane sniffed. "Some on the board felt we should have a little more distance between the two companies, especially Les Eastbrook." Sloane did not mention the other key reason for divesting himself of shares: his decreasing belief in Celestian.

"Yet Celeste and Antioch were separate companies already."

"To increase the perception of their separateness then; Eastbrook dislikes even the appearance of a possible conflict of interest. Can you believe he turns down free pens from companies we do business with?"

"And your meetings with Quint MacPherson?"

"Quint was a new CEO and kindly sought my advice. I was happy to assist. I'm only sorry the advice was unable to stave off the dissolution of the company."

"The overlapping board memberships?"

"Lincoln, you know as well as I do the difficulty of finding fully qualified people with the time necessary to devote to meeting the demands of being a board member, especially of a new company. Such positions devour time and effort like a dozen mistresses."

Lincoln considered as Sloane's eyes drifted to his former lover. What was her name? She cast him a calculating smile. He gazed out the panoramic window as a large, blue and white cabin cruiser hugged the far bank of the Charles on its way downstream.

"Basically I think we would be within our rights with the Celeste issue, although the SEC will press us on it," Lincoln concluded. "The possibility that the new company may have made Antioch's financials somewhat misleading to auditors, Wall Street and investors is to some extent strong."

"That falls more within your field," Sloane said. "I'm not an attorney or an accountant." Then, as a smile spread across his face, he added, "Maybe you should talk to Sandy or," he looked up and down the row of Lincoln's minions, "one of your attorneys."

Lincoln looked back at him with a friendly look that also carried a warning. This was serious and no time for levity. "I will."

Sloane nodded.

"Finally, the SEC is concerned about a meeting you had with a Dr. Chen Yu on Tuesday, this past August sixth in Laussane, Switzerland. The SEC alleges that you pressured Dr. Yu to rewrite his report on the laboratory-grown heart valve trial to make it appear more positive and optimistic to shareholders and to Wall Street."

"I did no such thing," Sloane declared, straightening in his chair and raising his voice. "Nor would I ever even consider such a thing."

"It appears the SEC has information that is at odds with your recollection."

Sloane sniffed and leaned his head back to look up at the conference room's exposed beam ceiling. Yu would pay for speaking out of school. Moments later, his thoughts organized, Sloane looked back across at Lincoln. "It is true that I asked Dr. Yu to shift the focus of the report from the unfortunate deaths of the clinical trial subjects to the possible avenues of enquiry that might lead to determining what had gone wrong and fixing the problem safely and rapidly."

"Merely a question of emphasis then?" Lincoln asked, his pale eyes locked on Sloane's face.

"Yes, merely a question of emphasis. Absolutely no substantive changes at all, none whatsoever."

"You sold 50,000 Antioch shares that morning from your personal account."

"I did, just as I had sold various amounts every month for the past year or so."

"Why?"

"I felt, and my financial advisor reinforced my belief, that I was too heavily invested in Antioch stock. Diversification is my watchword."

"Yet at the same time on CNBC and several other business programs, in the press and in 13 interviews we have found thus far you extolled the virtues of Antioch stock and that it would end its slow decline and quickly rebound to attain new highs."

"I believed it would. It did."

"Briefly."

"It will again after this mess is cleared up."

"You realize how it may look to those with a conspiratorial mindset?" Lincoln asked, tapping his gold pen on the stack of papers before him. "The SEC and the courts just imposed a $9 million fine and two months in prison on a CEO for insider trading."

"I don't see—," Sloane began before Lincoln interrupted, "This is extremely serious, especially since you did not do it, correct?"

Before answering, Sloane sipped his soda, setting the can down before him exactly in the same spot where the can had left a circle of condensation on the slate coaster. "One-hundred percent correct."

"If it cannot be avoided, you may need to agree to pay a fine and disgorge any gains you made from selling the stock, even though you did absolutely nothing wrong, of course."

"How do I pay if the stock went up after I sold it? I lost a possible profit."

"Not in the long run. You avoided a significant loss."

Sloane's jaw went rigid. "I did nothing wrong. Talk to my financial advisor, Alan Benson-Harris."

"We will. I am certain he will support your personal financial decisions, but even so, it looks somewhat questionable, if I may use such a loaded word. I would never think so, nor would anyone at this table, but some suspicious and vile individuals may think that you sold out of fear that the stock would decline and not recover."

"I had no such fear."

"Of course not."

"If I have to pay to make it go away, I have to pay," Sloane conceded, "But there's no way on this earth I am going to admit any wrongdoing."

"May the thought perish once and forever," Lincoln consoled him. "There may have been a slight, shall we say even a mild recklessness with the codes, rules and regulations on the part of the auditors, the board and Sandy's people related to the loan, the categorization of the drugs, and the stock sale, but it far from rises to the level of lying, let alone to the level of a fraud upon investors and, of course, it casts no hint of wrongdoing on you in any way, manner or form. Rest assured, absolutely none."

Chapter 24

Thursday, September 11, 2008

Moonlight shone through the slits in the white horizontal blinds near Arden's side of the bed as he awoke. Squinting at the clock, 2:12 am, he cursed his body for waking him at such an hour. Hoping a change would help him return to sleep, he carefully rolled over to avoid waking Marisela. He need not have been so careful. Her side of the bed was empty, save for a jumble of rumpled sheets and a pillow lying lengthwise. He glanced through the semi-darkness of the bedroom toward the bathroom door. It stood open. He heard nothing save a palm brushing against the window. Where was she? Not up cleaning again. She had experienced trouble sleeping since the burglary even with the alarm and losing her job had done nothing to alleviate her sleepless nights—or his.

Hoping she would return soon, he closed his eyes but let his mind wander to ensure he stayed awake until Marisela returned. He considered Marisela's idea to get a dog, but rejected it; too much work and the house was empty most of the week. A lonely life for a dog. A gun? He hoped not. He did not want to shoot anyone by mistake.

Thoughts of the challenge of living on one income and the gradually falling stock market intruded as they often did whenever he let his mind wander. They were getting by, but Marisela's severance pay would soon run out and they would have to start using their savings to cover living expenses. Once they did, they would be pushing retirement even further into the future.

He had not had a full night's sleep in months. They had lost so much on Antioch, and now the market was trending down with a grim determination. The economic news only worsened. On September 7, the government took over Fannie Mae and Freddie Mac, effectively nationalizing them: so much for a free market economy. Oil prices slumped below $101 per barrel for the first time since March on fears of a global slowdown. Stocks, however, staged a late rally on news of a possible buyout of Lehman Brothers, the troubled investment bank. When Arden last checked, the Dow had gained 164 to close at 11,433. With snippets of worrying news continuing to leak about the SEC investigation of Antioch, its stock was down another 3 percent. Arden had watched the CEO, Sloane, on a business channel predict a rapid recovery for the company after the "groundless, baseless and unfounded" SEC allegations were cleared up and the heart valve clinical trial was brought to a successful conclusion. Arden got the impression Sloane could talk you into giving him your place in the last *Titanic* lifeboat and feel blessed for having been given the opportunity.

Whatever happened, Arden knew Marisela would want to buy and hold, waiting for the long-term trend up. Timing the market, he knew, rarely worked, yet watching the value of their investments dwindle was like watching your child die of malnourishment. Convincing Marisela to sell would be a monumental task and, even if he succeeded, what would happen if he missed the rally that was certain to come at some point in the future? Even if they did sell, given their loses, they would still not have enough to retire for years.

At least Sam still had enough in her conservatively invested college fund to go to any college that accepted her. The thought made all Arden's other financial worries seem far less dire.

Where was Marisela?

Arden found her in the living room, sitting on the sofa, feet up, cradling her knees in her arms. She clutched one of the sofa's throw pillows, her white nightdress gleaming in the semi-darkness. Her violets sat on a shelf near the kitchen, a light set to a timer affixed to the underside of the shelf above casting its glow on the blooming blue, red and white plants below, and onto Marisela.

"You okay?" Arden trodded across the carpet to sit beside his wife.

"Fine. Couldn't sleep."

They had been married too long for Arden not to detect the lack of conviction in the first word of her answer. He pushed thoughts of a quick return to bed from his mind as he rested a comforting hand on her shoulder.

"Just can't sleep." Even as the last word left her mouth, the tears came.

Surprised, Arden drew her to him, discarding her pillow to the floor.

"I can't sleep," she repeated, wiping tears from her eyes with the backs of both hands. The red on the last knuckle of her left thumb caught the violets' light. "I get to sleep, then wake up an hour or so later, afraid." She looked at him. He could just see the whites of her dark eyes. "Terrified."

"Of what?"

"I lie there listening, trying to make sure no one's in the house."

Arden glanced around the living room. "No one is, just us: you and me and Sam. Don't worry. It won't happen again."

"I know, I know, but...." The tears burst forth again.

"We have the alarm system, and the burglars came during the day anyway."

"I can't seem to get past this fear, and I'm so mad at us, at me for not making sure no one could break in."

"Professionals will be able to break in every time, unless you want to live in a prison." Arden rocked her as if she was a baby. "Risk is a part of life. We had our one bad experience. It won't happen again. Try to think about all the years we've lived here and in other places and no one ever broke in. A once-in-a-lifetime thing, just bad luck."

Marisela exhaled with a deep, long sigh. Changing course, she asked, "Will I ever find a job?"

"You will. It's just a bad job market right now; too many people looking and too few jobs. We'll be fine. We have plenty saved."

"For retirement."

"For in case something goes wrong."

Moments later she asked, "How are you feeling?" Her gaze met his from inches away.

"Trouble sleeping like you, but I'm alright. We've come through rough patches before. We will this time."

"Your heart?"

"Results tomorrow, but I feel fine." He had seen his cardiologist the week before. Why had the office called him back in so soon?

"Do you want me to go with you?"

"No. I'll call if it's anything important."

She fell silent, her head resting against his chest. He felt her wet face against him, moistening the hair on his bare chest. It was a long time before she said in a little-girl voice, "I'm afraid of burglars, of never finding a job, of running out of money, of never retiring, that things will never get better for us, for Sam. All the time, especially when I'm home alone, I'm terrified. I'm never free from it. I'm so afraid."

Chapter 25

Friday, September 12, 2008

Arden sat across a cluttered desk from Dr. Trevelyan, his cardiologist, at Mount Herman Medical Center. The view out the window from the hospital's north tower was of Beverly Hills and the Santa Monica Mountains; a million-dollar view, which every patient would have happily foregone if it meant avoiding the reason for their visit to the hospital.

Arden had not expected the results from his myocardial perfusion stress test and a second test the name of which he could not remember, so quickly.

Dr. Trevelyan said, "Four of your arteries have some discernible plaque buildup."

Arden felt the world stop. All his attention focused on Trevelyan's pale, well-scrubbed face. A buzz seemed to fill his ears.

"But at this point, I would not recommend surgical intervention."

Relief flooded Arden's body, although having arteries blocked sounded dire. What did it mean? Was his heart going to stop? Was he going to die?

"We should make some modification to your diet, increase your exercise, and we can discuss a drug regimen to moderate your cholesterol levels," Trevelyan said. "No sign of arrythmia on your EKG, so we'll stay with the same medication for that. Let me know if you notice any palpitations and we'll have you do another Holter test. My real worry is your mitral valve."

Arden tensed. His stomach tightened. Fear grew in him like some vile snake uncoiling in his gut, preparing to strike.

"We can monitor the valve for a time, check it in six months and then every six months after that, but I recommend we replace it in the near future."

"Near future?" Arden asked, dreading the answer.

"A year, maybe two."

"Replace it with what?"

"A porcine valve is one option or there are some fine mechanical valves on the market, although they require you take Coumadin, a blood thinner, which increases the risk of stroke slightly."

Arden hated the sound of risking a stroke to avoid a heart attack. Choose your poison?

The cardiologist flipped closed Arden's file and added, "Far better than either a porcine or a mechanical valve would be a lab version grown from your own stem cells. A company has one in development. If, when the time comes, it looks like it may be ready in a reasonable time, we can discuss waiting and going that route. It would be a vast improvement, if it proves effective. You used to work for the company developing it, didn't you? Antioch Pharmaceuticals."

Chapter 26

Saturday, September 13, 2008

"Neat goggles," Sam commented as they made their way through the sporting goods store on Sepulveda.

Arden and Marisela stopped beside their daughter as she fingered a pair of bright red swim goggles.

"Are your old ones worn out?" Arden asked, eyeing the price sticker.

Sam's anticipatory smile faded. "No, but they're old and faded, and I don't like the color. They look like a rotten orange."

"When they wear out, we'll get you a new pair," Arden said, turning to move on.

"But the lenses on mine are cloudy."

Arden turned back to his daughter. "A little or a lot?"

Sam sighed. "A little."

"Let's wait a while and we'll get you a new pair for next summer."

"Maybe I'll use some of my money," Sam said.

"Swim goggles or Purdue?" Arden asked with a smile to lessen the sting of his words. "Your choice."

Feeling bad that he had to watch every penny and mad at himself for not being able to buy Sam whatever she wanted or at least needed, Arden turned to lead the way farther back into the store. Maybe he should have taken some of those lucrative consulting jobs from ex-parties in his mediation cases. How much could it hurt his reputation? How much would it hurt his self-image? Too much.

At the gun area, a short, thin young man with circular glasses leaned over a thick binder stuffed full of papers that stuck out at various angles, many dog-eared and some torn. When Arden, Sam and Marisela stopped at the counter, their gazes ranged over the wide array of guns from pistols and revolvers up through rifles and semi-automatic quasi-assault rifles displayed in racks on the walls and in the glass counter display cases.

"Good morning," Arden said, "we're interested in buying a handgun for our home."

The young clerk looked up, but did not straighten. His eyes flitted over Arden and Marisela, then lingered on Sam as she stood just behind them. "You have to be 18 to purchase a rifle or shotgun, 21 for a handgun. Proof of age required at purchase. A DROS is $19."

"DROS?" Arden asked, frowning.

"Dealer Record of Sale. There's a 10-day waiting period, and for a handgun you need a Handgun Safety Certificate."

Marisela asked, "How do we get a certificate?"

"Pass a Department of Justice HSC test administered by a certified instructor after completing a safety demonstration with the handgun being purchased."

Arden nodded as he thought that this was going to be more complicated, costly and take far longer than he had thought. Maybe a dog would be better. On the other hand, guns don't eat and you don't have to walk a gun every day.

"You must present clear evidence of identity and age, a driver's license will do, as well as proof of California residency for the purchase of a handgun. A utility bill or property deed will fulfill that requirement. Any questions?"

"Can we get the gun that Matt Damon used in the *Bourne Ultimatum*?" Sam asked, slipping in between Arden and Marisela.

"I don't think we should buy a gun just because it was in a movie," Arden cautioned, casting a disapproving look at Sam, who did not notice as she leaned over the counter, eyeing the handguns in the display case. "Is there an inexpensive model we could look at?"

Marisela said, "I don't want a gun made by the lowest bidder."

"The Glock 17 is a fine piece," the clerk said with a smile at Sam. "Police forces around the world use it, as does Jason Bourne; sturdy, reliable and good stopping power. Let me show you. My name's Aaron, by the way. What's yours?"

After a stop at the library for books, Arden, Marisela and Sam arrived home. Buell stood in his front yard pruning a shrub near the teetering fence between their lots.

"Maybe we should just tear the fence down," Arden said loudly as they walked from the car toward the front door.

"Go ahead," Buell said.

Her voice low, Marisela warned, "We need a fence."

Arden ignored Buell and whispered with a put-on evil smile as they entered their house, "Maybe I'll just wait to negotiate with Buell until after we get the gun."

Chapter 27

Monday, September 15, 2008

Late Monday morning, a blank newspaper crossword from his shrinking supply from work under his arm, Arden stood in the hall outside conference room 3 at Equitable Mediation. The parties were inside, seated, ready and waiting for their mediator.

"Delaying the moment of truth, Never Fail?" Donna Levin asked with a grin as she rushed past him, a thick mediation file folder in one hand and a white mug of steaming, aromatic coffee in the other.

"Savoring the final calm moments before battle," Arden said. Actually, he had been trying to remember the details of the case. He thought he knew them, but a nagging thought that he had forgotten something important lurked at the fringes of his memory like a small child playing hide and seek in the back of his mind. What had he forgotten? Or had he? Why couldn't the burglars have hit him in the back or knees? Why his head?

"What, Marisela didn't make shortbread today?" Donna asked, surprised. "Must be an easy case."

"They all are."

"Once they're settled."

"I settle them all."

"Hence, your well-earned nickname."

Donna disappeared without hesitation into her assigned conference room.

Arden sighed. It was time to enter the lion's den. It was a tough case and Arden had forgotten to make shortbread, but something else nagged at his mind that he feared he had forgotten. He told everyone Marisela made the shortbread, but he and Sam had been making the cookies since she was three, every Sunday morning. This past weekend, however, even with a difficult case on Monday, they had not found the time to bake. Arden had spent his time looking over their investments (to little gain), strategizing about the Buell fence issue (with little inspiration), and helping Marisela shop to replace more of their stolen things with limited success. He had also shown Marisela some job sites he had found last week at work that offered lab positions.

As he opened the conference room door, Arden realized that for the first time in his life, for all his bravado, not only was he worried that he had forgotten something, he was uncertain whether he would be able to find an equitable mediated settlement for his case. He had struggled for months to find that golden zone of agreement where the party's acceptable range of positions overlapped, where agreements were born, nurtured and matured into long-term settlements. He had experienced his fair share of failed mediations, but invariably because for some reason, often emotion, one party refused to see that an agreement was better than their best alternative. With this case, he was not sure he had figured out where—or even whether—a possible equitable settlement even existed.

"Financial services firm Lehman Brothers filed for bankruptcy protection today after 158 years in business," the television anchor reported after dinner as Arden sat at the table after dinner and peered at a blank *Austin American-Statesman* crossword he had taken from work. "Merrill Lynch, the world's largest stockbroker, agreed to be bought by Bank of America for $50 billion. The world's largest insurance company, AIG, is also in deep trouble, searching for ways to raise $40 billion in cash to stay afloat."

"Serves them right," Arden said. "Making risky loans."

"How did your case go today?" Marisela asked as she mended a pair of Sam's shorts.

"Fine. I thought I'd forgotten something important, but if I did, the parties didn't remember either. Couldn't reach an agreement, though. We meet again next week, so maybe it'll come together then."

"President Bush said his administration is working on ways to minimize disruptions to the US economy caused by the latest round of bank failures," the anchor said. "The Dow lost 504 points to close at 10,917, the worst day since the day after 9/11. The Nasdaq also fell, 81 points to 2,180."

Arden worried about the case at work. Had he missed something that would have led to a settlement?

"I was thinking that we might still be able to buy the Las Cruces house," Marisela said, "and rent it while we work another few years before we retire. If we really cut back, do you think we could swing it?"

"It would be cheaper to retire somewhere else other than Las Cruces," Arden said, marveling at his wife's continued optimism, even as their world fell apart. She really liked that house. "The house is fairly expensive. There are other nice places to retire."

"That means going through the hassle of finding another town we like, another house we like, and we'd lose the good faith money we put down on the Las Cruces house."

"Ten grand." Arden sighed. "We lost more than ten times that in a day."

Marisela focused on her mending.

"I think we just have to face it," Arden said, "we're down hundreds of thousands of dollars, you don't have a job, and it could take a year to sell this place, if we can even get anywhere near our asking price." He met Marisela's gaze across the remains of their spaghetti dinner, which they had yet to clear away. They put off a decision last time they discussed it, but this time he said, "We should walk away from the Las Cruces deal."

After an hour of discussion, Arden finally called Roxanna, their real estate agent. They had worked with Roxanna before and Arden felt bad killing the deal and, along with it, Roxanna's commission at such a deathly slow time in the real estate market.

"Ten grand gone, just like that," Arden said after he spoke with Roxanna. "She might be able to get some of our deposit back if the sellers can't get approved for a mortgage on their new house. Have to see."

Arden finished his crossword with half his mind as he thought about their shrinking options. "Maybe we can go looking for another place this spring."

"Can we afford it?"

"Maybe look at cheaper places: St. George, Bend or Ashcroft." Arden tried to think of more ways to cut spending and more ways to make money. "Any luck on the job front?"

"A few more papers to edit and another 10 hours of bench work at the lab, but no real job prospects. Any extra cases on the horizon?"

"A couple. I'll take anything that comes along now. Otherwise, we won't be able to retire until we're 95."

"It can't be that bad."

"Six years, I think. Best guess."

Marisela finished mending the shorts and asked, still looking down at her sewing, "When did your dad pass away?"

"He was 61."

"In six years you'll be 62. When did your uncles die?"

"Fifty-seven and 60. All from heart disease."

Marisela nodded. She looked solemn and had been subdued since Arden had told her the cardiologist's recommendations.

"Take care of yourself, Arden," she said, lifting her gaze to meet his.

Arden nodded. There was no point worrying about such things. Fear did not make things any more or less likely to happen, it just made the waiting worse. They were already doing everything they could to cut costs, make money and find Marisela a job. Everyone needed money, especially now, and everyone died.

"Sources close to the SEC investigation report that allegations against Richard Sloane, CEO of Antioch Pharmaceuticals, include insider trading, making false representations and possible conspiracy charges," the anchor reported. "Sloane is alleged to have used one of Antioch's jets to ferry his family on exotic vacations, allowed his daughter to rent an Antioch apartment near Stanford University at far below market rates, and sold blocks of company stock just ahead of negative news about a clinical trial, even while promoting the stock on television and in newspaper interviews.

Shares of Antioch tumbled today to below $3, before stabilizing at $3.06."

Arden rose and punched the button on the remote to turn off the new television. Turning on his heel, he asked, "Do you believe that guy? Sounds like he used Antioch as his personal ATM."

"At least the SEC is onto him."

"So he'll finally get punished for what he's done."

Chapter 28

Tuesday, September 16, 2008

The chainsaws roared to life just as Arden and Sam stepped out
their front door on the way to work and school. Rusty joined in
with a wheezing series of yelps before he lost interest and coiled
back down on Harry's porch to sleep as best he could amidst the
cacophonous chainsaws. Marisela had already left to meet an ex-
colleague from Antioch who was working in UCLA's pathology lab.
She had heard the lab might have an opening. Arden stalked across
his lawn, Sam close behind, to confront the crew that was cutting a
large branch off the American ficus in Buell's yard.

"A little aggressive pruning, isn't it?" Arden asked with a smile.
A cherry picker held a worker who was cutting through a foot-thick
limb as two other hard-hatted workers held a rope attached to the
limb to ensure that when it fell, it fell in the yard, not on a house.

"No," one of the Hispanic workers replied. "Taking her down."

Arden frowned. The magnificent old tree shaded his yard.
Looking up at its green, leafy mass of branches, he wondered why
anyone would ever even consider cutting it down.

"Homeowner wanted it down, so down it comes."

Buell. Arden cursed and glared over at Buell's house. Worth an
argument? Probably not, Arden reluctantly concluded. Unlike the
fence, the *ficus* was clearly on Buell's property.

When he arrived home from work, the beautiful ficus was gone and Arden found a foreboding buff envelope from the IRS and a white business envelope from their health insurance company in the mail.

"Wrong time of year for a tax refund," Arden told Marisela as she handed him turkey burgers to grill for dinner. "Ah, avian burgers with guacamole," he said. "Very nice."

Stuffing the envelopes in his back pocket, Arden stepped out onto the back patio, ignited the barbeque burners and laid the burgers on the grill. As they sizzled, he wiped his hands off on a towel, took the insurance letter out of his pocket, tore it open and read it.

"Our health insurance co-pays are going up from ten to 25 bucks for an office visit and from $25 to $75 for an ER visit," he called to Marisela through the open patio French door. "Prescription prices are also going up."

"You weren't planning on getting sick, were you?"

"Sam's asthma drug will be $50 instead of $35."

"At least she's been having fewer attacks this year."

Arden tore open the second letter, read it and frowned. "The IRS says we owe them $76."

"What? Why?" He heard the clatter of utensils and plates as Marisela set the table.

"Something about stock dividends and capital gains." Arden shook his head as he tried to decipher the IRS codes and their Byzantine explanation. "I don't know." What had he done wrong? What had he forgotten? Had the burglar's blow dislodged some crucial piece of information about their taxes from his memory? He certainly had not broken any tax laws, at least not as far as he had been able to tell when he had done their taxes. Then again, who could ever tell? "I'll have to figure it out after dinner."

"Didn't you want to go shopping tonight to replace some more of the missing stuff?"

"It'll just take me a few minutes to figure it out," Arden promised.

Just after 11 pm, Arden appeared in the living room and told Marislea, "The IRS is taxing us on the dividends from stocks we owned."

"I thought our stocks were all way down last year," Marisela said as she sat on the sofa and read a novel, *Morality Play* by Barry

Unsworth. "I finished editing another research paper. A few more dollars for the retirement fund."

"Great. That was my mistake. I thought that since the stocks were down, we couldn't have any taxes due on them, so I skipped that tax form." Arden was relieved that he remembered why he had made the error. At least his memory was still functioning.

"But if the stocks were down, how can we owe any tax?"

"Even though they were down, the stocks still paid dividends." Arden sat on the sofa beside her. "You would think that if the government wanted to encourage economic activity, they wouldn't tax selling stocks or any investment, or any spending at all." She put her bookmark in her novel, closed it and stood up. Arden rose to follow her upstairs to bed. No shopping tonight. "If they didn't, people would move their money around to find the most profitable investments, instead of leaving them in some investment that lagged just to avoid taxes. They'd also spend more money."

"Isn't that what got us into this mess?"

"Burrowing money did, which, oddly enough, is what the government is doing a lot of to get us out of this mess, as well as keeping interest rates low to encourage even more borrowing; bizarre."

They entered their bedroom and Marisela slipped out of her T-shirt. Even distracted by their financial woes, Arden admired her in her white bra.

"If the government didn't tax spending and selling," she asked as she unclipped the front of her bra, "how would the government get any money?"

"They could tax your net worth each year or your income, regardless of the source. It could be a flat percentage or, better yet, an escalating percentage," Arden said as he stepped over and held Marisela close. She felt wonderful. "The more you make, the more you pay. Like that CEO of Antioch, Sloane; who needs $11 million a year? After you earn a million a year, you should be taxed at 50 percent or more. That would be far better than how it is now."

"Maybe, but those are the rules we have to play by." Marisela kissed him.

"Dumb rules; dumb $76 rules."

"Shut up," Marisela said and kissed him again as she reached down to unbutton his pants.

"You're going to be tired tomorrow," Arden warned.

"I don't have a job; you do. Maybe you want to get some sleep?"

"Not for a while," Arden said as he kissed the side of her neck. "Not for a long while."

Chapter 29

"Basically they're amenable to a settlement, as usual," Lincoln assured Sloane, "but we need to put something on the table that will interest them and satisfy them."

"I'm willing to play ball," Sloane said, "maybe pay a fine."

"You or Antioch?"

"Both." As they trudged across the heather, Sloane wondered if the company's insurance would cover both fines, but did not ask. There would be time to find out later, after he had ensured the answer would be in his favor.

Just down the Scottish Highland slope one of the Wirehaired Pointing Griffons froze and pointed. Lincoln stopped, raising his 12-gauge side-by-side Purdey shotgun.

Sloane asked, "How many arms and legs do they want?"

Lincoln silenced him with a disapproving glance. Sloane frowned. He had not wanted to come on this silly grouse hunting expedition anyway. He had about agreed to suffer the boredom of shopping for clothes and jewelry with Maddy in Edinburgh, but Lincoln's enthusiasm for the hunt had won him over.

The Ghillie, dressed in camouflage to blend in with the heather and gorse, motioned to the dogs. The Griffons darted forward, flushing a pair of grouse. Lincoln raised his shotgun, led one of the birds and fired. Even before Sloane could tell if the bird had been hit, Lincoln fired again. With his ears numb from the blasts, Sloane tried to see what had happened.

"Did you hit them?" he asked, his voice sounding strange to his battered ears.

Lincoln turned back and grinned. "Of course." With a frown he looked down at Sloane's Perazzi shotgun. "You could at least give it a try."

"Not really my thing." Sloane watched his footing as they set off down the wet, steep hill toward where the Ghillie was collecting the two birds to add to Lincoln's growing bag for the day. Sloane was about to say that he had not grown up in Montana shooting the wildlife as Lincoln had, when he recalled that Lincoln liked people to believe his family was old money from Connecticut.

"How much are they thinking?" Sloane asked instead, sliding on a clump of wet gorse before he regained his footing, nearly dropping his shotgun. Did the damn thing have a safety? Last thing he wanted was to blow his attorney's head off by accident.

"Two million for the firm and $250,000 for you, for misstatements," Lincoln said, not even puffing after their trek across the glen and up into the hills above Loch Awe. The deep blue of the loch ran for 41 stunning kilometers through a gash in Argyll and Bute in the western part of the Scottish Highlands.

Sloane nodded. "Reasonable, but no admission of guilt, since I'm not guilty of a damn thing."

"Of course not. I suggest we pass along to the SEC a new set of policies and procedures on oversight, public statements about the company relating to the stock price, and regarding reports on clinical trials."

"Sounds acceptable," Sloane said, cautious, but thinking it was not going to be as horrendous as he had feared.

"Another $5 million for you for insider trading, most of it disgorgement."

"I did not insider trade," Sloane declared and stopped to emphasize the point.

"No admission of guilt is required."

"There will be none."

The Ghillie set the Griffons off on another search for more soon-to-be-unfortunate grouse.

Lincoln asked, "You have already resolved the other issues?"

"Yes," Sloane said, thinking of all the money he had spent straightening our broken plasma televisions, Stanford apartments, health insurance co-pays, and use of the corporate jet for his family. You would think he was guilty.

Lincoln said, "I settled the other pertinent matters."

Sloane nodded. Lincoln was alluding to certain issues relating to Sloane's various mistresses over the years and their use of company aircraft, cars, chefs, plastic surgeons, fitness clubs, and credit cards.

Sloane asked, "That should settle it?"

"Basically that is what my sources are suggesting, but nothing official yet."

Following his attorney along the slope at an angle, Sloane stopped to admire the splendid ruins of Kilchurn Castle far below on the breathtaking northeastern shore of Loch Awe. People would love to come see this place, if there was a decent lodge, just across from the castle. Maybe six hundred and up a night. Could be a nice sideline investment.

Making a mental note to investigate the possibility, Sloane returned to the issue foremost in his mind. "I want this wrapped up." He knew the board would not give him much more time. He had already heard rumors several board members were negotiating with his supporters on the board for his removal. He knew his supporters would hold out only for as long as they thought they could get more concessions from the others before him. "The sooner the better."

"I'll see what I can negotiate with the SEC," Lincoln promised as he walked and reloaded his shotgun with long-practiced ease.

"I pried open a side window," Angel told the enraptured young audience of Hispanics as they either lounged against the cinder-block walls, arms crossed to display their muscles and tattoos, or sprawled on the concrete floor of his cell at the LA County Jail. "In fast. Then I hear something come at me."

"*Christo*," one of the young men, a lone panther tattoo on his right forearm, exclaimed in rapt awe.

"Pair a snarling dogs," Angel said, at ease as he leaned back on his bunk against the cinder-block wall.

"You *vamos*?" another acolyte asked.

Angel cast the young inmate a look of complete disdain. "Got down and called 'em over."

"They bite you?"

"Petted them just like stroking my girl's pussy. Got them eats from the fridge, got what I wanted and left—with the dogs."

Laughter filled the cell.

"What'd you do with them?"

"Sold 'em to a guy where I work," Angel said. "Wanted the dogs 'cause he was afraid someone would break into his house."

His audience roared with laughter.

"Where's my candy bar?"

The audience fell silent as the deep voice cut through the laughter. Angel looked up at a muscular inmate framed in his cell door. The young men gathered around Angel fell silent. A couple nearest the door slipped out of the cell past the enormous inquisitor. Angel calmly stared up at the older inmate.

"My candy bar," the inmate repeated. Topping 250 pounds, the Hispanic had tattoos in Aztec motifs and 32nd Street gang symbols on his bare arms and around the sides and, Angel guessed, the back of his neck, which now rippled as the inmate's corded neck muscles tightened. "I left it on the bottom bunk this morning."

"Ain't seen it, Homes," Angel said, keeping his steady gaze on the gangbanger.

"You're ass is where it was, *niño*." The inmate stepped across the cell to loom over Angel. His broad back blocked the light from the fixture built into the ceiling, casting Angel into darkness. Everyone else in the cell cleared out as if the bunk was on fire.

Angel knew the con. If Angel said he had eaten the candy bar the bear of an inmate would charge him triple for it. Then, with Angel seen as an easy mark, Angel would be shelling out every dime his relatives or friends sent him for the monster to spend on cigarettes and candy in the commissary or for phone calls. It would never end.

The gangbanger was standing close enough for Angel to smell the aromatic soap he used. This *chollo* was doing well inside. His ugly face never came near the vile soap the city issued to inmates. From this close, Angel could see the muscles in the *chollo*'s arms moving under the taut skin, like snakes seeking escape from a tightly closed bag.

"You don't want to do this." Angel kept his voice even, sounding compliant and reasonable, without a hint of opposition, let alone violence.

The inmate laughed. A sneer spread across his face, which had been pockmarked by acne. The thought crossed Angel's mind that even if he beat the man's face into raw *carne asada*, it would only improve his looks.

"You telling me what to do now, *niño*?"

"Just what you might want to consider," Angel said. "I'm no ATM."

"No?" the man half asked, setting his tattooed fists on his broad hips.

"I do have candy bars, if you want 'em." Angel scrambled off the bunk, slipped past the inmate and stood before the sink, his back to the inmate. Taking and opening an Adidas shoebox from the shelf above the metal sink, he turned and held out six candy bars toward the inmate.

"We might just get along, *niño*." The inmate grinned malevolently, his eyes growing as they focused on the chocolate bars. The tension in the inmate's body eased, his right hand reaching out for the candy treasure trove.

Angel's left fist lashed out in a short, direct punch at the inmate's groin. The inmate doubled over. Angel's right fist flashed up in an uppercut. A cracking sound reverberated in the cell. As the inmate started to collapse, Angel punched and kicked him repeatedly as he crumpled to the concrete floor.

Chapter 30

Wednesday, September 17, 2008

"I don't need your charity," Buell roared and slammed his front door in Arden's face.

After Arden stalked back into his house, Marisela asked, "How'd it go?"

"We should build a 40-foot stone wall and cast him into eternal darkness," Arden declared.

"Not well, then."

Arden slumped down at the kitchen table and grabbed a section of the newspaper Harry, his other neighbor, had given him. Arden forced himself to read, pushing thoughts of Buell and fences from his mind before his heart went off again.

"Dow's down again, especially the financials," Arden said, hoping Buell was heavily invested in stocks, especially banks. "Maybe we should get out of our stocks and keep it all in cash for a while."

"And miss the rebound when it happens?" Marisela asked, sitting across from him.

"If it happens."

"It will. It always does. What happened with Buell?"

"I told him I'd heard he'd lost his job and that I'd be happy to repair the fence, split the cost and he could pay me back when he found a job. Bascially, he told me to stuff it."

"Don't you think he must be under a lot of stress since he's out of work? I don't think his wife works."

"I was just trying to help him." Arden fought to control his temper. "Any luck at UCLA?"

"Nothing that remotely fits my background."

"Maybe something will turn up tomorrow."

"Maybe." Marisela sounded as if she thought the odds of anything turning up tomorrow were nonexistent.

"I got another case today," Arden said. "Should last a few weeks."

"Good," Marisela said, her voice flat.

How could he cheer her up when his outlook was as bleak as her's?

Hoping to take his mind off his troubles, he returned his attention to the paper. It did not work.

"The Feds just used $85 billion of taxpayer money to buy AIG, the Dow is down 449 and new home construction fell 6 percent to the lowest level since 1991," Arden reported, skimming the business section. He hung his head. "We wanted to retire next year and now it might be five or ten years away, if then, especially if stocks keep falling. We wanted to buy the house in Las Cruces and now we barely have enough cash for the down payment. Buell is being an ass over the fence, and…and," his eyes fell on another story in the newspaper, "China's selling tainted baby milk. What a world. What a crazy, insane bloody world."

Chapter 31

Tuesday, September 23, 2008

"Basically they're interested," Lincoln reported to Sloane in the CEO's Boston office. "But with one new provision."

"What?" CEO Sloane asked his attorney, his suspicion aroused.

"They like the new policies we outlined and the amount of the fines for you and for Antioch." Lincoln sat in a plush leather chair across from Sloane.

"But?"

"They want you to serve some time."

"Time? In jail? For what? I didn't do anything wrong." Sloane hit the leather blotter atop his cherry desk with his fist to emphasize the point.

"I fully and completely agree."

"So why on earth should I serve even a second of time in jail?"

"The SEC maintains that you made misleading statements about the clinical trial and the stock price," Lincoln said, pausing, before he added, "bordering on fraud."

"Bullshit. I was optimistic, as a CEO has to be."

"Regardless, the share price did fall after you sold stock."

"It went up."

"At first, and only briefly, then it declined in value rather precipitously."

"Antioch's a good company and the share price doesn't reflect that. It hasn't for more than a year."

"The SEC does not see it that way, Richard," Lincoln said, sounding like a caring uncle. "They also believe, and feel that they could make a reasonablly strong case, that you sold stock based on insider information about the trial and about Celeste."

"I explained why I sold."

"I know and it makes perfect sense, but the SEC in their greater wisdom disagrees with that particular interpretation of events."

"It's not an interpretation. It's what happened."

"I do not for a second doubt it, but the point at issue is what the SEC believes happened."

"I am not going to prison. I did nothing wrong."

"The SEC does not see it that way and, given the political and social climate these days, neither will 12 members of the public if the SEC turns this over to the FBI for a criminal investigation and, God forbid, it ends up going to trial."

Raging inside, Sloane fell silent. He adjusted the sleeves of his Brioni dress shirt.

"The SEC is willing to recommend to the court that you plead guilty to fraud and serve 6 months with 24 months probation."

"No."

"If it goes to a jury, you could receive a sentence of up to a dozen years in prison. No one likes CEOs these days. A year ago, we could have made a much better deal, but not now."

Sloane fingered an anitque sextant on his desk. "If I say no?"

"They take the case to the FBI and God only knows where it will end up. They are willing to drop the insider trading issue in exchange for settling the misleading statement issue as a fraud. It is a favorable deal. It is a compromise to avoid a far worse possible outcome for you and for the company."

"Six months?"

"Basically, it is the best I can do."

"You told them about all the charity work I've done? The balls, the banquets, the golf tournaments I established and ran, the regatta and opera nights? I raised millions for a dozen charities, orphans and inner city teens, sick kids, and I didn't ask for a thing in return. Not a damn thing."

"I know, I know and they know, and they admire your devotion to such charitable causes, but I have to be honest, it does not matter one iota at this point."

Sloane fell silent and considered as he gazed out the huge window across the Charles towards Cambridge. "I'm innocent."

"So are many people serving lengthy sentences in prison and even some who are unfortunately and unfairly languishing on death row from what I read in reports coming out of The Innocence Project."

Sloane pursed his lips as he considered Lincoln's words. This could not be happening. He had given his all to Antioch and now this? What had happened to the world? Christ, it was a mess. But what choice did he have? "Alright, accept the damn deal, but talk to them. Work something out so I don't have to serve any time; not a single damn day."

"I will endeavor to try my best."

"You can do it, Lincoln. You're the best. I know you can. You've managed things in the past, always have, always will."

"I'll see what I can do, Richard. Maybe I can arrange something."

"I am never going to see the inside of a jail, Lincoln. I am innocent of all charges. The sytem is fair. I should not, I cannot go to jail."

"They weren't interested," Chester, Angels' attorney, reported to his client as they sat in a cramped interview room at the LA County jail. "But they did make an offer."

"What?" Angel asked, sullen and angry, his ankle handcuffed to the rust-speckled metal leg of his chair. His hands hurt from hitting the other inmate over the candy bar.

"Plead to burglary and assault, get 25 years, you're out in 12 with good behavior."

"No."

"It's the best I can do," Chester said, widening his eyes and throwing open his arms to emphasize the sincerity of his point.

"Do better."

"Hell, I went to law school with the prosecutor, got him his first decent lay and set his son up with the mayor's daughter: it's the best I could get. It's the best anyone could get."

"No." Angel folded his arms across his chest and sat back in the hard plastic graffiti-covered chair. Each interview room had different furniture, depending on how recently it had been trashed by an inmate. "I don't deserve it."

"Deserving's got nothing to do with it. No just desserts here. This is the justice system, not a dessert menu."

Angel's glare would have cracked a stone wall.

"They have the iPod, you were IDed in the photo-array, and Diego and Cesar place you at the scene and with the stolen goods after the fact," Chester said. "Diego will testify that you knew the goods were stolen."

"I'll go to trial."

"We'll lose. No ifs, no ands, no buts, no question. You will lose and get 25 to life."

"They're offering 25," Angel said, thumping his heavy fist on the metal table, which rang, echoing in the tiny room. Pain coursed up his arm.

"You lose at trial and you'll only be eligible to get out in 25 years. Make the deal and you walk in a dozen or less."

Angel shook his head.

"You don't have a choice."

"I do," Angel said, his temper flaring.

Chester slipped Angel's thick file back into his leather briefcase. "You'll rot in here for months waiting for a trial date."

"May as well. If I plead, I'll rot in prison for 25 years."

"Twelve years with good behavior."

"I've never been on good behavior in my life."

The lab-grown heart valve principal investigator, Dr. Yu, emailed Sloane. Yu's team had isolated the agent in the culture in which the heart valve was grown that had caused the death of the six trial subjects. The patients were lethally allergic to that specific agent, as was 27 percent of the population. Yu and his team had high hopes that by replacing the agent with another similar, yet non-allergenic agent, future deaths would be avoided.

Sloane shot out of his chair at his home-office desk and pumped the air with his fist. The stock price would recover as soon as the news hit Wall Street. Sloane sat down to send an email to tell Lester Eastbrook to prepare a press release for immediate distribution. He emailed Maddy, Jennifer and the cute lawyer with the amazing tits whose name he had finally remembered to share the good news. Things were turning around. The SEC case was settled and the clinical trial was back on track. With a little luck, Lincoln would convince the SEC to waive the prison time. He was in perfect shape to remain CEO for a nice long tenure.

After work Arden brought the handgun safety certificates for Marisela and himself to the sporting goods store and picked up their new Glock 17. He bought a box of ammunition and felt like a criminal leaving the store. Normal people should not be carrying a plastic shopping bag with a lethal weapon in it. At least it was not loaded.

"Where should we keep it?" Marisela asked, her gaze roving around the bedroom that night.

"In a lockbox," Arden said. "I saw them online; one for the gun and one for the ammunition."

"If someone breaks in, how long will it take to unlock one box, get the bullets, open the other box, and load the gun?" Marisela shook her head in disbelief. "Is a thief going to wait politely while you do all that so you can shoot him?"

"I'm not keeping a loaded gun lying around."

"If it's locked up in pieces, what good will it do?"

"It won't be used accidently to shoot Sam coming in late some Friday night," Arden said, aghast at the thought of anything ever happening to his daughter.

Marisela let out a breath and sat on the end of the bed. "By the time you get it all together from the various safes, a burglar could have killed us all."

Arden sat beside her.

Marisela said, "Sam knows not to touch a gun."

Arden remained silent.

"We could hide it, so only we know where it is."

"Like we used to hide Christmas presents?" Arden asked. "She always found every single one."

"In your bedside table, behind that stack of history books you always have. No one would ever look there for a gun."

"We're getting a lockbox."

"You may as well take the gun back then and I'll never get any sleep."

They sat in silence. Finally Arden sighed, kneeled down and started pulling the history books out from his bedside table. In a few weeks, he promised himself, he would buy a lockbox and transfer the gun there, or at least the bullets.

The Antioch press release stated that CEO Richard Sloane was retiring, effective immediately. He wished to devote greater attention and time to his family and pursue certain outside interests. The board was reluctantly and with deep regret initiating an immediate global search for a new CEO to replace the irreplaceable Richard Sloane. Sources close to the board said Lester Easterbrook, Vice President for Marketing and Communications, was a frontrunner for the position.

Chapter 32

Wednesday, September 24, 2008

"Sebastian Carpenter." A stout man in worn blue jeans and a red sweatshirt introduced himself to Arden, who failed to suppress a grin. "Yeah, I know, Carpenter the carpenter."

"Were your parents seers or just fortune tellers?" Arden asked as he and Carpenter stood on his front steps. The sun's rays filtered horizontally through one of the fig trees across the street from Arden's house.

"With a name like Carpenter what else could I become?"

"What'd your father do?"

"Laid carpet," Carpenter said with a grin.

"Carpet—carpenter, close." Arden led the way over into the sun to the leaning fence that had become the cause of his increasingly hostile relations with Buell. "I need this fence repaired or replaced, and the one at the back moved 18 inches."

Carpenter frowned. "Should we be meeting with the other homeowners?"

"We should, but they're about as reasonable as pit bulls with the last bones in the yard."

Carpenter nodded with a knowing smile. "I've run into my fair share of that type." He carried a metal clipboard that had a box an inch deep attached to the back, all in shiny aluminum. "Let's see what we have."

After inspecting the leaning fence and the fence at the back, Carpenter returned to stand beside Arden as the sun warmed the air into the seventies. Arden had heard it would be in the mid-eighties today. Rare for October, but not unheard of in Los Angeles when the hot, dry Santa Ana winds blew in from the desert.

Carpenter asked, "You want to save a little money?"

"I'd love to save a vault full of money."

"If you want, we can reuse most of the boards and just replace the posts on the side fence. Your problem is that most of the posts are rotten. I won't be able to reuse all the facing boards, but most of them look fine. Which way do you want the boards to face?"

Arden frowned.

"The fence was built with the posts and stringers on your side and all the boards facing your neighbor. Since you're paying for it, I could put the stringers on his side this time and all the boards facing your property. You'll have a nice flush fence facing you. It would look nice from your side, not so nice from his side."

Arden chuckled as a broke into a grin. Carpenter stopped and glanced back at the side fence.

"What?" Arden asked, sensing that the carpenter was hesitant about saying something.

"Normally I wouldn't suggest it, in the interest of being a good neighbor and all."

"He hasn't exactly been a good neighbor."

"Well, your house is set farther back than his house and I assume you want the fence to enclose your backyard."

Arden nodded, beginning to see what Carpenter was thinking.

"We could build the fence from the back of your property to the front corner of your house."

Arden laughed. "Leaving a nice gap between the end of the fence and the front of his house that a Hummer could drive through."

"He could just add a gate from the fence to the back corner of his house, but most people like a fence to protect the side of their house. And it would leave his front gate hanging in the air. Cheaper, too."

"How much for both fences?"

Carpenter gave Arden a quote.

"I'd love to, but at that price, I can't afford it right now," Arden said.

"Business is a little slow these days and I have a crew that just had a job cancelled. I could knock 10 percent off the top."

"That's kind of you, but my wife's out of work and money's tight." Arden wondered how much the materials alone would cost and how he could find time to do it himself.

"I could help you do it," a voice announced from behind Arden. He turned and saw his retired neighbor Harry striding toward him, an eager smile on his face.

Chapter 33

Tuesday, September 30, 2008

"How about St. George," Marisela asked. "Warm, dry climate, small town and close to a bunch of gorgeous national parks in southern Utah."

"What's the cost of living?" Arden asked as he sipped tea and she drank decaf coffee after dinner.

"Two-bedroom house for a little over $100,000."

"Sounds great. Maybe we could go take a look next summer."

"Assuming I have a job by then."

"You will." Arden coughed, hacked and used a tissue to blow his nose.

"Tea helping?"

Arden nodded. He had been sick for several days with an energy draining cold. Getting up and going to work had been a struggle, but he had done it every day. There was no way he was going to risk Kennelwhite transferring even one of his cases to another mediator. "If we sell this place, maybe we can look somewhere else. Bend looks like a possibility, too, as well as Ashcroft."

"Beautiful old homes in Ashcroft," Marisela said. "And closer to Purdue, Boston or Atlanta, depending on where Sam ends up going."

That night, his head still draining like Niagara Falls, Arden could not sleep. Besides his mucus-clogged head, financial worries

roiled his brain, casting the future into a frightening poverty-filled
black abyss. He rolled onto one side. He could not sleep. He rolled
onto the other side. Still no sleep. He needed a good night's sleep.
He had a tough case in the morning and had to be in top form.
He had requested the case for the extra money. He had to settle
it quickly and well or he might not get any more extra cases, especially since Kennelwhite had expressed concern that Arden's plate
was overflowing. Fool; Arden never had enough cases to even keep
him halfway busy. Arden closed his eyes and told his mind to stop
thinking. His body needed sleep to finish off his cold once and for
all. Go to sleep, he ordered his body. Neither his brain nor his body
listened.

Financial news crashed through his mind, causing a tidal wave
of worry. Being sick in bed each evening, he had watched even
more newscasts that usual. On September 25, the FDIC had seized
WaMu, Washington Mutual, and sold its banking assets to JP Morgan for $1.9 billion. The next day, as it seemed that the financial
future of the United States was on the brink of destruction, the
House failed to pass the Emergency Economic Stabilization Act,
228 to 205. The same day, the FDIC announced that Citigroup
would buy the banking operations of failing Wachovia. To sweeten
the deal for healthy banks to take over failing banks, the US Treasury changed the tax law so that a bank acquiring another bank
could write off all of the acquired bank's losses for tax purposes.
It made failing banks far more attractive to buyers, although their
toxic sub-prime mortgage assets were still worth a penny on the
dollar, if that. More than 280,000 jobs had been lost in the United
States in September, furthering the decline in jobs that was making
it harder with each passing day for the consumer—what the pun-
dits called the engine of the US economy with mind-numbing rep-
etition—to reverse the worsening financial nightmare into which
the world appeared to be sliding. Worst of all, yesterday, September
29, the Dow had suffered the largest single day point drop in its
history, a whopping 777 points. In an upbeat note, Ford's sales were
up in September some 34 percent from the year before. Should
have bought Ford stock, Arden thought with a rueful smile in the
dark of their bedroom.

Or maybe, he thought as he turned over once more, he should
have hijacked a freighter off Somalia. He had read on one of his

news websites that pirates had hijacked a Ukrainian freighter off the coast of the African nation carrying more than $30 million worth of Russian arms, including 30 T-72 tanks, grenade launchers, anti-aircraft guns, and ammunition. The pirates were demanding $20 million for the safe return of the crew. Even a tenth of the ransom would set Arden and Marisela up for a nice comfortable retirement in New Mexico for the rest of their lives.

Barring hijacking ships, if Marisela did not find a job, they might never be able to retire. Worse, the trend at work was toward fewer cases, and cases that were farther afield. Having to travel to a case seemed more glamorous, but they usually paid less since Equitable had to factor in travel costs when bidding on the job, decreasing the pay for the mediator.

Arden rolled over again, trying not to disturb Marisela. Knowing Marisela's opposition to selling any stocks, he had assuaged his own worries to an infinitesimal degree by changing his retirement account allocations. Instead of buying 75 percent stocks, new money from each paycheck going into his retirement account would now buy bonds or go into money market accounts. He hoped the change would preserve at least a little of their capital until the markets settled down. Unfortunately, the new money going in was only a couple of thousand a month compared to the hundreds of thousands they already had in the market—or had had. Worse, bond funds seemed to be falling right along with stocks—so much for diversification—and money market accounts were paying a meager one percent. It made stuffing your money in a mattress appear to be the most rational course.

Unable to sleep, Arden slid out of bed, checked that Marisela was still asleep, and staggered downstairs to make another cup of tea to attempt to clear the pounding ocean of mucus in his head. If it did not, maybe he could find a crossword or three to do. Unlike their financial problems, Arden knew he could solve crosswords.

Chapter 34

Wednesday, October 1, 2008

It was turning into a good day. His cold largely gone, Arden drove home from work listening to his favorite all-news station and heard that the Dow had clawed its way back to 10,800.

"After the devastation of the past few days, this could mark a bottom and the beginning of the end of the bear market," an analyst from a stellar Wall Street firm prophesized. "The bottom of the housing market may be in sight and the American people are poised to open their pocketbooks this winter, which should buoy the spirits and stocks of many retailers."

Arden made a mental note to check his retirement funds when he got home on the new computer Marisela had bought. Maybe they had recouped a little of what they had lost on Antioch.

As he strode in the door, Sam announced, "I got accepted to Purdue." Beaming and holding a letter in her right hand, she added, "Special early acceptance to aeronautical engineering."

A broad smile spread across Arden's face. He rushed to his daughter and hugged her, lifting her off the floor. "Congratulations, Samantha. That's fantastic." He kissed her cheek and squeezed her tight before setting her down. "Guess I better start pulling for the Boilermakers, as well as my Trojans. Luckily they never play each other. But what about MIT and Georgia Tech?"

"They don't send out admission letters until the spring, but whatever they decide, I want to go to Purdue. It's my first choice."

"Why?"

"Twenty-two alumni have been selected for spaceflight." Sam beamed with eager anticipation. "And Purdue's awarded more aerospace degrees in the past 10 years than anyone else in the country."

"Doesn't Leah go there?"

"She's in pharmacy," Sam said of her best friend.

"I'm proud of you, Chicklet, so proud," Arden said. "We should go out for dinner to celebrate."

"Are you sure?"

Thoughts of their finances intruded on his joy and Arden said with a wry grin, "Takeout from Tito's Tacos?"

Chapter 35

Saturday, October 4, 2008

"So the cop gives me a ticket because the tail lights on Harry's trailer weren't connected," Arden explained to Marisela as they repaired the leaning fence late Saturday morning. "Harry's son-in-law has his truck this weekend and my car didn't have the connection to hook them up."

"I am sorry about that," Harry said as he dug a new post hole six inches over from one of the old ones. The new fence would be right on the property line, now marked by a long piece of twine stretched between two stakes Arden and Harry had meticulously sited. Harry added, "I'll pay the fine."

"No way," Arden said. "That wouldn't be fair. We were hauling lumber to repair my fence."

"Half Buell's fence. Maybe he'll pay half," Harry said with a wry grin.

"How much was the ticket?" Sam asked as she hammered boards off the old fence with marked enthusiasm.

"Three hundred and five dollars," Arden said, watching Marisela, who winced at the figure; more than six hours of freelance editing.

The work progressed well. They knocked the boards off the old fence and dug new post holes in the hard, dry earth. Sam and Marisela dribbled gravel around the creosoted posts before Harry and Arden secured them into place with cement they mixed in a black bucket. Rusty, Harry's ancient coon dog, dragged himself over to keep an eye on things although by midmorning his eyes were shut as he snuffled and twitched, deeply asleep on the sun-warmed grass.

In the afternoon, a timid, high-pitched voice asked, "Would you like some lemonade?"

Arden looked up from hammering a stringer into place to see Lisa, Buell's young daughter, holding a tray loaded with plastic cups and a brimming pitcher at a precarious angle. He sprang to his feet to rescue it.

"Thank you, Lisa," he said, touched by the gesture. "That's extremely kind of you."

After Harry, Sam, Marisela, and Arden drank their lemonade, Arden asked Sam to grab his wallet from inside.

"No charge, Mr. Jeffries," Lisa said as she gathered her cups and empty pitcher.

"No, no, I insist."

"No, please." Lisa carried her tray and accoutrements toward her house and called out, "Thank you for fixing my fence. I was afraid it'd fall on me or Laurice."

"Who's Laurice?" Harry asked as the little girl disappeared into her house next door.

"Her unicorn," Marisela said.

By late afternoon, they had finished repairing the fence along Buell's property, albeit stopping right at the front of Arden's house, leaving Buell's house exposed and his gate hanging free and clear. Then they turned their labors to the fence at the back of Arden's property that ran along Leesing's lot.

They started taking down the old fence, hammering boards off and digging to loosen and then lift out the posts. They had just begun when two boys in their early teens scrambled out of Leesing's house and, without a word, started helping.

"Leesing's boys," Marisela whispered to Arden.

"With them, we may just finish by nightfall."

After refueling with a pizza dinner Marisela brought out, they did finish just as dusk was turning to night. Arden thanked the Leesing boys, who nodded and, without a word, clambered like cats back over the relocated fence.

"I hope they don't get into trouble," Marisela said.

"I saw Leesing watching out the window a few times," Arden said, worrying as he considered the matter.

"Should you go say something to him?"

"Probably make things worse for them." Arden thought for a moment and said, "They'll be fine. They did the right thing."

Chapter 36

Monday, October 6, 2008

"The Dow's falling," Marisela reported as Arden shuffled into the kitchen for breakfast. He had suffered through another worry filled, sleepless night.

"It's been doing that for a year," Arden said, thinking it was a death by a thousand cuts: every day you lost a little more of your money, until you had none left. At least then, he thought, he would have nothing more to lose. "It went down a little faster in September with the banks failing, but—"

"It's falling a lot faster today," Marisela warned as she handed Arden a bowl for his cereal. Sam sat at the kitchen table, her nose in an old *Aviation History* magazine, new iPod earphones filling her head with music. Marisela had broken down and replaced her stolen iPod.

"Bush just signed a recovery plan to buy failing bank assets; should help." Arden also had read that the law had been changed so banks did not have to show the value of troubled assets on their books. He was unclear what that meant, beyond making banks appear sounder than they were. It did not seem honest to Arden or to do anyone much good, other than to fool the gullible—and maybe voters.

Settled in with his Life cereal at the kitchen table, Arden changed the channel on the television from a local morning show to a business channel. The Dow was down more than 500 points. Arden stared at the figure. "My God." He turned the volume up as he noticed that Marisela was chewing the skin just above the nail on her right thumb.

"Stocks are plunging today as the government's $700 billion bank bailout plan and attempts by European governments to prop up faltering banks appear to have failed to comfort jittery investors," an anchor said, unable to sit still in the face of such dire excitement. "The Dow is below 10,000 for the first time in four years."

Arden rose and staggered into the den to collapse onto the sofa. He stared at the screen and watched the carnage. "Should we sell?"

"Don't you think it's a little late for that now?" Marisela asked as she sat at the kitchen table with a bowl of Cheerios and a cup of coffee. She had not touched her cereal. "It should come back, won't it?"

"When? We have some time if we push our retirement back, but Sam goes to college next fall."

"How much has my college fund lost?" Sam asked, pulling out the earphones, suddenly interested in her parent's discussion.

"The Dow is down almost 800 points," the announcer reported.

Her forehead furrowed with worry, Sam asked, "Can I still go to Purdue?"

Chapter 37

Tuesday, October 7, 2008

As soon as Arden's eyes opened he had one thought in his mind. He was downstairs with the business channel on before the warmth of his body had even taken the chill out of his black bathrobe. As the LCD picture came to life and his eyes spotted the stock index prices, hope surged within him. By the close yesterday stocks had recovered somewhat from their early 800-point loss and today the Dow, Nasdaq and S&P were continuing their recovery.

"The Federal Reserve's plan to loosen credit by promising $900 billion to banks to get them lending again has slowed the bleeding in stocks today," the anchor read from the teleprompter, beaming with hope and excitement. "The Fed has announced a plan to loan $1.3 trillion directly to companies outside the financial sector to help ease the credit markets and restart the flow of lending in the financial system. Many analysts and traders on the floor are saying this could mark the turning point, the bottom of the bear market."

Arden smiled. The worst was over. The government's actions were finally having an effect. If stocks rebounded, they just might be able to buy a nice house somewhere relatively cheap outside of Los Angeles to retire next year, especially if Marisela could find a job, any job for even just a year or two. Sam's college fund would recover and they could help her out a little, too. He looked forward to telling Marisela the good news as soon as she awoke.

Just after lunch at work, Arden checked the stock market. He was astounded by what he saw. After their opening rally, stocks had changed course by mid-morning and plummeted thanks in part to a speech by Fed Chairman Ben Bernanke. Speaking to a conference in Washington, Bernanke spoke of "financial turmoil" and warned of dark days ahead: "Economic activity is likely to be subdued during the remainder of this year and into next year."

By the time the markets closed back east, just as Arden finished his can of stew for lunch, the Dow had lost 500 points. In two days it was down almost 900 points. The S&P 500 index lost 5 percent to close at its lowest level since 2003. In a week, the Dow was down a staggering 1,400 points or 13 percent. Arden read online that financial stocks were hard hit as worries over sub-prime mortgages sent Bank of America, Morgan Stanley and Merrill Lynch down 20 percent or more. The dollar had slumped against other currencies. At least, Arden thought, he and Marisela were not trying to retire overseas. With all the debt the government was taking on, soon the American dollar would not be worth a peso, if he had any money left by then to even buy a peso.

Arden checked Sam's college fund for the twentieth time in the past week and winced at the tiny figure her account now held. Thanks to a generous gift from Marisela's parents when she was born and regular contributions from Arden and Marisela, the year before she had had just over $166,000 for college. Now she had less than $82,000. Enough for two years at Purdue, but how could she afford her last two years? Worse, Sam had told him, many colleges did not offer enough courses to allow students to finish in four years anymore. Many bachelor degrees now took five years, which meant even more tuition and more fees to pay. There were always government loans, but the more the government offered to loan students, the more colleges seemed to charge.

"We could help her," Marisela said as they lay in bed that night, her head on Arden's chest.

"With what?" Arden asked. "We're down a fortune."

"Maybe her funds will come back," Marisela wished, although even she did not sound like she believed that would ever happen.

"If they're down 50 percent, they need to go up 100 percent to get back to where they were," Arden said, "assuming she doesn't take anything out. If she does, which she'll have to for her first two years of college, there's not a chance what she has left will ever go up enough to pay for her last two years at Purdue."

"What are we going to do, Arden?"

"We've cut back. You're looking for a job. You're working every hour the lab will give you. I can't get any more cases. There aren't any more. We're doing everything we can."

Marisela placed her hand on Arden's heart as it beat.

"How's your heart?" she asked.

"Still beating."

After a long silence, Marisela asked, "What are we going to do about Sam?"

Chapter 38

Friday, October 10, 2008

By Friday, Arden was in a state of shock. If he had been told he was living through a second Great Depression he would have nodded without question at the validity of the comparison.

"Do you think the stock market will ever turn around?" Marisela asked Friday evening as they sat at the dinner table. Sam had hurried upstairs to peruse the web for summer jobs, now crucial to her dream of earning an aeronatucial degree from Purdue. Marisela had spent the day looking for a job as she broadened her search to anything for which she was even remotely qualified. Arden knew how Sam and Marisela felt. He had spent part of the day calling more than two dozen colleagues asking for any freelance mediation work and had come up empty. There were fewer cases and the cases that were available were in high demand.

The dirty dishes from a fajita dinner sat scattered across the table between Arden and Marisela. Arden eyed his wife, whose optimism about the future of the stock market had always been as solid as Jefferson's belief in the inevitable spread of freedom.

Arden asked, "Do you now how long it took stocks to recover after the Great Depression?"

Marisela shook her head with a look that told Arden she dreaded hearing the answer.

"Twenty-four years."

Marisela blew the air out of her mouth. "At least the worst is over."

Arden grimaced. Tell the truth or coast along on optimistic hopes? Maybe there was something they could do if they knew the truth. "The worst may not be over. I was reading about it. The Great Depression hit in waves. There was a big drop in stocks in 1929, then a partial recovery with some stocks going up 50 percent before there was another drop, and then yet another drop. It came in waves over several years."

"Years?"

"Years."

On Wednesday the Dow had climbed 341 points raising hopes that the worst was over before ending down 179. US, European and Asian central banks cut interest rates in an attempt to aid the global economy, while rumors spread that the US government might take an ownership stake in failing banks, just as the Swedes had done in the 1990s. The Swedes nationalized several failing banks, recapitalized them with a massive infusion of government/taxpayer cash, and sold them again, making a profit. The Swedes, however, had faced a local crisis, not a global catastrophe.

On Thursday, the Dow rallied again, rising 261 points before giving it all back and more to fall 679 points to close at its lowest point since 2003. It was the third largest one-day point loss ever. As the drop quickened, panicked investors dumped stocks across the board. Bank lending remained tight as nervous institutions continued to hoard cash. No investment seemed safe. Even treasury prices fell, raising their attendant yields. Oil, gas and gold fell as the dollar—perceived to be a safe haven—rose against other currencies. Auto makers suffered. GM lost 31 percent on Thursday alone, while Ford lost 21 percent on reports that auto sales would hit recession levels in 2008 and worsen in 2009. Arden was happy he had not followed his earlier whim to invest in Ford after their recent excellent sales figures.

Friday brought hope once again as the Dow raced up more than 400 points before dashing all confidence by giving it all back and more to close down 117 at 8,451.

Arden could recite the numbers by heart. From October 6 through 10 the Dow had fallen 22 percent. It was the worst week in the Dow's 112-year history; at least up until now, Arden thought, fearing what the next week would bring. He wondered if a stock market could fall to zero. The Dow, Nasdaq and S&P 500 were all down more than 40 percent from their highs in late 2007. Paper losses on US stocks totaled $8.4 trillion from the 2007 market highs.

European markets were also falling, while fears of a global recession had hammered Asian markets, crippling Arden's and Marisela's international and emerging market funds even worse than their US funds. So much for diversification, Arden thought. Diversification just meant you lost money in a dozen different sectors instead of just one.

Marisela rose from the table and took a chicken out of the freezer for Saturday's dinner. Arden perused a *Washington Post* he had picked up after a client left it in a conference room. Arden's eyes fell on a story, whose headline asked, "The End of American Capitalism?" With the government considering nationalizing banks and having already bailed out AIG and taken over Fannie Mae and Freddie Mac, the era of hands-off capitalism, the story argued, was over. Since the Reagan deregulation presidency, the United States had favored clearing the playing field to allow business to conduct business any way it saw fit. That era was now over. Wall Street banks and business had shown that a lack of regulation could lead to risk taking that could cripple the world's economy.

Deciding now was as good a time as any to tell Marisela the awful news, Arden said, "We're down about $600,000."

Sam appeared at the entrance to the kitchen, a letter in her hand. She appeared to be on the verge of a smile, but it would not come.

"What's up, Chicklet?" Arden asked, forcing a smile for his daughter.

Sam pursed her lips, shifted her weight from one bare foot to the other, and said, "I won a scholarship."

"That's fantastic," Arden exclaimed, rising to hug his daughter. Marisela gave her a kiss.

The scholarship was $1,000, named for Richard Bong, a World War II ace fighter pilot. Sam had penned an essay about the glories of flight to win the award.

Arden opened his mouth to say they should go out for dinner tomorrow night to celebrate, but the thought of their stock losses silenced him. Even Tito Taco's seemed too expensive now.

"A grand isn't going to help much to pay for Purdue," Sam said, shoulders slumped as she held the letter at her side.

"Every little bit helps," Marisela said, giving her daughter a reassuring hug.

"I still only have enough for two years at Purdue, and that's only if my stocks don't go down any more." She sighed. "My counselor said that Purdue's tuition is going up next year."

Arden bit his lip and decided to broach the topic he had been avoiding ever since the market started to tank. "Maybe you should look into going to another college, maybe in California. In-state tuition's a lot lower than out-of-state."

"UCLA and USC are fine schools," Marisela said with an encouraging smile.

"Purdue has the best aeronautical engineering program in the country," Sam insisted, her body stiffening in the defense of her dream.

Arden glanced at Marisela, whose eyes pleaded with him.

"I don't know—" Arden began.

"I've worked hard. I got straight As and did swim team, student government, edited the newspaper, ran the Darfur simulation, volunteered at the senior center, taught kids to read in East LA, and, and for what? I want to go to Purdue. If I ever want to go into space, I have to go to Purdue."

"You may not be able to, honey," Marisela said, her arm still around Sam's shoulders.

"It's the only school I want to go to."

Arden glanced at Marisela, whose eyes still pleaded with him.

"We'll see what we can do," Arden said, hoping they could put off the dreaded decision a little longer: Sam's college or retirement. "Your college fund will cover your first two years and who knows what'll happen in two years." Only in the past week had Arden realized just how much could happen in a week, let alone two years.

Chapter 39

Saturday, October 11, 2008

Arden was thinking of a six-letter word for 17 across, GI's helmet, when he spotted Sam crossing the mall parking lot toward his ancient Kharmann Ghia.

"Any luck?" Arden asked as Sam climbed into the coupe.

"I gave them my resume and filled out an application," Sam said, as she clipped on her seatbelt. She had come up with the idea of approaching businesses in person to try to increase the chance of finding a job over just applying by email. "The manager said they wouldn't be hiring anyone anytime soon. No one's eating out anymore; the economy."

Arden nodded. What could he say? He wanted to make it better. Their funds were down so much that if he took $100,000 out of their retirement accounts to fund Sam's last two years of college, it would push their retirement well into their 70s, if not 80s. If he did that, his heart would fail him before he ever retired.

"Maybe you can get some student loans." He started the car. It had been repaired since the burglary and seemed to run better than it had before being struck by the burglar's truck.

"And owe a hundred thousand by the time I graduate?" Sam glared out the window as if she was ready to lash out at anything or anyone she saw. "Is college even worth it?"

"Of course. Without a college education, your mom and I wouldn't have as good jobs as we have. We wouldn't have our house or nearly as comfortable a life."

"Mom doesn't even have a job."

"She did for a long time, and the odds of her getting another one are far greater given her education than if she'd never been to college," Arden said, his anger rising at Sam's attitude. "You'll make far more money over your working life if you go to college than if you don't."

"Uncle Peter doesn't have a college degree."

"He's an exception. He could sell air to a fish." Arden shifted gears and pulled out of the mall's lot. "A college degree's like a high school diploma used to be. You have to go to college."

Sam nodded, sullen, accepting the argument, but not the debt that seemed today to go along with it.

Arden said with an enticing grin, "Remember, you need at least an engineering degree to ride on a Space Shuttle."

"Maybe I should just live at home, go to UCLA and be done with it."

"Did you even apply?"

Sam pursed her lips and admitted, "As a fall back. I won't hear until the spring, but I should get in."

Arden looked with admiration over at his daughter. UCLA was tough to get into; few applied as a fall back. "You still want to go to Purdue though?"

"Of course." She looked down at the stack of resumes on her lap.

Arden could not let her fail at 18. "Then Boilermakers it is."

His pep talk was not working. Years ago, a few words from him would have cheered her. "It'll work out, I promise."

Sam kept staring down at the stack of resumes in her lap. After a few moments, she said, "If I don't get a car, that'll help, I guess. I'll live in a dorm and never leave campus."

"I'm sure your friends will have cars, and if you never leave campus, you'll study more, get higher marks and I'll be coming to see you launch in the Shuttle before you're 30."

"They're retiring the Shuttle."

"Then in whatever space craft they're sending into space after you graduate."

No response.

As they waited at a stop light, Arden reached over to lift his daughter's chin and turn her head toward him. "No smile for me? Not a one? Not from my Chicklet, the astronaut?"

Sam reluctantly smiled and then giggled.

"Where to next?" Arden tried to sound upbeat.

After a long pause, Sam said, "A pizza place on Sepulveda is hiring drivers. I heard that people aren't eating out as much, so they're ordering in more."

"I'm not having you delivering pizza at night," Arden said, shaking his head. "No way."

"I have to make money somehow, Dad."

"No. What else is there?"

Sam pulled out a list of places to apply from under her stack of resumes. "A firm that cleans out repo-ed houses needs crew-members."

"Sounds like hard work."

"Maybe I'll get some exercise in the bargain. Astronauts have to be in good shape."

Chapter 40

Monday, October 13, 2008

Arden finished the *Los Angeles Times* crossword in his head—no memory problems there—and waited for Marisela, who was talking to Sam upstairs.

"How's she doing?" Arden asked Marisela as she descended the stairs.

"Like me, looking for work: a part-time job, a summer job or any job she can find in West Lafayette or even Indianapolis."

"She'll need a car if she gets a part-time job in Indianapolis." Arden recalled that Indiana's capital was 60 miles from Purdue. "A car will cost more than she'll make."

"She's desperate." Marisela slumped down on the sofa beside Arden. "I have an interview tomorrow at Presser Labs."

"Fantastic."

"Bench work. Pays about 30 percent less than I was making, but…"

"But you need a job." Arden reached over and squeezed her hand.

"Sam found a few work-study positions at Purdue to apply to."

"Great."

"She's still worried."

Arden swallowed, considered, and said, "Tell her we'll loan her the money to finish at Purdue."

Marisela stared at him. "Can we?"

"With the Las Cruces house gone, we'll have more money available than we did."

"And retirement?"

"Years away anyway. What's a couple more years either way going to matter?"

Marisela kissed his hand. "That's why I married you." She stared over at him, beaming. "How's the heart?"

"Went off a little yesterday, but not for long. Oddest sensation, as if you've lost control of your body."

She sat, holding his hand with both of hers. "Take care of yourself, Arden."

"At least the market rallied today," Arden said. "The Europeans got their act together, which sparked a rally. The Dow was up the most ever, 936 points. The British, French and German markets all climbed, too, about 10 percent."

Marisela nodded, heaved herself off the sofa and said, "I should get a dinner together for tomorrow in case the interview goes long."

"Mom called," Arden said, rising to help, if he could. "Dad needs two crowns, $1,500, and Mom needs new glasses and sunglasses, $750."

"Ouch."

"They don't have the money. They've spent ten grand on prescriptions alone this year already."

Marisela took ground beef out of the fridge and began adding bread crumbs, BBQ sauce, egg, and spices to make a meatloaf.

Arden hesitated and then said, "I told them we'd pay half."

Marisela stopped. "Can we afford that?"

"They don't have the money. They can't find jobs at their age and I don't want them to work anyway. Mom's asthma isn't good and she's already lost one husband. I don't want her to lose another."

Marisela closed her eyes an instant and then mixed the meatloaf ingredients by hand. After a few moments, she nodded, giving in, but not agreeing.

"A few grand either way won't make any difference." Arden leafed through the newspaper on the bar and saw a photo of Richard Sloane. Arden skimmed a brief story about Sloane's deal with the SEC. "Six months in jail?"

"What?"

"The CEO of Antioch," Arden said, shocked. "Sloane lies to investors, insider trades, alters a report, loots the company, and sends the stock price plunging, then cuts a deal with the SEC and gets six months."

"Is that all?"

"A two-hundred thousand dollar fine for him, personally," Arden read. "He made ten times that last year alone. Antioch will pay $40 million, plus the story says it'll cover a $5 million fine for Sloane on charges directly related to his position with the company."

"I wonder who gets the fine money?" Marisela asked with an acquisitive grin.

"We lose the money and the SEC gets the fine. One hundred and twenty-six thousand dollars gone; almost as much as he was fined and that's just us, not counting the thousands of other people who owned Antioch stock. He should be shot."

Marisela looked at Arden with a patient look as if he was a little boy in the midst of a temper tantrum.

"I'm serious," Arden said. "If we execute someone who kills one person—which I disagree with on principle—we should certainly execute someone who impoverishes thousands of people."

"We're not impoverished."

"We're much poorer because of him."

"It's not like he robbed us with a gun on the street."

"He didn't have to. He got far more doing it his way." Arden shook his head. "In a way it's like treason."

"Treason?" Marisela asked, amused at the comparison.

"It is treason. What he did goes against everything this country was founded on."

"People like Sloane shake your faith in the system, in the economy, in the country. Gibbon was right, when a people stop believing in their society, the end is near. People like Sloane make you wonder if the end isn't coming soon."

"It isn't that bad, Arden," Marisela said as she finished mixing the meatloaf and scooped it into two bread pans.

"He's far more of a threat to the country than Al Qaeda, North Korea or Iran, far more."

"Come on, Arden. Al Qaeda kills people."

"Sloane and his kind kill dreams, about retirement and dream homes and college. He takes your money and with it, your dreams. Far more dreams than Al Qaeda ever killed people. Shakes your faith in the whole system when someone can get away with such egregious acts."

"They're punishing him, aren't they?"

"He should be crucified."

"Calm down, Arden."

"Anger is the anvil of justice, Marisela. If no one got angry, who would ever go to the trouble of seeking justice?" Arden shook his head. "How can people like us believe it's safe—well, not safe— fair to invest in stocks if people like him just rip us off?"

"The country's survived scandals before, hasn't it?"

"Now they seem bigger, more common. Like the entire system is corrupt; designed for the rich."

"Hasn't it always been?"

"It's far worse now. I read that the rich are far richer compared to the poor than they ever have been in American history."

"You just hear about it more now, I think. The media's every-where and trumpets every scandal day after day for months."

"That doesn't make the crimes any less vile."

"No, but it doesn't mean they're any worse."

Arden threw himself down into a chair at the kitchen table again. The chair rocked, protesting the abusive treatment before settling onto its four wood legs. "Sloane should forfeit everything and spend the rest of his life in prison. Even if he does, he'll have had a far nicer life overall than most of the people he screwed."

Chapter 41

Thursday, October 16, 2008

"The Dow fell 733 points yesterday," Arden read at breakfast from a *Los Angeles Times* that his neighbor Harry, an early riser, had given him. "Eight percent."

"So much for a recovery," Marisela said as Arden stalked off to their home office to check the market on the Internet.

When he returned, he reported, "Antioch's down another couple of bucks. We just lost another $18,000. Could have almost paid for Purdue for a year."

His gaze fell on another story in the newspaper. "My God, do you believe it?"

"What?" Marisela asked as she ate a blueberry bagel with cream cheese.

"Sloane is suing Antioch for wrongful dismissal. They refused to pay his $36 million severance package."

Marisela extracted the calendar section of the paper.

"Wish I could have a little of that $36 million," Sam said, reading a list of work study positions from Purdue for the fall.

"He was paid $11 million in total compensation last year," Arden read, shaking his head in awe. "His salary was $1.5 million and he earned $1.8 million as a performance bonus."

"Wasn't the stock falling all of last year?" Marisela sipped her morning coffee, adulterated with plenty of sugar. "What would he have got if the stock actually went up?"

"Ah, here it is. He was eligible for $2.8 million as a performance bonus but only got $1.8 million because the stock was down; unbelievable. That's not all the money he made," Arden said, reading on. "He was given $1.2 million in Antioch stock and options worth $3.6 million."

"They aren't worth that now, are they?"

"They're worth a lot more than our Antioch stock. I bet he got them for a lot less then we did. He also received $562,000 in other compensation ranging from the use of two cars—a Cadillac Escalade and a Mercedes—a company jet, an executive health plan, catered meals, six country club memberships, a $250,000 housing allowance, a maid service, a driver, and a retention bonus last year of $265,000. A retention bonus? Who would ever quit such a job?"

"I'd take it for only $200,000 a year," Sam said with a grin, dipping her spoon into her bowl of toasted oats.

Arden fell silent as he read the rest of the article. "He wants a $36 million severance package because the board terminated his contract three years before it expired. And that's after he received 9, 11 and 13 percent raises the past three years."

Marisela shook her head in amazement. "Who approves paying anyone that much?"

Finding the information in the article, Arden said, "A compensation committee approved the raises. The committee was made up of executives from other Fortune 500 companies." Arden paused and thought for a moment. "Of course their own compensation is judged in relation to the compensation of other executives, including Sloane. Talk about scratching each other's backs." Arden set the paper down. "What a crook."

"Sounds like they caught him and are going to punish him."

"A small fine and a few months in prison? It's beyond nuts, it's surreal, and now he wants his $36 million severance package?"

"It's the way things are."

Arden stared across the breakfast table at his wife. "That may be, but it isn't the way things should be. It isn't fair. It isn't equitable."

"Calm down, Arden, there's nothing you can do about it."

That afternoon as they sat in a light-blue interview room, Arden told Detective Ranjan, "I want to lodge a complaint against Richard Sloane, CEO of Antioch Pharmaceuticals."

Seated on either side of a narrow, artificial-wood table, Arden noticed the shadow of a frown cross the detective's smooth face. "On what charge?"

"He knew Antioch's stock was falling and that a clinical trial his company was conducting was failing, yet he repeatedly told the public—me included—that the stock would recover and that nothing was wrong."

"So he's an optimist," Ranjan said with a patient look that looked long practiced.

"In public he was optimistic," Arden said, leaning forward as he made his points. "In private, he was selling his company stock." Arden slammed down the newspaper story from that morning that outlined the SEC investigation, the charges against Sloane, and the settlement.

Ranjan picked up the newspaper business section and skimmed the article. The farther he read, the more a patient smile formed on his face, reminding Arden of the smile his father had displayed when Arden, as a boy, had suggested something logical and fair, but completely impractical.

"It appears the SEC has already charged him and settled the matter," Ranjan said, setting the paper down between them with great care.

"It wasn't a criminal case."

"He negotiated a settlement with the SEC."

"He wasn't charged under criminal statutes."

"He reached an agreement with the SEC and a court ratified it."

"He never faced a judge. He never faced a jury. You need to charge him with fraud."

"The SEC already did that."

"He was never criminally charged, just procedurally by the SEC."

Ranjan exhaled. Arden knew the detective's patience was nearing an end. "Mr. Jeffries, it's like in baseball. A player gets disciplined for taking illegal drugs, but the police never get involved."

"Almost never. I want Sloane arrested."

Ranjan shook his head. "It doesn't work that way."

"Why not?"

"One branch of the government responsible for overseeing securities trading investigated him, charged him and negotiated a settlement. Another branch of the government, the police—me— can't charge him again for the same things. It's sort of like double jeopardy."

"He wasn't in jeopardy the first time. I looked into it. If you cooperate with the SEC the odds of you serving any time in jail is about the same as me starting as running back for the Chicago Bears this Sunday."

"I'm sorry, Mr. Jeffries, but I can't help you." Ranjan rose. "I am sorry."

"Don't you have a white-collar crime department?"

Ranjan shook his head.

"Why not?"

"We have fraud investigators."

"Let me talk to one of them."

"She couldn't help you. Sloane's been charged and fined."

"It isn't fair. It isn't equitable."

Ranjan shrugged.

Chapter 42

Friday, October 17, 2008

Throughout the week Arden followed the furious highs and viscous lows on Wall Street with occasional flashes of hope and increasing all-encompassing fear. Some mornings Arden made or lost more money before he woke up than he earned in a week. The Dow Jones index rocketed up more than 900 points on Monday, meandered aimlessly on Tuesday before plummeting more than 700 on Wednesday, and roared back up 400 points on Thursday. The index swung back and forth nearly 600 points on Friday alone. As a day trader, Arden thought, he could have made a fortune…or lost one.

On the drive home Friday, Arden listened to his usual news radio station. Alaska Senator Ted Stevens took the witness stand for a second day at his federal corruption trial in Washington to announce that he always paid his own bills. He denied accepting $250,000 in home remodeling for free and said that he had tried to oversee the renovations, but his senatorial duties often got in the way.

"In the way of lining your own pockets," Arden told the radio.

The announcer reported that drug-maker Pfizer had reached a settlement of nearly $900 million over two painkillers. The agreement ended thousands of lawsuits targeting Celebrex and Bextra, which the suits claimed increased the risk for heart attacks and strokes. As Arden reached home he thought that drug companies were doing rather well to be able to pay a $900 million settlement. He had just put his laptop and bag down on the hall table when the doorbell rang. Arden answered the door to find Buell standing before him.

"When are you going to finish the fence?" Buell demanded without preamble.

"It's finished," Arden said, suppressing a smile.

"It isn't. When are you going to finish it?"

"Soon."

"When, soon? Next week? Next month?"

"Soon in a geologic sense."

Buell didn't see the joke. "I want that fence finished."

"We established it is on my property and that it is mine. I fixed it to my liking."

"People can walk right into my backyard."

"Not my problem."

"Finish the fence."

"No."

"Finish it."

"My fence is finished."

His face reddening, his fists clenched, Buell appeared to be on the verge of continuing the conversation by other means when Arden said, his voice low and forceful, "Now please get off my property or I will be forced to call the police and have you arrested for trespassing. I am sure you are aware exactly where the property line runs or would you like me to show you?"

That evening, the fence issues settled at least to his own satisfaction, Arden considered the problem of Richard Sloane, CEO of Antioch, and of the burglary. The police and the insurance company had taken care of the burglary rather well. The police had arrested the burglars and they would be punished. All Risk Insurance had replaced all of their missing belongings in exchange for the $500 deductible and all seemed well, save for the loss of his grandfather's scimitar. Arden missed the heirloom, but it would not ruin his life. The alarm and the gun they had bought had eased Marisela's and Sam's fears, even if Arden had already forgotten half of what he had learned in the gun class. He wondered if he even remembered how to load the gun. He reminded himself to buy a lockbox. At least Marisela and Sam were sleeping better and Marisela's thumb was healing.

The CEO Sloane, however, was another matter. The police were no use with Sloane, nor was insurance. After ruminating on the issue for more than an hour, Arden called an old friend, whom he convinced to see him on a Saturday.

Chapter 43

Saturday, October 18, 2008

"To be completely honest, you don't have a hope," Antoine Phillips said as he chalked his tanned and calloused fingers from a bag on his belt. He and Arden stood in a parking structure near Brentwood early one fine Saturday morning. "You can't sue over losing money in an investment."

"You can if the agent or representative lied or misrepresented an asset," Arden countered, remembering that tit bit from law school so many years before. "In August last year, some of Bear Stearns shareholders sued the firm over the collapse of a subprime-backed hedge fund."

"Best of luck to them winning that one; hard to assign clear liability to anyone."

"There seems plenty of blame to go around," Arden said. "The government pushed home ownership and kept interest rates low, so banks loaned money to those who couldn't afford a mortgage. The loans were bundled into bonds and sold through Wall Street to investors, who didn't have a clue what was in the bonds because the ratings agencies gave them all triple-A ratings, in part because they weren't doing their job and in part because the Wall Street banks gamed the system. Many people defaulted on their first mortgage payment. Who loans money to someone who can't even make the first payment?

"You've been doing your research."

"My future's at stake." Not to mention Sam's.

"Proving that Sloane knew Antioch would decline in price makes it contingent on you to prove he could predict the future." Phillips climbed over the low concrete wall of the parking structure. His toes encased in insanely tight rubber-and-leather rock shoes, he wedged them in a notch that ran horizontally along the outside of the structure.

"Sloane was selling his own stock," Arden said, looking with apprehension over the wall and down seven stories to Beverly Drive. "Even while publicly he said the stock would go up."

"Corporate officers owe a duty to the company," Phillips said as he edged along the ledge, shifting his toes and hanging on with his fingertips to the outer lip of the concrete wall, "and part of that duty is to withhold or at least present in the best possible light negative information if disclosure of said information would harm their company's financial future."

"Seems a clear case of insider trading to me and to the SEC," Arden said as he shuffled along between car hoods and the inside of the wall to keep pace with the agile Phillips.

"Did Sloane admit any wrongdoing?"

"No, but he must be guilty. Why else pay the fine and serve six months?"

"To avoid a trial, legal fees, continuing bad publicity, and I am certain a dozen other completely valid reasons his attorneys can devise well before you even file your brief."

"He still sold his stock when he said it would go up."

"I'm certain if he doesn't have a good reason for why he sold the stock now, he certainly will by the time you ever get to court. People sell stock for a million reasons, even if they think it's going to go up, and all he needs is one reason."

"I just want an equitable, fair settlement for what he did to me and every other shareholder," Arden said, turning sideways to slip between a parked red Mustang and the wall as Phillips inched along. "I have a right. I owned—I own—a lot of company stock, not to mention working for Antioch for 22 years."

"Contrary to popular belief, shareholders legally have few rights. They do not own part of the company."

"They do."

"Legally they own a share of company stock, which gives them few, if any rights over the company itself. It's far from the same thing."

"You're sure you're safe doing this?" Arden asked, peering down again over the wall. The cars below looked like kiddie cars from so far above. "Shouldn't you have a safety line or something?"

Phillips shook his head. "Nah, nothing to it." He held up one hand to show that he could hang where he was using just one hand. "I need to increase my finger strength. I'm tackling McKinley in the spring and Mont Blanc in the summer, if all goes well."

"If it doesn't, Lynnette is going to be a wealthy widow, assuming you have good life insurance."

"Haven't fallen yet."

"Just takes once." Arden sighed. "I didn't get anywhere with the police either." He felt as if the rock he was trying to roll up the mountain was never going to come even close to the summit. "They said the SEC settled it."

"Sounds about right."

"But they didn't treat it like the crime it is."

"That's a tough nut. White-collar crimes aren't clearly defined in legislation and aren't enforced much, other than the 'honest services' rule."

"Haven't heard of that one."

"The government charges most white-collar criminals in the financial sector with violating the honest services laws, which state that you must provide honest service to customers. If they ever repeal that law, white-collar crooks are going to have a field day." Phillips reached the corner of the structure and the attorney skirted around the angle like a spider on a web. "Even when the government charges someone with a white-collar crime and there's no plea bargain, which only occurs in 5 percent of cases, and actually secure a conviction, the sentences are light. Most of those convicted of the savings and loan fraud during the 1980s served less time than the average burglar."

"Yet they stole so much more." Arden shook his head, discouraged, as he slipped past more parked cars. "So much for justice, let alone equity in punishment."

"Criminal justice is more concerned with deterrence and rehabilitation these days. Justice and punishment don't really come into it anymore." Phillips paused to dip first his right and then his left fingers in chalk from the bag he wore on his belt. "It's hard to even know a corporation or business executive has broken a law," Phillips said as he started along the western wall of the structure. "Illegal activity is often mixed with legal business activity, so it's complex to detect, let alone explain. It has low visibility given the media's love for violence and action. Responsibility is diffuse and most victims don't even realize they've been a victim because there's no violence and the costs are spread across thousands, if not hundreds of thousands of victims."

"I know I've been a victim."

"I dread trying to explain white-color fraud or insider trading cases to a jury. I just finished a case that was a nightmare. I'm trying to explain to the jury of laymen how you tell that a CEO decreased the value of his company on purpose by accelerating accounting of expected expenses, delaying expected revenue accounting, and using some off balance sheet transactions to make a company's profitability appear poor to make it a target of a takeover bid. I thought I had him, since the new buyer paid off the CEO with a $100-million severance package because he bought the company at a substantially lower price. The takeover artist made billions when the stock recovered. The shareholders lost a fortune. The company may be broken up and sold off so their original stock is worthless even if they kept it through all the turmoil."

"A clear case."

"Not guilty."

"They should all be locked up."

"The jury or the CEO?"

Arden chuckled. "CEOs."

"Little risk of that."

"Sloane didn't decrease the value of the stock on purpose. He just knew it was going down and said it wasn't while he sold his own stock."

"Prove it and that's insider trading—maybe."

"I'd just like to get Sloane in the witness box and let a jury hear what he did."

"I've found it's damn near impossible to prove criminal intent in insider trading or misstatement cases, and even if you win they lead to light penalties," Phillips said, bitter even as he inched rapidly along the edge of the parking structure. "Penalties for convicted corporations are light. The vast majority are fined less than $5,000 and all of them less than $25,000 as long as they cooperate and promise to revise their policies. Even probation is rarely imposed for the executives involved, while jail or prison time is unheard of."

"At least Sloane got some time in jail."

"He must have been egregious then, although the climate these days is pretty anti-CEO."

"I read that the FBI estimates white-collar crime costs the United States $300 billion annually. Companies seem to break the law all the time."

"Every corporation has broken the law at some point, but corporations can't be put in prison and it's impossible in most cases to identify the specific executives who are guilty since they can always say the board approved their decisions."

"Companies seem to have all the rights." Arden heard an approaching siren.

"Since 1886, Santa Clara County v. Southern Pacific Railroad," Phillips said, sounding like he was making a closing argument to a jury, "it's been held that a corporation can be defined as a person. Corporations have all the same rights as you and me."

"Ridiculous. Freedom of speech, freedom of religion—do corporations pray?"

"The Global Church of Mammon, I believe," Phillips said with a grin. "Looked at another way, counting the huge number of executives at corporations through the years, the rate of criminal activity is extremely low. It's all in how you count it."

"Industrial accidents caused by scrimping safety measures, environmental pollution, fiduciary fraud, unsafe products, medical fraud, insider trading, misstatements, and a dozen other white-collar crimes; makes your head spin." The siren grew louder.

"I'd love to help, Arden, but I don't see my firm touching this case, unless every partner in the firm lost money on Antioch, and probably not even then."

A police cruiser pulled up behind Arden, lights flashing, siren wailing.

Arden suppressed a sigh of disappointment. He raised his voice to be heard above the siren, "I'll have to find another attorney to take the case."

"I doubt you'll be able to find one, unless you're willing to pay up front," Phillips warned as the siren fell silent. The police cruiser's lights still flashed red and blue. "No one with an iota of intelligence is going to take on a civil action against Richard Sloane for fraud."

Two officers stalked out of the cruiser, hands on their holsters.

"What's going on here?" one of them asked, taking in the scene.

"Maybe I'll have to file the case myself," Arden told Phillips.

"Good luck with that, my friend. Even if you find some traction in court and manage to win, it'll bankrupt you. Sloane's D&E insurance will pay for the finest attorneys in the country. If a miracle occurs and you win, a settlement just might benefit your children, but more likely your grandchildren after all the appeals."

"What is going on?" the officer repeated, more slowly and with greater force behind every word.

Ignoring the officer, Arden said, "Not every man who acts as his own attorney is a fool."

Phillips grinned and said, "Not every one, just most."

"What's going on here?" the officer demanded and this time his words carried a definite note of dire warning.

"Just practicing mountain climbing," Phillips said. "I'm an officer of the court. I have my identification right here," he said, taking one hand off the wall to reach in a zipped pouch around his waist. Both officers rushed forward to prevent him from falling, but stopped when Phillips remained securely where he was dangling, now by one hand.

"Don't believe him, officer," Arden said, "He's practicing his second-story B&E technique."

"Who are you?" the second officer demanded, squaring his broad shoulders in his bullet-proof vest toward Arden.

"Just a bystander," Arden said. "I thought he was going to jump." Arden started to walk away.

"Hold on," the first officer ordered.

Arden stopped, then thought of something to ask Phillips. "Did you ever stay in touch with Terry McGhee?"

Chapter 44

Tuesday, October 21, 2008

"These CEOs shouldn't be allowed to lie on television and tell the public that their company's stock is bound to go up when they know their company is heading south fast," Arden told Terry McGhee, an old law school classmate and now an aide to Senator Short. Arden had not seen Terry in more than 20 years, but had kept track of his career via the USC law school's alumni newsletter. The pair stood just outside double doors behind which a $2,500-a-plate fundraiser for the Senator was entering the dessert phase at the Biltmore Hotel in downtown Los Angeles.

"There are dozens of reform bills being drafted right now," McGhee reassured Arden. "The Senator's confident they will remedy the problems in the financial system."

"Making it illegal for CEOs to lie?"

"You can't make it illegal for people to be wrong about their predictions," McGhee said. The aide laughed. "If we had a law like that, every politician would be in prison for life." Then, realizing what he had just said, McGhee added as his eyes flitted around the empty foyer, "Well, most politicians."

A woman in a slinky red silk dress slipped out the doors behind McGhee and, with an appraising glance at Arden, sinuously wound her way down the hall toward the powder rooms.

Wrenching his gaze from the woman's pert derriere, McGhee said, "In any case, there's a tidal wave of support right now to reform the financial sector."

"I hope they make it so that if a CEO says a company is doing well when they have information that the company is about to collapse, they're charged with a crime."

"They would be now by the SEC for fraud or making misstatements," McGhee said. "Those laws are already on the books, so nothing needs fixing there."

"They're rarely enforced and the penalties are laughable for CEOs making ten or twenty million a year."

"Some do serve jail time, in the egregious cases."

"If they're stupid enough not to cooperate with the SEC or the FBI. Worse, they usually serve time for obstruction, like Martha Stewart, not for their real crime. What sort of a signal does that send?"

Applause rose to a crescendo from the banquet room behind McGhee. "Look, Arden, I know you're mad about this and I agree, as does the Congressman and his party, that something needs to be done to correct the flaws in the financial regulations. Rest assured they will be. Wall Street is going to be reformed. Regulators are going to have all the power they need to make sure risk is managed."

"Can it be, and is that the problem?"

McGhee frowned.

"Risk is inherent in investing," Arden said. "The problem isn't risk. It's that the rules for the big firms and CEOs are different than they are for the rest of us. If I take on too much risk and lose, no one bails me out."

"The system was in danger, Arden."

"If it was, then it deserved to fail."

"This was just a black swan, an extremely rare unexpected event. We'll fix the few kinks in the system, get things back to how they were and all will be right with the world again."

"Will it? I wonder when the same guys from the same big Wall Street firms who are now in the Treasury Department and the Fed who got us into this mess are now in charge of creating and enforcing rules to ensure it doesn't happen again."

"They know the system best."

"The system that led us into this mess."

The hint of a glare flashed across McGhee's face at his old classmate. "I can promise you that the Senator and his colleagues want to ensure this will never happen again by passing stringent and enforceable finance and investing laws to correct the flaws in the current structure of regulations."

Arden shook his head and looked down at the plush carpet. "The more I think about it, the more I think we already have too many laws and regulations."

McGhee frowned again.

"I read that we have more than 40,000 federal criminal offenses on the books, not to mention state and local ordnances," Arden said.

"Sounds like a stout wall against the forces of disorder," McGhee said with the hint of a grin.

Arden ignored his levity. "We'll pass laws to ensure that this particular type of catastrophe won't happen again, just as we did after the Great Depression. Then, no matter what laws are passed, bright executives on Wall Street will figure out some new way to make money that skirts the letter of the law, but certainly not the spirit of it."

"The new laws will be robust, I promise you."

"They can never cover every eventuality. The executives and traders who bend the rules say they didn't technically break this or that law," Arden said. "They think that if they don't break any laws based on the narrowest interpretation of each law, they're acting legally, as if morality and fairness don't even enter into it. Passing more laws isn't going to change that culture, and it's impossible to pass laws to rule out every single way to make money immorally."

"Have some faith, Arden. We've come a long way from the Robber Barons of the 19th Century."

"Have we? We used to have loan sharks illegally charging 20 percent interest so we passed laws against that. Now we have credit cards legally charging 22 percent interest. We used to have millionaires who paid no tax so we passed laws to tax the wealthy, but now the wealthy have enough money to pay creative young accountants to figure out ways around paying any taxes at all. We used to have politicians who were in office forever, fattening their wallets with bribes from those they helped procure government business. Now we have politicians flying in corporate jets, taking extravagant vacations, and lining up lucrative jobs after they retire from the very industries they are writing laws to regulate, not to mention having their campaigns funded by companies for which, once elected, they'll then write laws for. No wonder laws favor the big firms."

"I think you're exaggerating a little, Arden. The system, for the most part, works well." McGhee put a reassuring hand on Arden's shoulder. "I need to get back inside."

Arden sighed. "Could you tell the Senator something for me?"

McGhee looked wary, but said after a quick glance around to make sure no one was within earshot, "You got me through second-year torts. I'll do what I can."

"Tell the Senator that the public's belief in the American system is shaken a damn sight more by CEOs and Wall Street bankers who bend the law than by guys who stick a gun in your face and take your wallet."

Chapter 45

Wednesday, October 22, 2008

As the sun slanted its late afternoon orange-gold rays through the narrow window in Arden's office, he debated whether to bother checking his stocks. He glanced at the time on the bottom corner of his computer screen: five minutes before an all-staff meeting. Might as well.

The Dow was down 514 points. Arden groaned. He checked several news sites and found that recession fears were being blamed for the drop as a number of large companies reported weak earnings in the third quarter and forecast worse to come. Stocks across Asia, Europe and Latin America dropped as well, which meant Arden's and Marisela's international, US and emerging market funds were also all down—again.

Arden read that credit-rating agencies had drawn fire at a hearing at the US House of Representatives. Standard and Poor's, Moody's and Fitch gave AAA bond ratings to securities tied to subprime mortgages, which later turned out to be worth about a penny on the dollar, if that. The chairman of the House Oversight Committee, Democrat Henry Waxman of California called it "a story of colossal failure." The head of Standard and Poor's, Deven Sharma, said, "A number of the assumptions we used did not work."

"No kidding. I wonder how Standard & Poor's stock is doing," Arden mused, his anger increasing. "If they're even dumb enough to risk their company's value on the stock market."

Arden felt a disturbing rumble in his chest. His heart beat was off.

Buell was waiting for Arden when he arrived home.

"I demand that you finish the fence," Buell said, blocking Arden's path to his front door as Arden climbed out of his orange Kharmann Ghia.

Arden closed his eyes, took a deep breath and said, "I have several witnesses, Harry, Leesing and even your daughter, who will swear you said the fence was mine. As such, I am free to repair it any damn way I please. Now get off my property now, please."

Chapter 46

Saturday, October 25, 2008

Arden sipped coffee from his favorite mug. From Del Rio Steel, it was a reminder of the toughest case he had ever mediated. Thirteen other mediators failed before he settled the case in an afternoon. The mug had a chip on one side, so he sipped from the other side. Marisela and Sam were still asleep. The house was quiet. It had turned cold. Hundreds of thousands of furnaces in the Southlands lent the faint aroma of smoke to the air, which Arden found pleasant, reminding him of evenings at his grandfather's as a boy sitting by a crackling cedar fire on freezing, Iowa winter nights. Now, encased in his black, plush robe and sheep's wool-lined slippers, he felt comfortable and relaxed. He had almost succeeded in pushing thoughts of his emasculated retirement portfolio and the lost house in New Mexico from his mind, although such worries crept around the edge of his consciousness like a black wraith, intruding on his thoughts as he tried to finish an Edinburgh *Scotsman* newspaper crossword in his head. At least he had remembered to spell "harbour" with a "u" for one of the answers. Then a thought entered his mind unbidden about Sam's denuded college fund. He felt furious at the whole financial debacle and felt he was on the verge of doing something dramatic, yet what could he do?

He checked his heart; all was well. He had not told Marisela of an attack a few days before. She had enough to worry about. She had garnered an interview for a job, albeit lower paying, at Presser Labs. The interview, she said, had seemed to go well, but they had not called, emailed or written, not even to thank her for coming in.

Rising, Arden strolled into the living room. As he passed the living room's picture window, his gaze was drawn to the right side of his front lawn, where Buell, in blue jeans and a gray sweatshirt, dug near the sidewalk. With a wicked grin, Arden opened his front door and ambled out to the sidewalk and along to where Buell sweated as he dug his first posthole of the day to finish Arden's fence.

Arden sighted along the property line, closing one eye to be certain. "Good morning," he said, toasting Buell with his chipped coffee mug.

"Morning," Buell muttered, using a shovel to try to deepen the hole, which appeared to be blocked by the root of one of the jacarandas, magnolias or eucalyptus trees that shaded the quiet street.

"If it wouldn't be too much trouble," Arden said, his voice the soul of good neighborliness, "would you mind keeping your building materials and tools off my property?" He gestured at a 6-by-6 that lay across the property line, and a shovel, hammer and trowel that sat crowding his rose bed.

Buell glared at him, eyes slits, lips forming a narrow, angry white line.

"I just don't want my roses damaged," Arden explained, still smiling. "I'd hate for you to have to pay to replace them. Some are rare, the pink Damask, for example, and rather expensive."

Breathing audibly through his nose as he glared at Arden, Buell yanked the post back onto his property. He grabbed the shovel, hammer and trowel, and threw them onto his lawn. The hammer stuck in the turf and rocked from the force of the throw. "Satisfied?"

"Yes, and thank you." Arden nodded his thanks and, his slippers padding on the flagstone walk, strolled back toward his front door. He could feel Buell's glare follow him with every step and, if looks could kill, Marisela would have been widowed.

Chapter 47

Monday, October 27, 2008

"You identified the two burglars in the photo-array for Detective Ranjan," the assistant DA, Joseph Fernandez, told Arden as the attorney consulted his notes in one of the DA's conference rooms.

"I told Detective Ranjan that I was far from certain," Arden said. "I *was* hit on the head just after I saw them."

A tall, thin man wearing a light suit who moved with measured ease, Fernandez looked at Arden with disbelief.

"You're sure you can't do anything about pressing fraud charges against Richard Sloane?" Arden asked.

The attorney shook his head. "As I said, the SEC dealt with that issue. There's nothing more I can do. You might be able to file a civil case against him. You're certain you can't ID the burglars?"

Arden shook his head.

Fernandez sighed. "At least you can testify about what happened that day."

Arden shook his head.

The attorney stared at him and frowned.

"I can't," Arden said.

"You were there. You told the officers all about it."

"I don't remember now." The assistant DA stared at him, reminding Arden of the way his mother looked at him when he was five and insisted he had not broken the record player. "My memory's been hit or miss recently. Today, it's all miss."

"Are you sure?"

"Certain."

"Yet you remembered everything when you spoke with Ranjan."

"Not everything."

"Enough to ID the burglars."

"That was then, this is now."

"Now, after we talked about Sloane." Fernandez peered at Arden. Arden thought he detected a warning deep in Fernandez's dark eyes. Even so, Arden fell into a patient silence.

"You're certain you don't remember them?"

"I remember waking up, going to work, losing a fortune in Antioch stock due to that criminal Sloane, and arriving home. I even remember reaching for the doorknob, then nothing."

"A selective memory loss." Fernandez nodded as if he understood.

"The doctor said it might be like that."

"It comes and goes?" Fernandez sounded understanding.

"Like the tides."

"Maybe it'll come back for the trial."

"Maybe, but I wouldn't count on it."

"Notice any patterns?"

Arden shook his head.

"I do." The assistant DA set his pen down carefully and set his elbows on the table between them. Leaning forward, he said, "Enough of this bullshit," his voice low and angry. "You're pissed because I won't prosecute Sloane. Get over it. The SEC charged him. He'll pay his debt to society."

"He's serving barely enough time to pay a day's interest on his debt."

The attorney's face hardened into an angry mask. "I'll subpoena you to testify."

"I don't remember."

"I can have you arrested as a material witness."

"I do not remember." Arden enunciated each word slowly and carefully, as if talking to someone who was hard of hearing.

"You don't cooperate with me, I'll put you in jail on a material witness warrant until such time as your memory returns."

"If I remember law school correctly, a material witness warrant is for a witness who is a flight risk, and is not to be used preventatively or to coerce testimony. Isn't that correct?"

"An obstruction of justice charge suits me just fine."

Arden could see a few ways around that charge, but remained silent. Why reveal your entire arsenal before the battle is joined?

Fernandez appeared to take Arden's silence for acquiescence. "Now," he said, leaning back in his chair and appearing to relax, "do you remember the two burglars you saw in your house on the afternoon of August 5?"

"No."

"You told detective Ranjan that a wallet he recovered was your property."

"I was mistaken."

"You found a $2 bill hidden in it, which you stated was yours." The ADA checked the notes before him and said, "You said you collected $2 bills because of the painting on the back of the signing of the Constitution."

Arden opened his mouth to correct the attorney's error, but closed it. "I don't collect $2 bills and I have no idea what's on the back of one."

"No interest in American history?"

"Not recently. I'm reading some novels my wife recommended. Reality is too depressing, even if it has passed."

"You won't cooperate?"

"I would if I could, but I can't, my memory being what it is. I am sorry."

Fernandez swallowed and worked his mouth, as if his anger was making it hard to speak. Finally he said, "I had one onerous gentleman in custody for 33 months on an obstruction charge."

"You file charges against Sloane and I'll see what I can remember. As I said, my memory comes and goes. It seems worse when I am under stress and I am very stressed about Richard Sloane."

"You've been watching too much TV, Mr. Jeffries. I don't make deals like that, ever."

"Then I don't remember."

"Thirty-three months. Do you remember?"

"My doctor will back me up: memory loss."

"Jail's a rough place."

"I don't remember."

Fernandez paused and blew the air out of his mouth. "At least your daughter can testify about the iPod."

"Leave her out of this," Arden snapped.

Fernandez stopped and stared at Arden. "Mr. Jeffries, you're daughter is a witness to a crime, as are you. I will call her and expect her cooperation when, where and however often my office requires it. If not, she can join you in jail on an obstruction charge."

"If you do, I will cooperate with the defendants."

"What?" the ADA asked, shocked.

"I'll take the stand for the defendants and state that they are not the men who burgled my home."

"Your memory coming back?"

"Selectively."

"That would be most unwise, Mr. Jeffries. You refuse to cooperate?"

"I don't remember."

"Thirty-three months, Mr. Jeffries."

"I don't remember."

"You might in 33 months."

Chapter 48

Tuesday, October 28, 2008

"You eat my candy bar?" a deep voice demanded.

Torn from considering the best course to take with Sam, Arden looked up from his bunk to behold a muscular inmate at the door to Arden's LA County Jail cell. "I didn't see any candy bar."

"You're ass is right where I left it," the muscular inmate said, making it sound like an accusation of murder.

Arden bit back the response that no one should leave chocolate bars sitting around a jail. The other prisoner topped 6 feet and his muscular arms sported tattoos of an iron cross, a pair of SS lightning bolts, and various other intricate designs Arden never wanted to get close enough to decipher. "I am sorry for your loss, but I didn't take your chocolate bar."

The inmate glared down at Arden, his clenched fists resting on his trim waist.

"I'd be happy to buy you a candy bar," Arden offered in the interest of an equitable solution to the impasse. The smell of sweat, urine and fried food permeated the jail; a smell he had yet to get used to and hoped he never would.

"Three for eating mine." The inmate's face was set in a scowl. Arden noticed a faint white scar that ran from the flattened bridge of the inmate's nose up and across his forehead in a jagged line. Arden had already learned that inmates were segregated by ethnicity, gang affiliation and sexual orientation for their safety, but this inmate saw nothing wrong with extorting candy from a fellow Caucasian, heterosexual, non-gang member.

"I think one is more reasonable," Arden offered, shifting on the bunk and trying to slip past the inmate to stand up. He would have added, 'since I didn't eat your chocolate bar in the first place,' but thought that would be detrimental to an equitable and peaceful resolution to the negotiations.

"Three," the inmate repeated, shoving Arden down onto the bunk as Arden started to slip past him. The bunk squeaked and groaned as Arden landed on it. "Four if you keep up yer bitching."

Arden eyed the entrance to the cell. Two inmates walked past. Neither paid any attention to the drama unfolding in the cell.

"Why don't we go over to the concession and get a couple of candy bars," Arden offered with a reassuring, even friendly grin. "We can eat them and talk about it."

"Three." The inmate put his hands on the metal side of the bunk above Arden. He looked down at Arden as he flexed his arms, the muscles rippling the tattoos as if there were snakes under the skin. "I eat all three."

"Three seems excessive and unfair."

The inmate laughed. "Four then, motherfucka."

"That's unreasonable."

The fist hit Arden with amazing speed. He hadn't even seen the inmate take his hand off the top bunk before Arden's head slammed back against the cement wall.

"Five, now," the inmate said, dragging Arden off the bunk.

The inmate hit Arden again. Arden's head felt as if a sledgehammer had hit his left cheek. A blow like one from a baseball bat swung by a home-run slugger struck the side of his head. His brain screamed from the pain. His cheek bone felt broken. A searing pain coursed through his head like a million-volt charge.

"I think we should talk about this," Arden managed to begin to say as the inmate propelled him toward the door through the fuzzy world Arden now perceived via a battered brain and half-closed left eye.

The inmate jerked Arden to a stop and slammed him back against the rear wall of the cell.

"Six."

"I don't see…"

Another blow crashed into the side of Arden's head.

"You okay, buddy?"

Arden heard the soft, youthful voice like honey in his ear, as if from a great distance.

"Sit up. Come on, up you come."

Arden felt himself maneuvered into a sitting position, the wall cold and hard against his aching back. His face, forearms, biceps, sides, stomach, and chest roared in agony. His head exploded with shooting pains every time he moved even the minutest amount. Forcing his eyes open, Arden kept them slits as the light assaulted his brain, intensifying the pounding in his head that made the cell walls vibrate nauseatingly.

"Can you talk?" the honeyed voice asked.

Arden kept his head still and tried to move his eyes to the side from whence the mellow voice came. The movement of his eyes caused a stabbing pain on the edges of his eye sockets as if someone was driving rusty spikes into them with a 64-pound sledgehammer. Desperate to know who was helping him, Arden slowly and with the greatest care turned his head.

The man wore an inmate's blue scrubs. Despite his youthful voice, the inmate was older than Arden. A silver-gray stubble added a sheen to his chin and cheeks, reflecting the light from the single, harsh recessed florescent fixture in the ceiling. The inmate's hands were warm and strong as they helped Arden to his unsteady feet and eased him gently onto the lower bunk.

"Thanks," Arden managed to mumble, although the single word sent a mind-splitting tsunami of pain throughout his head.

Half an hour later, the inmate had bathed Arden's face gently with a towel, checked that nothing was broken and introduced himself.

"Santee?" Arden was able to mumble.

"From Santee, just east of San Diego. Born and bred. Great town—50 years ago."

Arden winced as he tried to find a position that would ease the spasms of pain coursing through his battered body. "I need a doctor."

"Might not be the wisest course." Santee shook his head, causing his stringy gray hair to swish across in front of his eyes before he pushed it behind his ears with his long-fingered arthritic hands. His youthful voice seemed out of place in such an aged body. "Nothing broke. Last thing you want is it getting around you tole the guards somebody beat on you."

Arden would have pressed the matter, but the last thing he wanted to do was talk. Besides, he feared he could not get to his feet unaided, let alone reach a guard to ask for a doctor. Santee's kindness seemed out of place. "What are you in for?"

"Never ask anyone that," Santee said, then added, "This and that. Last time cops got me for a robbery. I was going to ask them which one, but thought better of it. You?"

"Obstruction of justice and contempt of court." Arden ran his tongue around the inside of his mouth. All his teeth were intact, although several were loose and he felt blood along the gums. He spat blood onto the floor to clear his mouth.

"Contempt? What'd you do? Piss on a judge?" Santee asked, laughing. "You ever hear about the drunk who decided he had to take a hellacious squirt while his long-winded attorney presented his case. Everyone in the courtroom hears liquid hitting the floor. Turns out the drunk decided he may as well let loose right there. He was already going to jail and, given it was February in Denver, jail was warmer than the streets. What'd you do?"

"Didn't cooperate with the police about a burglary."

"Cops got all the advantages anyway without us helping them any."

Then Arden remembered. "I have to call my daughter." He struggled to his feet, the room spinning as nausea engulfed him. By flinging an arm out to steady himself against the bunk, he managed to remain upright.

"I'll help you along to the phones," Santee offered, taking Arden under an arm. "Be a wait, but I can stand in line for you while you sit and rest a time. Just be careful what you say on the phone."

"Why?" Arden asked as they shuffled toward the cell door.

"Screws tape every call."

"That legal?"

"It's their phone."

Arden stopped and groaned as pain shot down his back. Santee kept Arden upright. "I can't have my call taped."

"It important?"

Arden nodded, then stopped, deeply regretting having moved his head.

"Sit down. I'll be right back."

A few minutes later Santee returned and, glancing at the cell door to ensure no one was watching, offered Arden a neon yellow, plastic mobile phone.

"If you stand right next to the window, you can get a signal," Santee said. "Don't talk long. Guards watch for anyone standing near a window, watching for contraband cell phones."

"How'd you get it?" Arden asked, accepting the neon yellow phone.

"Wife brought it in with my daughter. Guards thought it was a toy. Only thing, I don't have a charger, so talk fast. I figure you got two minutes of juice left. Still need to find me a charger."

Arden caught Sam between classes. After a quick explanation for how he was able to call her from jail, he said, "Sam, I don't want you to tell the police that the iPod is yours."

"I already did."

"Say you were mistaken."

"All my songs are on it."

"Must be on dozens of other kids' iPods, too." Arden stood just beneath the cell window, his eyes flicking back and forth across the section of the common area he could see through the open cell doorway. No guards yet. Santee stood slouched against the door jam, thumbs hooked around the top of his blue scrubs, rubbing his back against the metal doorframe as if he had an especially stubborn itch.

"I don't get it, Dad. Why wouldn't you want me to help the police put the guys who robbed us away?"

"It just isn't right. I'm running out of time, Sam. I need you to do it, please. Tell them you aren't certain the iPod is yours."

There was a long pause. "I can't do that, Dad."

"Please, for me. It's important."

The cell phone faded and then came back.

"Can't they just use my statement?"

"They will, but it'll weaken the prosecution's case, and the defense will demand to know why you aren't there to testify in person."

The signal faded again and came back, weaker.

"I can't, Dad."

"Sam, can you help me, please? This is important. It's the right thing to do."

"People are supposed to cooperate with the police."

"Not when the law's wrong."

"I can't, Dad. It'd be wrong."

"It'd be right. People should get what they deserve for their crimes."

"The burglars will, if I testify."

"No, they won't."

"I don't know...."

"Didn't I raise you to recognize what is right and just?"

The phone went dead.

Chapter 49

Wednesday, October 29, 2008

"What happened to you?" Marisela asked, shocked at the sight of Arden as he sat down gingerly across from her in the LA jail's loud, congested visiting room.

"Just a little disagreement over a candy bar," Arden said as he shifted in the metal chair to try to ease the assortment of raging pains in his battered body. "I'll be fine."

"Your face…Your eye is half closed and…."

He met her worried eyes through the thick Plexiglass that separated them and assured her, "I'll be fine. Nothing broken." He thought some of his ribs might be, but they would heal if he left them alone. He stared at her, longing to touch her, hold her, smell her, kiss her. He could do none of that. The jail only allowed non-contact visits. Unfortunately, Arden thought as he shifted again and winced, there was no such rule between inmates.

Arden asked, "Where's Sam?"

"She was going to come, but she and her friends are having a car wash to raise money for her for Purdue."

"Nice friends."

"An excuse to flirt with boys in their cars. She got a work-study position at Purdue. Ten bucks an hour for 10 hours a week in the Department of Engineering office."

"Fantastic."

"She's decided to live near campus, share an apartment with three other girls, and do without a car."

"Our little cost-cutter."

Marisela pursed her lips and sighed. "You shouldn't be in here."

"I'll stay out of trouble from now on," Arden promised. He tugged at the blue scrub's tie at his waist. It seemed too tight, aggravating the bruises on his hips and back, but he feared his pants falling down if he loosened it.

"The ADA said you could get out of here right now."

"I can't."

"You said you'd never forget what the burglars looked like." Marisela stared at Arden.

Couples, young women with babies, and parents and children from toddlers to teenagers sat in the long row of chairs facing their inmate relatives through the scuffed and marred Plexiglass between them. Each couple spoke via a black telephone, just as Arden did with Marisela.

"I thought I would remember," Arden said, "but when I looked at the photos the police showed me, I just wasn't certain."

Marisela tilted her head to one side, pursed her lips and gave him the look he knew after decades of marriage. She did not believe him.

"I just wasn't certain," Arden said. He glanced around the room, the burble and low rumble of dozens of conversations filled the silence between him and Marisela. Looking back at her, he noticed that she had not brought the newspaper crosswords he had asked her to bring.

"Why didn't you cooperate? They'll be free now, free to go out and rob and hurt someone else. This time," Marisela said, leaning toward Arden, angry, "they might kill someone."

"I couldn't."

"Why?"

Arden sighed. "They cost us a few hundred bucks for the insurance deductible, my grandfather's scimitar, and some time to replace the stuff they took."

"I haven't slept since then," Marisela shot back, her face cold and hard. "Neither has Sam. We're afraid half the time and terrified the rest of the time if we're home alone, which is always now with you stuck in here. And they attacked you."

"Maybe it affected my memory," Arden said. He felt too sore and weary to explain, let alone to argue.

"It didn't affect your memory. It affected your good sense. I don't believe you're doing this, Arden."

"I have no choice."

"Of course you have a choice. Cooperate with the DA and put those bastards away forever."

"I can't do that."

"Why in the name of God not?"

Arden hesitated.

"Why?"

Arden closed his eyes and then opened them. "Sloane robbed us and thousands of other stockholders of hundreds of thousands of dollars and he got a few months in jail and a tiny fine," Arden explained in a rush. "Those burglars took a few thousand dollars worth of stuff and they're facing 25 years to life. Was that fair? Was that justice? The punishment should fit the damage done by the crime."

"You aren't the one to decide that," Marisela exploded, drawing looks from those around them, as well as from a roving guard, who stalked down the row of visitors with a stern look.

Arden smiled at the guard and nodded, as if to say there was nothing wrong and that they would keep it down. After stopping to glare a warning, the guard resumed his patrolling.

"I can't believe you convinced Sam not to cooperate with the police," Marisela whispered into the phone.

"I did?"

"She told me some lame story about it not being her iPod. She finally admitted you convinced her not to help the police. You've gone insane. Teaching our teenaged daughter not to help the police when some vile…some vile scum broke into our house and stole our things, terrifying us all."

"It wasn't fair."

"Your damn right it wasn't fair. You're crazy." Marisela's jaw was set as if it was stone. "What happened to you? I thought I knew you. I thought you were a good man." She glared at him with a look that made him want to say he had changed his mind. "I just hope you can live with your decision."

They fell silent, staring off into space, each stealing glances at each other after brief, tense intervals.

After a time, Marisela looked right and left and leaned closer to Arden, her nose almost touching the Plexiglass. After a moment's hesitation, her knuckles white as she clutched the phone, she said in a cascade of words, "When I was in college, I didn't press charges against someone. Years later I heard another victim finally had the guts to do it. When she did, dozens of others came forward to say he'd done the same thing to them. I could have prevented all of it, but I didn't. Since then, whenever I think of it, I feel like I'm going to vomit over what I didn't do."

Arden frowned, confused, staring at his wife. "What happened?"

Marisela looked down, ran her hand across the marred, graffiti-covered surface of the counter between them and said, "When I was in college a professor, someone I trusted and thought was my mentor, was talking to me late one night after class and... and...."

Arden gasped. "My God, I..."

"It was 20 years ago," Marisela said, before he could say any more, dismissing the episode with a shake of her head and a wave of her hand. "I told myself I didn't even know for certain what had happened, but I was just lying to myself so I wouldn't have to tell anyone about it." She leaned back, closed her eyes for a moment and said, as if talking to herself, "In a way it set me on the path to the life I have now. I applied to CSLA, transferred, met Dr. Graham, and she got me interested in biochemistry. She encouraged me and I went on to do my masters and doctorate. If I'd stayed where I was I never would have done any of that." She opened her eyes and looked at Arden. "I wouldn't have got the job at Antioch...or met you." She paused, staring at him, her eyes softening. "You were the first man I dated after it happened."

After a long moment, Arden whispered, "Why me?"

Her dark eyes met his and held them. "I thought I could trust you."

Arden nodded, struggling to assimilate what she had said.

"I should have stood up to him years ago, when it happened," Marisela said. "Then he couldn't have hurt anyone else."

Arden reached out to hold her hands but the cold, thick Plexiglass blocked him. "You were young and scared."

"So was the girl who pressed charges," Marisela shot back, bitter, pulling her hands away, even though he could not reach her anyway. Her eyes, fierce, glared at him as she said, "You aren't young or scared."

"I couldn't send the burglars away for the rest of their lives. It wouldn't fit their crime."

"It may fit one of their future crimes. Then you can try to explain to the victim's families why you let them go." Marisela rose, but still held the phone.

Looking down at Arden, she seemed to be considering whether to tell him something else. He stared up at her, still taking in all she had said. After a long silence, he asked, "What?"

She shook her head once, as if to herself, paused and said, "Buell was digging a posthole. He hit a buried telephone cable. They billed him for the repair, probably more than the fence cost us to repair."

"Maybe there is justice in the world," Arden said, wondering at the sudden change in the conversation. "Not much, but some."

Chapter 50

Wednesday, October 29, 2008

"This is the luckiest day in your short life," Chester announced to his client as he rumbled into the interview room at the jail.

Angel looked up, sullen and ready for another sparring match with his lawyer over his firm decision to go to trial.

"The witness who placed you at the scene—the homeowner—refused to press charges, identify you or even participate in the case."

"*Loco?*"

"If he is, you better hope he stays that way. I heard that he even told the ADA he'd help us if the DA went ahead with the case," Chester said, his shock at the news still showing. He pranced around the room with glee, dancing with his black briefcase as if it were a slim, beguiling partner. "Never seen it happen and I've seen some extremely weird things in my time."

"What now?" Angel asked, confused and uncertain what it all meant.

"So what now? Now you're a free man, my Angel," Chester exclaimed, slapping his client on the shoulder with a flabby hand. "Fly, fly away, my Angel—and to show your gratitude, I could use a new stereo for my car: iPod capable, CD, with some killer speakers."

Chapter 51

Friday, October 31, 2008

Arden stood outside the LA County Jail at the north end of downtown Los Angeles, the early morning breeze tickling his face with its cool fingers. The horizon was lightening behind the twin towers of the stark, overcrowded jail. Slit windows lent the gray towers the appearance of a medieval castle ruled by a dour tyrant.

Late the day before Arden had been hauled into an unannounced conference with his attorney.

"The DA's dropped the case against the burglars and the obstruction charge against you," his attorney announced.

"Why?" Arden asked, stunned at the turn of events.

"Without you, his case is weak. If you testify for the defendants, his case is non-existent."

Relief flooded Arden's stressed, exhausted and battered body. With it came a great sense of victory; he had stood up to the DA and had not cooperated in a prosecution he believed to be unjust.

"Don't feel too special," his attorney warned. "You're just one of 60,000 inmates released early this year because of overcrowding. Guess they feel safer releasing you than a serial rapist."

In the cool morning air, Arden wiggled his aching shoulders in the T-shirt he now wore. It was an XXL. He wore a medium. The leather belt holding the 48" jeans up around his 36" waist had a worn hole six holes along from where he had it cinched in the first hole. The socks and shoes on his feet were also clownishly large as he shuffled along the sidewalk toward where family and friends could park to pick up inmates.

Earlier that morning, the discharge officer had handed Arden a plastic bag of clothes.

"These aren't mine," Arden said, eyeing the unfamiliar garb.

The officer grunted, grabbing a bag for the next prisoner about to be discharged behind Arden.

"I said these aren't mine," Arden repeated, holding up the line and earning glares from the mixture of Latino and black men behind him.

"Take those or you can go back inside and wait until we find your clothes," the officer said in a monotone. "Could take a day or two; your choice."

Arden sighed and shuffled over in his prison sliders—flip-flops—to the long, narrow holding room with a nicked wood bench down the middle. The bench showed cigarette burns and gang graffiti between where other free men were changing into their or someone else's clothes. At least Arden had been given the bag containing his own wallet, watch and keys.

Arden stood in front of the jail and looked southwest up at the lights of the skyscrapers clustered in downtown Los Angeles. After jail, they represented a different world. A gust of wind caught his face, chilling him. The windbreaker he had been issued was huge but its size allowed him to wrap it twice around his torso, keeping him warm as he waited for Marisela.

Just released inmates trudged past him, many heading toward the bus stop at the end of the block or Union Station three blocks up Vignes Street. Men shuffled their feet along the broken sidewalk. Arden realized that, like him, many of the inmates had got the wrong clothes back. Some of the men spoke in low tones. None seemed excited to be free. They reminded Arden of a shift change at a foundry. In the glare of lights from the jail, he saw many a suspicious look. He was the only white man in sight.

Arden frowned as another of the released inmates emerged from the metal jail doors, which closed with a metallic click. The young Hispanic inmate hesitated as he left the building before sauntering toward Arden, joining the stream of men heading back to their lives.

"I know you," Arden exclaimed.

The young Hispanic slowed as he approached Arden, but did not stop.

"Wait," Arden urged the young man. "We've met before."

The young man, his head down, jacket collar up—apparently he had got his own clothes back—kept walking. His dark eyes were narrowed and, although he kept looking straight ahead, Arden felt that he had seen Arden. Just as he was about to pass, Arden grabbed his arm. In an instant the man jammed Arden's head back against the concrete wall of the jail, a thick forearm wedged into Arden's neck, constricting his breathing.

"What up, Homes?"

"You robbed my house," Arden managed to splutter as pain shot through his head from bouncing off the jail's wall. Terror rose in him like a monster.

The forearm eased on Arden's windpipe, just for a moment, then was reapplied with even greater pressure.

"So what."

Arden gasped, smelling the nicotine on Angel's breath. Angel looked right and left as other inmates trudged past, paying only the briefest passing attention to the altercation. Angel's eyes came to rest for a moment on the security camera pointed at them mounted high on the wall near the jail's main entrance. Angel released his hold on Arden and continued walking toward the bus stop.

Arden swallowed, felt his neck and, concluding he could breathe again, rushed after Angel.

"Don't follow me," Angel threatened, stopping to shoot a warning glare back at Arden, who halted mid-step.

"I just wanted to talk."

Angel took in Arden's bruised face. "You should learn to shut up."

"I did."

Angel stopped, stared at Arden and a grin spread across his broad face. "You the one?"

Arden nodded.

Angel watched a couple of black inmates push past Arden, "Why?"

"Why'd you rob my house?"

Angel sniffed, pursed his lips and, glancing right and left, said, "I'm free on that."

"Why then?"

Angel snickered, as if he had been caught in a white lie. "Needed some cash."

"What were you so desperate to buy?"

Angel shrugged and one end of his mouth turned up in a half-smile. He shrugged.

"You robbed me and my family for money you didn't know what to do with?"

"I found a use for it."

"What?"

Angel looked around. No one was near. "Just stuff. Help my *mami* out. Save for electrician school. Get some nice things."

"You could get a job."

Angel straightened. "I got a job."

"Good, good," Arden said, not wanting to anger the muscular young man.

"Minimum wage." Angel spat. "If I still have it."

"I hope you do; beats robbing houses and ending up here."

"You ever work in a metal-fabricating plant?"

Chapter 52

The long black livery car conveyed Sloane from a private airport near Boston to his house in Chestnut Hill. He had just returned from meeting with his attorneys in New York about his severance suit against Antioch. It was 37 degrees with a crisp wind gusting out of the southwest, but there was no snow on the ground and he felt good to be home. Although he owned five houses, he had always considered Boston home. He would miss it the most if he had to go to prison, even if it turned out to be a Federal minimum security camp in Florida. He still had great faith in his attorney. Lincoln would find a way out of this mess.

"Maddy!" Sloane called as he stepped through the 18-foot double mahogany front doors. "Maddy!"

He walked through the marble foyer. From the balcony, he surveyed the great room. Pumpkin, skeleton, and black cat decorations adorned the walls and windows. They had been put up for a planned Halloween party which Maddy, out of shame for Richard's conviction, had been forced, she claimed, to cancel. Sloane's comment that they had attended parties at Michael Milken's in Los Angeles did nothing to change her mind.

"You're home," Maddy announced as she came bustling out of the south wing. She rolled a carryon bag the size of a bar fridge after her across the marble floor, which clicked on the ochre grout between the 20-inch diagonally laid tiles.

"Going somewhere?" Sloane asked, miffed at his cool reception.

Maddy stopped. "Edgar St. Pierre asked me for a visit."

"Edgar?"

"To his little place in Vermont."

"Should I get ready?" St. Pierre was a good man to know.

Maddy shook her head. "He just invited me."

"Well, have a good time," Sloane said, confused. "When will you be back?"

She stood straighter, looked him in the eye and said, "I am not coming back, Richard. I want a divorce."

Sloane stood in shocked silence.

"You have made such a mess of things," Maddy said, shaking her head and pursing her lips with distaste as if she had just tasted month-old milk. "It is not in me to go on living with someone who would needlessly squander such an opportunity, not to mention such a position."

"Squander?"

"The SEC fine and stepping down as CEO." She shook her head at the horror of it all.

"I didn't squander a damn thing," Sloane roared. "I did my best for the good of Antioch, for you and me."

"You threw it all away. Prison time? Really Richard. Who goes to jail over such things?"

"I had no choice. The board forced me to make the deal. If I hadn't, I would have faced a jury and been in prison for years."

"Ridiculous."

"Ridiculous, but there was no way to avoid it." He was about to tell Maddy that Lincoln might still come through, given time, when she said, "People like us do not go to jail, Richard."

"Apparently we do," Sloane said, amazed at his wife's position. No way he would mention Lincoln's plans now.

"I still love you, Richard, but I really cannot stay," Maddy said, turning with her bag toward the elevator.

"Why the hell not?"

"There is really no need to curse, Richard."

"Why not?"

"I have needs, expectations, social standing, Richard. I can't just throw it all away like you did." She continued on her way.

"I did not throw anything away." He rushed after her.

"I thought I knew you, but apparently I was mistaken. You just are not who I thought you were."

"You are making a mistake."

"I think not."

"I will be a CEO again," Sloane vowed, his voice rising in anger, echoing off the great room's distant glass wall.

"You will be lucky to become CEO of some struggling little biotech startup in Bangalore."

"Wait and see."

"No, Richard, I will not wait for the man you apparently have become."

"Because of Edgar St. good-damn Pierre?"

Maddy jabbed the button for the elevator to take her down to the garage and her waiting silver Maybach 62 S sedan and driver. "He is still CEO of Richardson Development and Construction, as well as serving on the board of nine other companies. What positions do you hold? I know him. I know what he values and how he conducts himself. You, well…" As she stepped onto the elevator, she added, "Don't worry, dear. Edgar will take excellent care of me." The elevator door closed and she was gone.

"Silly bitch," Sloane said, turning to head to the bar for a drink. "Good riddance and may Edgar tire of you after one fucking boring night in bed with the missionary position the most adventurous position she'll try, and she doesn't even like having her tits fondled."

Chapter 53

Angel lay on his elbows atop Tiffany with a pillow under her rump. The position with the pillow changed the angle of entry and vastly improved the sensations he felt as they had sex. Angel had missed sex during his short stint in jail.

As they lay side by side afterward, Angel smoked a Marlboro Red. Tiffany lolled beside him, a towel beneath her so she would not have to change the sheets. Angel stared at her breasts for a while, reaching over to fondle them and play with the nipples until Tiffany squirmed and whined, "That's too much. I'm sensitive there."

With nothing to touch and nothing to say, Angel reached over to the chipped bedside table and grabbed the remote control. He clicked the power button for the television. Nothing happened. He clicked it again.

"It doesn't work," Tiffany said. "You have to go turn on the TV, then the remote works to change the channels and the volume."

Angel swore and dropped the remote on the bedside table.

"Don't break it," Tiffany snapped.

"It's already busted."

"You going to buy me a new one?"

Angel took a long drag on his cigarette.

Someone shot off rounds for an early morning Halloween celebration. Tiffany sat up, clutching a pillow to her ample breasts.

Angel wondered why she bothered to hide her best assets. Didn't he deserve a nice view? He grabbed the pillow. She grabbed it back. "I'm cold."

"Turn on the heat."

"It's shut off. If you hadn't got caught on that last lick, we could have heat and a new TV, maybe a nice big one."

"Had a beauty of a flat-screen in the truck."

"You sell it?"

Angel nodded.

"Where's the money?"

Angel shrugged. Should have kept the money for trade school, but it wasn't enough anyway. Tiffany fell silent, staring down at Angel as he cradled his head with one hand and held his cigarette with the other.

"If you got a little cash, we could get a TV, maybe some other nice things," Tiffany tempted, leaning down to kiss him between drags on the cigarette.

Angel nodded, staring at her dangling tits. He pursed his lips at the thought of having to get more money. A nice lick and he could be in Phoenix and be an electrician before he knew it. Never have to do this shit again. He did not need this, not after getting sprung on the burglary with life inside hanging over his head.

"Just one tiny bit of work and we could fix this place up nice."

Angel glanced around the bedroom. The carpet had beer, burrito and God-only-knew-what stains scattered around the sagging bed. The television was a cathode-ray model and only 32 inches. The door to the bathroom had peeling white paint and the walls had an array of water stains from the ceiling. Angel knew the rest of the one-bedroom apartment wasn't in any better condition. "Move."

"That takes money," Tiffany said.

Angel nodded. Everything took money. Trade school took money. Living took money. Breathing took money.

He closed his eyes and considered. The colleges were in session. Lots of busy *pendajo* students in libraries who thought nothing of leaving their $800 laptops on a table for a minute while they went to grab a book, use the *bano* or buy a soda. Hard to fit in on a campus though; had to dress differently and hide his tattoos. He couldn't remember if he had the right clothes that fit anymore since he had lost some weight in jail surviving on a baloney sandwich for lunch and a slop of meat, potatoes and unidentifiable sauce for dinner.

Free on bail, Diego had spent recent evenings using a baseball bat to remove the side mirrors from cars, making a nice stack of cash. A Mercedes mirror cost $450 new, $250 used. Angel knew a mechanic who would give him $100 for each mirror as long as the mounting bracket was still usable. Angel was a lot better with a screwdriver and rubber hammer than Diego was with a baseball bat. *Idiota* destroyed more mirrors than he sold.

"What are you thinking?" Tiffany asked, clutching her pillow and peering down at Angel with her luminous dark eyes.

"Work." Thinking through the possibilities: colleges, cars, LAX or maybe hit *El Tigre*'s and take all his hot property? Maybe another house? Options. Dump Tiffany. Maria was looking fine and interested. Her apartment was a damn sight nicer than Tiffany's dump. He would need some cash for a new girl. What would pay the most for the least time and risk? Try the airport and the metro. If they didn't pay, try another house, maybe. And if someone was home? No way he would face 25-to-life again. Never again. Angel looked up at Tiffany and asked, "Cesar still selling that three-eight?"

Chapter 54

Arden waited and waited for Marisela outside the jail, but she did not come. The day before after a long wait to use the phone, he had left her a message that he would be released the next day. Alone in front of the jail, he listened to the rumble of morning traffic on the 101 Freeway. He heard fireworks and the occasional gunshot as people celebrated Halloween early at various isolated points across the Southlands. With no one in sight and the hour since he was released long passed, he gave up. Maybe she had not heard the message.

Arden trudged down Vignes Street under the weak October morning sun to Union Station to catch a bus to the Westside. After a long wait for the right bus, and an even longer ride with many stops and three transfers, he finally reached Santa Maria. He trudged home. Rusty woofed a half-hearted greeting from Harry's front porch before circling back down to sleep. Arden's house was dark, the blinds shut. Was everyone still asleep?

Inside he found mail, including a bill from the city: $500 for not maintaining a fence in a safe manner, and another $500 for not removing or moving a fence that stood on someone else's property. Regrettably, he had been late fixing and moving the fences.

Glum at the prospect of another $1,000 gone, he spotted a note on the kitchen table:

Arden,

I do not know you anymore. I thought I did, but now you do not seem to know right from wrong. I can't trust you anymore and until I can, Sam and I will have to live apart from you.

I am sorry.

Marisela

Chapter 54

Thursday, November 20, 2008

Richard Sloane strode up a side street of the Bund in Shanghai on the west bank of the Huangpu River. Where Britain, Russia, the United States, Germany, and Japan once maintained powerful banks and obscenely wealthy trading houses, Sloane now passed an Armani store with suits in the display windows starting at $1,500. Sloane had a dozen in his closets at his various homes. After inspecting a double-breasted tan suit, he found the building he wanted and entered its simple, yet elegant interior.

On the lift to the fifth floor he checked his email, more from habit than from anything else. He was so used to being involved he still expected 150 emails a day asking for his input, advice or a decision. Even now, he received at least 50 a day from friends and business associates arranging parties, speeches and exploring possible business relationships. He smiled at an invitation to the Kentucky Derby in the spring from Ken Lim, CEO of Great Northern Golf and Athletics. Ken was trying to entice Sloane to join Great Northern, but Sloane was far from certain he wanted to leave the pharmaceutical industry.

Sloane checked an email from Jennifer DeCarlo, who was supposed to be waiting for him back at the hotel. She had sent him a photo of her in a red silk gown she wanted to buy, asking if he liked it. He did. At $1,999 it was a steal, she said. She had been fantastic in and out of bed since Maddy left. If he had had to pay for such service the past three weeks, it would have run at least $2,000 a night. She knew so much and all of it related to pleasing a man. He often even had trouble staying in control until he was inside her. He told her to buy the silk gown. She could model it for him tonight, at least for a few minutes until she would no longer need it.

The lift door silently slid open and Sloane stepped into a simple reception room. A mix of heaven-sent aromas reached his nose and made his mouth twitch in anticipation. A middle-aged Chinese man in a dark suit stood guard at a polished wood lectern. Having established that he was expected—the man at the lectern spoke perfect English, accented to mimic public schooling in England—Sloane was ushered into the restaurant. He marveled at a massive crystal chandelier-like feature that dominated one end of the room. Ceremonially escorted to a table with a view over the river, the Pudong district and the rest of glittering Shanghai lit for as far as the eye could see, Sloane met his party of two.

"We hope your trip over was smooth," Gentao Lo said, as the trio sat down after shaking hands.

"It was," Sloane said with a smile and a nod. The corporate jet the pair had sent had been the epitome of comfort. After a nice hour with Jennifer trying a new position she had read about where she put a pillow under her rump to change the angle of entry, which proved extremely sensual, he had slept most of the way across the Pacific in the aft cabin's Queen-size bed. He was fresh for the meeting.

While the three men made small talk and perused the á la carte menu, a delicate glass of lime jelly with pieces of dragon fruit, fresh mango and shrimp topped with a garlic foam appeared as if from nowhere.

With experience doing business in Asia, Sloane was far from surprised that business was not mentioned as they savored their multi-course meal: candied lotus roots with osamanthus and stuffed with slow-cooked grains; drunken chicken poached with Shao Xing wine and covered in shaved ice; Shanghai smoked fish; crispy beef strips with sun-dried pickled orange peel; double-boiled clear chicken consommé with Chinese vegetables; *xiao long bao*; and a red cooked braised pork knuckle served on a large square plate and swimming in a thick, sticky soy-based sauce. They sipped Long Jing tea and a fine Rhenish Guigal Côte Rotie.

It was only as the efficient white-coated waiters whisked away the remains of their extravagant meal and brushed the crumbs off the immaculate white tablecloth with tiny horsehair brushes that Sloane's mind turned to the reason for his long, if comfortable and entertaining flight across the Pacific. Even so, he said nothing as a waiter poured their after-dinner Remy Martin Louis XIII brandy from its sparkling Baccarat decanter. The hum and buzz of the restaurant had subsided as other diners departed for home, nightclubs or other rendezvous. After an appropriate interval, Gentao set his brandy snifter down, glanced at the third man at the table, Stephen Chin and, with an imperceptible nod from his partner, began, "We are more than happy that you decided to visit Shanghai. If we might raise the issue of our possible business together, Stephen and I have been wondering if you had yet had an opportunity to fully consider our offer?" Gentao's intense black eyes focused on Sloane and did not waiver.

"I have," Sloane said, "and it is an extremely generous and tempting offer."

"We carefully considered all the potential candidates and after much thorough and lengthy discussion the board unanimously agreed that our company and your background, experience and contacts are a fine, even a perfect match," Chin chipped in. Sloane knew that Chin and Lo had been friends for more than two decades after meeting while studying for their doctorates in biochemistry at the University of Minnesota. Their company, GenChin, had made them both billionaires.

"We would like tonight to formally invite you to join our firm as Chief Operating Officer of Phoenix Pharmaceuticals," Gentao said with great formality and gravitas.

Antioch's stock had been pummeled in the recent downtown, exacerbated by the SEC investigation and the problem with the lab-grown heart-valve trial. GenChin, Inc. had taken the opportunity to purchase Antioch Pharmaceuticals at a bargain-basement price. Now renamed Phoenix Pharmaceuticals, the reissued stock was rising with the SEC investigation behind it and the heart-valve trial back on track and headed for rapid FDA approval.

Sloane paused, smiled and said, "I formally accept your generous and kind offer." The offer would begin a month after he walked out of the federal detention facility having served the six months required under the deal Lincoln Avery had negotiated with the SEC.

The trio rose, shook hands and embraced, broad grins and back slaps all around.

When they sat back down to enjoy their brandy, Sloane smiled. Maddy was wrong. He was back on top again and not at some struggling startup in Bangalore. With China booming, his compensation for the new position was more than 15 percent greater than it had been with Antioch. China was the new land of opportunity. Go east young man. Given some time and intensive Cantonese lessons, Sloane planned to move from COO of Phoenix Pharmaceuticals to CEO of GenChin. With such grand thoughts, he toasted his new bosses and savored the brandy as it coursed down his throat like liquid gold.

Chapter 55

Sunday, December 7, 2008

Arden awoke at 5 am. He tried to get back to sleep. He tossed. He turned. Sleep eluded him, even though he lacked the will to get out of bed. With Marisela and Sam still at her parent's house, he was lonely and depressed. He had to summon the energy to breath, let alone to do anything.

After lying in bed for far too long, he finally berated himself enough to get dressed and drag himself downstairs for breakfast. He had to eat. He did not want to. After an intense internal debate, he finally accepted the need. With his cereal poured, he was holding the milk when he remembered that his Sunday morning television business report was on.

Arden clicked on the television in the living room. An analyst was reciting the dire economic numbers. "Between June 2007 and November 2008, Americans have lost on average one quarter of their net worth. Housing has fallen 20 percent from its peak, the S&P 500 is down 45 percent from its 2007 high, while total retirement assets have fallen 22 percent from $10.3 trillion in 2006 to $8 trillion in mid-2008."

Arden clicked off the television.

His stomach felt as if it was filled with bile, his face and body ached from his beating in jail and he felt as if death in the form of a massive heart attack would be a welcome release. The house was silent, as if nothing lived in it anymore, not even him. He had brought a crossword down to do at breakfast, but couldn't force himself to face doing it. What was the point?

He ate a few tentative bites of cereal before tossing the soggy remainder in the trash. It tasted like wet cardboard.

In their home office, he unsubscribed from the seven news and business websites that sent him alerts. He was glad he had already canceled his newspaper subscriptions in their attempt to save money. No news had become the only form of good news.

It was 7 am. He knew he should not go back to bed, even though it seemed the most desirable course. He looked around for something to do. He considered calling Marisela to try to talk to her again, but it was far too early on a Sunday morning. With nothing to do, he finally settled on a novel, Barry Unsworth's *Morality Play*, which Marisela had recommended but he had never read, because he never read novels. His favorites were nonfiction: American and world history, and biographies. He took *Morality Play* from a bookshelf and settled down on the sofa to try to read about a world far different from his own.

Chapter 56

Monday, December 8, 2008

Why did Monday bring the toughest cases? Probably, Arden thought as he dawdled down the hall toward conference room 7 at Equitable Mediation, because you felt a little out of practice after the weekend and a touch less sure of yourself. Today it was far worse than usual. He walked slower the closer he got to the conference room door. He was not surprised at his lack of drive. It took a superhuman effort for him to just get out of bed each morning. He missed Marisela and Sam as if a part of him had been removed. His attempts to convince Marisela to come home had been met with a barrage of unyielding refusals. Anguish and an unspeakable pain engulfed him, making every movement, every thought an unbearable effort. He felt tired all the time, barely ate and his level of caring about anything had plummeted to below zero. Nothing seemed to be worth the bother.

"You have Cain and Abel and their sister in there?" Donna asked as she cruised past on her way to her case in room 5.

"I fear so," Arden said, his voice flat.

"Watch out if Cain has the jawbone of an ass with him," Donna warned with a snicker.

"That was Samson, not Cain." Arden was about to thank Donna for a kind card she had sent after his release from jail, but she was already through the door into her conference room; no hesitation there.

After a deep breath, Arden stepped into his conference room. He said hello to the three siblings who had been feuding for four years since their father's last breath over the metal fabricating business he had left them. The company employed 65 people, owned a building and a dozen trucks, as well as an assortment of equipment, all of which produced a steady, healthy eight-figure profit.

Most recently during the protracted negotiation process, Arden had suggested allowing the sister who for years had been heavily involved in the company to have control of the firm in exchange for the two brothers having a larger share of the profits. The sister rejected the proposal, refusing to even consider negotiating percentages to make the deal work. She wanted control *and* a greater share of the profits.

Arden said good morning and sat down, as usual without any notes or laptop. He set the blank *New York Times* crossword he had splurged on beside him on the conference table—maybe it would reignite his interest in crosswords—and decided on a new approach.

"We've been trying to mediate a deal of some sort," he began, "unsuccessfully. We have caballed together three possible deals, which subsequently and rapidly collapsed." He paused. "I have been mediating disputes for many years and on rare occasions, extremely rare, I reach the conclusion that an equitable deal is impossible. I have reached that conclusion in this case."

All three siblings looked at him across the conference table with a mixture of disbelief and disdain before they all started speaking at once.

"We were told you never fail."

"Never."

"Never-Fail Jeffries, they said that's your nickname."

"You always find a fair solution."

"We were promised."

"There must be a solution to this mess."

Arden weathered the angry accusations with serene indifference. As it died down, he said, "You may think it's me and you are free to select another mediator, or you can try taking the case back to court."

"None of us wants to go back to court," the older brother said. "We already tried. The court's settlement broke down before it even took effect."

"We were lucky to convince the judge to allow us to try mediation," the sister said. "He only did because we selected you as the mediator."

"You're why we choose arbitration," the younger brother added.

"That may be," Arden said, "but when it comes down to it, I can't write an agreement that will close every loophole to get around the spirit of the agreement. No one can. That's why the law failed you and why mediation is failing. Your case, like so many others, has certain factors that make it unique, so the law doesn't specifically cover your dispute down to the most specific detail. That being the case, you have to be willing to make an agreement work. If you search for loopholes and try to play gotcha with each other, then any agreement will fail and I promise you, you will all be worse off in the long run." At least Arden hoped that would be the result, yet even as he said it, he wondered whether it was true as doubt flooded his mind. He knew now that for some it made them far better off to sneak through every loophole, bend every rule and seek every advantage regardless of morality, ethics or the law.

"Can we try again?" the older brother asked, pleading, glancing at his siblings for support. The other two joined in with the same question.

Arden sighed, looked around the table at the eager faces and said, "Yes." Relief showed on the three faces across the table, but the emotion vanished as soon as he added, "But not with me. This firm has many other fine mediators who would be more than willing to take on your case and attempt to assist you."

"Why not you?"

"Your reputation—"

Arden shook his head. "I've run out of options. I've done everything I can for you. I am sorry." As he picked up his crossword and started toward the door he added something he believed was impossible, "I hope you find a mediator who can discover an equitable and just resolution to your issue."

Chapter 57

Saturday, December 13, 2008

"Richard Sloane, ex-CEO of Antioch Pharmaceuticals, is in Los Angeles today," the morning news anchor said.

Arden had just turned on the television and his finger was poised over the button to change to the History channel.

"Sloane, who was allowed for undisclosed health reasons to postpone serving six months for misstatements after an SEC investigation, will speak to the Southland Business Growth Organization about ethics in the modern, global business environment. He just signed a mid-six figure contract with Kerrera House Press to write a book on the same topic. Tickets sold out early for the $300-a-seat talk at 3 p.m. today at the convention center."

Arden stared at the screen.

"Mr. Sloane recently accepted a new position as COO of Phoenix Pharmaceuticals, part of the global biomedical powerhouse, GenChin. On a personal note, he also just became engaged to Jennifer deCarlo, an ex-swimsuit model and actress." An image flashed on the screen of a young beauty in a bikini made with a bare minimum of red material.

Arden hung his head, staring down at his half-buttered English muffin as he wondered where the world was heading. It made no sense to him anymore. Was there no shame left in the world? Porn stars became famous and felt no compunction about making public their background. Drug addicts became successful self-help speakers and authors by detailing their addiction, while those who had never broken the law struggled to work two minimum-wage jobs to stay an inch above the poverty line. Criminals from G. Gordon Liddy, whom Arden had heard now had a radio show, to Michael Milken, who was listed as a philanthropist first and felon a distant, if mentioned at all, second, were not even rehabilitated; their fame rested on their crimes. Now there was Richard Sloane: criminal and expert on ethics because he had none. The way to fame and fortune was through infamy first, which then transformed into fame, fortune and status.

It was outrageous. Society was sick. This should not be. It could not be. Something had to be done. Now. If not, the disease would spread and destroy everything. What sort of world would Sam live in if nothing was done? Sloane, a crook, kept his wealth and position, even enhanced it, while Arden lost everything.

Leaving his English muffin on the counter and the television on, Arden stalked out of the kitchen and, taking the stairs two at a time, hurried upstairs to the empty master bedroom. He opened the gun safe, which had arrived just two days before, and removed the Glock 17. He took ammunition out of a second safe and loaded the handgun. He stuffed the Glock into a red backpack he took on day trips, and went downstairs. After getting the number from information, he called the convention center.

"I'm sorry to bother you, but I fear you may be my last hope," Arden told the receptionist as he stood in the kitchen, the backpack resting on the counter. "I have a package for a Mr. Richard Sloane."

"He's speaking here this afternoon, so you can come and probably give it to him a little before 3 pm," the receptionist offered with a mellow, agreeable voice.

"That would be fine, except I was told he needed the contents of the package to prepare for his talk," Arden said, sounding anxious and worried. "Something about a change in his speech."

"I don't know—," the receptionist began to say before Arden interrupted, "This is my first day with the messenger company and all they gave me is a name, no address. My boss hates me already."

"I am sorry—"

"The dispatcher said Sloane was staying at a hotel downtown, but that doesn't narrow it down much. Is there any way you could find out where he's staying or if he has a contact number? I'd hate to lose this job, the economy being what it is. My wife just lost her job and our savings are down to nothing and our daughter is going without so many things. A treat for her is a pack of M&Ms."

Silence.

"I'd really appreciate your help," Arden said, his voice pleading. "I need this job. I'm desperate. Please."

After a pause, the receptionist said, "Hold on," and put Arden on hold.

Arden hoped and prayed. The minutes ticked by and he had about decided to drive down to the convention center to make a plea in person with another story, when the receptionist returned to the line. "Mr. Sloane left a contact number and I just called it. He's staying at the Excelsior Arms, suite 1911."

"Thank you so much," Arden gushed, "for me, my wife and our little baby, Sam."

Arden knocked on suite 1911. No answer. He knocked again. Nothing. He loitered near the door, his gaze flicking up and down the empty hall. The elegant five-star hotel had winged armchairs set on either side of a flower arrangement atop a lyre table at the end of the hall. Forcing himself to calm down, Arden walked over and sat in one of the chairs, taking a *USA Today* off the ornate lyre side table. He found the crossword and started it in his head. The backpack with the Glock in it was wedged beside him against the arm of the winged chair. In less than two minutes he finished the crossword. He frowned. He must be distracted to take so long or maybe the concussion had affected his memory.

Arden flipped through the paper, glanced at an older couple who exited their room to walk to the elevators, and tried to admire the floral arrangement, which filled the hall with a pleasant spring-time aroma. It did not make waiting any easier.

After an hour, the elevators opened for the fifteenth time. Arden lowered his paper and recognized Richard Sloane from his television appearances. He was less tanned then Arden remembered and, unlike his standard suit and tie for interviews, wore khaki trousers, tasseled loafers and a red polo shirt. He carried several newspapers under one arm and held a muffin wrapped in a napkin as he strolled out of the elevator.

Arden stood, dropped the newspaper on the table beside the flowers and, grabbing his red backpack, hurried down the hall to intercept Sloane before he reached his suite. Sloane's room was near the elevator and he had already used his card key to open the door when Arden reached him.

"Mr. Sloane," Arden said, his voice louder than he had intended. "May I have a word?"

Sloane turned, a smile on his face, which faded into a look of uncertainty when he saw Arden. "Have we met before?"

"Not in person, but our lives collided in August."

Sloane frowned and his eyes flicked from Arden to the door to his suite. Arden unzipped the backpack and pulled out the Glock. Sloane froze. A quizzical look crossed his face, as if it was a joke, but the look passed, replaced by one of fear.

"My wallet's in my suite," Sloane said, raising his hands and dropping the newspapers and blueberry muffin. The napkin fluttered to the carpet. "You can have it."

"I don't want your damn wallet. What good would a few bucks do me after you cost me $126,000?"

Sloane frowned. The ding of an elevator instantly brought both their gazes to the elevator bank.

"Inside," Arden ordered, "now."

Shoving Sloane into the suite with his free hand, Arden kept the gun aimed at the ex-CEO's back. Arden kicked the muffin into the suite, leaving a trail of crumbs, and shut and locked the door. The newspapers and white napkin still lay in the hall. Arden followed Sloane into the main room of the suite. Larger than the first apartment Arden had rented after college, the room had a Carrara marble-topped bar near the door, a pair of sofas, a dark marble fireplace, 60" flat-screen television, and a balcony with a glass-topped table and four rattan chairs with thick, welcoming white cushions. The heavy drapes were open, flooding the space with light.

Arden checked the two doors leading off the room, but kept the gun aimed at Sloane, who stood motionless in the center of the room, his hands raised. One door led to the bedroom; empty. The second to a bathroom; also empty.

"No one else here?" Arden asked, listening and not hearing anyone in what he guessed was a second bathroom he could see through another door across the bedroom. He would have rushed over to check, but by then Sloane could have bolted from the suite.

"No one," Sloane said, sounding calm for having a handgun pointed at his chest.

Arden motioned for Sloane to sit on one of the sofas. "Put your hands down."

"What do you want?" Sloane asked once he was seated, his hands now resting rigid on his thighs.

"I want to know why you lied to me and thousands of Antioch stockholders?" Arden's anger surged to the surface. "Why you said repeatedly that the stock would recover, that the clinical trial would work, and that the SEC investigation would find nothing, when not one word of it was true?"

Sloane swallowed, pursed his lips and narrowed his eyes for an instant before his face took on a relaxed, even friendly appearance. "I believed our researchers would discover what caused the unfortunate setback with the clinical trial and remedy the problem rapidly."

"But they didn't," Arden shot back.

"Not yet." Sloane sounded calm and reasonable. "Although the PI—principal investigator—thinks he knows what caused the deaths."

"Then why didn't he fix it?"

"He's trying. It takes time to check whether the proposed solution works, and then test and verify it to the satisfaction of the FDA in a safe and prudent manner. It's an extremely long process. Many drugs take years to reach the market, even ones that never have a patient unfortunately succumb during a trial."

Arden hated hearing what sounded like prepared sound bites. "What about the stock price?"

"I honestly believed it would bounce back. Antioch was—is a good company. It was undervalued. Now everything is, but even before the drop Antioch was trading significantly below its real intrinsic value."

"Yet for months you were selling off your own Antioch stock."

Sloane sighed. "As I explained to the SEC investigators, my wife was remodeling our new home in Newport, I wanted to buy a new racing sailboat, and my wife and daughter were spending money like Bill Gates was their loving uncle. In short, I needed money. Selling the stock was the easiest route to obtain it." He held out his hands, palms out as if that explained everything.

"You sold the stock even when you say you believed it would go up?"

"Yes."

Arden glared at Sloane, daring him to justify his behavior, but Sloane just sat there, meeting Arden's glare with an even, patient look. The bastard did not even look scared anymore.

"Why did you lie?" Arden demanded.

"I never lied."

Arden lifted the gun, which had fallen lower as they talked, and gestured at Sloane with its muzzle. "You lied repeatedly. The SEC found you guilty of misstatements."

"No, they did not."

"They did," Arden yelled, rising to advance at Sloane, who remained seated, as Arden waved the gun to emphasize his point.

"The SEC investigated allegations of misstatements and various other miscellaneous charges," Sloane explained, even as Arden, gun in hand, loomed over him. "In order to avoid a prolonged distraction for myself and the company, Antioch's attorneys recommended a settlement. The board agreed. I strongly, vehemently and at length argued against such a course, but the board had made up their mind. I could not sway their decision, much to my continuing regret. We negotiated a settlement, involving a fine and some token jail time, but absolutely no admission of guilt; that I firmly refused to do. I did not plead guilty nor was I found guilty. I was not guilty of anything."

"Then why serve prison time?"

"At the board's firm request, in the best interest of the shareholders, and to avoid a long trial with the attendant further bad press for Antioch and the stock price falling even farther."

"Which it did anyway."

"You can hardly blame me for the global financial meltdown," Sloane said, his mouth bordering on a disbelieving smirk. "If the market had remained healthy, Antioch would have quickly recovered after the SEC concluded their baseless investigation. Our researchers will test their remedy for the clinical trial problem and once that issue is resolved, I am certain the stock price would have skyrocketed well above where it was before this series of unfortunate events."

Sloane glanced at the gun, then up at Arden's face. "I firmly believed in Antioch and everything we did. That's why I'm still leading the reformed Antioch. The laboratory-grown heart valve will work. The team just needs more time, and it will help thousands of people facing the horrendous prospect of having their chest cut open, their ribs spread, their heart stopped, and a valve replaced, not to mention months of slow and painful recovery."

"And the SEC?"

"The SEC had some former personal enemies of mine on their investigation team who were intent on destroying me. Even so, they found next to nothing, but they hold all the cards. They interpret the laws, and financial laws can be interpreted extremely broadly and in a multitude of ways."

"Not that you ever would."

"The board and the shareholders would oust me in a week if I did not carefully follow every applicable law."

"You sound like an angel, but I agree with the Roman saying, 'He who profits from a crime, commits it.'"

"What crime?"

"Crimes: lying to the public and your shareholders, and looting a company of millions of dollars."

Sloane leaned forward on the sofa. He appeared to be fighting to control his anger at the temerity of such accusations. "For years I was the first in at Antioch and the last out the door, every single day. I worked my tail off for that firm. The board wanted the stock price to rise and I delivered for nine years, year after year after year. I was responsible for it all. When it came down to it, every decision every one of our 21,000 employees made was my personal responsibility. I worked 100 hours a week and everything I did was for the good of the company, the shareholders, the employees and our customers."

"The cheap apartment for your daughter. The corporate jet for your family's personal use. The low-interest loan. All for the good of the company? For the good of the shareholders?"

"Every CEO has perks and for God's sake, Antioch's a billion -dollar company. An apartment? Even if Britanny paid triple the market rate it wouldn't have affected our P&L one one-thousandth of a percentage point."

"That's not the point," Arden yelled. "You acted unethically."

"I did nothing illegal."

"The SEC disagreed."

"No, they did not or they would have sicked the FBI on me, just as they did on Fannie Mae and Freddie Mac, Lehman Brothers and AIG."

"So you aren't so bad because others are even more crooked?"

"I never said that."

"You didn't have to."

"You can't compete without playing somewhat close to the gray areas."

"You went far into the black."

"The board, the outside auditors and our accountants all supported every decision I made and every thing I did."

"I regret ever working a single minute for you."

"You worked for me?" Sloane asked, surprised.

"Twenty-two interminable years in Antioch's HR department here in Los Angeles. My specialty was dispute mediation, until you cut the HR staff. I took early retirement and joined a mediation firm." Arden chuckled.

"What?" Sloane asked, frowning.

"Just remembering that we used to kid about when we'd get our big break and some director or VP guilty of bedding his secretary or of insider trading would offer us a few million to keep quiet," Arden said. "We joked about the life of ease we'd live once that happened. Then one day just recently it happened."

A week before, Arden stared down at the check: $120,000.

"You saved CSM International hundreds of millions," Gordon Hayes, CSM's project leader for the Peruvian mine nationalization, told him as they sat in Arden's office at Equitable Mediation. "We avoided nationalization. Had a little legal trouble over the subsidiary we set up, but no big deal the legal boys couldn't sort out for a couple of hundred billable hours." Hayes chuckled. "In Reno you warned us about that, didn't you?"

Arden stared down at the check. "Why isn't this made out to Equitable Mediation?"

"Already paid them. This is just a little token of our CEO's appreciation for your help, personally."

"It should go to Equitable," Arden said, his voice a monotone.

"You're the one who saved our asses. Why so glum? One of our rivals got nationalized and lost a fortune: mines, processing plants, equipment, and enough of a stockpile to supply the global market for a month."

Arden stared at the check. With divorce on the horizon, Sam's college fund and his retirement accounts denuded, and Antioch stock being exchanged 100 for one of a new Chinese company that had purchased it, Arden needed every penny he could get. "Equitable has rules about accepting gifts from clients."

"As well they should," Hayes agreed as he stood and came around Arden's desk to stand beside him. "Gifts can affect the outcome of mediations. But in this case, the mediation's over. In fact, there wasn't any mediation. You were just advising us on the nationalization issue, so no harm, no foul." He grinned down at Arden. "Your advice was worth ten times that amount," he added, flicking his index finger at the corner of the check in Arden's hands.

One hundred and twenty thousand would cover all of Sam's college costs, plus some for graduate school. One hundred and twenty thousand would put retirement almost back on their original schedule.

"I can't accept this," Arden said.

"I told our CEO we should have tripled it," Hayes said, shaking his head and pursing his lips. "I completely understand. I wouldn't accept table scraps when I'd saved the entire meal."

"No, I can't."

"I'll get him on the phone and see what we can arrange to make it a respectable amount: $500,000? A million? What floats your boat?"

"It's not the amount," Arden almost shouted. "The amount has nothing to do with it."

"The amount always has everything to do with it," Hayes said, shocked, but still keeping a jovial expression.

"No, it doesn't," Arden said, forcing himself to calm down.

Hayes stared at him.

"You would need to pay me enough so I'd never have to work again," Arden said. "If I accepted the money, any money, I couldn't work ever again as a mediator."

"Why?"

"I wouldn't be me anymore."

"It's just a piddling hundred and twenty grand," Hayes said with a dismissive wave of his manicured hand. "Firms have been known to pay more than that to an assistant secretary of mining in some foreign land without batting an eye."

Arden sighed. There was no point arguing; people rarely change their perceptions, let alone their beliefs. "The rule is that mediators are only allowed to accept gifts of nominal value." He handed the check back. "Please give it to Equitable Mediation if you want to express your thanks for my work."

"Should have taken the money," Sloane said, back in the hotel suite, "it would have made no difference."

"It would have made a difference to me."

"Bribes, gifts and favors are the way they do business in most of the world. They're just user fees. You have to do it to conduct business. There's nothing inherently wrong with them."

"Nothing wrong with a bribe?"

"It's the normal way of doing business and everyone knows it. Without favors the system would grind to a halt. Nothing would get done. Favors are a way of determining who can get things done and rewarding them. Bribes grease the wheels."

Arden shook his head. "I don't believe you; no remorse and no recognition that you did anything wrong."

"I didn't do anything wrong."

"No excessive perks."

"I have a demanding job and am justly compensated for it. Few could do it."

"No insider trading?"

"I sold stock every month as a matter of routine."

"No lying to stockholders."

"CEOs have to be optimistic. It's part of the job's description."

"Everything you did was for the good of the company, for the shareholders."

"Of course."

"You'll never understand." Arden raised the Glock and aimed it at Sloane's head. "For all the shareholders who listened to your lies and lost a fortune. For all the dreams you killed; all the retirements, college funds and thousands of other dreams that are now dead, thanks to you."

Sloane met Arden's anger with steady eyes and thin compressed lips.

Arden's index finger pressed the trigger. He felt it give. Sloane straightened, raising his head, preparing himself to be shot. His face rigid, the CEO waited for death. His face showed no fear, just a rigid resignation.

"You can't do this," Sloane whispered. "You shouldn't do this. It's wrong."

"Sometimes a killing is more than justified, it's equitable, fair and just."

Chapter 58

Arden sat in the driveway of his Santa Maria home in his 1974 Kharmann Ghia. He was glazed with nervous sweat that had turned cold, chilling his body as if he has just stepped into a walk-in freezer. Eyeing the red backpack with the Glock in it on the passenger seat beside him, he struggled to remember what he had just done. He knew what he had done; he had sought justice.

Clutching the bag, he staggered toward his house.

"Arden," Harry called from next door where the retiree was washing his car as he listened to a portable radio. Rusty snoozed on the porch. "Just heard that CEO, Richard Sloane, is dead. Didn't you used to work for him?"

"I have to confess to the murder of Richard Sloane," Arden told Detective Ranjan at the police station three hours later. Arden had been thinking about what to say ever since Harry told him the news. At first, he had thought he would just ignore it and go on with his life. Who could link him to Sloane? He would be free and clear. No one he knew had seen him and the few people who had probably would not remember him. He knew the difficulty first-hand of identifying criminals. Besides, the list of possible suspects who hated Sloane must be the size of a thick phonebook. Even if he was caught, what jury after hearing his story would convict him?

Then the thought stuck him, no one would know why Sloane had been shot. The act would lose its meaning if no one knew. A man, albeit a piece of slime, would be dead for no reason. Arden had to tell someone. He had to explain. People had to know why, even at the cost of his freedom.

"I am not a violent man," Arden told Ranjan. He felt exhausted and speaking took great effort. "I've spent my life doing my best to fairly mediate disputes in an unbiased and objective fashion. My education, training, career, and life have been devoted to the peaceful resolution of conflicts, disputes and disagreements. My goal has always been fairness and equity."

"That's all well and good, but how do you explain shooting Sloane?" the detective asked with a frown. Ranjan sat knee to knee with Arden, each in an armless straight-backed gray plastic chair. The room, painted a cool blue, was Spartan from the simple light fixture in the center of the ceiling to the tan blend carpet. With no table between them, Arden knew it made it more likely a suspect would open up to a detective and confess. The same principle applied to mediation.

"Well?" Ranjan asked, tilting his head to one side as he looked into Arden's eyes.

Arden wanted to say what he felt precisely so Ranjan would understand. Arden took his time. As a mediator, he was used to taking his time, but he could tell that Ranjan, like most Americans, disliked silence. Asians often used that American dislike to their advantage, sitting in silence during negotiations as the Americans gave more and more away in an attempt to end the silence. Funny, Arden thought, how similar getting a confession was to settling a dispute.

"We have enough evidence to convict you even without a clear motive," Ranjan said, giving in to the silence. "To tell you the truth, I could not really care less about your motive, except for curiosity." He glanced at his watch; nice touch, basic but effective. "I'm off duty in a few minutes, but it would be nice to know why you did it, if you want to tell me about it."

"The law defines right and wrong, detective," Arden began, leaning toward his interrogator. "But it shouldn't define how people behave."

Ranjan frowned.

"If we live our lives merely to avoid breaking the law, then our society is going to collapse. We must abide by what is right, instead of just what is legal." Ranjan still did not appear to understand. Arden tried again. "The law is like the brick wall at Wrigley Field,. Morals and ethics are the warning track. Without the warning track, we'll run headlong into the wall."

"We have plenty of people doing that here every day," Ranjan said with a wry grin. "But why'd you do it?"

Arden frowned. "Have you ever been the victim of a crime, Detective Ranjan?"

"Had a car stolen," Ranjan said, hesitating, wary. "My wife lost her purse once."

"A crime like that makes you mad, doesn't it?"

"Not enough to kill someone."

Arden nodded. Ranjan was probably far from a violent man, having seen too much violence as a police officer. Seeing violence made some more sensitive to it, others oblivious to it.

"It all started with a crime," Arden said. "No, two crimes, against me personally. Then the system kicked in and the way the crimes were dealt with was so uneven, so unrelated to the damage done by each that finally I just couldn't stand it any more. The system failed and I had to do something to set it right."

"Tell me exactly what happened. I should remind you that we are recording this."

"I take full responsibility, since I set out this morning to kill Richard Sloane for what he did to me, my family, and to all the Antioch shareholders, but I can't remember what happened."

Ranjan looked as if he did not believe Arden, but said nothing.

"I remember getting up this morning, hearing Sloane was in town to give a talk about ethics, getting my gun and driving to the hotel." Arden's words came out fast as he struggled to remember what had happened during the gap in his memory. Maybe if he spoke fast, his mind would forget to forget. "I waited near his suite. When Sloane stepped out of the elevator, I met him and forced him into his room."

"Did you hit him?"

"Of course not. I just ordered him inside."

"What happened next?"

"I confronted him about lying about the stock, the SEC allegations and his lies about the clinical trial. He denied it all, even when I threatened to shoot him." Arden looked down at his hands in his lap. He shook his head. "I couldn't believe it. He actually believed what he did wasn't wrong. He thought everything he did was for the good of the company, for Antioch, for all the shareholders."

After a long pause, Ranjan prompted, his voice low and even, "Then what happened?"

"I threatened him with the gun and I think that he finally got mad. It was hard to tell."

"Why?"

"He hid it well. He just sat there. But I was... He wasn't mad that I was going to kill him. I think he was mad because I had the effrontery to question his ethics and his morality, and that I didn't believe he'd given his all for the company. He didn't understand that what he'd done was wrong. He had no comprehension of it at all."

Another long pause. "And then?"

"I must have had one of my memory blackouts from the concussion," Arden said, shaking his head and frowning, "because I swear I don't remember shooting him. I remember I had the gun pointed right at him. He wasn't even sweating. Sloane looked as if he thought he was being martyred. He actually believed he had done what was best for the company and would now die for it—for the company."

Arden paused, vividly remembering that moment, so recent, yet so long ago.

"At that moment I realized that shooting Sloane wouldn't accomplish anything." Arden looked over at Ranjan, looking into his eyes. "I remember that I swore. I released my finger on the trigger. I remember saying that I could no more shoot him than he could ever realize that what he did was wrong."

"So you didn't shoot him?" Ranjan asked, leaning over to close the distance between them.

"I swear on my daughter's life, I don't remember that part." His voice quiet, Arden added, "But I must have."

Ranjan rose and, his face taking on a formal appearance, announced, "Thomas Jeffries, I am placing you under arrest for the attempted murder of Richard Sloane."

Arden's head jerked up and his eyes locked on Ranjan in wonder. "Attempted murder?"

"Sloane isn't dead. After you left, Sloane—hale and hearty—called 911, and then promptly suffered a heart attack and hit his head on a marble end table."

Chapter 59

Monday, December 22, 2008

"Merry Christmas," Arden's attorney boomed out as he stepped into the interview room at the jail. "This is the luckiest day of your life."

Exhausted, stressed and constantly scared after nine days in jail, Arden looked up at his lawyer in complete confusion.

"Sloane isn't pressing charges."

Arden frowned.

"Don't look so glum."

"The DA can press charges."

"Not likely if Sloane doesn't cooperate. Sloane claims it was all a misunderstanding."

"The DA's dropping an attempted murder case?"

"Sloane is on a first name basis with the Attorney General and the local party head honchos, so the DA is disinclined to do anything Sloane doesn't devoutly desire."

So much had happened so fast that Arden's mind had difficulty processing it all.

"I hear Sloane promised a substantial contribution to the DA's reelection campaign if she drops the case, not that I'd tell anyone that," Arden's lawyer said. "The DA also helped Sloane negotiate his prison time down to parole."

"Based on what?" Arden asked in disbelief.

"His poor health after his heart attack and a promise to leave the country for an extended period. Keep him out of the public eye for a while, especially when the DA runs for re-election."

Arden closed his eyes at the lack of justice in the justice system, let alone in the world. "Why would Sloane drop the charges?"

"Doesn't want the story on every news website in the world that a disgruntled stockholder tried to put a bullet in his heart, if he has one. It'd make him appear less than the wonderful, top-of-the-line CEO he wants to appear to be."

"Why does he care what people think of him?"

"He has another CEO gig lined up."

"He's worth millions. Why ever work again?"

Arden's attorney shrugged. "You've got to be the dourest looking man I've ever seen who just got handed his freedom as an early Christmas present."

Arden rose as the shocking news sank in. "I'm free?"

"Just the paperwork to process. You'll be home before you know it."

Arden finally smiled and said, "Maybe I'll even get my own clothes back this time."

Chapter 60

Saturday, January 3, 2009

"Jason Sardina, the President's special Middle East envoy, is in the region today for intensive talks with Israeli and Palestinian leaders," the radio announcer reported.

"Good luck with that, Sardina," Arden said, clicking off the radio as he arrived home from a weekend day at work to catch up on what he had missed while he had been jailed. He reminded himself that he needed to retune his car radio's buttons to music stations. He had heard enough news to last him a lifetime.

Arden lingered in his front yard. He had read that to combat depression, you should do things that used to give you pleasure. They would not at first bring any pleasure, but with time they would once again. He tried to admire the rose bushes along the new fence Buell had completed at far more cost than he had expected after hitting the phone line. Maybe, just maybe, sometimes there was a certain twisted justice in this unjust world, Arden thought with a wistful smile.

Glancing back at his empty house, Arden's good feeling fell away into the dark abyss that had enveloped him since Marisela and Sam had moved out. They had to come back. He had to explain, better, more convincingly. There had to be, somehow, an equitable settlement between them to restore their life to what it had been.

Arden sighed and tried to force himself to enjoy the warm evening. The Santa Ana winds were blowing. They were forecast for several days and, Arden knew, they would soon bring the dust, pollen and pollution that the more usual breeze from the coast normally pushed into the desert. With it all would come irritated eyes that felt as if an infection was coming on, sinuses full of gunk and, if they lasted long enough, a sore throat. But for now, the desert breeze just pumped up the air temperature to a balmy 76. Heaven. It barely cheered Arden at all.

Arden turned to head inside to force himself to eat some dinner. Belatedly awakening from a nap, Rusty woofed at him from Harry's front porch. Arden's gaze fell on the wood fence that bordered Harry's property. It leaned toward Arden's rose bushes. Arden shambled across the grass and, prodding in the grass with his foot near the sidewalk, felt for the property marker. Finding it, he sighted along from the property marker and saw that the fence was on Harry's property by at least six inches, assuming the property line ran parallel to the one on Buell's side of Arden's lot.

"Enjoying the evening air?" Harry called, as he meandered over from his front porch to lean against the aged fence, sweating Guiness in hand. "You hear the government's going to pay people to buy a new house? Has to be what they call a primary residence." Harry leaned over the fence and, lowering his voice said, "You have to have lived in your current house for five years, but they don't seem to plan to check if you're living in the new place. Thought I'd buy a place, rent it, get the tax refund, and if anyone asks, just say I was planning on moving to the new place right soon."

"Probably work," Arden admitted, sighing at the state of the world.

"It's $6,500. Nice pile of money."

"You could use the cash, I'm sure."

"Might as well get a little of my taxes back."

Arden nodded. If anyone was going to take advantage of the government, why not Harry?

Arden said, "I was just admiring the new fence Buell built and thinking we should talk about *your* fence."

Harry grimaced as he gave the top of the fence a gentle pull and push. The fence creaked and moaned and, as he let go, swayed back and forth as if it was about to collapse. Harry said, "Looks like we should get to fixing it soon before it falls down."

"True. *Your* fence is looking its age."

"You free next Saturday? Maybe we could figure out what we need to fix it and get started on her. I'll bring the cold beer." He held up his beer. "Should be able to get it done in a day if we split up the work and cost."

Arden pursed his lips, slowly smiled and said, "Yeah, I'm free Saturday for you…and *our* fence."

Chapter 61

Saturday, January 10, 2009

Arden awoke with a start. He had been napping after helping Harry repair their fence all morning. Using the holiday season as a softener and the promise of a new start for the New Year, Arden had finally convinced Marisela to let Sam visit for dinner. Arden had been so excited by the prospect of Sam's visit that he had not slept more than an hour the night before. Looking at the clock on his bedside table, he realized he had been asleep for more than two hours. Even so, he had some time before he had to start getting dinner ready, although Sam should be home soon.

He was still deciding whether to get up when he heard a sound downstairs. It sounded as if something had snapped, but had a deeper grinding tone to it.

Eyes wide open, Arden strained to listen in the semi-darkness of the master bedroom. The alarm had not gone of. He cursed himself. He had not set it. Sam would be home soon, so he had not bothered. Swallowing, he sat up. Maybe it was a crow on the eaves, a cat on the roof or the fridge grinding away. He sat up, fully clothed, the covers over his legs, listening. He debated whether to go downstairs.

He had about decided that it had been nothing when there was a crash from downstairs. There was no mistaking it now. Someone had dropped a kitchen appliance or a television.

Arden flung back the covers and raced around the bed to Marisela's side to grab the cordless phone. He hit 9-1-1 and, even as he did so, rushed back around to his bedside table. As the phone rang and he tried to both listen to the phone and for any more noises from downstairs, he used his free hand to shift a stack of books in front of the safe that held their Glock handgun.

"9-1-1 emergency, what is the nature of your emergency?"

"Someone's broken into my house," Arden whispered as he opened the safe.

"Did you say someone's broken in?" the man on the line asked, his voice even, calm and precise.

"Yes," Arden said, biting off the word. Arden gave his address and the nearest major intersection.

Sounds of someone moving around downstairs reached Arden's ears. He took the Glock, which the police had returned after the charges were dropped, out of the safe. Continuing to cradle the phone with his shoulder against his ear, he ran around to Marisela's side of the bed to open the second safe in her bedside table. He took out a loaded magazine. He slid the magazine into the Glock's handle. It slid home with a reassuring click. He switched the safety off.

More noises downstairs of things being moved. Looking around and feeling cornered, Arden retreated into the walk-in closet. No way would he be surprised from behind this time.

"Where are you, sir?" the 9-1-1 operator asked.

"In my upstairs bedroom closet."

"Stay there. I will have officers on the scene shortly. I will alert them to your location. Please stay where you are."

Arden nodded. More noises.

"Sir?"

"Yes, fine. I understand," Arden whispered.

Arden licked his dry lips and swallowed, trying to still his racing heart. It was probably off beat already. His eyes were locked on the open bedroom door through which he could see the top of the stairs just across the carpeted landing.

Drawers and cabinets were being opened downstairs. Someone cursed. Whoever it was did not know anyone was in the house. On Friday Arden had left his car at the mechanic's a few blocks away for an oil change, so there was no car in the driveway or in the garage. Arden prayed that Sam would not come home, not now. He glanced at his watch. His body shuddered. She should be home from swim practice at any moment.

"My daughter is on her way home," Arden said.

"Does she have a cell?" the 9-1-1 operator asked.

"Yes."

"Give me her number. I will have her called and told to stay where she is or in a safe place until you contact her."

Arden gave the dispatcher Sam's name and cell number. "Tell me the second you reach her."

Arden heard a footstep on the second stair; it had creaked for years. "Someone's coming up the stairs," he whispered.

"Can you close the closet door? Does it have a lock? My officers should be there shortly."

"I'll try." Arden shuffled toward the closet door. He held the handgun in front of him, pointed at the open bedroom door. The weapon felt heavy and cold. Sweating, his heart beating loudly—at least it was not skipping beats—Arden started to close the closet door. It had no lock. As he did so, through the slit of open doorway he spotted a head on the stairs. At the same moment, Arden heard the front door downstairs opening and Sam's rumbling ringtone of a Space Shuttle liftoff.

Arden's mouth went dry. His arms and legs went cold. Through the half-open closet door, Arden saw the burglar stop on the stairs and turn toward the sounds downstairs.

"My daughter's home," Arden said. Terror rising in him, Arden opened the door and raised his gun. He heard sirens. "I have to go."

"I have officers on their way. Do not leave the closet."

"I have to. I have a gun."

"I do not want you poking around with a gun when my officers arrive. You will get yourself shot."

"My daughter's here."

"Stay where you are!"

Arden dropped the phone. The sirens grew louder. Gun leveled before him, Arden rushed across the bedroom. "Sam! Run! A burglar's in the house!"

Arden reached the top of the stairs. The thief bolted back down the stairs, a gun in his right hand. Just beyond the foot of the stairs near the front door, Arden spotted Sam. Her eyes were wide, her posture statue-still and her red cell clutched in her left hand. The burglar was running down the stairs toward her, .38 revolver in his hand.

Arden aimed at the burglar's broad back and pulled the trigger. The thief stumbled as blood erupted from the back of his neck. He collapsed in a sprawl at the bottom of the stairs. Blood splattered all over the stairs, the banister and Sam, whose screams mixed with the wail of approaching sirens as Angel lay dying at the foot of the stairs.

The End

About the Author

K. Scot Macdonald is the author of the novel, *The Shakespeare Drug*, two non-fiction books, *Rolling the Iron Dice* and *Propaganda and Information Warfare in the 21st Century*, and has contributed to two edited volumes and to *The Writers' Journal*. He lives in California with his wife, daughter, and two Scottish terriers. To find out more about him, visit KScotMacdonald.com.

About Kerrera House Press

Kerrera House Press is an independent press dedicated to producing the books you keep. Visit us at KerreraHousePress.com for more information about our authors and our latest books.

Reader Resources

For a reader's guide, character bios, and more about the story and writing of *In Justice Found*, please visit KerreraHousePress.com.